Susan R. Sloan is a former attorney who lives on an island in Puget Sound. This is her third novel. Visit her website at www.sloanbooks.com

Also by Susan R. Sloan

Guilt by Association
An Isolated Incident

Susan R. Sloan

ACT OF GOD

A *Time Warner* Paperback

First published in the United States
in 2002 by Warner Books, Inc.

First published in Great Britain
in 2002 by Time Warner Books

This edition published by Time Warner Paperbacks in 2003
Reprinted 2003

A CIP catalogue record for this book
is available from the British Library.

ISBN 0 7515 3258 4

Typeset by Palimpsest Book Production Limited,
Polmont, Stirlingshire
Printed and bound in Great Britain by
Clays Ltd, St Ives plc

Time Warner Paperbacks
An imprint of
Time Warner Books UK
Brettenham House
Lancaster Place
London WC2E 7EN

www.TimeWarnerBooks.co.uk

For Howard,
My biggest fan

And for Bear,
My best friend

Acknowledgments

As always, I thank my agent, Esther Newberg, who keeps the checks coming, and my editor, Jamie Raab, who always seems to make magic out of mud.

I am particularly grateful to Kasey Todd Ingram, Sue Klein, Nancy Mack, Sally Sondheim, Pamela Teige, Alan Weiss, and Lee and Alicia Wells for their support and assistance.

And last but not least, I am indebted beyond calculation to Betta Ferrendelli, the little search engine that could, and to Susan Roth and The Author's Edge, without whom this book would just plain not have made it.

PART ONE

'We should do only those righteous actions
which we cannot stop ourselves from doing.'
— *Simone Weil*

I

He worked quickly but with extreme caution, knowing that one false move could prove fatal. Wearing several layers of latex gloves and a surgical mask, he powdered the correct measure of aspirin tablets with a mortar and pestle, added the appropriate amount of methyl alcohol, and then proceeded to whisk vigorously until the fine granules began to dissolve in the liquid.

He had chosen his product carefully. It had taken him two weeks to find a reasonably anonymous, out-of-the-way filling station with a methyl pump, and to collect enough cheap, unbuffered aspirin, being sure to buy no more than one bottle at a time from any supermarket or drugstore or quick-stop shop within a twenty-mile radius of Seattle. He then drove well out of the city to acquire the quantity of fertilizer he needed. Lastly, he made the rounds of auto supply stores, traveling as far north as Bellingham and as far south as Olympia to purchase the batteries, one battery per shop.

And all along the way, he was careful to pay for everything with cash, leaving no credit trail. After that, it was simply a waiting game – waiting for those blocks of time, like now, when he could steal into the garage and work undisturbed.

As soon as the aspirin was sufficiently whisked, he began to filter out whatever undissolved powder remained in the alcohol, repeating the process again and again until the liquid was clear and he could pour it into a Pyrex dish and set it aside.

Next, he turned to the battery, draining the sulfuric acid from it into a glass beaker. Granted, this was an extra step, when he could simply have bought the required amount of acid, but he decided it was far less conspicuous.

He took an old electric frying pan, retrieved from a thrift store for just this purpose, and filled it with cooking oil, which he heated to exactly one hundred and fifty degrees. As soon as the alcohol in the Pyrex dish had evaporated, he added the acetylsalicylic acid crystals that had formed in the dish to the sulfuric acid, and placed the beaker in the warm cooking oil, letting it sit there until the crystals dissolved. Then he removed the beaker from the oil and very slowly began to add the sodium nitrate, being careful not to let the foam overflow.

There was a real element of danger to what he was doing if he didn't do it properly, but the procedure couldn't have been simpler. All he had to do was follow the recipe that was available to anyone with access to the Internet, skipping over the disclaimers that popped up every second sentence about how illegal it was to do what the author of the recipe was describing be done in step-by-step detail.

After cooling the mixture slightly, he dumped it into a measure of crushed ice and water and watched as brilliant yellow crystals began to develop. He processed the crystals according to the instructions, then pulverized them into face powder consistency. The final step was to mix the powder with the specified amounts of wax and Vaseline, and pack the plastique into a glass container.

He checked his watch. The entire process had taken a little over three hours, just as it should have, just as it had taken to prepare each of the other containers that now lined the shelves of a locked cabinet in the far corner of the garage.

He set about cleaning up after himself, placing the frying pan, the Pyrex dish, the beaker, the whisk, and the remaining materials in a plastic garbage bag for discreet disposal into the depths of Puget Sound. Then he washed down the garage as though it were a surgical suite.

This was the last batch he had to make. Now it was time to put it all together, to remove the plastique from the glass receptacles, fill the duffel bags, attach the detonator he had fashioned from a light bulb, and affix the clever timing device he had found on the front seat of his car two days ago.

4

There was an informal rule observed by the people with whom he had come in contact: admit to nothing and involve no one else in what you're doing. Still, the timer had been provided to him – perhaps, he decided, as a form of silent affirmation.

He loaded the finished product into his vehicle, covered it with a blanket, and went into the house, to sit down in front of the television set as though he had been in his chair all evening. Then, as he habitually did on a night before work, he watched the news and went to bed.

But he didn't sleep. He waited until almost midnight, when the breathing beside him was deep and regular, and then he got up, slipped silently into his clothes, and left the house.

The night was cold and damp, quite typical of February. He climbed into his car, shifted the gear into neutral, and let the vehicle roll down the driveway and out into the street before starting up the engine. During the past weeks, he had made several dry runs, testing different routes to and from his destination, timing himself, and checking traffic until he was satisfied. Now he turned confidently onto the route he had chosen, circling around the back of Queen Anne to Denny Way, forking right onto Boren Avenue, and driving up First Hill. Reaching Spring Street, he made a little jog across Minor, then turned down Madison, and parked.

At this time of night, the street was deserted, the shops and restaurants closed. The area, appropriately nicknamed 'Pill Hill' some years ago, was dominated by Seattle's major hospitals, and the swing shift had given way to the graveyard shift over an hour ago. He had planned for that, of course.

A splendid Victorian mansion, set off by carefully manicured lawns, occupied the northeast corner of Madison and Boren. He was relieved to see that the building was dark and silent. The security guards who protected the grounds during business hours were gone, and no night watchman was on duty. It meant there were no late evening activities in progress, a glitch that would have significantly altered his schedule.

Neither of the two gates in the high iron fence that surrounded

5

the house was locked at this hour, a foolhardy practice he had determined in advance. Not that a locked entry would have stopped him, of course, it would just have slowed him down, and perhaps made him a bit more vulnerable.

He climbed out of his car, looking in all directions to make sure there was no one in sight. Then he hefted his plastique-filled duffel bags and carried them through the Madison Street gate. Just inside the fence, a high hedge of laurel bordered the property, making him all but invisible from the street. Nonetheless, he wasted no time. He went quickly along the path at the side of the building to the basement access he had spotted during one of his exploratory visits, pulled open the trapdoor, descended the concrete steps, and set about positioning the duffel bags in exactly the right place for maximum effectiveness. Then he checked one more time that the detonator was properly connected.

The very last thing he did before leaving the scene was to check the timer, just to reassure himself that it was set for two o'clock, and that the little green indicator beside the AM designation was lit. Then he got back into his car and drove away.

2

Dana McAuliffe looked far more like a high school cheerleader than an accomplished litigator approaching forty. She had thick, honey-colored hair, neither curly nor straight, that was gradually feathered in front and then fell softly around her shoulders. Her warm brown eyes required just a hint of mascara for accent, her cheeks were naturally rosy, and her unpowdered nose was highlighted by a generous splash of freckles. Were it not for the tailored gray suit and leather pumps she wore, one might almost have expected her to break into a high leg kick and a hearty 'rah-team-rah.'

Instead, she leaned back in her chair and smiled calmly at the nervous gynecologist seated across the desk from her.

'Don't worry,' she told him. 'As I said over the telephone, this kind of case rarely goes to trial. And now that I've looked over the papers, I can assure you that even if it does, we'd be in a very strong position.'

It was the first Tuesday in February, and although the office building's heating system rarely pushed the temperature above sixty-eight degrees, Dr. Joseph Heradia was perspiring freely.

'You see, I've never been sued before,' he said in distress. 'Twenty years of practice, and I've never been sued. Some people would probably say I've just been lucky all these years, and never got caught. But I've looked into my heart, and I know I did the best I could for those poor people.'

'I know that,' Dana assured him. 'And I can understand their reaction. But I'm sure, once they've had time to calm down, they'll realize you weren't to blame.'

'In vitro fertilization doesn't come with any guarantees, I told them,' he persisted. 'I tell everyone that going in. Sometimes

7

you can fool Mother Nature, sometimes you can't.'

Dana sighed. 'I think the Jensens probably wanted a baby more than anything, and you were their last hope,' she said. 'Hope can be a hard thing to let go of.'

The gynecologist nodded. 'I told them they should think about adopting.'

What a world, Dana mused. People wanting babies who couldn't have them, and people having babies who didn't want them. She had told Heradia the truth, as she did with all her clients. It was a bogus case – it had no legs.

'Maybe they'll think about that now,' she suggested.

The short, pudgy son of Guatemalan immigrants slumped in his seat. 'It's just that I feel so bad for them,' he said.

He was a good man, Dana reflected, not for the first time. 'Let me talk to their attorney,' she said, without bothering to mention that she knew him to be the type who would take on any case for an adequate retainer. 'If I can get them to understand that there is no blame here – not on you for not being able to work a miracle, and not on them for not being able to conceive a child – I think we can make this all go away.'

'I sure would appreciate it,' he said, confident that he was putting his problem in the right hands. 'And thanks for seeing me on such short notice. I guess we've kind of flipped the professional coin here, haven't we?'

Dana smiled. 'That's what coins are for.'

Heradia rose to leave. 'Look, I'd really like to buy you lunch or something,' he said, 'but I have to get back to the clinic. Will you take a rain check?'

'Sure.'

Dana walked him down the hall and through the reception area to the front entrance, giving him one last reassuring nod as he departed.

As soon as the solid oak door had closed behind him, Angeline Wilder leaned over the edge of her desk. 'Isn't he one of those abortion doctors from Hill House?' the receptionist for the law firm of Cotter Boland and Grace whispered.

8

'Is he?' Dana replied with a blank expression. 'I thought he was a gynecologist.'

'Well, I suppose he could be both,' Angeline conceded. 'But I'm sure he's one of them.'

'How do you know?' Dana inquired. 'Do they wear some sort of a badge, or do you just know them all by sight?'

'No, silly,' Angeline said. 'There was a story on the news about them the other night, you know, about how many abortions they perform up there every year, and he was one of the ones they identified.'

'I see.'

'He isn't a client, is he?'

'He may be,' Dana told her. 'So, given what you've heard about him, if he should come in again, be very polite. After all, you never know when he might whip out a curette.'

'What's that?' the twenty-one-year-old asked.

'Nothing you'd need to know about, unless you happened to be pregnant,' Dana replied.

The receptionist blushed to the roots of her already red hair. 'Well, I most certainly am not. I'm not even married.'

'In that case, don't give it a second thought.'

The attorney walked back to her office, shaking her head. Joseph Heradia had been her gynecologist for the past twelve years, and to her knowledge, a kinder, gentler, better man did not exist.

She thought about the couple who wanted a baby. The Jensens were probably good people, too, she decided, just desperate. And desperate people sometimes got caught up in doing irrational things. She flipped through her Rolodex file for their attorney's telephone number, and was reaching for the receiver when her intercom buzzed.

'Yes, Angeline?'

'Ms. Purcell's here,' the receptionist announced. 'She said to tell you it's one-thirty, and she's sorry she's late.'

Dana glanced at her wristwatch in surprise. Heradia had stayed much longer than she realized. Her chat with the Jensens' attorney would have to wait until after lunch.

'Tell her I'll be right out.'

9

*   *   *

Lunch with Judith Purcell had begun as a daily event when the two were assigned adjoining desks on the first day of second grade, and continued, if not quite as regularly, right up to this moment. Now that they were both working in Seattle, it had settled into a more or less weekly routine. They had been best friends for so long, and knew each other so well, that there were few surprises left between them.

'You didn't get the commission, did you?' Dana asked as soon as they had been escorted to their customary window table at Al Boccolino, their lunchtime restaurant of choice.

'No,' Judith confirmed. 'They loved my concept, but alas, not my bid. I think they would have gone with me if I'd been willing to drop my price, but I'd already cut it to the bone.'

Judith was an accomplished, if not yet renowned, sculptor. The commission in question was for the lobby of the city's newest waterfront office building, and Judith's proposal had been for a fanciful pod of gray whales done in glass, steel, and ceramic. As bid, the eighteen-month project would have enabled the artist to cover her costs, with barely any to spare.

When she was married, Judith's moneymaking ability had not been as important as indulging her creative spirit. But her first husband had died suddenly of a heart attack, she and her second husband had married and divorced in a very short period of time, and now she needed to support herself and her twelve-year-old son, Alex. A life in the arts was beginning to seem frivolous.

'I'm sorry,' Dana said. 'I really thought you had that one in the bag.'

'Me, too,' Judith admitted with a resolute shrug. 'But the truth is, I have only myself to blame. Instead of preparing for a real career, like you did, I thought I would be able to count on having a man around to support me.'

Aside from their physical dissimilarities, Judith being small and dark to Dana's above-average height and fair complexion, the attorney knew there was one basic difference between them. Judith had been raised to define herself by the man at her side, while Dana had been raised to define herself without anyone at her side.

'I still like the idea of you having your own gallery,' Dana said. She had been trying for almost two years now to move her friend onto more stable financial ground. Small loans from Judith's mother kept food on the table, and the half dozen Purcells that had made their way into Dana's home paid the artist's mortgage, but neither was going to be a long-term solution.

Of late, an idea had begun to form in the back of Dana's mind, of a joint venture, perhaps, where she might front the money for a gallery, but not be involved with the actual operation, since she admittedly knew next to nothing about art.

'I'd die to have my own gallery,' Judith agreed. 'But I just don't have the capital. And I doubt there's anyone out there who would be willing to gamble on me.'

'Well, who knows,' Dana said as their bowls of pasta arrived. 'Maybe Providence is getting ready to smile on you.'

'It would be nice,' Judith said with a sigh.

3

Summer was definitely Joshua Clune's favorite time of year. It was then, when the cold went away and the nights were mild, that there were plenty of places to sleep. And, too, when the tourists came, there was always more money. It was getting from October to April that was the problem, when the spaces under the overpasses and in the bus tunnel were taken, and the missions were full.

It was also in the summer that the scar that ran from his temple to his chin didn't hurt so much. Joshua hid the scar as best he could beneath long brown hair and a reddish stubble, but he knew it was there – a painful reminder of the car that had skidded out of the night years ago, and plowed into the doorway where he slept.

In the winter, Joshua suffered.

He had come from Wisconsin, slowly making his way west, walking, hitching rides when he could, until he reached Seattle and the end of the continent, and then he stopped. Someone told him he should go south to California, where the weather was even warmer and the people were rich, and he could get a suntan and put some meat on his bones. But he was tired of traveling, and besides, Seattle suited him.

He met people like Big Dug, a giant of a man with a full black beard, who showed him the ropes, and helped him settle in. Big Dug didn't trust the city shelters. He said there were too many stories about what happened at places like that, where there was little if any supervision. So, under the older man's tutelage, Joshua acquired a big cardboard box that had been used to deliver a desk to somebody's office, and he rummaged around in Dumpsters until he found a plastic tarpaulin. He cut the tarp in two, folding one half underneath his box to keep the cardboard dry, and draping the other half over the top to shut out the wind and rain and cold. Then, for a couple of dollars, a thrift shop provided him with a blanket.

'All the comforts of home,' he told people with a big happy smile.

Big Dug showed him where to go to relieve himself and where he could bathe, when he felt it necessary, and then he introduced him to Hill House, taking him up Madison to Boren, and pointing out an enormous gray mansion on the corner.

'It's like a clinic, but it's a whole lot more than that,' Big Dug told him. 'They bring a soup kitchen to the waterfront, and give you a hot dinner every night, and it's good food, not slop. If you do drugs, they can help you get clean. If you want to work, they can help you find a job. And if you're sick, they take care of you. And it doesn't cost anything, if you can't afford to pay. Only thing is, they don't want any of us sleeping up there. That's the rule, and we all know it, and we don't break it.'

'Why is that the rule?'

'I think it's probably got something to do with insurance,' Big Dug said. 'You know, in case there was a fire, or something, and somebody got hurt.'

'Is that why I can't go there?' Joshua asked, his hazel eyes taking in two well-dressed people as they walked through the gate. 'Because I might cause a fire?'

'Sure you can go there. You can go there first thing in the morning, if you need to, or any time of the day you want to, but you just can't sleep there, that's all, 'cause if they found out, they might get mad, and then it could ruin things for all of us. Do you understand?'

Joshua kicked at a crack in the cement pavement. 'Uh-huh,' he said.

'Okay, then,' Big Dug said.

Doctors in Wisconsin had classified Joshua as retarded when he was six years old, at which point his mother, who had four other children from three different men to raise, handed him over to the state.

'Life's tough enough,' she explained. 'I don't have time to do for no dummies.'

The state educated Joshua as best they could, encouraged him to be an upstanding citizen and to embrace true Christian values, taught him to be as self-sufficient as possible, and turned him loose, according to law, at the age of twenty-one. He was functional and he could follow simple instructions.

He got jobs washing dishes in restaurants, or mopping floors and cleaning toilets in office buildings. But with no one to remind him, he sometimes forgot to go to work, and then his employer would get mad and fire him, and Joshua would have to look for other restaurants and office buildings. When he didn't have enough money to pay for a place to sleep, he slept on the streets.

He left Wisconsin one day without even noticing. He just got in a car with a fellow who offered him a lift, and ended up in Minnesota. He never knew the difference. After all, there were restaurants and office buildings in Minnesota, too.

By the time he reached Seattle, Joshua was thirty-two years old. In all that time, he had never known a real home-cooked meal, or a night's sleep in a soft bed, or the warmth of another human being. But he knew right from wrong, and he knew he was not supposed to sleep at Hill House.

4

The official name of the building, imprinted on a small brass plaque affixed to the front door, was the Seattle Family Services Center. But for almost fifty years, it had been known throughout the city simply as Hill House. A spacious three-story Victorian that dated back before the turn of the twentieth century, it was one on a very short list of elegant dwellings gracing First Hill to have survived the onslaught of progress. The rest had been systematically gobbled up by the insatiable need of a municipal medical community for more modern complexes of steel and concrete.

By the early 1950s, the mansion had fallen into serious disrepair. An anonymous benefactor then quietly purchased it, restoring the gingerbread facade to its former glory with a fresh coat of paint and installing a new roof. The lawn was tilled and seeded, the front was decorated with little stone benches, the back was fenced around a children's playground, and the interior was remodeled into an efficient multipurpose clinic.

Hill House sat quietly on the corner of Boren Avenue and Madison Street, behind a high sculptured iron fence and a dense border of laurel bushes that had grown up over the past half century to provide an ample measure of privacy. Neither the people who worked at the center nor those who frequented it had any wish, nor made any attempt, to conceal their presence there. Nevertheless, they came to appreciate the buffer that the hedge provided from the little knot of protesters who verbally assaulted them from the sidewalk on a regular basis.

The group had appeared one day, some dozen and a half years ago, pushing and shoving, shouting, intimidating, and even threatening. Over time, the number of protesters dwindled, and several of their more extreme actions, such as vandalism and stalking, had been curtailed by the passage of new legislation, but their purpose remained the same.

Many things happened at Hill House, including multilevel counseling, a full range of obstetric and gynecological services, and comprehensive day care. But the only activity that concerned the sidewalk people, as the center's employees came to call them, was what they devoutly believed to be the immoral procedure of terminating pregnancies. Every single day, for almost two decades, the staff and patrons of Hill House had alternately been damned and prayed over, entreated and spat upon.

'Personally, I would never have an abortion, and I don't assist at them,' Shelly Weld, one of the clinic's obstetrical nurses, informed a member of the group one day. 'But I would never presume to tell anyone else what to do.'

'If you continue to dwell in the house of the devil,' came the dour reply, 'your soul will burn in hell for all eternity.'

Altogether, some ninety people worked in the nine-thousand-square-foot building. Among them were four physicians who specialized in obstetrics and gynecology, three family practitioners, two radiologists, two anesthesiologists, one pharmacist and an assistant, nine registered nurses, eleven nurse's aides, and seven laboratory technicians. In addition, there were two social workers, three psychiatrists, eight psychologists, sixteen licensed day care providers, three receptionists, one administrator and his two assistants, two secretaries, one accountant, two bookkeepers, two clerks, two security guards, and six maintenance people.

Moreover, at least three hundred others passed through the iron gates every day, seeking one kind of service or another.

The center's administrative and business departments were located on the first floor, just off the front entrance, and the laboratories, the pharmacy, and the consultation rooms shared the back of the building with the counseling unit. A surprisingly well-equipped mini-hospital occupied the entire second floor.

And each morning, some seventy children between the ages of two months and five years found their way to the third-floor day care center. The vast majority of these children were the offspring of personnel from the surrounding medical community, including the center itself; parents who prided themselves on having their sons and daughters in the most highly regarded facility in the city, and who knew how lucky they were. At any given time, as many as fifty other youngsters languished on a waiting list.

At two o'clock in the afternoon on the first Tuesday in February, the sky was overcast, the temperature hovered around fifty, scavenging crows squawked at one another from their perches in the laurel bushes, and the scent of cinnamon from a nearby bakery hung in the air.

In addition to the staff and the children, there were six couples and five women in counseling. Seven women were undergoing a variety of laboratory tests. Three mothers and their newborn babies were rejoicing with family and friends in second-floor rooms. One woman was preparing for a termination, two women were in labor, an expectant father and grandmother paced the maternity lounge, and nineteen people were waiting in the lobby for one type of service or another. At that moment, the building held close to two hundred and fifty people.

On the first floor, psychologist Frances Stocker, a robust sixty-year-old woman, had spent her morning counseling parents of an autistic son, a woman contemplating divorce, and a pregnant fifteen-year-old. She was just settling into a session with her next client, Grace Pauley, a frail, nervous woman, who was finally seeking help after years of spousal abuse. If Frances ever questioned her choice of profession, she needed only a day like this to remind herself of how much what she did mattered, and how meaningless her life would otherwise be.

In a consultation room just down the hall, radiologist Caitlin Callahan was reviewing the ultrasound recording of a suspected ectopic pregnancy. The single mother had just come down from the day care center, where it was her habit to lunch with her three-year-old daughter, Chelsea.

On the second floor, obstetrician Jeffrey Korba, tall and balding at forty-two, was holed up in his office, washing down a chicken salad sandwich with a soda before his second delivery of the day, and wondering if he would have time to call his wife. They had parted this morning on an argument about a washing machine, of all things, and he was sorely regretting it.

In one of the mini-hospital's four holding rooms, Shelly Weld was monitoring Denise Romanadis's contractions, and estimating that she could probably give Korba another five minutes to finish his lunch before Hill House's seventeenth set of triplets would require his attention. In another room, Betsy Toth had just finished preparing Joyce O'Mara for an abortion, and was awaiting Joseph Heradia's return from an outside appointment. As she had quite often during the past two weeks, the twenty-year-old nurse's aide found herself wondering, with a little tingle of anticipation, if she and Andy might be pregnant, and hoping he wouldn't be terribly upset if they just happened to jump the gun a little bit. After all, their wedding was only a few months away.

At one end of the third floor, whose newly papered walls featured tumbling brown teddy bears amid brightly colored streamers, Ruth Zelkin, the ebullient, fifty-three-year-old director of the day care center, had finally gotten the last of the toddlers, towheaded Jason Holman, down for his afternoon nap, and was heading for a much needed coffee break.

At the other end, Brenda Kiley was feeding the adorable four-month-old Gamble twins, Christopher and Jennifer. Fraternal though they were, the chubby siblings had identical China blue eyes, fuzzy blond hair, and wide, happy smiles.

Outside Hill House, Jesse Montero, the forty-two-year-old head custodian, had just finished stowing several boxes of light bulbs in the utility shed behind the building. Having taken a moment out of sight for a few puffs on a forbidden cigarette, he was in the process of securing a padlock on the shed door.

Carl Gentry, one of the security guards, stood at his post on the front porch. He was forty-six years old and recently divorced, and he was thinking about the woman he had met last night and not left until after breakfast this morning. He was hoping that she had enjoyed their time together as much as he had, and he was wondering how long he should wait before he called her.

What happened next happened so suddenly that afterward no two accounts of it were identical. One or perhaps several powerful jolts shook the ground as though a volcano were erupting, or an earthquake were taking place. Walls and windows cracked across a three-block area. Hill House first appeared to some to shudder and then it shattered, or as others reported, it shattered almost immediately, sending pieces of debris spewing over the lawn and hurtling over the laurel hedge. Some witnesses later reported that the mansion seemed actually to rise with the explosion and then collapse into itself, fire breaking out in one or maybe a number of places directly thereafter.

From an operating suite in Swedish Hospital two blocks to the east of Hill House, Janet Holman heard what she initially thought was a crash of heavy equipment, and then felt the whole building around her shake.

'What was that?' the orthopedist demanded through her surgical mask. 'An earthquake?'

'Sure felt like it,' one of the nurses replied.

'Here, take over for me for a minute,' Janet directed the senior resident who assisted her. 'I just want to make sure Jason's okay.'

At the Madison Medical Tower just across the street from the clinic, the windowpane blew out of Helen Gamble's cubicle, raining shards of glass over the billing clerk's desk and chair. Ignoring the fact that she was bleeding from several deep gashes around her head and neck, Helen jumped up to peer through the gaping hole. It was an instinctive action, of course, taken to reassure herself that whatever might have occurred, the twins were safe at Hill House. Her maternal concern turned to absolute terror.

'What was that?' Judith Purcell wondered aloud, a piece of bread halfway to her mouth. 'Surely, it can't be a thunderstorm at this time of year.' The restaurant was perhaps a mile from the corner of Madison and Boren. Still, they both heard and felt the rumble. 'Maybe it's a bomb.'

The two women stared at each other. Then Dana thought of the train tunnel nearby and shrugged. 'More likely an accident,' she said. At that moment, she had no way of knowing that her friend was right, or that it would have anything to do with her.

Faster than it would have seemed possible, the hundred-year-old mansion was reduced to little more than a pile of burning rubble.

Frances Stocker was thrown to the floor by the force of the explosion. Her heavy metal desk, overturning on top of her and pinning her to the floor, crushed her legs in multiple places, but almost certainly saved her life.

Her client, the long-suffering Grace Pauley, was not so lucky. She was tossed aside like a rag doll, landing at an odd angle, her head almost completely severed from her body.

There was nothing left of the consultation room where Caitlin Callahan had been reviewing an ultrasound. There wasn't much left of Dr. Callahan, either.

The right side of Jeffrey Korba was blown away. He lay in a gathering pool of his own blood and was pulled from the wreckage by rescue workers with barely a moment of life left in him.

Neither Shelly Weld nor her patient, Denise Romanadis, as full with life as the woman had been, were recognizable by fellow workers. Their bodies had to be pieced together afterward, their identities determined more from a process of elimination than anything else.

The ten-week-old fetus that Joyce O'Mara had been about to abort did not survive. Joyce barely survived herself. Betsy Toth sustained a fractured spine that would leave her paralyzed from the waist down.

All things considered, Ruth Zelkin was lucky to lose only her eyesight as the third floor collapsed under her. In the final count, she would also lose ten members of her staff and fifty-six of her children – among them, two-year-old Jason Holman.

Brenda Kiley saved the Gamble twins. She did so by using her own body to protect them from the major impact of the explosion. Unfortunately, there was no one to protect her.

Jesse Montero was shielded from the full thrust of the blast by the utility shed. He began with only minor cuts on his face and arms from flying glass and debris, but later incurred severe burns on his hands and arms as he tried desperately to save some of those who were trapped inside.

Two-hundred-and-ten-pound Carl Gentry was thrown from his post on the front porch as though he were nothing more than a sack of flour, his head coming in direct contact with one of the stone benches as he landed. He lay with a fractured skull and a broken neck, conscious, but unable to move.

Joseph Heradia, returning from the meeting with his attorney just seconds after the explosion, managed to pull the security guard away from any further harm.

'Oh my God,' the gynecologist exclaimed, as he surveyed the scene around him. 'What's happening?'

Inside the hedge of laurel, more than two hundred men, women, and children lay wounded or dying or already dead. It would later be determined that a dozen had miraculously escaped injury. One of them was three-year-old Chelsea Callahan.

Firefighters and paramedics reached the scene within minutes; police close behind. They were greeted by doctors, nurses, and staff members from nearby hospitals, already in the throes of a massive rescue effort. The wounded were removed as quickly as they could be extricated from the burning building and whisked off to various facilities for treatment, determined by the severity of their injuries. Authorities later verified that the immediacy of medical attention was in all likelihood responsible for most of the lives that were saved.

Carl Gentry was among the first to be lifted onto a gurney

and taken off to a hospital. And fuzzy though his mind was, as he was being wheeled away, something that had not occurred to him earlier now struck him clearly. This first Tuesday in February was also the first day in the eight years since he had come to work at Hill House that the sidewalk people had not appeared.

5

The bombing of Hill House shook Seattle to its very core. Not just literally, within the half-mile radius of the mansion itself, but figuratively as well.

There were few in the city who had not had some sort of association with the center at one time in their lives, if not as an employee or a patient, then perhaps as a friend or family to an employee or patient, or to a child who had been so carefully nurtured on the third floor. Or possibly, the link had come through the facility's extensive outreach efforts: its neonatal and well-child clinics, its indigent care and clean needle programs, its youth and drug crisis hotlines. Whatever the connection, it was now being sharply felt.

As word of the disaster spread, people found themselves stopping in their tracks, stunned and incredulous, unable to comprehend.

'What could have happened?' they asked one another.

'Why?'

Reporters from Seattle's two daily newspapers raced to the scene. Cameramen from the local television stations had their Minicams rolling when they were still blocks away. What greeted them was total devastation. Lenses, zooming in past the ring of fire trucks that had answered the call, registered the gruesome sight of body parts, mingled with fragments of furniture and equipment, smoking and smoldering in the blaze. Microphones caught the awful sounds of dying, the frightened whimpers of infants, the agonized screams of adults. The smell of burning flesh, fortunately unrecordable, was sickening. The historic mansion was gone.

'In a matter of minutes,' the fire chief confirmed with a catch in his voice. 'There was nothing we could do. This has been mainly a search and recovery operation.'

'How many?' reporters asked.

The chief sighed as he surveyed the destruction. 'We don't know yet,' he said. 'All these . . . parts . . . will have to go to the morgue to be sorted out. It could be days, even weeks, before there's positive identification, or even an accurate count.'

It was a photographer from the *Seattle Times* who caught what would become the quintessential shot of the event. Thirty-eight-year-old Janet Holman, still wearing her hospital scrubs, stood in the middle of the grisly wreckage, holding a small, dismembered arm in a blue-striped sleeve. On her face was an expression of disbelief, dismay, and dawning horror.

'We have a breaking story to report,' newscaster Joyce Taylor was telling her television viewers within minutes of the incident. 'A massive explosion of as yet undetermined origin has just occurred at Hill House. We don't have many details at this point, as authorities are just now reaching the scene, but we're told that the explosion has completely destroyed the mansion and killed or injured a great many people.'

For Dana McAuliffe, the association with Hill House was personal. Not only had she been going to the clinic for gynecological services for over a decade, she had been there not more than a month ago for her annual checkup.

'I can't believe it,' she exclaimed, when she returned to the office after lunch. 'I thought it was a train wreck.'

'I heard it on the radio,' Angeline Wilder assured her. 'It's really spooky, you know, what with that doctor having just been here.'

'Good lord, you're right,' the attorney gasped. 'And he was on his way back there.'

Angeline shook her head. 'They shouldn't have done that story the other night. I bet that's what did it. I bet someone set a bomb.'

*   *   *

24

'I want answers, and I want them now,' Washington's governor bellowed from his office in Olympia, some sixty miles away.

'Nobody knows anything yet,' his chief of staff replied.

'Don't tell me nobody knows,' he retorted. 'Somebody has to know something – they're just not talking. Well, I'm the goddam governor of this state, and I want answers. So, go get me some. And keep the media out of my face until you do.'

'You're going to have to make a statement about this fairly soon,' his aide said.

'Of course I am,' the governor replied. 'That's why you're already on your way out of here, right? I'm running for reelection this year, and I don't intend to make an insensitive fool of myself by saying the wrong thing.'

It didn't take investigators long to determine the cause of the disaster. Once firefighters had the blaze under control, members of the King County bomb squad were on the scene, bolstered by several teams from the FBI. Entering the area, which had already been cordoned off by the police and sealed from public access, they went to work, systematically combing the rubble of Hill House for whatever they could find. And what they found were fabric remnants, traces of fertilizer and other chemicals, and the remains of a small timing device.

'It was a bomb all right,' the head of the squad declared. 'And whoever set it knew exactly what he was doing. The stuff was positioned for maximum results.'

'Will that help you catch whoever did this?' someone asked.

'It's a starting point.'

At a quickly arranged press conference, a spokesman from the Seattle mayor's office did what he could to assure an apprehensive population that everything possible was being done to protect the community and to resolve the crisis expeditiously and professionally.

'Let there be no mistake,' he said firmly but calmly. 'This was not just an attack on one isolated building. It was an attack on the entire city of Seattle. We do not take it lightly, and we intend to do whatever is necessary to track down the person or persons responsible.'

'Tell us what you know so far,' entreated a reporter from the *Post-Intelligencer*.

'I want to,' came the response, 'but unfortunately I can't. In this case, we must balance the people's right to know with the need for an unhampered investigation. I'm sorry, but that means there can be no briefings, no information, no leaks from the police or any other investigating authority to anyone until we have something of material substance to report. And we ask you all to understand and respect that.'

'You mean, don't call us, we'll call you?' the reporter suggested sardonically.

The spokesman shrugged. 'For now, let's think about the victims and their families, and the grieving that has to take place,' he said, deftly diverting the crowd. 'Let's all be there to offer our condolences and our prayers to these people, and give us a few days' breathing space.'

'In a most heinous act of terrorism,' NBC's Tom Brokaw reported on the evening news, 'more than two hundred people, including an estimated seventy children under the age of five, were either killed or seriously injured today when a bomb destroyed an abortion clinic in Seattle, Washington.'

'Whatever your opinions on the subject,' Kathi Goertzen, KOMO news co-anchor, felt compelled to suggest, 'the Seattle Family Services Center was much more than just an abortion clinic. It was an integral part of our community. Over the years, it was a helping hand for millions, a refuge for thousands, and a last resort for hundreds. Hill House will be sorely missed.'

'The Coalition for Conservative Causes is a peaceful and law-abiding organization that does not advocate violence of any kind against anyone,' executive director Roger Roark read from a hastily prepared script. 'We deeply regret the loss of life at the Seattle Family Services Center. While we accept no responsibility

26

for those who have made a holy war out of an unborn child's right to life, we cannot help but consider how many times, in such righteous wars, guiltless people have been sacrificed for the greater good.'

'We are horrified by the destruction of Hill House, and by the deaths of so many innocent people,' Priscilla Wales, president of FOCUS, the acronym for Freedom of Choice in the United States, declared in an impromptu telephone interview from her San Francisco headquarters. 'However, if you consider the current political climate, and the resulting rhetoric of the CCC and other organizations like it, who want you to believe that two wrongs do indeed make a right, you can see why we're not particularly surprised by this terrorist act. A disaster of this magnitude was totally predictable, really just a matter of time. The question is – how much longer are we going to continue to put up with it? How many more lives are going to be lost before we elect officials who will step up to the responsibility for protecting the rights of women in this country?'

'This is what happens when our legislators turn a blind eye to the double standard of killing helpless babies and then protecting their killers,' said the soft-spoken, Houston-based Prudence Chaffey, pro-life activist and co-founder of AIM, the acronym for Abortion Is Murder. 'And the worst of it is that such acts of frustration and desperation will likely continue until the people of this country are willing to rise up as one and repudiate all forms of murder.'

'A special hotline has been established in an effort to help authorities identify the victims of this catastrophe as quickly as possible,' veteran KING telecaster Jean Enersen announced. 'Police are asking people who think they know someone who might have been at Hill House at the time of the bombing to please call this number.'

* * *

27

'My mother isn't here,' eight-year-old Justine Pauley told the woman who answered the hotline. 'I think maybe she was at Hill House today.'

'And why do you think that, honey?' the operator asked.

'Because she told me not to worry if she wasn't here when I came home from school.'

'Can you describe her for me?' the woman inquired gently.

'She's thin.'

'How old is she?'

'I'm not sure. Pretty old, I guess.'

'What does she look like? What color is her hair, her eyes?'

'Brown,' Justine replied.

'Honey, is your daddy home? Can I talk to him?'

'No, he's not here,' the child replied. 'But I'm not worried about him, 'cause he doesn't come home until real late sometimes.'

'Are you alone?'

'Oh no,' Justine assured her. 'My brother is here with me.'

'That's good,' the operator said, relieved. 'How old is he?'

'He's six.'

Joshua Clune would not come out of his box. No matter how hard Big Dug coaxed and cajoled, his friend would not budge.

'I've been looking for you,' the bearded behemoth declared. 'Did you hear the news?'

'No,' Joshua mumbled.

'Somebody blew up Hill House this afternoon, and it burned right down to the ground.'

There was no response.

'I heard almost everybody's dead.' There was still no response.

'Are you sicker?' Big Dug asked. For the past week now, Joshua had been suffering from a chest cold. Yesterday, he had coughed up blood, and Big Dug had taken him to Hill House, where he was examined by a doctor and told to come back today for further treatment. 'Did you go see the doctor again like you were supposed to? Did he give you some medicine?'

'Go away,' Joshua said.

'I'd get you some soup, but I don't know who's going to feed us tonight, and I don't have any money.'

'I don't want any soup.'

With some effort, Big Dug got down on his knees and peered inside the box. Joshua was curled up in his blanket like a baby.

'Hey, what's the matter?' the man asked. 'You're shivering.'

'Go away,' Joshua repeated. 'I don't want to talk to you now. I have nothing to say. I want to go to sleep.'

'Okay,' Big Dug said with a sigh, hefting himself back up. 'I'll come by later and see how you're doing.'

As soon as Joshua heard the heavy footsteps moving away, he let out a deep sigh of relief. It was all his fault, and he couldn't tell Big Dug. He couldn't tell anyone. They would all blame him, and Big Dug wouldn't want to be his friend anymore.

He hadn't meant to do it. It was just that he had the appointment, and the doctor had told him it was important, and he was afraid he would forget. But he knew he wasn't supposed to sleep at Hill House.

'I'm certainly not saying that we should condone what took place in Seattle today,' the Reverend Jonathan Heal was quick to tell his televangelical flock on his nightly cable Prayer Hour. 'I say only that it's not hard to understand why it happened. I myself know the frustration, the outrage, of having to stand by helplessly while more than a million blessed babies are murdered in this country every year, each one of them given no more significance than an unwanted piece of garbage. So the grief that we as true Christians feel by the loss of so many innocent lives at Hill House must be taken in context with the fundamental wrong of taking any life – born or unborn.'

In homes all across the country, people murmured, 'Amen.'

'I have no idea what tortured soul was driven to commit such a deed as this, but I will pray for him,' the Reverend continued, warming to his subject, and beginning to sweat through his customary white suit and ruffled shirt. 'Because I believe, in his heart of hearts, he decided that he was not only justified in doing what he did, but that he had no choice. Surely, he must have felt that, at the highest level, he was committing nothing less than an act of God.'

Throughout the afternoon and into the evening, from local newscasts to *Nightline*, the bombing of Hill House – and the fact that every international terrorist group in the world was denying any responsibility for it – was the major topic of conversation. It eclipsed everything else of interest.

This was not, however, just any first Tuesday in February. As happened every four years, it was the day of the New Hampshire primary, and the voters from that state had gone to the polls to declare their preference for both Democratic and Republican presidential candidates. On any other evening, the event, which unofficially signaled the start of the election campaign, would have been on everyone's tongue, even the late-night gagsters. This evening, however, the story was almost an afterthought on the news, and Leno and Letterman were not making jokes.

6

The authorities were as good as their word. While regular medical bulletins on the various victims were issued during the days that followed the bombing, there was no information forthcoming about the investigation itself.

The media, its ranks already swollen to national proportions, scrounged around for anything that would fill air or print space. The overwhelmed medical examiner's office confirmed that there were so far one hundred and sixty-three dead, the majority having perished at the scene. Some forty of the most seriously injured were still in various hospitals around the city. Another thirty had been treated and then released. Perhaps half a dozen were still unaccounted for.

Reporters hovered outside the boundaries of the clinic, watching rescue workers dig through the wreckage, waiting for word on the missing. They camped outside the homes of victims, begging for interviews. They stood shifts at the various hospitals, anticipating a rise in the death toll.

By Saturday, funerals had begun to take place, and memorial services were being conducted. Among the most poignant was one held by a group of homeless people who had depended on Hill House's waterfront soup kitchen for one decent meal a day. Over five hundred strong, they lined Alaskan Way, down near the ferry terminal, armed with candles donated by a shop in Pioneer Square, and prayed throughout the night. Several local churches, hearing about the vigil, quickly organized their congregations to bring a hot dinner for the participants.

The governor and the mayor attended as many of the ceremonies as they could, with the media close behind. Politics had taken second place to Hill House. The results of the New

Hampshire primary and speculation about the upcoming South Carolina primary had been sandwiched between round-the-clock bulletins from Seattle.

Sensing a national photo opportunity, the two front-running presidential candidates, seeking to go into South Carolina on a high note, both announced they would fly to Washington to meet with the survivors and the families of the victims. Upon hearing this, the mayor's office promptly planned a huge public memorial service, and designated Memorial Stadium at Seattle Center as the site.

Condolences poured in from all across the state and many parts of the country. And money, tucked inside cards and letters, found its way to the families of the victims. Outside the iron fence along Boren and Madison, flowers and small remembrances began to appear, a trickle at first, that soon became a deluge.

Joseph Heradia was one of the lucky ones; he had not been killed or even injured in the explosion. More important, as far as the investigation was concerned, he was an eyewitness.

'I was just crossing Boren,' he said, repeating to Dana McAuliffe exactly what he had told the police. 'The laurel bushes were between me and the clinic, but I heard what sounded like, well, sort of a sonic boom – very loud. And then the ground was shaking under me so hard I could barely stand. I grabbed hold of the gate, and stuff started flying in all directions. The next thing I knew, I was inside the fence, on the lawn, and let me tell you, it was total chaos.'

'I can only imagine,' Dana responded, thinking how a meeting run long had more than likely saved his life.

'The police asked me if I'd seen anybody who looked suspicious, someone who didn't belong at the clinic, or who was heading away from the scene rather than toward it, but I really couldn't help them. I wasn't thinking about that at the time.'

'Maybe in a few days,' she suggested, 'something you may not even realize you noticed will come back to you.'

He looked at her with hollow eyes. 'What kind of crazy

people would blow up a bunch of innocent children like that, not to mention mothers with their newborn babies? What kind of world are we living in, anyway? And if this is what it is, why would anyone want to bring new life into it?'

'Sometimes, I wonder,' Dana murmured.

'The police also asked if I knew of anybody who had a grudge against me or against Hill House. I really can't bring myself to believe that the Jensens would've had anything to do with this, but I had to tell them.'

'Of course you did,' she assured him. 'Don't worry. If they're not involved, there's no harm done.'

'They're good people,' he said. 'I don't want them to get hurt by this.'

'I'll talk to their attorney,' Dana promised. 'Give him a heads-up. He'll explain to the Jensens that you didn't have a choice. It'll be all right.'

Marilyn Korba huddled in the tiny waiting room just inside the second-floor Intensive Care Unit at the Harborview Medical Center. The cramped space held a shabby sofa, three cracked vinyl chairs, and a television set that worked on only one channel. It had been her home for the past eighty-four hours, ever since the call had come, telling her that her husband had been critically injured in the Hill House bombing.

Family, close friends, doctors, and nurses had passed in and out with food, blankets and pillows, small talk, and medical updates, but most of it was just a jumble in her head. Other than her sister, who had been with her from the start, and the daily telephone call to her mother, who was taking care of the children, all she could focus on was that the last words she had exchanged with Jeff had been in anger over a stupid washing machine. Now there was a very real possibility that she would never hear his voice again.

For just a few minutes at a time, she was allowed in to see him. He lay in a small, sterile, curtained-off room, blessedly unconscious, what remained of his once vigorous body attached by a dozen different wires to machines that blinked and flashed and bleeped, and connected by tubes to life-sustaining drips of blood and glucose and saline. Marilyn had never seen anything so frightening in her life.

'I don't want him to wake up in pain,' she told the doctors anxiously. 'You can give him something for that, can't you?'

'Of course,' the doctors said, nodding solicitously, not wanting to suggest to her that it was unlikely he was going to wake up at all.

Marilyn and Jeffrey Korba had both been born and raised in the Seattle area, meeting at the University of Washington, and marrying right after graduation. They lived with Marilyn's parents while Jeff went through medical school. In his last year of residency, they bought a modest home of their own in Issaquah and started their family, two boys and a girl coming in rapid succession. In all their years together, except of course for those nights when Jeff was on duty at the hospital, they had never been apart for more than a day at a time, and they had never once gone to sleep on an argument.

'I wish they'd let me stay in there with him,' Marilyn told her sister. 'I don't want him to be alone.'

'He's not alone,' her sister assured her in a soothing voice. 'God is with him.'

After surgery to remove the metal fragments that had lacerated her eyes beyond repair, Ruth Zelkin was moved to a private room on the third floor at Virginia Mason Hospital. Although the Zelkins could hardly afford the expense, her husband, Harry, had insisted, knowing that the family would want to be in constant attendance, and not wishing to disturb another patient.

He was right. Four of their five children lived in or near Seattle, as did Ruth's two sisters, her brother, Harry's brother, and all their families. At least a dozen people surrounded his wife's bed at any given time.

'The children,' Ruth moaned as soon as the anesthesia had begun to clear from her brain. 'What about the children? What about the staff?'

'Don't think about that now,' Harry told her gently. 'There'll be time later on. Right now, you need to concentrate on getting well.'

She turned toward the sound of his voice, fear creeping into her tone, as she whispered, 'How many?'

Harry looked acutely uncomfortable, and for an unguarded instant, he was glad she couldn't see his face. It was too soon, he thought; she wasn't strong enough to hear. Their oldest daughter took her mother's hand.

'You need your rest, mom,' she said. 'Talk later.'

But Ruth set her jaw in that not-to-be-denied expression her family knew so well and managed to half lift herself from the bed. 'How many?' she demanded.

Her daughter placed both of her hands on her mother's shoulders and pushed her gently back against the pillow.

Her husband sighed. 'Ten members of the staff were lost,' he said.

'And the children?'

Her daughter shook her head vehemently, but Harry shrugged. 'Fifty-six,' he told his wife.

Ruth Zelkin's world, which was already gray, suddenly went black.

The nursery where Jason Holman had spent most of his brief life was dark, heavy curtains blotting out the sun so that his afternoon naps would not be disturbed. Janet Holman sat in the big maple rocking chair where she had nursed her son through infancy, and held and soothed him whenever he was hurt or frightened. She had been in that chair, in that room, since Tuesday night.

She hardly needed light to see the crinkly smile that brightened his face when she lifted him from his crib, or the little arms that reached up for her, trusting her implicitly to defend and protect him from whatever evil might lurk in the big bad world. In truth, she couldn't have said whether it was day or night, nor did she care.

Outside the room, people came and went from the spacious Bellevue condominium, walking softly, speaking in whispers.

They needn't have bothered; Janet never heard them. She just sat there, gently rocking back and forth, as she always did when Jason was fretful, and stared into the lightless space, in a world of pain so excruciating, so overwhelming, that all she wanted was to go wherever it was that Jason had gone.

'She hasn't eaten or slept since it happened,' her husband, Rick, told everyone. 'I try to talk to her, but I don't think she even hears me. She just sits there, staring at something I don't see.' He was red-eyed with sleeplessness himself. 'We have to make . . . arrangements, you know, for the funeral and everything. But she won't even discuss it. It's almost like, if she doesn't have to talk about it, then it didn't really happen. I don't know what to do . . .' His voice trailed off.

'Look, why don't you let me take care of the arrangements,' his brother offered. 'You just take care of Janet.'

'If I only knew what she wanted,' Rick murmured.

'You try to get some rest,' his sister-in-law suggested. 'Just leave everything to us.'

Rick slipped into the nursery and leaned over the rocking chair, wrapping his arms protectively around his wife, hardly aware that the minister had followed him in and now stood silently in the shadows.

He knew exactly how Janet felt. Jason had been the only survivor of thirteen years of trying to get pregnant. 'My brother is going to make the arrangements for the funeral,' he murmured into her hair. 'It'll be exactly the way you want it, simple and private, no fanfare, no media, just family and friends to say goodbye to Jason.'

He felt her whole body convulse. 'He can't be alone,' she said in a strange singsong sort of voice that didn't sound like her at all. 'You know how he hates to be alone.'

'He won't be alone,' Rick said soothingly, although at this point, he had little faith that there would be any Supreme Being to look after him.

'No, he won't,' Janet agreed, in that same frightening tone, 'because I'm going to go with him. Then we'll be together, always.'

'Please, honey, don't talk that way,' he said in as calm a voice as he could muster, while ever so slightly tightening his grip on her shoulders for fear she would somehow find a way to slip away from him. 'You know you can't go with Jason.'

'Of course I can,' she replied in the darkness, her words chilling him to the bone. 'So you see, tell your brother, there'll be no need for any goodbyes.'

At that, the minister felt compelled to step forward. 'Dear girl, don't despair,' he said. 'Jason is in loving hands. He's with God now.'

Janet Holman peered up at the man as though she had never seen him before. 'God?' she asked, clearly perplexed. 'God who?'

Jesse Montero had never been much of a churchgoing man. He always figured that his wife prayed enough for both of them. But on the Sunday after the bombing, he got up, somehow managed to dress himself in his one good suit, and was the first one into the car.

'What are you doing, Jesse?' his wife asked. 'You should be in bed, like the doctor said.'

He waved his bandaged arms impatiently. 'I am going to thank God for saving my life,' he said through the dressings that covered most of his face. 'Now, hurry up and get the children. I don't want to be late.'

The church was filled for the morning mass. The priest was not surprised. It was always like that after a disaster, people wanting to feel closer to the Almighty.

Margo Montero glanced at her husband, on his knees in the pew, a rosary clamped between his mittened paws. She had slept beside this man every night for the past sixteen years, through good times, bad times, and very bad times: unemployment, illness, hunger, homelessness. And this was the first time in all those years that she had ever seen him truly frightened.

Helen Gamble couldn't stop crying. Aside from a few minor broken bones and some lacerations, the twins, having been released from Children's Hospital, were safe and sound in their West Seattle rambler. Helen's husband, Walter, cut a business trip short and flew home as soon as he got word. But even with her husband by her side, the tears still flowed uncontrollably.

'It's nerves,' the doctor told Walter. 'Don't worry, it'll pass.'

'It's for all those poor babies who won't ever come home,' Helen told a reporter from *People* magazine who had played on her sympathy to get a foot in the door. 'And for Brenda Kiley, who I owe so much more than I can ever hope to repay. And for all those other people who died . . . so many of them. I can't believe this has happened.'

The first thing she did, after making sure the twins were all right and in good hands at Children's Hospital, was to go to Raymond Kiley, put her arms around him, and assure him that Christopher and Jennifer would never know a day without his wife's name being spoken.

'They will understand,' she declared, 'that there were two women in this world who gave them life.'

'We always wanted kids,' Raymond said. 'We were never lucky.'

'You have two now,' Helen assured him.

Brenda Kiley was laid to rest on Monday. Ignoring her own injuries, which had turned out to be far worse than those of the twins, Helen dressed Christopher and Jennifer in their Sunday best, and took them to the private service for friends and family only.

Then she went home, put the twins up for their nap, and wept.

Three-year-old Chelsea Callahan, who had escaped injury in the blast that killed her mother, was placed in foster care while Child Protective Services tried to find a relative who would take her.

The foster family reported that the only word the little girl seemed able to say was 'Momma,' and that she cried herself to sleep every night.

After evaluating the results of an eight-hour surgery, the doctors at Virginia Mason concluded that Betsy Toth would never walk again. Her fractured spine had been reassembled, but the nerve damage was too great. The twenty-year-old nurse's aide would spend the rest of her life in a wheelchair, and have only minimal use of her hands and arms.

Andy Umanski sat by her side, holding her hand, and watching her sleep. She had slept most of the last five days, which was a blessing, he decided. The stronger she was when she heard the news, the better. She certainly didn't look very strong to him right now. In fact, she seemed so fragile – pinioned, as she was, to a very scary-looking contraption that rotated her whole body face-up or face-down – that he was afraid she might slip out and fall. At the moment, she was facing up. He leaned over and rested his cheek on her hand.

'I had a dream,' she murmured, waking for a moment, and seeming to know that he was there. 'I dreamed we had a baby boy with brown eyes and blue hair. Isn't that silly? I told the doctor there had to be some mistake, but he said there wasn't; that this was a special little boy, meant just for us.'

Andy squeezed her hand. 'Good for us,' he whispered, and watched as she drifted back to sleep. In the two years he had known her, and particularly during the last six months, after they had become engaged and began planning their wedding, it was always the first thing on her mind, having a big family to make up for being orphaned at the age of eight. He sighed heavily. There would be time, too, but not yet, to tell her that there would be no babies.

Ironically, Shelly Weld and Denise Romanadis, who had shared their last moments of life together, were buried on the same day; Shelly after a large, boisterous Catholic service, and Denise after a small, quiet Greek Orthodox ceremony.

In both cases, the funerals had been delayed because it had taken the medical examiner's office almost a week to reconstruct the bits and pieces of the two women's bodies. And all they could do was pray that they had gotten at least most of it right.

They needn't have worried. Both caskets were closed and both bodies were cremated. Shelly's parents chose to scatter their daughter's ashes over Puget Sound. Denise's remains were interred in a family crypt.

The mayor was an honored guest at the Weld funeral in Seattle. The governor startled Denise's mourners by making a brief appearance at the Romanadis family church in Northgate.

Joe Romanadis, standing with his three surviving children, was overwhelmed when the governor actually came up and hugged him. It was a great media opportunity. A tape of the moment topped the news broadcasts that evening, and a photograph made the front page of the *Post-Intelligencer* the following morning.

'Hey dad, you're famous,' his thirteen-year-old son said.

'I don't want to be famous,' Joe told him, tears in his eyes. 'I just want them to catch the son of a bitch who did this.'

Frances Stocker's daughter drove her mother from the hospital to Whidbey Island. The psychologist's legs were in casts up to her hips.

'There are so many steel pins in those legs,' the doctor quipped, 'you be sure you don't meet up with any "magnates."' He was very proud of his handiwork. Going in, he hadn't really been sure whether he would be able to save both legs.

'I don't want to be a burden on you,' Frances said to her daughter. 'I'll go home as soon as I learn how to get around.' She was discharged from the hospital with a quantity of antibiotics, a prescription for pain pills, and a pair of sturdy metal crutches.

'Mom, you're not a burden,' Gail Stocker replied. 'You'll stay until the doctor says you can go.'

'The doctors are overcautious,' Frances said with a sniff. 'I'll be an expert on those stilts by the end of the week.'

Gail sighed. Her mother had never been one to listen to

anybody, least of all her daughter. 'Good,' she said. 'I'll enter you in the Boston Marathon.'

'I just don't want you waiting on me,' Frances grumbled. 'You have enough to do, what with your job and all your animals. I don't know why you think you have to take care of me.'

'Because I can,' the veterinarian replied. 'For the first time in my life, I have the opportunity to really do something important for you. So let me.'

Frances smiled to herself. Her mother's daughter, she thought wryly – capable, independent, and stubborn. But in truth, the idea of being alone right now was not particularly appealing. Just simply knowing that another person was near at hand was what mattered most of all, especially during the night when it was dark and quiet. When she lay by the hour with eyes wide open, alternately perspiring and shivering, and wondered why she had been spared, when so many others had not. It was nice to know then that someone was there, someone to whom she was connected, someone who cared.

It was easier to stay awake than to sleep. In her nightmares, Frances was back in her office, seeing Grace Pauley perched in the chair just across the desk. Why had the desk protected her, and not that poor woman who had so needed protection? For the rest of her life, she knew she would see that frail figure, those fragile features, that desperate expression, etched on the inside of her eyelids.

It didn't take Carl Gentry long to discover that a broken neck wasn't necessarily fatal.

'I thought people died when their necks got broken,' the security guard said to the doctor at Swedish Hospital a week after the bombing.

'Some do,' he was told. 'But many don't. It all depends on the type of fracture. The fact that you remained conscious could have given you a clue.'

The upper part of Carl's body was strapped to some kind of a board, and he seemed to be numb from the waist down. He raised his hands and gingerly touched the medieval collar screwed into his neck and head. 'What is this thing?' he asked.

'Torture,' the doctor replied with a smile. 'You know that old song about the head bone connected to the neck bone? Well, that collar is what's holding your head to your neck, and your neck to your spine.'

'Well, all I can say is it's giving me one hell of a headache.'

The doctor nodded. 'And it probably will for a while. Savor the pain. It's a good sign; it means not all the nerves were damaged.'

Carl looked at the doctor. 'Tell me straight, doc, will I be okay? Will I walk again? Will I – will I be able to function?'

'All indications so far are that I am a superb surgeon, a bit of a miracle worker, actually,' the doctor replied with a twinkle in his eye, 'and that you will in no way damage my reputation.' He saw the uncertainty in his patient's expression. 'The numbness you're experiencing should wear off in time,' he added. 'How much time, I admit we can't predict with any real consistency. It could be as long as several months before you regain certain capabilities, but everything should come back pretty much the way it was. For now, though, you'll just have to take my word for that, and be patient.'

The security guard sighed with relief. 'Thanks,' he said, a little embarrassed. 'I was kind of worried, you know. You see, I'm only forty-six.'

Four days later, there was a visitor, slipping into his room like a vision. For a moment, he couldn't quite place her, and thought perhaps she had come for the man in the next bed. But then she came close and he smelled her perfume, and then she spoke and he remembered. It was the woman he had met the night before the bombing, the one he had been thinking about the next day, at the very moment he was being tossed off the porch.

'It took me this long to find you,' she told him, half hidden behind an enormous bouquet of flowers, 'or I'd have come sooner.'

'I'm really glad,' he said. 'I've been thinking about you a lot, but, well, under the circumstances, I wasn't really sure, you know, if you'd want to see me again.'

'Whew,' she declared with a sigh of relief, depositing the flowers on the bed stand and herself in a chair. 'I was going to feel very foolish, rushing to your side like this, if you'd forgotten all about me.'

A big smile spread across Carl's face. His headache seemed to vanish, gone in a rush of sensations that he could swear he felt the whole length of his body.

The injuries to Joyce O'Mara were extensive. For days, the doctors at Swedish Hospital were unsure whether she would survive. They removed one kidney and a lung, reconstructed her rib cage, repaired her aorta, made every effort to locate and control all the internal bleeding, and then monitored her around the clock for any signs of infection, liver damage, or failure of her other kidney.

'Barring any unexpected complications, I think she's going to make it,' the lead doctor finally felt confident to report. 'But I don't mind telling you, she is one very lucky lady.'

Donald O'Mara, Joyce's husband of eight years, felt the sting of tears in his eyes. 'I can't thank you enough,' he said. 'The whole staff. I know how hard you've all worked.'

'It's going to be a long recovery,' the doctor cautioned. 'She'll have to adjust to a body that isn't going to work quite the same as the old one did. There will probably be some things she won't be able to do again, and others she'll have to learn to do differently.'

'Don't worry,' Joyce's mother said. 'She's coming home to North Bend with me. Everyone is coming home with me. I'll take care of her. I'll take care of everything.'

'We're going to move her out of Intensive Care in a couple of hours,' the doctor told them. 'One of the nurses will let you know what room she's going to.'

The moment the doctor was gone, Donald slumped into a chair, deserted by every ounce of the energy that had kept him going until this moment. As harrowing as the two weeks prior to the bombing had been, this last week had been ten times worse. 'I don't know what we'd do without you,' he said to his mother-in-law.

'It's a perfect solution,' she replied. 'I have plenty of room and the children will be the better for the distraction. What better place for all of you to be than on the farm?'

Donald sighed. 'For the sake of the family, we make an agonizing decision not to have this child, based on overwhelming medical advice, exhaustive religious debate, and endless hours of prayer, and look what happens.'

'God works in mysterious ways,' she suggested.

Her son-in-law looked horrified. 'You think all this devastation was the work of God?' he asked.

At two o'clock in the afternoon on the third Tuesday in February, two weeks almost to the minute after the bombing of Hill House, Jeffrey Korba died. His injuries were just too massive for him to survive.

'He's at peace,' the doctor told his sobbing wife. 'I realize how hard it is for you to understand this now, but it was for the best. Had he lived, he would not have been the man you knew. It's better to remember him the way he was.'

Marilyn nodded, thankful, at least, that she was by his side, holding his hand, when he took his last breath. She had been able to tell him how sorry she was about the damned washing machine.

'Do you think he knew I was there?' she asked.

'We know so little of what the mind processes in a state of unconsciousness,' the doctor replied. 'But we constantly hear about people who come out of comas and relate whole conversations that were carried on around them. So yes, I believe he knew.'

Marilyn looked down at her husband. 'I guess I have to go on somehow, don't I?' she murmured.

'Do you have someone to help you?' the doctor inquired solicitously.

'Oh yes,' she said. 'My mother – she's taking care of the

children. And of course, my sister is here with me. There are lots of people . . .' Her voice trailed off, and she looked up at the doctor with an almost childlike need for reassurance. 'But Jeffrey was my whole life, you see. I don't know what I'm going to do without him.'

7

Joshua Clune took the medicine the doctor had prescribed for him and got over being sick. But he didn't get over the bombing of Hill House. It was all he could think of, every day, every night. And it didn't help that for almost a month now it was all anyone seemed to want to talk about.

'We're not as safe as we used to be,' Big Dug told him, as the two sat huddled on a bench near the ferry terminal in a cold damp rain. 'They didn't just feed us, they looked after us, too.'

'I know,' Joshua mumbled, wishing his friend would go away and let him be. 'I'm sorry.'

'Of course you're sorry. We're all sorry. Life here won't ever be the same.'

'I couldn't help it,' Joshua said, his stomach in knots.

'Of course you couldn't, none of us could,' Big Dug assured him. 'It isn't like any of us wanted this to happen.'

'I didn't, really, I didn't,' Joshua told him, finding it suddenly difficult to breathe.

'It's just that nobody knows what to do. The churches will feed us, but what about everything else? Like your medicine when you got sick. Who's going to give that to us now? I have to tell you, everyone's pretty worried.'

At that, Joshua couldn't stand it anymore. Tears filled his hazel eyes and rolled down his cheeks, into his reddish stubble. 'I'm sorry,' he choked. 'I didn't mean to do it.'

'Mean to do what?' Big Dug asked.

'I did it,' Joshua gasped, no longer able to hold it in. 'I caused the fire.'

The big man blinked. 'What are you talking about?'

'The fire,' Joshua repeated. 'I caused the fire, and I'm so sorry. I didn't mean to do it.'

'It was a bomb,' Big Dug told him. 'A bomb caused the fire.'

'No, it was me,' Joshua said forlornly. 'You told me. You told me not to sleep there, but the doctor said for me to come back first thing in the morning, and I was afraid I'd forget. I forget things, sometimes, and if I forgot the doctor, then he would get mad and tell me to go away, and I wouldn't get my medicine, and I wouldn't get well.'

'You slept at Hill House that night? The night before the bomb went off?'

Joshua looked miserable. 'You told me not to, you told me if I did, it could start a fire,' he sobbed. 'Now I don't know what to do. I burned down Hill House and nobody will ever want to be my friend again.'

Big Dug might have looked like a lumberjack, but he had once been a schoolteacher. 'Listen to me, very carefully,' he said, his voice as gentle as he could make it. 'You didn't burn down Hill House. What I said about sleeping there, I didn't mean for you to think that just sleeping there was going to cause a fire. It takes a lot more than that.' He stopped and peered down at his younger friend. 'You did just sleep there, didn't you?'

Joshua nodded. 'In the back. There's a little shed next to some bushes. It's real dry and cozy in between there. I just wanted to make sure I didn't forget to go to the doctor. Do I have to tell?'

'Well, I guess that depends,' Big Dug replied. While there was little open hostility, there was not much love lost between the police and the homeless in the city of Seattle, and not much sympathy, on either side. 'Did you see anything, or hear anything, you know, that looked suspicious?'

'I don't think I did,' Joshua said, shaking his head. 'It was pretty dark, and I was sleeping.'

'Then, if there wasn't anything, I don't see any reason for you to have to tell.'

Joshua heaved a huge sigh of relief. 'And no one has to know I was there, except you and me?'

47

'I guess not,' Big Dug said. 'We can just keep it between ourselves, if you like.'

A broad smile spread across Joshua's face. 'That's what I'd like,' he said. 'If we could just keep it between ourselves. Do you promise you won't go and tell any of the others what I did?'

'I promise,' Big Dug assured him with a smile, getting up from the bench and lumbering toward the water fountain.

Joshua rose to follow him. 'Besides,' he said with renewed cheer, 'if there was anything to see, the delivery man will tell.'

Big Dug stopped in his tracks. 'Delivery man?' he asked. 'What delivery man was that?'

'The one that brought the packages.'

'Someone brought packages to Hill House? The night you slept there?'

Joshua nodded. 'He took them down to the basement.'

When the bombing of Hill House was six weeks old, the mayor of Seattle sat down with his chief of police.

'Are we any further along than we were, say, a week ago?' he asked, a clear note of desperation in his voice.

'I think so,' came the reply.

The two men had known each other since boyhood, and the mayor generally knew better than to push the methodical police commander. But now *he* was being pushed, and pushed hard, and he didn't like it. 'Can you give me something, anything?' he begged.

'I know the media blackout has been tough on you,' the chief said. 'But it's made all the difference to us. At this point, I can confirm that this was not an act of international terrorism.'

'Well, that's something, anyway,' the mayor said. 'It'll relieve some of the pressure.'

'I can also tell you that we now have a person of interest.'

'You mean someone you think you can charge?' the mayor exclaimed, almost popping out of his seat.

'I believe so. But we're not ready to go public with that yet. We want to be sure we've got everything in order first.'

'When?'

'A couple more days, maybe.'

The mayor sighed. 'Why does that sound like another eternity?'

'It won't be much longer,' his friend promised.

'All right then, can I say that the investigation is still ongoing, and has been quite productive, and that your office will likely have a statement to make, say, by the end of the week?'

The police chief thought for a moment. The mayor was not alone. He, too, was under the gun, and feeling the pressure. His department was being ridiculed by the media, and after almost thirty years on the job, his competence was being questioned by the city council.

He was almost certain of his culprit, but he had been dragging his heels on an arrest because his case was wholly circumstantial. The thing he needed to lock it up tight was just one piece of direct evidence, and he knew, if it came to that, he'd give his pension for it. However, he also knew he couldn't wait forever. He sighed. 'I think that would be all right,' he said.

The news came late Saturday, with a simple statement from the chief of police that began: 'We now have a person of interest in custody,' and ended: 'We thank all of you for your patience and understanding.'

According to officials, the arrest was the culmination of the largest investigative effort in city history. Seattle authorities, in cooperation with several federal agencies, had sifted through the wreckage of Hill House with the proverbial fine-tooth comb. They had collected anything that might conceivably be related to the crime, examined and then reexamined each piece of potential evidence, interviewed literally dozens of people, and run down every possible lead.

What was extraordinary was that it had all been done with amazing calm and efficiency, despite incredible public pressure and the white-hot glare of a national media blitz.

8

Once a year, Dana McAuliffe fixed pancakes for breakfast. The singular occasion was the Sunday closest to March 19, and she made the effort because her husband, Sam, was a sucker for the buttermilk kind with fresh blueberries in them. March 19, which this year just happened to fall on a Sunday, was Sam's birthday.

For the first two years of their marriage, Dana had lovingly and laboriously prepared the batter from scratch, squinting over the tiny print in her antiquated version of the *Joy of Cooking*, measuring cups and spoons firmly in hand, hoping to achieve the right blend of flour, buttermilk, eggs, and seasonings. Then one day she happened to come upon a packaged mix at Costco, and never looked back. If he noticed the difference, Sam never let on.

Molly certainly never noticed. The nine-year-old freckle-face with brown pigtails loved pancakes every bit as much as her stepfather did, and the preparation process was still a happy mystery to her. It was a most fortunate circumstance for Dana, whose least favorite activity in life was cooking.

'If I'd wanted to be a cook,' she often grumbled to herself, usually during the frenzy of getting a meal on the table at the last minute, 'I'd have gone to cooking school instead of law school.'

Dana was every inch her father's daughter, from her height and her striking features, to her keen intellect and her single-minded determination to succeed as an attorney. She had cut her teeth on the law in Port Townsend, Washington, watching how it was practiced by the dedicated crusader for individual rights who was both her idol and her mentor.

'The law is the only thing that keeps us civilized,' Jefferson Reid told her from the time she was old enough to understand. 'Without it, we would have destroyed ourselves a long time ago.'

The eldest of four daughters, and in many ways the son her father never had, Dana was a double graduate of Stanford University, her father's alma mater. She began her career by spending two hectic years in the King County prosecutor's office before joining the small but prestigious Seattle law firm of Cotter Boland and Grace.

'I don't have to take this job, you know,' she told her father when she called to discuss the offer with him. 'I can come back to Port Townsend. We could set up that partnership we talked about when I was a kid. Remember – Reid & Reid?'

'Yes, but you're not a kid anymore,' he replied wisely. 'You wouldn't be happy practicing small-town law. It might suit me to a tee, but not you, my girl. Not yet, anyway. Right now, there are big-city lights in your eyes and dreams in your head, and you have to follow them wherever they take you. From everything I hear, Cotter Boland is a top-level firm, doing first-class work, and it sounds like an offer that's probably too good for you to pass up.'

She could always count on him to know her better than anyone, probably better even than she knew herself. Port Townsend was a fine place to have been raised. Dana treasured the years she had spent there, growing and learning, and she would always think of it as home, but it was undeniably provincial, and to be honest, dull. Seattle, on the other hand, was the largest city in the Pacific Northwest, and it offered all the excitement, sophistication, and opportunity she could hope for.

'Are you sure you don't mind?' she persisted.

Jefferson Reid, who was very good at reading people, especially his daughter, smiled into the telephone. 'I'm sure,' he said.

She took the job.

Eight years later, having devoted herself to her work, at the expense of almost everything else in her life, she was invited to join the partnership of Cotter Boland and Grace; the first woman to whom such an offer had ever been tendered. She was thirty-five years old.

'A healthy dose of feminine perspective ought to do this stuffy old place some real good,' Paul Cotter told her. He was then fifty-eight, and the managing partner of the firm that had been started by his great-grandfather more than a century before.

The first time that Dana took her place at the foot of the huge mahogany conference table, she knew she had achieved what she had dreamed about since the days when her father had let her play hooky from school and had taken her to court with him, sat her down in the first row, right behind the defense table, and let her soak it all up.

'Your mother's a wonderful woman, who has no head for the law,' he would tell her. 'So I will share it with you.'

Two years after joining Cotter Boland, Dana married a young attorney who had followed her to Seattle after law school. They rented a lovely little place near Green Lake and had Molly. But when her husband realized that he had quietly been shuffled from a dubious first to second and then to third place in Dana's affections, he headed back to California with an aerobics instructor who was all boobs, and butt, and teeth. Neither she nor Molly had heard from him since.

It was difficult for Dana, trying to balance the demands of her job with the requirements of single-parenthood, knowing that Molly usually came out on the short end of the stick. Then one day, when she could no longer avoid thinking about her parents' roomy house in Port Townsend, and the significantly less hectic schedule of a small-town practice, Sam McAuliffe came into her life. Sweet, solid Sam, who took over the care and feeding of her and her daughter as though he had been doing it from the beginning.

He wasn't handsome, as her first husband had been, nor was he an attorney, which didn't bother Dana at all. He was a violinist with the Seattle Symphony, and gave music lessons during the off-season to supplement his income.

It was crazy because they were so very different, and yet they fit together in ways she would never have thought possible. Best of all, he accepted her ambition and her drive and her passion for her work.

'You need me,' he told her one day when they had known each other for six months. 'I can be there for you, and I can be there for Molly, too, when you have to be somewhere else. I know it could work for us, and I really don't think you can afford to pass me up. Besides, I'm in love with both of you.'

His brown hair was thinning at forty-one, he was seriously myopic, and he was what would have been called homely back in her grandmother's time. But he had the most beautiful hands she had ever seen and a lopsided grin that spread all over his face when he was happy. Dana always said it was the grin that got her. But in the end, it was Molly who persuaded her to accept Sam's proposal; the girl was only three and she needed a father.

In the six years that had passed since the three of them had married, Dana never once regretted her decision. The little house they bought on 28th Avenue West in Magnolia was always filled with warmth and laughter and music, and Sam didn't seem to care what place he held in her affections.

By the time his forty-seventh birthday came around, Dana was convinced that she had it all perfectly balanced – career, child, and marriage.

The telephone rang right in the middle of the pancakes.

'Something's come up,' Paul Cotter said without preamble or apology. 'We need you down here right away.'

Cotter Boland and Grace was eminently successful at the practice of law. A modest office by general standards, its seven partners and nine associates were rarely idle. The firm had long ago earned a reputation for being brilliant, conservative, and pragmatic, and for honoring diligence over flamboyance. The managing partner and his two-man executive committee, made up of senior partners Elton Grace and Charles Ramsey, chose their clients with scrupulous care, and rarely accepted a retainer for a case they did not feel was either possible or appropriate for them to win. They won far more cases than they lost, and

53

few of their clients ever regretted the high price tag.

The firm worked out of a modest suite of offices on the seventeenth floor of Smith Tower, once renowned for being, at forty-two stories, the tallest building west of the Mississippi. A number of prominent firms in the city had since relocated to newer, more fashionable quarters, but Cotter Boland had chosen to stay. The eighty-five-year-old structure boasted marble walls, an exquisitely carved Indian head ceiling in the lobby, and ancient copper elevators manned by operators who knew every tenant by name.

Paul Cotter's office was a spacious corner rectangle that overlooked Puget Sound from one set of windows and the King County Courthouse from the other. By the time Dana arrived, speeding all the way down from Magnolia, the rest of the partners were already assembled.

'Glad you were able to join us,' Cotter said, as though his summons had offered a choice, and steered her to the empty chair beside his own, in a grouping around an exquisite Oriental coffee table. 'We waited, of course. We didn't want to begin without you.' There was a general murmur of assent.

Dana sat, but with the distinct impression that whether they had waited or not, she was the only one in the room who had no idea what this was all about. Reacting to Cotter's tone of voice over the telephone, she had not taken time to change, and now noticed with some discomfort that all six of the men wore suits and ties as though this were a regular business day. She tucked her legs in their casual slacks under her chair, and brushed a hand across her flour-streaked nose.

'As I'm sure you've already heard, a young naval officer by the name of Latham has been arrested in connection with the bombing of Hill House,' Cotter continued, turning to her. 'We've agreed to represent him, and we'd like you to take first chair.'

Dana blinked, clearly stunned. She had of course followed the story from the very beginning, or more accurately, the speculation in lieu of facts that surrounded the tragedy. And when news of the arrest broke, she found herself listening with a real sense of satisfaction, even going so far as to offer a private little prayer that the prosecution would be swift and the punishment totally appropriate. It never dawned on her that her law firm, much less she, herself, might be involved.

Cotter Boland and Grace was a practice that, at least during Dana's tenure, had always resisted this sort of high-profile case, far preferring to operate in the background rather than the limelight.

'I wouldn't have thought this was our kind of thing,' she murmured.

Cotter shifted in his seat. 'Normally, it isn't,' he conceded. 'But we're doing it this time as a favor to a friend.'

Dana nodded slowly, filing this bit of information away for the moment. 'And the Navy isn't grabbing it?'

'Apparently not.'

'So, why do I get the honor?' she inquired with unusual bluntness. 'Because abortion is arguably, if not accurately, a woman's issue, and I'm the only woman on the letterhead?'

'No, because you're a first-rate attorney who can do the job,' Cotter replied smoothly. 'Of course, I admit we do think having a woman up front on this one will play a lot better with a jury.'

Dana felt the first stirrings of uneasiness in the pit of her stomach. 'I have a relationship with Hill House,' she informed them. 'I've been a patient there for over a decade. For goodness sake, my doctor was almost a victim.'

'Almost?'

'He wasn't injured. He got to the scene just after the explosion. But he's also a client.'

'In regard to the bombing?'

'No,' Dana conceded. 'He's being sued by a couple over a fertility procedure.'

Cotter took a moment or two to digest this. 'I don't think that constitutes a conflict of interest,' he said at length. He turned to the other partners. 'Do any of you?'

There was a general shaking of heads, and Cotter looked at her and shrugged.

Her stomach stepped up its complaint. 'Well then, is this the time to tell you that I'm not exactly pro-life?' she felt impelled to inquire, looking around the room. 'Or that I think the son of a bitch who blew up all those people should burn in hell?'

The six men exchanged startled glances. They had always known Dana to be a well-bred and soft-spoken woman. Paul Cotter cleared his throat.

'Do you think your personal views would prejudice your client?' he asked.

Yes, she wanted to shout, of course they would. So would any rational person's. 'They never have before,' she said instead, as her stomach protested.

The managing partner folded his hands in his lap. 'Then I see no problem.'

9

The King-County Jail was an eight-minute uphill walk from Smith Tower. And Dana walked it as often as possible. In her high-pressured life, staying in shape was something she had to fit into her schedule.

A solid concrete structure that fronted on Fifth Avenue and occupied the entire city block between James and Jefferson, the jail reflected an architectural style that could most kindly be described as functional. To add insult to injury, the city art commission, for some ghastly reason, had thought it appropriate to install a fanciful mosaic tile playground at the building's entry, entitled, of all things, Freedom Park.

The twelve-story, full-service facility, completed in 1985, had been designed to house just under eleven hundred inmates. It was currently operating with more than twice that number.

Dana crossed the absurd park, and with a deep sigh, pushed her way through the entrance doors. At the security gate, she exchanged her bar card for an ID pass, and was directed to the Number 2 elevator, which took her nonstop to the eleventh floor, and from there to a private interview room.

The room, which more closely resembled a closet, was an irregularly shaped, windowless space with concrete block walls, one of which was painted a garish purple for no discernible purpose, and a steel door with one vertical, four-by-twenty-four-inch tempered glass opening. The cramped area held a small metal table, connected to a chair on either side of it, and bolted to the floor.

Ordinarily, attorneys and their clients met in the public visiting room, and spoke to each other by telephone from either side of a thick Plexiglas panel. But certain law firms that had influence

57

in the city, or were handling a particularly high-profile case, could arrange to meet with their clients separately. Cotter Boland had both, and had no problem obtaining the private room.

Still, Dana looked around the cubicle with a heavy heart. Special treatment or not, it was a place she did not want to be, on a matter with which she did not want to deal.

'Do you believe that everyone in this country deserves a rigorous defense?' Paul Cotter had challenged her after the Sunday meeting had concluded, the other partners had departed, and just the two of them remained in his office.

'Yes, of course I do,' she had replied. 'But even a defense attorney has to have standards. There may not always be a mitigating circumstance for a crime, but at least there has to be some level of rationale that I can build on. If I can't believe in my client, I at least need to believe in the case.'

'And you don't believe in this one?'

'No, I don't,' she had told him, the queasiness in her stomach stirring again. 'Look, I'm not one of those radical feminists who believe that a woman has the right to abdicate all responsibility for her actions. But that doesn't mean I have any loyalty to the control freaks, either, who don't give a tinker's damn about fetuses and are just in it for the power trip. This case – well, I'm sorry, but I can't find a whole lot of rationalization in some lunatic going out and killing innocent people as a protest against killing innocent people.'

'And how exactly have you determined that he's a lunatic?' Cotter inquired. 'You haven't even met him yet.'

'No, I haven't,' she agreed. 'But there must be someone else, someone with more sympathy for his cause, who might be able to justify his actions, who would be better suited to represent him.'

'On the contrary,' Cotter declared. 'I think you're perfect for it.'

'Why?' she protested. 'Aside from your idea about having a woman up front, this is a major case, certainly the most visible case this firm has handled in the twelve years I've been here. You know as well as I do that I have no significant capital crime experience. Aren't you even a little bit concerned about that?'

'What I'm concerned about,' he said, 'is providing the client with the very best we have to offer.'

'Well, in that case,' Dana responded, 'does the client know that I've never sat first chair on a death penalty case before?'

'The client knows everything he needs to know,' Cotter responded. 'Namely, that the full resources of this firm will be put behind his defense.'

'Which means what, exactly?'

'It means that this will be a team effort, of course – all the way down the line. You won't be operating in an isolation ward. Nobody has any intention of abandoning you.'

It still felt like a case she knew she should be running, not walking, away from. 'Why do I think you know something that I don't know?' she wondered aloud.

'Because you're young and have a suspicious mind,' he replied with a smile.

Now, as she sat in one of the interview room's metal chairs, and opened her briefcase to extract a pad and a pen, Dana knew that it didn't really matter what happened here this morning, because the managing partner had given her an out.

'Go talk to the kid,' he had said, handing her the file. 'Get him through the arraignment. Then, if it really isn't right for you, just come and tell me, and I'll assign someone else. I believe it's a fit, but I won't force it on you.'

It was the only reason she was here, she knew, so that she could go back to Cotter and tell him she had done what he asked, and did not want this case.

Five minutes later, the door swung open, and twenty-five-year-old Corey Dean Latham, hands and feet shackled, and escorted by two guards, entered the cubicle.

There were four types of uniforms worn by the inmates at the King County Jail: blue for those serving misdemeanor time, yellow for worker inmates, red for accused felons awaiting trial, and white for those who were charged with a high-risk felony. Corey Latham was dressed in white, with the damning words

'ULTRA SECURITY' printed in big bold letters across his shirt and down the legs of his pants.

Dana's first reaction, as she watched him take the chair across from her, sitting ramrod straight with his manacled hands resting tentatively on the table in front of him, was one of unhappy surprise. He was not at all what she had expected, or wanted, to see. She had prepared herself for some religiously zealous martyr in the making, someone who was unkempt and unattractive, perhaps, or wild-eyed and obviously deranged, or clearly cold and calculating. Any of the above would have suited her purpose, and would have made things so much easier.

But the tall, slender, and undeniably attractive young man who sat so erect in front of her was clean-shaven, had neatly cropped brown hair, clear blue eyes, and the demeanor of an altar boy. He looked totally incongruous in the sinister white uniform.

Dana shook her head slightly as though to clear her mind, or her vision. Latham was an officer in the United States Navy, she exhorted herself to remember. Of course he would know how best to present himself in any kind of situation . . . or in any kind of uniform. The fact that he looked normal, she knew, did not automatically exempt him from having committed cold-blooded murder. After all, his dossier indicated that he was an assistant weapons officer on his submarine. Didn't that mean that killing was what the government had trained him for?

There, she thought with a small surge of triumph, she was back on solid ground now, which was where she would stay. She was certainly not about to let herself get suckered into believing he might be innocent.

Still, the blue eyes did not equivocate. They looked directly at her with an expression she could only interpret as sincerity mixed with enough confusion and naïveté to totally belie his circumstance.

'Mr. Latham, my name is Dana McAuliffe,' she began by rote. 'I'm a partner with the law firm of Cotter Boland and Grace. As I assume you already know, we've been retained to represent you, and I've been asked to come here and talk with you.'

'I've heard of your firm,' he said politely. 'But I don't know why you're representing me.'

'You're entitled to representation,' she explained. 'It's the law.'

'I know that,' he replied. 'What I don't know is why your firm would want to do that. I can't afford to pay you. I don't have that kind of money. Neither do my folks. My pastor here in Seattle told me the church would take care of it, but I know they don't have the money, either.'

'Well, we don't have to worry about that right now,' Dana responded, because she didn't actually know who was footing the bill. 'Let's talk instead about how we're going to help you.'

There was a pause. 'I don't know what I'm supposed to say,' he said.

'You can say anything you like,' she told him. 'Nothing we discuss here ever leaves this room.' He didn't respond. For some reason, she wasn't sure he had even heard her. 'It's called attorney-client privilege, or client confidentiality,' she added.

'I know what that is,' he said, and fell silent.

'Maybe we should begin by getting to know a little about each other,' she suggested after a while.

He sighed. 'I wouldn't know where to begin.'

'Well then, why don't I start by telling you something about myself?' she offered.

When he gave no reaction, she took it to mean assent. 'On the personal side, I'm thirty-nine years old,' she began. 'I'm married to the first violinist with the Seattle Symphony. And I have a nine-year-old daughter named Molly. On the professional side, I've been an attorney for fourteen years. I've worked at Cotter Boland and Grace for twelve of those years, and I've been a partner there for the past four. I think my firm is very good at what it does, but you don't have to take my word for it, if you don't want to. We have a long list of very satisfied clients who, I'm sure, would be more than willing to back up that statement.'

'I believe you,' he said. 'But you don't understand – I don't know what I'm doing here.'

Dana frowned. 'You've been informed of the charges against you, haven't you?'

He nodded. 'I know what they told me, but I don't know why they think I could have done such a horrible thing. Just because I'm in the Navy, that's supposed to mean I'm the kind of person who goes around killing people? I don't see how that follows, but that's what they said.'

'The police?'

'Yes,' he said. 'I've been trained to defend my country, sure, but that's a lot different than being trained to kill. I'm not a violent man. I'm a man of peace. That's why I'm in the Navy, to protect the peace. In any case, I know I'm a man of conscience. I could never go out and just kill a whole bunch of people like that. It goes against everything I believe in.'

'What *do* you believe in, Mr. Latham?' Dana inquired, taking advantage of the opening.

'Well, for one thing, I believe that life is sacred and precious,' he replied.

'All life?'

He looked at her as though perplexed by the question. 'Yes, of course,' he said. 'All life. How can you separate one kind from another?'

A small stab of appreciation darted down Dana's back. Without any prompting, he had given exactly the kind of answer that would play well with a jury – simple and forthright, and reeking of honesty. She felt tempted to believe him herself, and abruptly straightened up in her chair.

'It seems to me the state is prepared to do just that, separate one kind from another,' she suggested. 'As far as they're concerned, abortion is legal – murder is not.'

'I didn't kill those people,' he said softly.

'Whether you did or didn't isn't the issue right now,' she told him. 'You're being charged with the crime, and unless you enter a guilty plea and throw yourself on the mercy of the court, you're going to stand trial. So, the question is, how do you want to proceed?'

His eyes widened. 'Are you recommending I plead guilty to something I didn't do?'

'No,' she said. 'I'm obligated to present you with your

options. If you lose at trial, you'll almost certainly be facing the death penalty. If you plead now, I may be able to get the death penalty off the table.'

'I want to be completely exonerated.'

'I'm not going to kid you, Mr. Latham,' Dana said. 'This won't be an easy case to win. At the very least, it's got terrorist overtones written all over it. And we'll have to deal with the high body count, including all those children. Emotions are running rampant. People want to taste blood.'

'*My* blood?' he asked.

Dana chose her words as carefully as she could. 'This town, who knows, maybe even the whole country by now, is looking for a conviction here, *needs* a conviction here,' she told him. 'The pressure that's been mounting since this thing happened has been extraordinary. And in a situation like this, sometimes what the people need becomes far more important than a little matter of guilt or innocence. Given the tidal wave of media coverage that I guarantee you is building out there, we'll be trying this case in – and out – of the courtroom, under bright lights and a microscope. No one will be able to escape it. Not the victims and their families, not the jury, not you.'

'Does that mean I'll lose?'

Blue eyes met brown for a long moment, and the attorney was first to look away.

'Of course not,' Dana replied with more conviction than she actually felt. 'It just means that the odds won't exactly be running in your favor.'

'Do you think I did what they say I did, Ms. McAuliffe?' he asked suddenly.

'It doesn't matter what I think,' she replied.

'It does to me,' he countered.

Dana thought about that for a moment. 'I don't know,' she said finally. 'I don't know enough about you to form an opinion.'

He seemed to sag in his seat. 'Well, I guess you could say I had a pretty good motive,' he said, looking down at his manacled hands.

'And what was that?' she asked with a little sigh.

'My wife and I got engaged six weeks after we met, and we were married only three months when I went out on my last cruise,' he told her. 'I guess maybe we rushed things a bit, didn't know each other very well, didn't take the time to cover all the bases, so to speak. But we sure were in love. Everyone told us we should wait a year or two before we tied the knot. But what we felt, we knew it was the real thing, and we didn't want to wait.'

Dana didn't want to hear this, certainly not now, when she was almost out the door and clear of it. 'And?' she heard herself ask.

He looked up. 'Oh, we're still very much in love, if that's what you're asking,' he said. 'But I guess you could say things got a little stressed.'

'Stressed?'

'Well, just before I left on the cruise, Elise – that's my wife – she said she thought maybe she was pregnant,' he explained. 'I mean, she just dropped it on me, real casual like, right in the middle of dinner. Well gosh, who cares about chili when you're going to have a baby, right? I was totally blown away. And Elise was excited, too. I know she was. That is, until she realized that I still had to go away. I don't know, I guess she figured the Navy would just let me stay home with her or something. But of course, that's not the way it works. Lots of Navy wives go through pregnancy while their husbands are at sea. Sometimes, guys don't even get to be at the birth.'

'She was upset with you?'

'Well, I think maybe more with the Navy,' he replied. 'But I was so juiced about being a father, I could hardly stand it. Sure, I'd rather have been home with her, only there I was, out in the boat for three straight months, without even knowing if she really was pregnant.'

'Why not?'

'Because the Navy doesn't let you communicate about anything important when you're on patrol. The submarine service being so hush-hush, you know, nobody's even supposed to know where we are. It's a tough life out there, and it's all about maintaining morale, keeping up spirits. So they don't allow any "Dear John" letters, or the dog died, or little Billy fell off his bike and broke his neck, or anything like that. No birth, no death, just "Hello, everything's fine, and I miss you" kind of stuff. So just in case, I spent my time thinking up names, and doing the numbers every which way I could think of, to see whether we could afford to buy a little house somewhere, you know, where the schools are good.'

'And when you got back?'

His gaze wavered, and for an instant, Dana saw real pain in his eyes. 'Elise told me she'd been right about being pregnant, but that she'd had a miscarriage.'

'A miscarriage?'

He nodded. 'I felt awful,' he confided. 'Awful for Elise that she had to go through that alone, and awful for us that we weren't going to have a baby, after all.'

She looked at him a bit skeptically. 'How awful is awful?' she asked.

'I love kids,' he told her. 'I have two sisters back home in Iowa. Between them, they have four boys and three girls, all of them terrific. I can't wait to be a daddy.' Suddenly, the light went out of his eyes, and his face darkened.

In spite of herself, Dana took the bait. 'What?' she prompted.

'A week later, I found out that Elise hadn't really had a miscarriage, after all. She'd had an abortion.'

'Your wife lied to you?'

Corey nodded. 'She said she was afraid to tell me the truth because she knew how I felt about kids, and she didn't know how to tell me she didn't feel the same way. But I don't think that was it. I think, you know, she was just plain scared about having a baby so soon into the marriage, especially with me being away so much of the time.'

'You mean, she wasn't thrilled about being a single parent half the year?'

'I guess not,' Corey replied. 'You see, Elise may be a couple of years older than I am, but she's pretty immature in a lot of ways. And I wasn't there, and she had no way of contacting me, and she had to make the decision by herself. So the decision she made was that she wasn't ready to start a family.'

'Were you okay with the abortion?'

Unexpectedly, tears filled his eyes, and without thinking, Dana reached out and put her hands over his, perhaps to comfort him, perhaps to give him strength, she wasn't sure. All she knew was that she had never done that with a client before.

'No, I wasn't,' he admitted. 'First I was hurt when I found out about it, and then I was furious. Didn't I have a right to be? That was my baby she got rid of, a piece of me, a piece of both of us, a wonderful expression of what our love for each other was supposed to be all about.'

A sudden twinge of nausea rumbled through Dana's stomach and threatened to rise. She hastily withdrew her hands. 'Okay, you had a right to be angry at your wife,' she conceded.

'I couldn't understand how she could do such a thing. It goes against who I am, against everything I believe in.'

'Did she know how you felt about abortion?'

'I thought she did,' he replied.

'What happened then?'

'Well, finally, I guess I calmed down, and we went and got some counseling, and we talked and talked about it, and I tried to see things from her perspective. I joined a group through my church that helped, too. After a while, I sort of started to understand where she was coming from.'

'And you forgave her?'

Corey looked at Dana with an expression that was so raw and exposed that she could actually feel his anguish. 'I love my wife,' he said.

The attorney nodded. 'I understand.'

'Do you?' he asked, and she wasn't sure whether he was questioning her reply or simply seeking affirmation. 'There's so much peer pressure put on women, you know. Do this. Do that. You have to have this baby. You don't have to have this baby. Stand up for this right. Stand up for that. People pulling you in half who don't even know you, and who don't really give a damn about you. People who all they care about is their own agenda.'

'And when she decided to have the abortion,' Dana asked, as gently as she could, because of course she already knew the answer, 'Elise went to Hill House, didn't she?'

He nodded.

'And the police knew that?'

'I don't know, I guess they must have,' he said. 'They were at me for hours, wanting to know just how angry I was, and how far I would go to vent that anger. I tried to tell them, no matter how I might have felt, I don't believe that two wrongs make a right. My baby was already dead. How would killing all those innocent people change that?'

'But they weren't buying it.'

Corey shrugged. 'Like I said, I'm not saying I didn't have a good reason to do it. I'm just saying I didn't do it.'

Dana nodded slowly. 'Well, that's all we need to get into for the moment,' she said as she stuffed her pad and pen back into her briefcase. 'Look, I have to leave for a little while now. But try not to worry. I'll be back at two o'clock, and we'll go downstairs for the arraignment. That's when you'll be formally charged, and you'll enter your plea. I'll tell you exactly what to say, and when to say it. Other than that, I don't want you to talk about the case. No police, no reporters, no one here at the jail. Not even your friends and your family. Not a word to anyone. It's very important for you to remember that.'

With that, she snapped her briefcase shut and stood up, giving him what she hoped was an encouraging smile.

'Please,' he said, as she stepped past him on her way to the door, 'if you're going to be my lawyer, you've got to believe me . . . I didn't kill those people. Oh God, somebody's got to believe me.'

'Is that the delivery man you told me about?' Big Dug asked, thrusting a newspaper he had found at the ferry terminal under Joshua's nose. Taking up almost half the front page, a picture of Corey Latham stared back at the retarded man.

'I don't know,' Joshua said. 'It was pretty dark, and I didn't get to see him very good.'

'But does it look like him?'

Joshua shrugged. 'Naw, the guy I saw had a cap on his head.'

'What kind of cap?'

'The soft kind, that comes down around the ears.'

Big Dug fished a stub of pencil out of his pocket and proceeded to draw a knit cap over the man's hair in the photograph. 'Now what do you think?'

'Yeah, it could be,' Joshua said. 'That looks lots more like him. Why?'

"Cause that's the guy they say set the bomb at Hill House.'

'Really?' Joshua peered at the photograph with more interest, then shook his head. 'I couldn't say for sure,' he said.

Big Dug tossed the paper aside. 'Come on,' he said.

'Where?' Joshua asked.

'We're going to go find us a television set.'

They found one in their favorite bar on First Avenue. Between them, they scraped together enough money to buy a glass of beer, and the bartender let them sit at the end of the counter while they shared it. The television was tuned in to the fourth quarter of a Sonics basketball game, and the two men sipped the beer as slowly as they could, and waited for the game to be over and the news to come on. Sure enough, the top story was about the young naval lieutenant who had been arrested for the bombing of Hill House.

'Well?' Big Dug asked, as they showed a tape of the suspect being escorted into the King County Jail. 'Now what d'you think?'

'Don't say it so loud,' Joshua hissed, darting a look at the other patrons. 'No one else's supposed to know, remember?'

'What do you think?' Big Dug persisted, in a somewhat lower voice.

Joshua stared at the television screen, squinting up his eyes to get a better look. 'I don't know,' he replied. 'It looked more like him in the newspaper with the cap on. And he was wearing a dark jacket, too.'

'Then try to see him dressed that way.'

Joshua sighed. 'Maybe it was him,' he said. 'If the police say it was him, I guess it was him. It coulda been him. It kinda looks like him. But like I said, I couldn't say for sure. It was too dark. It coulda been anybody.'

Priscilla Wales sat in her San Francisco office, decorated over the years in what she only half jokingly referred to as Salvation Army eclectic, and contemplated her options. It didn't matter that it was after midnight. One time of day was just like any other time of day as far as she was concerned.

It hadn't always been that way. There was a time when she had rushed home to her son every evening to fix his dinner or to help him with his schoolwork or simply to be near him and watch as he grew into an excellent young man. And after he was grown, when he was away in college and then at law school, there were the nightly telephone calls when they would talk for hours about anything and everything, like best friends.

But all that ended abruptly two months ago, when a drunken driver had taken her son's life at the age of twenty-four.

What was left was her work. FOCUS – Freedom of Choice in the United States – kept her going now. And after more than two decades of dedicated effort, Priscilla believed the organization finally had the break it had been waiting for. A suspect in the Hill House bombing had been charged with the crime, and if indicted, faced a trial that was certain to provide the broadest possible media coverage.

It was becoming clear that this year's presidential election would feature two candidates who could not have been further apart on the issue of abortion. Since one of them was running on the unwritten but nonetheless clear 'let's-get-women-back-under-our-control' platform, it was all-important that the other one win the White House.

What better kickoff could the campaign have, Priscilla reasoned, than a conviction in this case? It would be an unequivocal statement that dominance over women would no longer be tolerated in this country, and that violence toward them would be dealt with swiftly and severely.

The fifty-one-year-old civil rights attorney sat back in her chair, pondering exactly what she and her organization might do to further that effort.

Priscilla had just turned fourteen when a boy who lived down the street cornered her in his garage and raped her. Too ashamed to tell her parents she was pregnant, she got a name from a friend of a friend and made her way to a dilapidated building in the seediest section of San Francisco. She barely survived the procedure.

Lying in the hospital, while doctors fought to stop the bleeding and control the infection, Priscilla made a pact with God. If He let her live, she would become a crusader for the rights of women in America. It was years before the Supreme Court would rule on *Roe v. Wade*.

God let her live, and she kept her promise. She graduated *summa cum laude* from law school and promptly hung out her shingle. By the time she got there, however, things had changed. Abortion had become the law of the land, but constant efforts to undermine it needed to be deflected. After twenty-five years, she was still waging the battle.

The tall, gaunt brunette knew this was the line in the sand. This was where the hard right had to be stopped, or women's rights would be set back a hundred years. Her lip curled up at one corner. That was exactly where the ultrarightists of the nation, like Roger Roark of the Coalition for Conservative Causes, were heading, she thought. Repeal a woman's right to choose, and could the vote be far behind? She made a note to schedule a meeting with her board of directors in the morning, to formulate a plan that would aid in the conviction of Corey Latham.

'Oh God, somebody's got to believe me.'

Dana jerked awake at the sound of the voice in her head, and glanced at the clock on the nightstand. The green digital display read three-twenty-three, exactly nineteen minutes since she had last looked at it. Sam was snoring softly beside her in the big four-poster bed. His low rumble was usually a comforting sound to her but tonight she found it irritating.

'*Somebody's got to believe me.*'

That's what Latham had said, and she couldn't seem to get the words out of her head. They had followed her out of the jail, back to Smith Tower, and throughout the rest of the day. Now they were replaying in perfect rhythm with Sam's breathing.

Dana punched up her pillow and leaned against it. Who was Corey Latham? she wondered.

In the dark, she went back over everything he had said and done. Part of being a good attorney was the ability to evaluate people and situations quickly and accurately. His recitation had been simple and straightforward, without the slightest hint of fanaticism, and without any indication that it was rehearsed. She had listened carefully for that. His gestures and expressions had been totally consistent with someone who was confused about the circumstances in which he found himself. She could find no misstep.

Dana sighed. If Corey Latham were in fact the cold-blooded terrorist who had committed this crime, he was certainly hiding it well. She recalled the panic in his eyes and voice, on the way down for the arraignment, when she told him that he would enter his plea, but there would be no bail.

'You mean I have to stay in this place?' he cried. 'I can't go home until the trial? I can't go back to my boat?'

'This is a capital case,' she explained, experiencing a sudden rush of sympathy for him that made her actually regret having to say the words. 'There is no bail.'

At that, his knees seemed to buckle, and one of the escorts had to prop him up to keep him from falling. When the elevator doors opened, both guards bolstered him between them and, as though heading for the gallows, marched him toward the courtroom. Only when they were about to enter did he regain his composure, and she heard him mutter under his breath, 'Suck it up, sailor.'

Like a turtle exposed to danger, Corey seemed to retreat into himself, withdrawing his emotions, protecting himself from the judge and the proceedings going on around him, doing and saying only what he was told to do and say, nothing more.

Dana watched the shutdown with a mixture of fascination and compassion. When she left him to go back to his cell, he barely acknowledged her.

That image of him bothered her for hours afterward, and still tugged at her. But it was her own feelings that bothered her even more. It was almost as though she had in some way followed him into his shell, and taken on his pain. She had never before connected with a client on anything other than a professional level, and she did not want to do so with Corey Latham. Certainly not about this, anyway. Because, whichever way it played out, it was clearly going to be a no-win situation.

Dana disagreed wholeheartedly with Paul Cotter. It was unfair, if not inappropriate, for him to ask her to take this case simply because he wanted a woman up front. And despite his attempt to gloss over it with platitudes about her legal prowess, there was no mistaking his message – abortion was a woman's issue, and he intended to dismiss it as such.

She smiled to herself. On that basis alone, she would have no problem dropping this case right back in his lap.

10

Corey Dean Latham was born on the tenth of September in Cedar Falls, Iowa, a picturesque little city in the middle of a state that was, give or take a bit, right in the middle of the country.

He was the only son born to Dean and Barbara Latham, and the youngest of three children by eleven years, his birth having been unplanned, but certainly not unwelcome. His father was a mathematics professor at the nearby University of Northern Iowa. His mother worked at a local Christian preschool.

A self-sufficient child, with brown curls, bright blue eyes, and endless curiosity, Corey loved his family, his golden retriever, and his Red Flyer best in all the world, if not always in that order. He had a gentle disposition, a ready smile, and a disarming charm.

By the time he reached his teens, he had developed a keen sense of right and wrong which, combined with a personal code of honor to do no harm, earned him the respect and admiration of both his peers and his elders. As he moved into adulthood, he was looked upon as one of the brightest lights the community had ever produced.

Growing up, he excelled at sprinting and acting, splitting his time between the track and the theater. His father often joked that he didn't know which Corey was better at, running lines or running between the lines. In his junior year, he won the state championship in the hundred-meter sprint, and also won the lead role in his high school's production of *Hamlet*.

Whether they were aware of it or not, Dean and Barbara Latham raised their two daughters to marry young, have large families, and stay in Iowa. They raised their son to leave.

'There's a great big world out there,' Dean suggested when the boy was about to enter his senior year in high school. 'Go take yourself a good hard look at it before you decide what to do with your life.' What he didn't say aloud, but fervently hoped, was that his son's choice would not be the theater.

Perhaps because Iowa was a landlocked state, Corey had always had a deep and abiding fascination for the sea. He took that fascination, along with a strong middle-American sense of duty and patriotism, excellent grades, and the blessing of a career congressman, to the U.S. Naval Academy at Annapolis.

'This is the finest young man I have come across in many a year,' the congressman wrote in his letter of endorsement. 'It is my privilege to sponsor him, and I have every belief that given the opportunity, he will do his family, himself, and his country proud.'

Corey had barely turned eighteen. It was the first time in his life that he had been outside his home state, and he was totally unprepared for what greeted him. The sudden, unfamiliar freedom, the constant carousing, and the easy access to drugs, alcohol, and women, combined with the rigorous training, rigid class system, and unabated, academy-endorsed hazing, tested his morals, threatened his determination, and wreaked havoc with his studies. For the gentle, sheltered Iowan, the mental and physical brutality was shocking. He finished the first quarter in the bottom ten percent of his class, and would likely have quit a dozen times over had it not been for a very experienced and understanding academy chaplain.

The Lathams were good people who believed in traditional family values. They had raised Corey on an abundance of affection, tempered with occasional discipline, and the constancy of the Methodist version of Jesus Christ, the Bible, and the Golden Rule. His religion was as much a part of who he was as were his good looks or his lean body or his quiet sense of humor.

For months, the chaplain met with the plebe on an almost daily basis, helping him to find his footing, and encouraging him not to give up, but to stick it out. He shared anecdotes about previous plebes, and the ways they had found of coping.

Corey listened and absorbed. By the end of the year, he had regained his balance and added a thick layer of toughness to his Midwest hide. When he graduated from the academy, he was in the top ten percent of his class.

In return for his education, Ensign Latham owed the Navy the next five years of his life. He spent the first twenty-four weeks of it at the nuclear power school in Orlando, Florida, after which he was sent to Charleston, South Carolina, for twenty-six weeks of nuclear prototype training. Then it was thirteen weeks in Groton, Connecticut, for the submarine officer basic course. And everywhere he went, he worked hard and excelled. Finally, he was rewarded with the prestige assignment to the Bangor Naval Submarine Base, located near Bremerton, Washington, where he was assigned to the crew of a Trident class submarine, the USS *Henry M. Jackson.*

His first patrol, which began in the middle of August, was a disaster. Submerged for sixty-eight straight days, he was subjected to the endless criticism of a neurotic engineer, packed into a steel fortress without an inch of privacy or a ray of sunshine, forced to breathe fetid air, unable to sleep, worried every moment about fire or leakage or worse, and scared to the point of constant nausea about living cheek-to-jowl with a formidable nuclear arsenal. He returned to Bangor at the end of October with a gastric disorder and a sickly pallor, twelve pounds lighter and ten years older.

'I think I know what hell is,' he told his roommate, who already had two patrols under his belt.

The roommate laughed. 'There's only one cure,' he replied. 'Go out and get laid.'

There were a few girls who had wandered through Corey's life during the last several years; fine young women from good families with whom he spent pleasant evenings that never progressed past the preliminary fondling stage. The church in which Corey had been raised considered intercourse inappropriate outside of marriage. His parents had both been virgins on their wedding night, at the age of twenty-two, as had their two daughters when they married, one at nineteen, the other at twenty. And their son was without experience at the age of twenty-four.

His roommate, Zach Miller, took him to Seattle, on a series of bar-hopping excursions through Belltown, a section of the city frequented by yuppie singles. He met three girls in rapid succession, each of them pretty, each of them available, each of whom invited him to come in when he escorted her home. In all three cases, he bought them dinner, took them to the movies or to a concert or to a sporting event, and said good night at the door. A girl who thought so little of herself that she was willing to go to bed with him on the first date was not what he was looking for.

'What's the matter?' his roommate asked.

'Nothing, I hope,' he replied.

Zach was usually in bed with at least half a dozen different girls during the months between his patrols. But as far as Corey was concerned, what his roommate was doing was like drinking out of a paper cup that was discarded soon after it was used. There was no way he could explain that he was looking for just one cup – clean, reusable, and made of the finest porcelain.

'I intend to test the product before I buy,' Zach told him. 'After all, a lifetime is an awfully long trip to take with someone incompatible in bed.'

But for Corey, sex without love was much like a church without God. He knew how long a lifetime was, and he was in no hurry.

Three weeks later, he met Elise Ethridge, and his world turned upside down.

'Hi,' she said, sliding up beside him at the bar of a fashionable Belltown watering hole, all tall, and slender, and golden. 'What's a nice guy like you doing in a dump like this?'

'Gosh,' he said before he could stop himself, 'I didn't think anyone ever said that for real.'

She laughed a deep, husky laugh. 'Well, I saw your uniform and I just couldn't resist. My name's Elise.'

'I'm Corey,' he replied a little breathlessly, because someone had squeezed in on the other side of her and pushed her against

76

him, and he could feel her warmth down the length of his body.

Elise reached into her handbag for a cigarette and stood waiting for a light. But Corey didn't smoke, and had no lighter. He glanced around in a near panic until he spied a pack of matches lying on the bar and grabbed at them. It then took him three tries to strike one up. She wrapped her hand around his to cup the flame, or perhaps to prevent his hand from shaking too much for the match and the Marlboro to meet. Green eyes looked at him through a lazy stream of smoke and he tried his best not to choke. Her perfume was intoxicating. He invited her back to his table.

Long before the end of the evening, Corey decided that Elise was the most mature and sophisticated woman he had ever encountered, which may have had something to do with the fact that she was two years his senior. Nevertheless, next to her, all the other girls he had known suddenly seemed silly and superficial, and he couldn't believe his good fortune when she agreed to go out on a date with him.

Zach did not seem particularly impressed with her, but then he was a good deal more experienced than Corey, and had a whole stable of willing women at his beck and call.

'She's a bit chilly,' he observed on the way home to Bremerton, as they stood on the top deck of the ferry, leaning over the rail, letting the wind blow in their faces.

'You mean, not the type to jump into bed with you on the first go-round?' Corey responded with a chuckle. 'I think I like that about her.'

After a couple of double dates, Zach took him aside. 'Take it easy,' he cautioned.

'Why?' Corey asked. He was now seeing Elise at every opportunity, sometimes just for a few minutes between round-trip ferry rides. They would step outside the terminal, weather permitting, and share a few lingering kisses in the dark. Or they would sit inside the lobby and hold hands, saying little, their eyes locked. When they couldn't arrange to meet in person, he would spend hours on the telephone talking with her.

'Because there's no need to get that serious this soon,' Zach told him. 'You're a country kid, still wet behind the ears. You've never even been in the sack with anyone. And she's a city girl, with a definite level of expectation. It's obvious she's got all your hormones going crazy, which doesn't exactly correspond to seeing straight, but you're from two different sides of the aisle here.'

'So what?' Corey protested. 'That doesn't mean we can't be in love with each other.'

Zach groaned. 'You're not in love, you're just in lust. Love takes time. So, do yourself a favor, slow down. Get to know her.'

'I know her.'

'No, I mean, get to *really* know her, before you do something stupid.'

'You don't like her very much, do you?' Corey observed.

'She's all right, I guess,' Zach replied with a shrug. 'Just a little too anxious, you know what I mean? Anyone that anxious always makes me nervous.'

But she didn't make Corey nervous. And she wasn't any more anxious than he was. His heart raced out of control at the mere thought of her. He proposed after six weeks, two days before he shipped out on his second patrol, and he and Elise were married a month after he returned, a week after he received his promotion to lieutenant, junior grade.

'Did you really think putting a ring on her finger was the only way to get in bed with her?' Zach asked after the ceremony.

'No,' Corey responded with a happy grin. 'I thought it was the only way to spend the rest of my life with her.'

The newlyweds honeymooned in Hawaii, and Corey had ten days to discover that Elise was anything but chilly. When they returned, it was to a cute little house with a detached garage they had rented on West Dravus, on the north side of Queen Anne Hill. They spent the remaining days of Corey's leave, in addition to several thousand dollars, furnishing their new home, and then began the process of settling into married life.

On most Mondays through Fridays, Corey would take the five-twenty car ferry to Bremerton in the morning, driving the short distance from there to Bangor, and the six-twenty ferry from Bremerton back to Seattle in the evening.

'Why do you have to work such ridiculously long hours?' Elise complained once she realized he would be abandoning their bed at four o'clock in the morning, when she didn't need to rise until nearly eight, and returning home too late to participate in the preparation of dinner, a chore she quickly learned she loathed.

'Someone has to protect the country,' he told her with a gentle smile because he didn't really want to be away from her so much. 'And for the next two years anyway, that means me.'

Corey continued blissfully on, seeing Elise for a few precious hours at night, occasionally enjoying the luxury of an uninterrupted weekend, and even making time to participate in a number of activities involving his new church, until August when it was time for him to go back on patrol.

His only contact with his bride during the next two and a half months was a weekly 'family-gram,' containing a maximum of fifty words – including salutation and signature – which was routinely read by his commanding officer, and to which he could not reply. It was a most unsatisfactory form of communication, but given the highly sensitive and secret nature of his work, it was all the Navy would allow.

He spent every wakeful minute of the tour dreaming of her, planning their future, reliving their nights and weekends together in such intimate detail that his reaction made him blush, and sent him searching for a square foot of privacy. He returned to shore at the end of October, eager to resume his storybook marriage with his very own princess.

On a Saturday afternoon in the middle of March, there was a knock on the front door of the house on West Dravus.

'Corey Dean Latham?' inquired one of two civilian men in dark suits, thrusting a badge in his face that identified him as a police detective.

'Yes,' he replied, perplexed because he recognized both the badge and the man.

'You are under arrest for the bombing of Hill House,' the detective said, 'and for the murder of one hundred and seventy-six people.'

'What are you talking about?' Corey asked, looking from one to the other.

The two men ignored the question. Instead, one of them moved in and began to run his hands up and down Corey's body, until he had assured himself that his suspect carried no weapon. Then he pulled Corey's arms behind his back and snapped handcuffs around his wrists. The other detective pulled out a card and began to read aloud the most chilling words the young naval lieutenant had ever heard.

'You have the right to remain silent . . .'

After a brief flurry over protecting one of its own, the United States Navy decided it wanted no part of the Hill House bombing. Once the King County Prosecutor's Office claimed jurisdiction in the matter, Bangor relieved the lieutenant of his duties, put his career on hold, pending the outcome of the case, and retreated.

11

'Okay,' Paul Cotter said pleasantly. 'You've met him, you've talked to him – what do you think?'

Always the consummate strategist and gentleman, he had not summoned Dana to his office first thing Tuesday morning, but had given her until well after lunch to make a decision.

'I think there's a pretty good case here for rush to judgment,' she replied automatically, the effects of her sleepless night not evident. 'When did the bombing happen, six, seven weeks ago? Hardly enough time to dot the i's and cross the t's. As far as I can tell, Corey Latham is not a fanatic, and doesn't appear to be emotionally unbalanced. In fact, he seemed perfectly normal to me. Of course, I'm hardly an expert,' she hastened to add. 'You can certainly have him examined by a psychiatrist, if you like.'

'Would you put him on the stand?'

'You'd almost have to,' she responded.

'How would he do in front of a jury?'

'I think he'd do just fine. He's a bright kid, good-looking, clean-cut. He gives straightforward answers to direct questions, and comes across as quite sincere. Any mother's dream.'

'Did you believe him?'

Dana had never let herself be much concerned about the guilt or innocence of a client, only with the merits of the particular case. As her father had told her, from the time she was old enough to understand what it meant, a defense attorney's job was to defend, no matter what, and getting caught up in believing or disbelieving your client very often got in the way.

Of course, a death penalty case might be different; she didn't know. It was true that Corey Latham was unlike any of the clients she had so far come across in her career. He was young, and cooperative, and very vulnerable, and could easily be destroyed by a system that more often than not didn't really care. But that wasn't going to be her problem.

'Let's just say, if I were a member of the jury, I might be persuaded to give him the benefit of the doubt,' she replied.

'It's odd,' Cotter mused, toggling a gold pen between the index and middle fingers of his right hand. 'I've looked at the file. What they've got may have been enough for a warrant, might even be enough for an indictment, but it's far from being conclusive. Yet everyone's running around the prosecutor's office like this thing was open and shut.'

'They're under a lot of pressure.'

'Yes, but they need a conviction here. An acquittal on a case this big would give them a black eye they'd never get over. If the kid's got even half a story to tell, why are they so hot to trot?'

'I'm no psychic,' Dana said with a shrug. 'But maybe they're counting on the emotion of the situation to sway the jury. Or maybe they figured they'd be going up against a public defender, and it would be a walk in the park. I don't think they ever expected Latham to come in with a top firm.'

'Or maybe we're not totally in the loop?'

Dana shook her head. 'I checked,' she replied. 'Brian Ayres is the prosecutor assigned to this case. I know him. I used to work with him. He doesn't play games. Probably because he doesn't have to. He's been around awhile, and he's one of their best. No, for whatever reason, I think he thinks he sees a solid case.'

'And you see reasonable doubt?'

'Absolutely,' she said without hesitation. 'So far as I can tell, the evidence is wholly circumstantial, which makes it wide open to interpretation. Of course, it's our job to see things that way, and their job to paint as convincing a picture as possible. But I don't see any walk in the park here, not at all.'

'Which brings us to the real issue, doesn't it?' Cotter suggested, getting down to business. 'You've spent some time with the boy. You seem to like him. At the very least, you're apparently impressed by what you saw. And you know how big this case is, how important the right defense will be. We want you to lead it. We think you have what it takes. And hell, who knows – he may even be on the level. So, what's your answer?'

Dana had her answer ready, worked out during the early morning hours as she waited for dawn and Sam to rise. She was not going to take the bait. She was not going to be maneuvered into defending Corey Latham. Whether she liked him or not was irrelevant. Whether he was guilty or innocent was irrelevant. Despite having the full resources of the firm to back her up, as Cotter had promised, she knew enough to know, even if he did not choose to acknowledge it, that she was in way over her head. It was *her* reputation at stake here, not the firm's. They could simply cut her loose if she became an embarrassment to them. No, it was her career on the line, and the small matter of the client's life.

She looked the managing partner directly in the eye, although she could not keep her stomach from churning. She had played the good soldier, agreeing to go to the jail, meet with Latham, and see him through the arraignment. But she had been resolved, even before she crossed Freedom Park, not to take this case, whatever she might find when she got inside. And in all honesty, as much as she felt for the young man – and she had to admit she did – nothing had transpired to alter that original decision. On the contrary, her encounter with Corey Latham had only strengthened her resolve.

For at least half a dozen perfectly rational reasons, she knew this was not a case in which she wanted to be involved, and not a cause with which she wanted to be associated. Certainly not as first chair, and not even as second, should it come to that.

Her plan was quite simple: do the groundwork she had been asked to do, and then go back to Cotter, report her findings, and sever all connection with the matter as soon as possible. That plan was still in place.

She opened her mouth to tell him. 'I'll take the case,' she heard herself say.

12

There were cases that made headlines, and there were cases that made lawyers. As low-profile as her experience at Cotter Boland and Grace had been to date, Dana knew that the Latham case, whatever the outcome, was going to make both.

'I don't have a clue what I'm doing,' she was confiding to her father over the telephone half an hour later. 'I don't know if I'm thrilled or petrified.'

'A good measure of each would probably be appropriate,' Jefferson Reid advised from his waterfront office in Port Townsend.

'I feel like I'm three years old again,' she said, 'and you're about to throw me into Puget Sound.'

'I remember,' he replied with a chuckle. 'And I also remember that you not only survived, you went on to lead the high school swim team to the state finals three years in a row, and set four records along the way.'

'So I did,' she conceded. 'But this is different.'

'Of course it is,' he agreed. 'Because this time, it isn't just about you.'

'That's what worries me.'

'Why?'

'I don't know,' Dana replied thoughtfully. 'I didn't want to take this case. I opened my mouth to say no, and yes popped out. I didn't want to like Corey Latham, but I couldn't help myself – I do like him. The whole country is out to crucify him for this bombing, whether he did it or not. I want to know that he's got the right person in his corner. Someone who won't just go through the motions, but will go to bat for him, you know what I mean? But why do I think that has to be me?'

'I assume because it's the only way you can make sure he gets the kind of representation you think he should get,' Reid suggested.

'But what if I'm letting my ego get in the way? I have no experience here. What if I'm not good enough?'

'You don't need me to tell you you're good enough,' he chided her. 'Look into your heart, my girl. Ask yourself why you really took this case.'

For a moment, there was silence at the Seattle end of the telephone, and the crafty, patient Port Townsend attorney leaned back in his chair to wait. He had taught his daughter well, and had little doubt she would work her way through to the truth of the matter. Without any help from him, she was perfectly capable of exploring her own motives and arriving at her own conclusions.

'It has nothing to do with any kind of commitment,' Dana said finally. 'I just felt sorry for him.'

'That's not an unreasonable place to start.'

'Guilty or innocent, he's scared to death. I mean, here's this guy who serves on a nuclear submarine, which is about as scary as it can get, and he's locked up safe and sound in the King County Jail, panicked to the point of paralysis. I just didn't think any of the other partners at the firm would know how to deal with that.'

'Then it would appear that the young man has himself the right attorney,' her father said.

Dana did not respond. On the surface, it might appear that her father was right. But then, there were things that he didn't know about.

'You've handled capital cases in your career, dad,' she said suddenly. 'Legal shenanigans aside, if you thought there was a chance your client was being railroaded, how did you deal with it?'

'Thankfully, that's happened just once in my lifetime,' he replied. 'And I must tell you, it didn't end particularly well. To this day, I believe he may have been innocent. I know he was railroaded. He was also convicted and executed, and I couldn't do anything to prevent it.'

'That's what I'm afraid of.'

'There are no easy answers in a death penalty case, and not many sleep-filled nights ahead of you,' he told her. 'As I think you're about to discover, defending someone who is guilty is tough enough, for all the obvious reasons. But defending someone who may be innocent can be terrifying.'

'We'd like an interview,' a reporter from the *Globe* said over the telephone, right in the middle of dinner. 'We're planning on a whole feature actually, in-depth, with pictures of you at the office, and at home with the family. And anything else you might want to include.'

'I'm sorry,' Dana replied, horrified by the request. 'I don't do interviews.'

'Are you sure?' the reporter asked, clearly dumbfounded. 'Don't you realize you're going to be famous? The whole country is going to want to know everything about you. Why, you're the new Marcia Clark.'

'No, I'm not,' came the curt response.

'Frankly, my dear, I'm giving you the chance to tell your own story, before someone else comes along and reaps the benefits of telling it for you.'

'I don't do interviews,' Dana repeated with outward calm, even as the hand holding the receiver began to shake. 'Please don't call again.'

'Who was that on the phone?' Molly asked. 'Your face is all red.'

'No one important, sweetie,' Dana declared, reclaiming her seat at the dinner table. 'Just someone trying to sell me something I didn't want to buy.' She picked up a bowl of potatoes and spooned a big helping onto her plate as though calls from tabloid newspapers were a regular happening in their cozy Magnolia home.

'I think you'd better assume that was just the beginning,' Sam observed later, when they were getting ready for bed, and out of Molly's earshot, and Dana had relayed the gist of the telephone conversation.

'They're like vultures, aren't they?' she said with a shudder.

Sam eyed her thoughtfully. 'I guess this is going to be a pretty big case for you, isn't it?' he asked.

'The biggest,' she replied in a breathless mixture of regret, exultation, and fear.

'Well then,' he said, 'before you get buried in it, let's find a way to store up some good times to tide us over. I have a few ideas. I'll talk them over with Molly.'

Dana looked at him – her comfort, her sounding board, her rock. If she sometimes took him too much for granted, she knew it was his sense of purpose, of balance, and of proportion that enabled her to be who she was and do what she did, and that meant more to her than she could ever express in words.

'I've lost count of the times I've said it before,' she told him with genuine affection, 'but I honestly don't know what I'd do without you.'

He grinned. 'That's okay, babe,' he said in his best Humphrey Bogart impersonation. 'Just play your cards right, and you won't ever find out.'

Sam McAuliffe was a happy man. At forty-seven, he had the profession of his choice, the wife of his dreams, and a step-daughter he couldn't have adored more had she been his own flesh and blood.

He may not have understood Dana completely, her drive, her intensity, her need to fight the good fight at every turn, but it didn't matter. He loved her unconditionally. She was everything he had hoped to find in a woman, fantasized about finding, through the long, lonely years of singlehood. There were so many times when he had thought he would never meet someone like her, never marry, never know the joy of having a family of his own. Then one day, there she was. He knew he would always be grateful to her, for wanting him, for letting him into her life, for allowing him to become a part of something so special.

If there was one small flaw in the otherwise perfect tapestry of their marriage, it was that he and Dana had so far been unable to give Molly the baby brother or sister that would have made their lives complete. They had often spoken of it, of how wonderful it would be if they could have a child together. It would be the ultimate expression of what they felt for each other. He knew Dana had never really had that with Molly's father.

But in six years, it hadn't happened. The closest they had come was one false alarm shortly before Dana made partner at Cotter Boland. Sam knew that time was not on his side, and he so wanted a child while he was still young enough to raise one. After the false alarm, he took himself to a doctor, unbeknownst to his wife because it was embarrassing, to see if maybe he had a problem. However, the tests showed that he was just fine, and he was told not to worry, but to relax.

'Things have a way of surprising you when you're least expecting it,' the specialist said.

Yet four years later, it was still just the three of them, and Sam was beginning to wonder if it simply wasn't meant to be, and if it was time to put the dream away, and appreciate what he already had.

Truth be told, he had enough to fill his plate. It was in holding hearth and home together that he truly excelled, filling in the holes of Dana's absences when she was overwhelmed by work. The Latham case was going to be the greatest test of his abilities, and he fell asleep thinking up ways he could protect his family from the media invasion that was bound to come.

'You must be out of your mind,' Judith Purcell declared, the moment she heard. 'You can't take this case.'

'I already did,' Dana told her.

'But how can you defend him?'

'I'm a defense attorney. That's what I do.'

'Oh, come on,' Judith persisted. 'You know what I mean.'

Dana fixed a level gaze on her friend. 'Sometimes, we have to make hard choices,' she said in a soft voice. 'We may not always make the right ones, but we do the best we can. And then we live with the consequences.'

13

Of all the single, separate moments in time that, for whatever reason, one was destined to remember for the rest of one's life, Corey Latham believed he knew the worst.

Certainly, there was the humiliation of being taken, in shackles, from his home, in broad daylight, for all his neighbors to see. Of course, there was the degradation of being marched into the county jail where he was stripped and searched, fingerprinted and photographed. Nor would he soon forget the frustration of being grilled for hour upon hour, until he felt that his brain was turning to oatmeal. But all that turned out to be merely a prelude to the sheer terror of being escorted to the eleventh floor of the King County Jail, thrust inside a cell that was little bigger than a closet, and hearing the heavy steel door slam and lock behind him.

That was the moment. When he knew, no matter what he said or did, he could not get out. He had lost the right to freedom of choice.

It was ten times worse than the *Jackson*, and that was bad enough. Even after three tours on the submarine, he was not even close to being comfortable with the claustrophobia or the dread of impending disaster. But he had chosen the Navy, and there were compensations aboard ship: the ability to move about, cramped though the quarters were; the camaraderie of his fellow officers; the knowledge that he was serving his country and fulfilling a vital mission.

This was something else entirely. This was black panic that could take hold of him at any moment of the day or night. This was knowing that he was caught, like a rabbit in a trap, in a situation he could not control, with an outcome he could not predict. This was hearing his heart pounding in his chest so loud he feared it would explode inside him, like a bomb – and the irony did not escape him. This was hour after hour, day after day, of nothing but his own thoughts, his own terror.

Ironically, it was pretending he was back on the *Jackson* that got him through. Pretending that this was just another tour, and that, as before, if he took it one day at a time, it would soon be over. In his mind's eye, his tiny cell became the missile stacks where he sometimes slept just to get out from under the prying eyes of his engineer. He ordered books to read, Ludlum, Clancy, Follett, and pretended that the dialogue in them was conversations with his shipmates. He likened the twenty-three hours a day that he was confined in the concrete coffin to the seventy-some days he spent submerged, and convinced himself how lucky he was to have a four-inch slit of window from which he could at least see the sky.

During the twenty-fourth hour, he was given the run of the day room; an ugly place, with a metal picnic table and bench bolted to the floor, a chin bar, and a shower. Three days a week, he was allowed time in the recreation area, an indoor/outdoor space, with a basketball hoop and a jogging track.

But always he was alone, in his cell, in the day room, in the recreation area. As a designated ultra-security inmate, he was not permitted contact with anyone other than his two escorts, whose purpose was not to make friends or conversation. It was the isolation that got to him the most.

'This is worse than hell,' he told Dana the day after the arraignment, when it had sunk in that he was there for the duration. 'I don't know how much more I can take.'

'I never promised you an ocean cruise,' she responded firmly. 'So you call it anything you like – hell, war, survival – but do what you have to do to get through it. My best guess, we're looking at months. The wheels of justice grind very slowly around here. So I suggest you consider it a test of strength, or a test of courage, or a test of faith. Whichever suits you best.'

Corey liked Dana McAuliffe. She was smart and assertive in a very feminine way, and he considered it a stroke of genius for the law firm to have assigned her to represent him in this matter. It filled him with a sense of confidence that his nightmare would someday be over, and he clung to her words as a drowning man would to a bit of driftwood.

Aside from unlimited access to his attorney, he was allowed visitors for only three hours each week: Saturdays, Sundays, and Wednesdays, between six and seven in the evening. They met in the visiting room, a long narrow space, divided down the middle by a thick Plexiglas wall, and partitioned into cubicles. They sat opposite each other in one of the cubicles, and conversed over a telephone. He hated that Elise had to see him in shackles, and that he couldn't touch her, or smell her, or even talk to her, except over the damn phone, but he didn't hate it enough to tell her not to come.

'You look pale,' she said, two days after the arraignment. 'Are you sick?'

'I'm not sleeping very well,' he told her. 'The food's not too good, and my stomach's upset most of the time.'

'Did they let you see a doctor?'

'Sure. He gave me Tums.'

Tom Sheridan came to visit. The pastor of the Puget Sound Methodist Church was a large man, fifty-seven years old, with a broad smile, a booming voice, light eyes, and prematurely gray hair that several of his colleagues had, for some metaphorical reason, perhaps, compared to a steel helmet. He sat calmly on his side of the Plexiglas wall, with the telephone wedged between his ear and his shoulder, and read to his parishioner from the Bible in his deep, persuasive voice.

'"They that wait upon the Lord shall renew their strength; they shall mount up with wings as eagles; they shall run, and not be weary, and they shall walk, and not faint,"' he recited from Isaiah.

'Oh yes,' breathed Corey.

And from Joshua,'"Be strong and of a good courage; be not afraid, neither be thou dismayed; for the Lord thy God is with thee whithersoever thou goest."'

'Amen.'

* * *

'How are you holding up?' Dana asked her client on Friday.

Corey shrugged. 'I'm doing a little better, I guess,' he said. 'I've been thinking about your test of faith thing, and I've been praying a lot.'

'Good,' she said with an encouraging smile. 'That means you're learning to cope.'

'You were right about months, weren't you?' he asked. 'I'm going to be here a long time, aren't I?'

Dana sighed. 'Longer than you'd like,' she conceded. 'Even mistakes can take a while to sort out.'

'That's what I hold on to,' he said. 'That this is just a mistake that's got to be sorted out.'

'I'm going to see Elise tonight,' she told him. 'Any messages?'

His eyes lit up at the mention of her name. 'Just tell her I love her,' he said. 'And I can't wait to see her.'

Ignoring the camera trucks and the swarm of reporters trampling the rosebushes, Dana walked up the front steps of the little brick house on West Dravus and rang the doorbell. It was six-thirty, and she had come directly from work, wearing what she referred to as an office uniform; in this instance, a tailored suit in soft taupe. Elise Latham answered the door in a short, clingy black dress that would not have been appropriate in a workplace.

'I'm having dinner with friends as soon as we're through here,' the young woman explained when she saw her visitor's eye wander.

Elise was close to six feet tall, which was almost two inches taller than Dana. And where Dana would be considered trim, Elise was thin, with just a suggestion of curves beneath the sleek fabric. Her hair fell straight and shiny to her shoulders, and was of a color halfway between platinum and straw. Her eyes were wide-set, thick-lashed, and frosty green. Her makeup was fresh and perfect.

'We expect the prosecutor will go to the grand jury sometime within the next ten days,' the attorney began when the two women were seated on a rattan sofa in the small living room. 'And at this point, we're pretty sure an indictment will be handed down.'

'Okay,' Elise said tonelessly.

'I know, in many ways, what's happening here is just as hard on you as it is on Corey,' Dana said. 'I want to assure you that we're going to do everything we can to get him through this as quickly, and as unscathed, as possible, and then hopefully get the two of you back on the right track.'

Elise sighed. 'Whatever.'

'In the meantime, I know I don't have to tell you, he's going to need all the support you can give him.'

'Sure, whatever you say,' Elise replied. 'I'll be there for him.'

'A prison perspective is always a little warped,' Dana told her. 'He's isolated, literally cut off from the world he knows, and from everything and everyone in it that he cherishes. More than anything, he needs constant reassurance that you're still on his team.'

'I'll go down to that awful place whenever I can,' Elise promised. 'I'll sit there. I'll smile. I'll make jokes. I'll tell him how beautiful the roses used to be. What more can I do?'

'Is that what you think he needs?'

'Is that all this is about – what Corey needs?' Elise inquired. 'Well, what about me? Maybe I have some needs, too, you know.'

'I know how lonely it must be for you, as well,' Dana assured her, glancing over the black dress.

'Oh, you don't know anything,' Elise cried. 'I only wish it was about being lonely.'

Dana peered at her. 'Are people making it tough for you? Here in the neighborhood? At the place where you work? Is the media bothering you? I can help with that, you know.'

'Look, being the wife of an accused terrorist isn't exactly a day at the beach, you know what I mean?' the young woman retorted. 'My whole life has become public property, to be pawed over by anyone with the price of a tabloid. I get letters. I get phone calls. All day, all night. It never stops.'

As if to emphasize her words, the telephone shrilled suddenly, and Elise jumped as though she had been shot.

'Let me,' Dana said firmly, already reaching for the receiver. 'Hello?'

'Murderer!' an anonymous voice shrieked in her ear, and hung up.

'Are they all like this?' the attorney asked. 'Calling you a murderer?'

'Half of them,' Elise replied wearily. 'The other half call me the wife of a murderer.' She shuddered. 'Oh God, I hate this place. I want to get out of here, go somewhere where nobody's ever heard of me, and start all over again. Only there *is* no place where nobody's ever heard of me anymore, is there? It's the lead news story all across the country – maybe even around the world, by now. So, I guess you could say that I'm just as much in prison as Corey is.'

'I see,' Dana murmured.

'No I don't think you do, Ms. McAuliffe,' Elise shot back. 'I had an abortion. My family is Catholic, and I had an abortion. Do you have any idea what that means? My parents were never supposed to find out about it, but the newspaper people and the television reporters just couldn't wait for the chance to tell them every gory detail. Now they treat me like I'm a leper. My own family. I begged them to let me come home, just for a while, until this gets sorted out. You know what they told me? That I'd made my own bed, and now I could lie in it. So maybe I need some support here, too.'

Dana contemplated her next words, as a little knot began to form in the pit of her stomach. 'If it's any consolation,' she said finally, 'I was raised Catholic, too.'

'Well then, maybe you do understand,' Elise conceded. 'I'm only twenty-seven years old, for God's sake. My life is over, and I don't even know what happened to it.'

'Look, Corey's defense may be my primary concern here,' the attorney said, 'but I want you to know that I'm available to you, too. Anytime, for any reason. Even if you just want to talk.'

'Yeah, okay, sure,' Elise acknowledged, her voice dull, her glance drifting past the conversation and out the window toward the street where other people were going about their daily lives as though everything were right in the world.

Dana considered the young woman. Her big green eyes, highlighted by just the right amount of mascara and shadow, were blank. No, not blank, exactly, the attorney decided, more like – empty.

'Do you think this whole situation could be anything other than a horrible mistake?' Dana asked. 'What I mean is, do you think your husband might possibly have set that bomb?'

'First the police, and now you.' Elise shook her head slowly. 'No, I don't think he did. I can't believe I could be married to anyone who would do such a horrible thing, and not know it. But how could I be sure to an absolute certainty?'

'Did you tell the police that Corey was here with you that night?'

'Well, yeah. We watched the ten o'clock news, we had some cocoa, and then we went to bed, just like we always do on weeknights. The police say I can't give him an alibi because I was asleep, but I would've woken up if he'd gotten out of bed. I always have before, like when he got up in the middle of the night sometimes to go to the bathroom.' She bit her lower lip. 'I used to get so mad at him for messing up my sleep when he did that. And now I'd give anything just to have him do it again.'

Dana nodded, thinking how typical the reaction was. It was exactly how she had felt when Molly's father first left. 'And there was nothing in his behavior during the weeks before the bombing,' she probed, 'that seemed strange or a little different or just out of place to you?'

Elise shrugged at that. 'He took the abortion hard,' she admitted. 'And of course I made it worse by lying to him in the beginning. But then he seemed to be okay with it.' She paused for a moment. 'I don't really know what you mean by strange behavior,' she said finally. 'I mean, how would I have recognized if he did anything different? Sure, we're married and all that, but when you come right down to it, the truth is, I hardly know him.'

Dana climbed into her car and sat there, with her hand on the key, for several moments. She was going to need Elise Latham as a witness, really the only alibi witness Corey had, for whatever it might be worth. And unless she was very, very careful, it could turn into a nightmare.

14

Once Corey Latham's name had been released to the media, it was only a matter of hours before the white frame house that had for thirty years sat quietly at the end of a tree-lined street in Cedar Falls, Iowa, became the center of a maelstrom.

'Please leave us alone,' Dean Latham tried to tell the horde of media people who swarmed across his front lawn and his wife's flower beds, mangling her azaleas. 'We have nothing to say.'

'But this is your chance to tell the world your side of the story,' they replied.

'We have no story,' he corrected them. 'We're just parents, and we're devastated that anyone would think our son could commit such a crime.'

'Have you talked to him?' someone asked. 'Did he tell you whether he did it?'

'He doesn't have to tell us anything,' Dean said with quiet dignity. 'Now please go away.'

The local police tried to help, but other than pushing the crowd off the Lathams' property, and making sure that the road was kept clear, there was really very little they could do. It was the people of Cedar Falls who came to the rescue.

'Those folks in Seattle just plain don't know what they're doing,' members of the community said earnestly, as they physically inserted themselves as a barrier between the cameras and the Latham home. 'If they knew Corey the way we do, they would know he could never do such a thing.'

'I've known that boy since he was born,' the minister of the United Methodist Church said. 'They don't come any finer.'

'That boy has been a role model since the day he stood up and walked,' declared the congressman who had sponsored him to Annapolis.

'I have no problem with Cedar Falls being known as the home of Corey Latham,' the mayor of the city was quick to add. 'He has always been a credit to this community.'

Barbara Latham's hands were shaking so hard she could barely pack the clothing laid out on the bed into the two suitcases. The long morning hours she had spent ironing were lost in her clumsy efforts to cram everything in. She took a deep breath and tried to relax. Dean would be home at any moment and was relying on her to have everything ready.

She had arranged for a taxi to take them to the airport in Waterloo, reasoning that it would make no sense to disrupt anyone else's day for such a short distance. Their plane was scheduled to land in Seattle at four-thirty in the afternoon, but because this was Friday, they would not be able to see Corey until the following evening.

Her son locked up in jail for a horrendous crime he couldn't possibly have committed, with a mere hour allotted for visiting just three days a week. The very idea of it was almost more than Barbara could bear. She had prayed every moment since the news had come that the police would realize their terrible mistake and free her son.

It seemed an eternity, but it was really only three days since Dana McAuliffe had telephoned. The attorney tried so hard to be encouraging, but Barbara knew an arrest for a capital crime was not something one could easily dismiss.

'Corey's a tough kid,' Dana had said, 'and I think he's holding up well, under the circumstances. But he's probably going to be indicted sometime in the next two weeks, and that'll be difficult for him. He tells me there's a very strong bond between you. So, I was thinking, if you can arrange it, seeing you would really help him get through this.'

'We'll come as soon as we can,' Barbara promised.

They were leaving Cedar Falls buoyed by an outpouring of

support, from family and close friends, as well as the entire community.

'Give him our love,' Corey's sisters directed their parents.

'Tell him we're praying for him,' the local druggist and his wife told them.

'We're one hundred percent behind him,' the high school principal assured them, taking it upon himself to speak on behalf of the entire staff and student body.

'Go with peace of mind,' the neighbors came by to say. 'We'll look after everything for you here.'

The flight to Seattle was uneventful, for which both Dean and Barbara were most grateful. They found the hotel they booked to be clean and impersonal, and within walking distance of the jail. They ate an early dinner and went to bed, hoping to sleep. But the bed and the city noises were unfamiliar, and each lay awake, trying not to move, lest they disturb the other.

To keep their minds occupied, the Lathams spent Saturday walking around the city in a droning rain, doing things they remembered doing from earlier visits, but without much enthusiasm. The gaggle of media people who had followed them from Cedar Falls trailed along behind them, cameras clicking, questions flying.

'Now I know how Princess Diana must have felt,' Barbara said to her husband.

They went back to the hotel and tried to nap, but both were showered and dressed an hour before it was time to leave for the jail. Dean turned on the television, only to find the local news reports filled with the latest rehash of the case. They even caught a segment about themselves, backed by shots from Pioneer Square. They looked like a pair of cornered animals.

Dana McAuliffe met them in the lobby of the hotel, walking right over when they stepped from the elevator, as though she knew them.

'Your son looks very much like you,' she told Dean.

She steered them past the media people and into a waiting

cab, although the King County Jail was barely a ten-minute walk away.

'You'll probably be a little shocked by Corey's appearance,' Dana cautioned them. 'You haven't seen him for a while, and being in jail is not exactly a nurturing experience. But I don't think *he* realizes how much he's changed.'

Barbara nodded. Without actually coming right out and saying it, the attorney was preparing them for what they would find, and asking them to be careful of their reaction. In a very professional but gentle way, she wanted them to help her protect Corey. Barbara liked her immediately.

'You told us he was going to be indicted,' Dean said as the taxi pulled up in front of Freedom Park. 'How do you know that before it happens?'

'Because the reality of the grand jury is that it comes from the presumption of guilt, not innocence,' Dana replied. 'It's strictly a one-sided show, put on by the prosecutor, for the purpose of establishing a prima facie case, which means there's enough evidence to allow the state to proceed to trial.'

'Is there enough evidence?'

'On the surface, probably, or Corey wouldn't have been charged in the first place,' the attorney conceded. 'But please keep in mind that it's a long way from an indictment to a conviction.'

They hadn't seen him since the wedding, but it was clear that Dana was right. They could see it through the Plexiglas wall, the moment he shuffled into the visiting room with his shackles and his escorts. He had lost weight. His face was drawn from lack of sleep, there were dark circles under his eyes, and his skin, popping with acne, had an unhealthy gray cast to it.

Barbara ached to put her arms around him, and hold him, and assure him that this nightmare would soon end. It was all she could do to keep from crying out. She glanced at her husband; he was fighting back tears of his own.

The three of them sat down awkwardly in one of the cubicles. Corey picked up the telephone on his side, and motioned to his parents to do the same.

'How is it going, son?' Dean asked, putting the receiver to his ear.

'Okay, I guess,' Corey replied. 'It's good to see you. How's everybody at home?'

'They're all just fine, and send their love. The nieces and nephews made cards for you. We gave them to your lawyer; she said she'd see that you got them. I guess just about everyone in town stopped by to wish you well. They want you to know that Cedar Falls is behind you.'

'I didn't do it,' Corey blurted suddenly, his eyes full of pain. 'I couldn't have. I couldn't have killed all those innocent people.'

'You don't need to tell us that,' Dean said. 'We raised you. We know who you are.'

'It's just a mistake,' Barbara said, taking the receiver from her husband. 'And pretty soon, the police and everyone will realize that, and then everything will get sorted out.'

'Do you really think so?' Corey responded wistfully. 'I don't know. In here, after a while, you get to feel like you've fallen through the cracks. It's like I'm in the *Jackson* at the bottom of the sea, the radar's gone dead and I'm running out of air, and nobody's going to get to me in time. Nobody's listening to me. No one believes me.'

'Mrs. McAuliffe seems to be listening.'

Corey nodded. 'Yes, she is,' he conceded. 'But that's her job. She's getting paid to listen, isn't she? It's not like it's someone objective – it's not like a member of the jury.'

Dana liked the Lathams. They were good people, warm, sensible, and supportive. It was obvious that they loved their son, but they did not appear to be unduly blinded by that love.

After their visit with Corey on Saturday, she had whisked them over to the Hunt Club, where the food enjoyed a reputation for excellence, and the staff was used to shielding its patrons.

They talked all the way through dinner, about Corey, about themselves, about their values. They spoke of their hopes for their children, and their pride in their son and his accomplishments was obvious.

Dana came away from the evening convinced of their sincerity. There was so much in the news these days about parents abdicating their responsibilities, and about kids going berserk. If Corey Latham had gone berserk, it wasn't because his parents had not been paying attention.

She had begun this case presuming innocence, but to be honest, assuming guilt. Less than a week later, she wasn't so sure. She remembered her bold assurances to Paul Cotter that the prosecution's case was circumstantial, and therefore, weak at best. Now she found herself feeling the first flutter of apprehension as she faced the possibility that she might be all that was standing between an innocent man and the gallows.

15

Brian Ayres was a senior deputy prosecuting attorney, criminal division, for King County, Washington, a job he had held for seven years. A slender man of slightly more than average height, possessed of an easy smile and an irrepressible enthusiasm for life in general and the law specifically, he reflected an ageless attractiveness that most people found difficult to resist.

At forty, there were gray streaks in his black hair and deep creases around his brown eyes. He blamed the streaks on the rigors of raising five children, and the creases on having to squint his way through mountains of indecipherable defense motions. However, neither seemed to lessen his appeal, or his considerable effectiveness in a courtroom.

Fourteen years earlier, he had been an ambitious young lawyer, fresh out of the University of Chicago, sharing a cramped office on the fifth floor of the King County courthouse with an equally ambitious Stanford graduate named Dana Reid.

'Hi, Punk,' he greeted her now as she poked her head in his office.

'Hi, Dink,' she replied.

They had given each other those nicknames years ago, after she had once observed that, without shoes, they were exactly the same height.

Once friendly associates, they were now friendly adversaries. Brian was already married with two children when they met. He sometimes thought things might have been different between them had he been single. Dana was the kind of woman one occasionally came across in the professional world, a woman who didn't know how beautiful she was, and probably wouldn't have cared if she did know. Her work was what mattered to her, and all she wanted to be admired for was her mind.

A couple of times a year, schedules permitting, they did lunch. It was their way of networking, of checking out life on the other side, of keeping in touch.

'Never would have thought this was your kind of case,' he said. He had to admit, if only to himself, that he had been hoping for an easy ride on the Hill House bombing. And it had tweaked him more than a little to hear that the Latham kid had been able to bring in a firm with the track record of Cotter Boland and Grace.

'Neither would I,' she admitted.

'How did you get suckered in?'

She shrugged. 'My number came up, I guess.'

He wagged his head. During the two years that they worked together, they had talked long and often about defense attorneys who walked with the devil. 'You should have stayed on the side of the angels,' he told her.

'So we used to say,' she replied softly, reflectively. 'Except that this time, I think maybe I am.'

Brian chuckled. 'Always the optimist,' he observed. 'So, to what do I owe the pleasure of this visit?'

'Just happened to be in the building,' Dana said, which was true. Her stop at the fifth floor had been on impulse. 'To be honest, though, I'm trying to figure out why you would risk your reputation on the prosecution of Corey Latham.'

'Good tactic,' he said with an approving grin. 'Is this the moment for me to start quaking in my boots?'

'No,' she replied. 'But I'd have thought you, of all people, would want to be pretty positive of a conviction before you exposed yourself in open court. I know you. I know how you hate to lose.'

'You think maybe I don't know what I'm doing?'

'No. I think maybe you've let yourself be pushed into action a little too soon.'

'Ah, rush to judgment!' He raised an inquisitive eyebrow. 'Am I hearing the first hint of a defense strategy here?'

Dana chuckled. 'You never know,' she said, the first salvo having been neatly fired.

'Then let the battle be joined,' he suggested with mock gallantry.

She blew him a kiss and departed. The door had barely closed behind her when Brian grabbed for the telephone.

'I want to know that all our ducks are in order on the Latham case,' he barked into the receiver. 'I won't have it coming back on us. Bring me everything, and I mean everything. I want to know, step by step, exactly how we got to this guy.'

It *was* a good tactic, he conceded as he hung up, her trying to put him that quarter-inch off-balance just days before he was due to present to the grand jury, and he couldn't deny she had succeeded.

Dana Reid McAuliffe was a very sharp lawyer, and Brian knew she was not above bending every rule and pulling out every stop in defense of a client. But he also knew, whatever else she might do, she wasn't one to bluff.

The senior deputy prosecuting attorney went back and pored over the files. The case was far from being a slam-dunk, he knew, but he didn't feel it would make him look ridiculous, and it would at least get the brass off his back. He didn't know whether Latham was guilty or innocent, and truth be told, he didn't much care. The evidence pointed at guilt, and his boss was champing at the bit to get to trial and to get the mayor and the governor and the media out of his office and off his telephone, and that was enough for Brian.

'I don't know what McAuliffe thinks she knows,' he told his assistant finally. 'But I'm okay going with what we've got.' He didn't bother to add that he had been a lot more okay about it before he learned that he would have Dana McAuliffe sitting across the aisle.

'It may not be the strongest case we've ever taken in,' Mark Hoffman agreed. 'But it's not the weakest, either. We've got the ID on the vehicle. We've got the fibers and the trace materials. We've got the neighbors. We've got the doctor. I've seen a lot worse.'

One week later, a grand jury did indeed find probable cause to indict Corey Latham on, among a laundry list of other things, one hundred and seventy-six counts of murder in the first degree.

'We're scheduled for trial in September,' he told the King County prosecutor.

'Good,' the prosecutor said. 'Now maybe everyone will get off my back.'

'Don't be discouraged,' Dana told her client. 'All this means is that the grand jury found enough evidence to move forward to trial.'

'But how could they?' Corey demanded, his voice rising until it bounced off the purple wall of the interview room. 'How could they find enough evidence to believe I killed all those people when I didn't?'

'It's because they only heard the state's side of the case,' she explained. 'Just remember that we'll have a side to present, too, and there's a mighty big gap here between probable cause and reasonable doubt. I promise you, this isn't going to be any rollover for the prosecution.'

Craig Jessup was a nondescript man of medium height and weight, average looks, and indeterminate age. An exceptional mind for details, a chameleonic ability to blend into any circumstance, and a true gift for gaining the trust and confidence of others were what made him unique, and gave him a distinct advantage over many in his line of work.

For twenty years, he had been one of Seattle's finest, advancing steadily, if not meteorically, up the ladder from foot patrolman to homicide detective to sergeant. It was known around that he was in line to make lieutenant. Then his partner was killed, supposedly caught in the crossfire between police and a black man. When it was quietly covered up that the black man had no weapon, Jessup retired.

Taking the best of what he had learned, he established himself as a private investigator, offering his services to attorneys who could afford to pay high fees for top-quality work. His biggest marketable asset was his skill at second-guessing the police with whom he had worked for so long. In less than a year, he was fully employed. For the last five years, his steadiest account had been the law firm of Cotter Boland and Grace.

'Let's go on the assumption that Latham didn't do it,' Dana told him the day after the indictments had been handed down.

'Is that for real?' Jessup questioned. He knew a little about the evidence, considered it sufficient, and believed himself to be pretty good at sizing up odds. 'When I heard you'd taken the case, I figured you'd go for something like diminished capacity, and try to plead him out.'

'Not at this point,' Dana said, not bothering to add that the client was opposed to any kind of a plea.

'You really think the badges got it wrong?' the investigator asked, doubt written all over his face.

'I don't know,' Dana told him. 'That's for you to find out. For now, as always, I'm assuming innocence. If I'm wrong, I'm wrong. But if I'm right, then there's something out there that your friends down at headquarters missed. So, take a look-see, will you?'

'Okay,' he said.

She handed him a copy of the case file, which she had relentlessly flagged and redlined, and a sheaf of notes highlighting her own interviews and impressions. 'Take all the time you need,' she said dryly. 'You've got until September.'

'What if you don't like what I find?'

'As always,' she said with a shrug, 'I'll have to live with it, won't I?'

There were many in Jessup's line of work who, for the right fee, would break the rules without thinking twice, on behalf of lawyers who both expected and encouraged it. But Dana knew he was not one of them. She knew he would bend the rules, if he could, and stretch an interpretation as far as it would go, as she herself would, but that was where it would end. He was, perhaps because of his background, perhaps in spite of it, incorruptible. Whatever way an investigation went was how he would present it. He could not be turned. It made him a formidable opponent, and an invaluable ally.

Jessup worked out of his Capitol Hill home, a compact brick house tucked between two huge gingerbread Victorians and unfettered by the trappings of children. He had taken the second bedroom as an office, overnight visitors being rare, in a move that turned out to be far more comfortable and economical than renting separate space had proven to be.

His wife saw to his bookkeeping, tracking his hours and expenses, preparing the monthly billings, and keeping a careful watch over the receipts and disbursements. It was part-time work for her, amounting to at most twenty hours a month, and she had no problem fitting it around her job as an administrative assistant at Providence Hospital.

'I can't believe you're working on this case,' Louise Jessup told her husband when he came home with the Latham file in his briefcase. 'Why would anyone want to help that animal?'

'My job isn't to judge,' he reminded her, 'it's to investigate.'

'But I know people who died in that bombing,' she argued. 'Innocent people, friends.'

'I know you did,' he allowed. 'But I still have a job to do.'

They ate dinner in silence. It was better than his trying to explain to her, for the millionth time, how important what he did was to the proper outcome of a trial. He had no trouble explaining it to himself. Holding the state to the highest standard of evidence was what made the system work. Checks and balances were what kept it honest. After all his years on the police force, Jessup knew that as well as anyone.

As soon as dinner was over, he retired to his office with a steaming mug of tea, and picked up the material Dana had given him. First, he scanned the pages to get the gist of what they contained. Then he went back to the beginning and read the file, word for word. This time, alongside Dana's notations, he added some of his own. When he was finished, he sat back in his chair, a shabby recliner that his wife hated, but where he did some of his best thinking, and sipped his now tepid tea.

After a while, he picked up a yellow pad, and began to write, slowly at first, and then with increasing speed as thoughts came to him. Every once in a while, he would stop and refer back to something in the file, and then he would continue his writing. After two hours of this, he read over what he had written, made a few changes, placed the pad and the file on top of his desk, and went to bed.

'What you find out,' Louise asked in the darkness. 'Will it help convict Corey Latham or acquit him?'

'I don't know yet,' he replied softly.

16

Margaret Ethridge's home in Bothell, just north of Seattle, was immaculate and filled with an assortment of overstuffed furniture and framed photographs that spoke of years of continuity.

Craig Jessup was welcomed into the living room and sat in a huge wing chair by the fire with a cup of fresh-brewed coffee.

'We told Elise, you know, right from the beginning, that it was a mistake,' Margaret said.

'What was a mistake?' Jessup asked.

'Marrying him, of course,' she replied. 'To begin with, he wasn't Catholic. What chance did she have of making a marriage work with a Methodist? And as if that wasn't bad enough, it all happened too fast. A matter of months, a few weeks, really. But would she listen? Not to a word of it. Oh, she knew exactly what she was doing, she said. We shouldn't worry. We shouldn't try to interfere. But of course, she *didn't* know what she was doing, and now look what's happened. She's ruined her life, and not just here on earth. Her soul is going to burn in hell for all eternity.'

'You mean, because of the abortion?'

The woman, an older, heavier, faded version of her daughter, wagged her head in obvious distress. 'This whole thing had disaster written across it from the start.'

'You didn't approve of Corey Latham?'

'It had nothing to do with him, personally,' Margaret said. 'The truth is, it was all so fast, we hardly had a chance to get to know him. He seemed nice enough, I guess, for a Methodist. No, it was *her*. You see, he didn't know, she wouldn't let us

112

breathe a word to him about it. But my daughter was on the rebound.'

Much of what Craig Jessup did when he worked a case, and what made him so valuable, involved sifting through countless perceptions and impressions to reach reliable conclusions, and it helped clarify his thinking to be able to bounce his ideas off another person. The only person in the world he trusted enough to be his sounding board was his wife of twenty-eight years. She had a sharp mind and a simple way of cutting right to the chase.

'Can you put aside your personal feelings about this case,' he asked her, 'and just consider the possibility that Latham might be innocent?'

'I'm not going to tell you it will be easy,' Louise replied. 'But since you've gone and gotten yourself involved in it now, I'll do my best.'

He told her the salient points about his visit with Margaret Ethridge.

'I can understand the family's disappointment,' she said. 'The Catholic thing, and all that. But to cut her daughter off at a time like this, that seems pretty heartless to me.'

Jessup nodded. 'I can't decide whether the mother is a woman who's trying to cope, or a woman who's trying to control.'

'Or someone who's afraid to get too close to what might really be there.'

'I've been renting rooms to naval officers for twenty years,' Evelyn Biggs confided on the front porch of her boarding house in Bremerton. 'Corey Latham was one of my favorites. He used to come in for cocoa and conversation in the evenings, especially when he had a problem he needed to work out. He called me his surrogate mom. I was proud to have him and that nice Zach Miller rooming together in my house. Why, he couldn't possibly have done what they say he did. You think I would have rented to a monster? Now that wife of his, that's another story. You ask me, she's the monster.'

'Why do you say that, Mrs. Biggs?' Jessup inquired of the gray-haired landlady who was every bit as wide as she was tall.

'Because it was so obvious. Right from the beginning. She snared him like a piece of fish for her dinner. Got her hooks in so deep, he didn't know up from down. How could he, him being so young and inexperienced, like he was? All the poor boy could do was wriggle, while she dragged him here and dangled him there. And then to kill his baby without a second thought? A long cold drink of water, that one.'

'Did you know her well?'

Evelyn shook her head. 'Never really got much chance. Right from the get-go, she started alienating him from everyone who cared about him, or anyone who might try to talk some reason into him.'

'And did you try to talk some reason into him?'

'Of course I tried. Zach and I both tried. What was the rush? we asked him. If this was right, it would still be right in a year or two, after they'd had a chance to get to know each other, and could separate the love from the hunger. But her exotic perfume must have been a lot stronger than our common sense. She led him around on a very short leash, and he followed right along after her just like a puppy. And of course, him being such a fine young gentleman, he didn't know what to do with all those hormones except marry her. And wasn't that a disaster?'

'What?'

'Why the wedding, of course. That boy came to me in tears. Seems he and the girl had their hearts set on this lovely affair up at the Kiana Lodge. It's such a beautiful place, sitting right out there on the water. Do you know it?'

'No,' Jessup murmured, 'can't say as I do.'

'Well, anyway, her parents refused to pay for it. Told Corey flat out, if he wanted a fancy wedding, he'd have to pay for it himself. Can you imagine that? Well, he came home all upset, of course, and he asked me what he should do. I should have told him to get out of that whole relationship as fast as he could. To my regret, I didn't. I told him, the groom pays for the ring, the rehearsal dinner, and the honeymoon, period. And if her parents wouldn't pay for the wedding, well then they could just march themselves on down to city hall and say "I do" right there.'

'What happened?'

Evelyn shrugged. 'The parents finally agreed to shell out for a peanut affair at the family church in Bothell.'

'A peanut affair?'

Evelyn Biggs rolled her eyes. 'That's what I call it when all they serve is a glass of sparkling wine and a few nuts in a bowl.'

'It sounds like there was trouble with that marriage before there even was a marriage,' Jessup told his wife.

'Yes,' she agreed. 'But where was it coming from – inside or out?'

'There are five of us,' Ronna Ethridge Keough, short and chubby and looking nothing at all like her spectacular sibling, told the investigator. 'Two brothers and three sisters. Elise is the oldest. I never thought much about it before, but looking back, I guess it really bothered her that she was the only one of us who wasn't married.'

'Your mother said something about Elise marrying Corey on the rebound,' Jessup prompted.

'Yeah,' Ronna said with a nod. 'She'd been dating this other guy, Steve – Dr. Steven Bonner, to be exact – for about two years, and was totally crazy about him. Never mind Cloud Nine, she was on Cloud Ninety. He was some kind of surgeon, really smart, really good-looking, really high on himself, with this mansion on Mercer Island, no less. It was obvious to me, anyway, that he had a roving eye for anything in a skirt, but Elise either didn't notice, or didn't care. She had dreams of where she wanted to go in life, and I guess she figured sleeping with Steve for two years gave her more than a leg up. It entitled her to a first-class ticket.'

'That sounds rather calculating, doesn't it?'

Ronna shrugged. 'Elise is nothing if not practical. She's bright enough for most men, but she always thought her way to the top was going to be through her looks. My mother was beautiful when she was young, and it didn't take a genius to see how long good looks last. I guess, at twenty-seven, Elise got scared. So one day she told Steve it was time to fish or cut bait.'

'Don't tell me. He cut bait, didn't he?'

'Well, that's what we all were sure he'd do. But the next thing we knew, they'd set a date, and she was floating around, wearing this three-carat rock on her finger. You could've knocked us over. My folks weren't exactly thrilled, I don't think they liked him much, but they didn't want to rain on Elise's parade. So they planned this really elegant wedding for her. Spent a small fortune they couldn't afford. I guess simple wasn't good enough for a surgeon from Mercer Island.'

'Let me guess,' Jessup suggested. 'He called it off at the eleventh hour?'

'Worse,' Ronna said with a sigh. 'He just never showed up. Left her standing at the altar in front of two hundred guests and melting ice sculptures. He didn't even have the courtesy to phone. He sent her a telegram, can you believe it? She cried for a month, and then she went out and found Corey.'

'I see what your mother meant,' Jessup said. 'It was kind of quick, wasn't it?'

'And then there was that awful abortion thing,' Ronna said with a sigh. 'My parents don't know it, but I went with her.'

'You went to Hill House with Elise when she had the abortion?'

Ronna nodded. 'She needed someone to be with her. To get her home afterward, and all. We were always the closest.'

'So you knew she lied to Corey when she said she had miscarried.'

'Yes, but what went on between them was none of my business.'

'What do you think of Corey?' Jessup inquired.

Ronna shrugged. 'I've met him exactly three times: at the engagement party, at the wedding, and last Christmas,' she replied. 'Elise didn't bring him around much. He seemed nice enough, a little immature for her maybe. But if you're asking me whether or not

I think he bombed Hill House, I'll tell you the same thing I told the police when they asked me. I have absolutely no idea.'

'Naive,' Zach Miller said. 'I think that's the word I'd use to describe Corey Latham. That and idealistic, too.'

'How so?' Jessup asked the former roommate.

'Well, he's a real decent guy, but it's kind of like he lives in this world that just doesn't exist anymore,' the lieutenant said. 'He's like right out of *Ozzie and Harriet*, if you know what I mean. The American flag, mom, and apple pie. I think he honestly sees himself as a knight on a white horse with right on his side, chosen by God to defend his country and protect the honor of women. Not that this is necessarily bad, mind you. It's just that he takes himself so seriously.'

'And what about his relationship with Elise?'

'Well, that was bound to happen, him being who he is, and all. He fell for her like a ton of bricks, right off the bat. Put her up on a pedestal so high, I doubt he could even see her.'

'Do you like her?'

'Barely know her. Met her at the bar the same night Corey did. As I recall, he met her first, but she made a play for both of us. He bit, I didn't. After that, she seemed pretty intent on the two of them not spending much time around the people he used to hang with. I think she saw us as a major threat.'

'To what?'

'To ruining things for her, I guess,' Zach replied. 'Corey might have been too smitten to see it, but desperation literally oozed out of her. The package might have been okay, but women who are that desperate always set my alarm bells off.'

'Any idea what she was desperate about?'

'God knows,' he said with a shrug. 'Maybe it had something to do with being twenty-seven years old and unmarried, although in this day and age there's no disgrace in that. A few of us tried to talk him out of tying the knot so soon. After all, what was the rush? But she was pushing hard, and he was so innocent. I think maybe he was afraid if he hesitated, he'd lose her.'

'Have you noticed any sort of change in Corey since he and

Elise got married? Or since he came back from his last cruise?'

Zach considered for a moment. 'He seemed a little more tense, maybe, but that could be related to things that have no connection to his marriage.'

'How did he handle the abortion?'

'He was furious, and he was very hurt. But then he told me he had started going to church a lot, and the minister there got him into some group that was helping him work through it.'

'Is he quick to anger?' Jessup asked. 'Does he have a short fuse?'

'Not that I ever noticed.'

'Do you see Corey as the kind of person who would blow up a building full of people?'

'Never,' the lieutenant declared. 'Whatever effect the marriage has had on him, his basic personality hasn't changed. And like I said, he's all about defending and protecting, not attacking.'

'Even if he thought he was avenging his unborn child?'

Zach sighed. 'Only if the guy snapped,' he said reluctantly. 'I sure didn't see any signs of it, and I don't know anyone who did, but if you push me to the wall, I'd have to say that would be the only way – if he snapped.'

'It sounds like the best friend is in his corner,' Louise observed. 'Even if he did equivocate there at the end.'

'No one seems to want to point a finger at the kid,' Jessup said. 'But no one wants to come up looking like a fool, either.'

'Corey Latham is a fine human being,' Tom Sheridan declared in his resonating pulpit voice. 'In fact, I'd have to say, they don't come any finer.'

Jessup had found the minister in his rectory office, a heavily beamed, Tudor style adjunct to his church, and Sheridan was quick to make his guest feel welcome, first by enveloping the investigator's hand in both of his huge paws, and then by holding a chair for him.

'He's a member of our Thursday supper club, you know.'

'No, I didn't,' the investigator said. 'What is that?'

'A number of churches here in Seattle have gotten together to provide hot meals to some of our homeless people. Puget Sound Methodist is responsible for Thursdays. Let me see now, Corey joined our church just about a year ago, I think it was, and to the best of my recollection, except when he was out in his submarine, of course, he never missed a Thursday.'

'That's good to know,' Jessup murmured, filing that tidbit of information away for the time being. 'Now, can you tell me something about the support group you got him into?'

'Oh yes, of course,' Sheridan said. 'It's not officially a church group, you understand, but it was organized by one of our parishioners. It's for people who have lost a child.'

'To abortion?'

'To anything,' was the reply. 'Death is death, and loss is loss, any way you look at it. And the loss of a child, well, that always seems to be the hardest for people to come to terms with.'

'Was Corey doing well in the group?'

'I'm told he turned out to be as much of an inspiration to the rest of the members as they were to him,' the minister said with a little smile. 'Corey's like that, you see. And it also might interest you to know that those are the folks who are raising most of the funds for his defense.'

'You sound like you'd make an excellent character witness,' Jessup said.

'Whenever and wherever I'm needed,' Sheridan said without hesitation. 'This is a travesty, you know, what they're doing to that boy. He reveres life and he abhors violence.'

'You'd testify to that, in court, under oath?'

'In a heartbeat. I'd do whatever I could to convince a jury that Corey Latham couldn't possibly have committed such a mindless act of destruction. Should it come to that, of course.'

Jessup stood up. 'I'm not the attorney,' he said, 'but I think you can pretty much count on it coming to that.'

'At long last, an unqualified endorsement,' Louise observed. 'Unfortunately it's coming from someone who's known the boy barely a year.'

'Maybe so,' he said with a shrug. 'But at this point, I don't think we can afford to look a gift horse in the mouth.'

There were about a dozen people in the rustic room, warmed in the cool spring evening by a crackling blaze in a rough stone fireplace that took up most of one wall.

According to their host, they met on a weekly basis, but were available to one another more often if any of them signaled the need. The common bond was that they had all lost a child, in one way or another, and were either trying to come to terms with the grief themselves, or trying to help someone else do so.

'It helps to know you're not alone,' Damon Feary told Jessup when the investigator knocked at the door of his Woodinville home on a Tuesday evening. 'We all have to deal with the pain, and there is comfort in knowing that there are others in the same place you are.'

'Corey Latham was grieving the loss of his child?'

'Certainly,' Feary said. The man was tall and lean, with wild red hair, and he lived in a rough log home that he had helped to build and that his wife had decorated with lace curtains and crocheted doilies. 'You don't always have to have known the child to feel the pain.'

Jessup glanced over the group. 'How many of these people have lost a child to abortion?'

Feary sighed. 'Three,' he replied. 'The two men over there on the sofa who, like Corey, didn't know until it was too late, and the woman by the window who allowed herself to be talked into an abortion, only to regret it later.'

'Tell me about Corey Latham,' the investigator prompted those gathered, blending easily into the fabric of the room, the mix of people.

'He's so young,' one woman said with a sigh. 'In many ways, practically a baby himself.'

'He has a very caring heart,' said another. 'In the midst of his own grief, he wanted to help others.'

'None of us has much money of our own,' a man said. 'We're just ordinary working people. But whatever we do have, and whatever more we can raise, will go to help defend him.'

'We've already organized an all-you-can-eat spaghetti supper, two yard sales, and a car wash, and we're working on a talent night,' a woman said. 'Anything, no matter how small, helps.'

They almost made Jessup feel like he should dig into his own pocket for a contribution. 'Do any of you think he was capable of bombing Hill House?' he asked.

'Never,' three people said together.

'Then why do you think he's been arrested?'

'It's a frame,' Damon Feary said, and several others nodded. 'They needed to blame it on someone, and given all the pressure the police were under, they had to come up with someone pretty fast. Somehow he just got in the way.'

Jessup nodded thoughtfully. 'Do you think the police fabricated evidence?'

Feary shrugged. 'I'm not saying they did that,' he replied. 'On the other hand, if they did, we all know it wouldn't be the first time.'

'There may have been a couple of coincidences that started them looking in his direction to begin with,' one of the other men said. 'After that, the police just shut their minds and ran with it.'

'I understand Corey was coming to these meetings pretty regularly,' Jessup said. 'How would you say he was coping with the abortion of his child?'

'I can only speak for the meetings he came to up until February,' Feary replied. 'Then I was out of town for a while. But I know the group got together while I was gone, so some of the others might know.'

There was a pause then, as the people in the room turned to look at one another, searching for the right words. Finally, the young woman who regretted having had an abortion replied.

'As with all of us,' she said softly, 'God was helping him to see the way.'

'I must be developing a suspicious mind,' Louise said. 'They sound like very nice people, but they hardly know the boy. Why would they go to such lengths to help pay for his attorney?'

Jessup nodded. 'And such an expensive one, at that,' he murmured, 'when there are so many other competent ones who could have been hired for less. I wonder if they're doing it because they really believe he's innocent, or because they're afraid he might be guilty.'

'After all the fine things they said to you about him,' Louise scoffed, 'how could they believe he was guilty?'

'Well, what have you got?' Dana asked.

'So far,' Jessup reported, 'a fairly consistent picture of a thoughtful, caring, nonviolent young man, who would no sooner blow up a bunch of people at a clinic than he would step on a sleeping cockroach. Unless, of course, he snapped. And to this point, we have no evidence of that.'

'Pretty much my conclusion,' Dana concurred. 'So, what are we missing?'

Jessup scratched his right ear. 'I'm not sure. There's something about this whole thing that bothers me. The first night I came home with this case, I thought Louise was going to leave me on the spot. She was that upset that I would even think of working on behalf of the – what did she call him? – the animal who bombed Hill House. But now that she's in it as deep as I am, well, she may not be entirely sure he's innocent, but she's come a long way from assuming he's guilty. And that bothers me.'

'Why?' Dana asked, not getting it.

'Look, here I am, barely into my investigation,' he explained. 'And there's Louise, already thinking this case hasn't got any legs. This is Hill House, for God's sake. She knew a lot of the people who died there. Some of them were good friends. At the very least, I'd expect her to be at the head of the lynch mob. But she's not. Instead, she's starting to convince me they got the wrong guy. What's wrong with this picture?'

Dana shrugged. 'I don't know, but I must admit, I'm with Louise on this.'

'Well, at the risk of ruining my reputation,' Jessup admitted, 'that makes three of us.'

'Good,' Dana declared. 'Now all we need to do is find twelve like-thinking people to put on the jury.'

'Well, it's obvious the prosecutor's office isn't about to let that happen,' Jessup observed. 'The minute the indictments were handed down, the floodgates opened, and out went the spin doctors to trumpet their position. A regular colony of marching pissants.'

In cases like this, despite the terrible tragedy and lingering consequences, Dana knew the tendency for most people would be eventually to drift back to their normal lives. It was already three months since the bombing, and the trial was not scheduled to start until September. She understood why Brian Ayres wanted to keep everyone's emotions fresh and churning until then. It was what she would have done had she still been a prosecutor.

'Translation,' she said, 'they're taking dead aim at the jury pool.'

'But why?' Jessup wondered. 'If their case is so good, why resort to cheap tactics?'

'Good question,' she replied.

'Will you ask for a delay?'

Dana shook her head. 'Corey doesn't want one. He wants to get out of there as soon as possible. He's asked for a speedy trial.'

'You could advise him.'

'I'm not sure another six months would make that much difference.'

'Are you going for a gag order then?'

'No,' she told him.

'Why not?'

'Because I'd get it, and it would look like we had something to hide,' she replied. 'This way, the evidence is the evidence. It won't get any stronger by them hanging it all out there. And it won't get any weaker by my trying to refute it.'

'So you're going to do nothing?'

'Absolutely nothing,' Dana confirmed. 'I want to walk into the courtroom and be able to say to the jury, here he is, take a good long look at him. Where's the monster the prosecution has been telling you about all these months?'

Prudence Chaffey sat on a peach velvet sofa in her gracious Houston living room on a muggy afternoon in May and served tea to the board of directors of AIM, which stood for something she believed in wholeheartedly: Abortion Is Murder.

'The Hill House trial is set to begin in four months,' she said, pouring from an elegant sterling silver service, and passing the cups with plates of frosted teacakes. 'For the future of this country, we must do everything in our power to make sure there is an acquittal. While I abhor the loss of life associated with the bombing, I firmly believe that Corey Latham is to be championed, not chastised for his courage.'

The only daughter of a Southern Baptist minister, she had married into a prominent Texas oil family when she was seventeen. By the age of fifty-three, she had buried two babies for whom she still grieved, raised four others into adulthood, and was enjoying nine grandchildren, with the promise of more on the way.

It didn't take her long to realize she had married too young, and with too many romantic notions in her head. By the time she had celebrated her fifth wedding anniversary, she knew that her husband, Harold, was a regular visitor to other women's beds.

She went to her father. But instead of being outraged, he only shrugged.

'Boys will be boys,' he said, and then suggested that she find an outside interest to occupy her time. There was no question of a divorce.

Prudence tried a variety of local charities, all of which were delighted to have the young society matron's name on their rosters, but none of them really appealed to her. Then *Roe v. Wade* became law, and as her father railed against it from his pulpit, she knew she had found the true cause she was looking for. What better purpose could one have in life than to help protect the rights of the preborn? True to her daddy's teachings, the sweet, round, strawberry blonde believed abortion to be an act against God.

'The timing of this incident couldn't have been more perfect,' one of AIM's board members suggested. 'What with the national elections coming up, and the party's strong stand on the issue. Demands for a Constitutional amendment against abortion have been pouring into our offices.'

'Yes,' Prudence murmured. 'One would almost think the young man had divine inspiration.'

17

'Okay, Corey, let's fill in a few more of the blanks,' Dana began, opening her briefcase across the metal table in the purple interview room, and pulling out a pad, a pen, and a stack of files. 'Let's start with the police. I want to know exactly when and how they got to you, and I need you to be as specific as you can.'

'The first time was when two detectives came to the base,' he told her. 'I think it was the first week in March. They asked some of us if we'd be willing to let them look in our cars. I remember one of the detectives was named Tinker.'

'Specifically, besides you, who did they look at?' she asked.

Corey thought about that for a moment, and then gave her the names of a lieutenant and three enlisted men from the *Jackson*. 'I think those were the only ones on my boat,' he added. 'But I heard they were talking to some guys from the other boats, too, and some civilians.'

'Altogether, how many would you estimate?'

'Maybe a couple dozen of us.'

'And, aside from the fact that you all work at Bangor, what did you have in common?'

'I found out later,' he replied. 'We all drove SUVs.'

'What else?'

'Our vehicles were all dark-colored. You know, black, green, brown.'

'Anything else?'

'I don't think so.'

'Didn't they all have identification stickers?'

'Oh yeah, well, sure. Everyone has to have the sticker, or they wouldn't be allowed on base.'

'Are the stickers located in pretty much the same place on everyone's vehicle?'

'Yes,' he replied. 'We have to put them on the lower left-hand side of the windshield, so they're clearly visible to the guard at the gate. It's regulation.'

'Are all the stickers the same?'

'Yes.'

'Exactly the same?'

'Well, not absolutely exactly.'

'What's different?'

'The Department of Defense sticker is the same, but we also have base ID tabs, and they have different colors: blue for officers, red for enlisted men, and green or yellow for civilians.'

'And the tags are clearly visible on the windshield?'

'Yes. That's one of the reasons why they do it that way. So the guards at the gate can pick up on a blue tag, and immediately know it's an officer's vehicle, and salute.'

'Okay,' Dana said. 'Now how did the police know about the abortion?'

At that, Corey looked blank. 'I don't know,' he said.

'Did you tell them?'

'No. They didn't ask me anything about that the first time. But when they came back, they just seemed to know.'

'Well, aside from you and Elise, of course, who did know?'

Corey had to think about that for a moment. 'Zach did,' he said at length. 'And a bunch of guys on my boat. I stopped in and had cocoa with Mrs. Biggs a couple of times, and I didn't exactly keep it a secret. My minister knew, and the people in the support group I was in. And I guess the staff at Hill House. I think that's all.'

Dana shrugged. 'Well, I don't know if it means anything,' she said, passing the pad and pen over to him. 'But I'd like you to give me all the names.'

'Sure,' Corey said, beginning to write.

'All right,' she continued when he had finished. 'So, the first contact you had with the police was when they asked to see your car. Detail the second for me.'

'Maybe a week or so later, Tinker and another detective came back to the base to ask questions.'

'Of all of you?'

'I don't think so. They talked to me, and they talked to another lieutenant on my boat, and to a couple of officers on the *Michigan*, and to one on the *Alabama*.'

'That's it? Just officers?'

Corey considered that for a moment. 'Yeah, I think so. I think it was just the five of us. I'm pretty sure it was.'

'What did they ask you?'

'They wanted to know what my relationship was with Hill House. How many times I'd been there. And how I felt about the abortion. And did I hold the people at the clinic responsible. Stuff like that.'

'How long did they talk to you?'

'Gosh, it must have been for an hour or more. I remember it was long enough so that they started asking the same questions two and three times, like they forgot they'd already asked me.'

'And then they went away?'

'Yes. But then the same guy, Tinker, and a couple of others showed up at my home a few days later, with a search warrant. They took stuff from my car, the garage, my closet. They kept telling me that what they were doing was so they could eliminate me as a suspect. I cooperated with them as much as I could.'

'And was that it?'

Corey nodded. 'Except for the day they came and arrested me.'

'Here's the list of people Corey says knew about the abortion,' Dana said, handing Craig Jessup the piece of paper Corey had written on. 'I don't know what it means, though, or if it'll do us any good.'

'Are you thinking this might have been a setup? That one of these people took advantage of a situation?'

'I have an obligation to explore every possibility,' she

responded. 'And to present any reasonable alternative to the jury.' She shrugged. 'Sure, there's always a chance he was set up.'

'Okay,' Jessup agreed. 'I'll see what I can find.'

'There's something else, too,' she said. 'When the police went to Bangor the second time, they were only looking at officers.'

'What do you mean?'

'They didn't talk to any of the enlisted men a second time, or the civilians. According to Corey, they only talked to the officers.'

Jessup's eyes narrowed slightly. 'Okay,' he said.

'She thinks it could be a setup,' Paul Cotter said over the telephone.

'A setup?' the voice at the other end asked.

'Seems a fair number of people knew the kid was angry over the abortion. She's got Jessup out snooping around. But I think the chances of him finding out anything are slim to zero.'

There was a thoughtful pause on the line. 'Does she really think she could back that up?'

Although the caller couldn't see him, Cotter shrugged. 'Frankly, with just a few months before trial, and the other side enjoying round-the-clock media coverage, I think she's just grasping at straws.'

'Probably,' the caller agreed. 'But you never know.'

'How'd you get your nose caught in the middle of this one?' Detective Al Roberts asked.

Although Craig Jessup was no longer a member of the police force, relationships that had been forged over twenty years on the job were lasting ones. The two men still met for drinks almost every week.

'Doing what my clients pay me to do,' Jessup replied with a helpless shrug and a heavy sigh. 'Right now, I'm just trying to get a handle on this whole thing, you know, doing what I have to do to get it clear in my own mind. Worst-case scenario, I go back to my client and tell her to start praying for a deal to keep her client off the gallows.'

Roberts laughed. 'From what I hear, that would take a lot of praying.'

'His head's already in the noose, huh?' Jessup murmured.

'Oh yes, and then some,' Roberts confirmed. 'Rumor has it, they've already ordered in the champagne – imported, too.'

'Well, between you and me,' Jessup confided, because he knew Al Roberts to be an honest cop, 'I don't see how they put this together.'

'Defense teams never do,' Roberts suggested with a smile. 'Isn't that the way it works?'

'Well, most of the time, I suppose,' Jessup allowed. He considered his friend for a moment, because he valued their relationship, and he didn't like to abuse it unless it was absolutely necessary. 'Listen, without doing yourself any damage, can you tell me how you came to like this guy for the bombing in the first place?'

'It isn't my case, you know,' Roberts replied. 'It's Tinker's, all the way. I have no real involvement, so I'm not privy to all the ins and outs. But as I understand it, they got a tip.'

'A tip?'

'Yeah.'

'What kind of a tip?'

'An anonymous tip.'

'An anonymous tip?'

'Yeah, so what?' Roberts responded. 'It's not unusual. We get them all the time. You know that as well as I do.'

Jessup hunched his chair a little closer and lowered his voice. 'This is the biggest case to ever hit this town, and from where I'm sitting, anyway, there's nowhere near enough to convict here. I'm looking at nothing direct, nothing material, no DNA, just a pile of assumptions. And now I hear you got to this guy through an anonymous tip. I don't know. You tell me they've ordered the champagne, but I see a case that just barely got them their indictments, and won't hold up on cross-examination. And you know I know enough to know that.'

Roberts frowned. 'You saying you think the kid's being railroaded?'

'Well, I sure wouldn't blame anyone if he was. Look at the criticism you got for keeping a tight lid on the investigation. People said you were making mistakes and then covering your asses. Look at the pressure you were under to find the bastard, whoever he was. Now your side's got people running all over the place, assuring everyone he's the right bastard, like for some reason you need to try your case in the court of public opinion instead of the courtroom, and the other side's not saying a word. Doesn't that strike you as peculiar? Let's face it, this thing is a major hot potato, for all of us, and an acquittal isn't something the department would recover from so easily.'

Roberts stared into his beer for a few moments, then picked up the glass and drained it. He knew Jessup was being straight with him.

'Let me get back to you,' he said.

18

At the age of forty-five, Tom Kirby was by far the oldest reporter on the staff of the investigative magazine *Probe*. He had knocked around the fringes of journalism since graduate school, without ever quite finding his niche. Not that he hadn't had his share of opportunities.

There were a few good years on the *Detroit Free Press*, and a couple more on the *Chicago Tribune*, but in both cases, booze had gotten in the way. Then came other newspapers, smaller and smaller dailies, then weeklies, and finally a tabloid. In each case, a step down from the job before. There was also a bad marriage in the middle of it all. He finally checked himself into a rehab center and got clean. But it was too late to resurrect any kind of serious journalistic career.

He became a jack-of-all-trades, doing odd jobs for people whenever he could find them. He had always been good with his hands. He knew basic carpentry, was a pretty decent painter, and had more than a passing acquaintance with cars. He taught himself as much as he could about plumbing and electrical repair.

A year and a half ago, he had landed at *Probe*, a glossy weekly that liked its readers to think it was mixing fact with its gossip, and providing less sensationalism and more integrity than most of the competition.

He shaved off his three-day stubble, combed his unkempt sandy hair, and put on his one good suit for the interview. It was at least ten years old, and he was relieved to find that it was only slightly tight around his midsection.

'I know your history,' the Los Angeles publisher, who was ten years his junior, told him. 'But I also know you did some good work once.'

'How would you know that?' Kirby asked.

'I was raised in Detroit,' the publisher replied.

'I can't remember that far back,' the reporter mumbled.

'Try,' the publisher said. 'Try to tell me what it was you went into journalism for.'

Kirby thought for a moment. 'I wanted to write something that was worthy of winning a Pulitzer Prize,' he said with a dry chuckle.

'What?'

Kirby scuffed his shoe against the plush carpet. 'I don't know – a series maybe, about people in trouble.'

'Any particular people?'

Kirby shook his head. 'Nah, it didn't matter. Just people who got themselves in trouble. I always wanted to understand what forces can drive a person to do certain things, and how they make the decision on whether they do good things or bad things. Maybe because I never understood myself very well, or why I did a lot of the stuff I did.'

The publisher smiled. 'I need a veteran here, someone with just that attitude, someone I can rely on to get a story and get it right, someone the kids fresh out of school can learn from. Are you clean enough to be that person?'

'I'm clean,' Kirby replied. 'I've been clean for two years now.'

'I know,' the publisher said. 'That's why you got this interview. But I also happen to know that you haven't worked much in the past few years, either. So the question is, will you be able to stay clean when the pressure is on?'

Kirby looked at the man through disillusioned eyes, hating that he had to beg for work on a rag that wasn't even good enough for toilet paper. 'I can't make you any promises,' he said, 'except that I'll try. I want to stay clean. I want to work. Hell, I need a job, okay, and this is the first interview I've had in eight months. You'd be going out on a big limb with me, but I'd do my damnedest not to let you down.'

The publisher had taken a chance, not that much of a chance, really, at least monetarily, and had not been disappointed with his bargain. Kirby had done his job, delivered his pieces on time, and earned the respect of his much younger co-workers. If he was drinking, it certainly wasn't apparent to anyone.

At the end of May, Kirby knocked on the publisher's door. 'I want to go to Seattle,' he declared.

'Why?' his boss asked. 'We've already got someone up there covering it.'

'I know,' Kirby said, 'but I think there's something there for me. I don't know what it is yet, but I can smell it.' He gave the publisher a cynical look. 'I think it might be my Pulitzer.'

'I know how busy you are, Ms. McAuliffe,' Corey said shyly one day, when he had been in the King County Jail for two and a half months. 'But do you think maybe you could come see me once in a while, even if it's not about my case?'

Dana peered at him in the half light of the purple interview room. 'What's the matter?' she asked.

He shrugged. 'It's just that I'm alone so much. I can have visitors only three hours a week, and the rest of the time I'm all by myself. I eat alone. I exercise alone. Nobody talks to me, except the guards, and they're not very sociable. And besides, I always have to watch what I say to them. I always have to be careful. It's just so hard, and I get so lonely.'

'Your minister can come more often,' Dana reminded him.

'I know, and he does, as much as he can,' Corey hastened to assure her, but then a sheepish smile spread across his face. 'It's just that, well, mostly he reads from the Bible, and while it's very uplifting and all that, it's not exactly the same as two people getting together and talking to each other, if you know what I mean.'

Dana smiled. 'I know what you mean.'

'You're really the only one who can come here whenever you want, and get the private room, and all. And I thought, well, maybe you could find a reason to come more often. Something you forgot to tell me, or a question you forgot to ask. And you know, if you didn't have anything about the case to discuss, maybe we could just talk about whatever we felt like. It's the monotony, you see. It's driving me crazy.' He stopped before he blurted out about the headaches, and the nightmares, and the bitter acid that was roiling around in his stomach now on a pretty regular basis. 'But I know how busy you are,' he said instead, 'and I'd understand if you didn't have time.'

Paul Cotter had long since removed the bulk of Dana's workload from her calendar, smoothly transitioning her clients to other partners and associates. The Latham case was now her only priority.

'I'll come every day, whether I need to or not,' she promised. 'And I'll stay as long as I can.'

'You're famous,' Sam told her when she finally made it home that evening.

'Why?' she replied. 'What did I do?'

'You made the cut on Jonathan Heal's Prayer Hour.'

'What are you talking about?'

'Apparently, once a week, he selects someone to elevate to his own personal list of living saints, and this week, it seems to be you.'

'Who is Jonathan Heal?'

'Ah, the joys of working sixteen hours a day,' Sam said with a grin. 'You get to miss the really important stuff. Jonathan Heal is this major televangelist, with a reputed following of millions. He goes around in this ridiculous white suit, preaching the gospel, and rakes in a fortune. I read somewhere that his real name is Jacob Hunsucker, but he changed it because he didn't think that name would inspire the flocks.'

'How did I get to be a part of all this?' Dana asked.

'Oh, your sainthood was conferred because you're representing the great protector of the preborn. According to him, you are noble, you are virtuous, you are the epitome of modern woman.'

'Do I leap tall buildings with a single bound?'

Sam chuckled. 'I think he left that part out. But he did get in that you are the only hope of a morally bankrupt nation.'

'Rubbish,' Dana declared.

19

Joan Wills had every intention of becoming a partner at Cotter Boland and Grace, and sooner rather than later, if she had anything to say about it. Recruited right out of the University of Washington Law School, she had worked for the firm for seven years, doing every bit of scut work demanded of her, and quietly biding her time.

There was no question in her mind that she was the sharpest associate in the office. According to her time sheets, she was by far the most sought after, and she had easily logged twice as many billable hours as any of the other eleven associates. Additionally, in the last couple of years, she had been acknowledged several times by the executive committee for bringing in significant business of her own. If that didn't qualify her for partner status, she didn't know what would.

She was certainly aware of Cotter Boland's less than profeminist history. But Joan figured she had an ace in the hole on that score. Dana McAuliffe had led the way. And as far as Joan was concerned, Dana McAuliffe walked on water.

Smooth as satin, soft as cashmere, hard as nails, and nothing less than totally professional, the firm's only female partner exemplified everything the senior associate wanted to be. Let her male counterparts idolize Paul Cotter or Elton Grace, Joan was perfectly content to learn at the feet of the person she had chosen to emulate.

When the invitation came for her to sit second chair on the Latham trial, the thirty-two-year-old attorney knew this was the final test. Office scuttlebutt had it that a new partner was going to be made next year, and that Joan was on a short list of three senior associates being considered. She felt confident, if she performed well on what was arguably going to be the most important case the firm had ever handled, it should all but assure her of the offer.

At the very least, she knew Dana would go to bat for her. During the past couple of years, the two attorneys had moved past being just colleagues to become friends. It would not have been unusual, for someone looking, to find them discussing everything from legal matters to shoe styles over yogurt in the lunchroom. Occasionally, when they worked late, they would go out to dinner together. And on one occasion, Joan joined Dana and Molly at the symphony to hear Sam play.

Despite some in the firm occasionally confusing them, the two women hardly resembled each other, with some three inches in height and thirty pounds in weight separating them. Although, as expected, tailored suits dominated their work wardrobes, Joan preferred the charcoal grays and navy blues to Dana's choice of soft colors. While both had blond hair, Joan's was more strawberry than honey, and she wore it somewhat shorter than Dana's flowing shoulder length. And where Dana's eyes were large and brown, Joan's were hazel and slightly slanted. Still, there was a sense of likeness about them that was obvious to most.

'I was sure one of the partners would have taken second chair on this one,' Joan said breathlessly. 'Or at least one of the boys.'

'It was my choice to make,' Dana replied with a shrug. 'And it was made with Paul Cotter's full approval.' In fact, Cotter had been downright enthusiastic when Dana discussed it with him.

'Don't get me wrong, I want the case,' the associate hastened to add. 'But I have to tell you, right up front, even if it costs me the job, I'm pretty much pro-choice.'

Dana smiled. 'That's okay,' she said. 'You're in good company.'

'Well, what I mean is, to put it politely, I'm not particularly sympathetic to our client.'

'Neither was I, at the beginning,' Dana conceded. 'But go spend some time with him, as I have. You might want to reconsider.'

Joan raised a cynical eyebrow. 'Come on. Are you going to tell me you think maybe he didn't do it?'

'No. I'm going to tell you I think maybe he deserves the benefit of the doubt.'

It was a nonanswer, of course, but Joan had enormous respect for Dana's intelligence and judgment.

'Interesting,' she murmured, but her mind was already beginning to whirl. If she had a hand in getting Corey Latham an acquittal, in the biggest case that had ever hit the state of Washington, she was certain the partners at Cotter Boland would not be able to deny her.

'My name is Joan Wills,' she told the alleged Hill House bomber from her side of the metal table in the purple interview room. 'I'm going to be assisting Dana McAuliffe with your defense.'

A hollow-eyed young man, accustomed enough to his shackles, she noted, to have become adept at the jailhouse shuffle, sat down and looked back at her without expression.

'Thank you,' he said politely.

'Don't start thanking me until we get you out of this,' Joan responded with a bright smile.

'Will you?' he asked in a dull voice that suggested he did not expect a reply.

'Shouldn't we?' she countered.

His eyes narrowed slightly as he looked at her. 'Did you have a choice?' he asked.

'About what?'

'Could you have said no, you didn't want to represent me?'

'Sure I could've,' she replied easily, because it was true. 'No one at my firm is forced to work on a case if he or she doesn't want to.' She paused for a moment. 'Actually, I wanted this case,' she added. 'You see, it'll probably make me a partner, even if we lose. But it'll definitely make me a partner if we win. Now, does that make you feel better or worse?'

He laughed, in spite of himself, it seemed. 'Better, I guess,' he said. 'You're a lot like Dana. You tell it like it is.'

'Don't worry, whatever else goes down, neither one of us is going to lie to you,' Joan assured him, pleased by the comparison. 'We guarantee to give you the bad news right along with the good.'

'I'd like to be able to do something, you know, to help you with my defense,' he said. 'But I don't know what more I can say other than I didn't do it.'

'Trust me, you're going to help,' Joan said. 'When we go to trial, you'll have the opportunity to get up on the witness stand and make that very statement to the jury, just as persuasively as you know how.'

'The thing is, I look in the mirror, and I see the me I think I am, the me that everyone who knows me knows I am,' he said, and she could hear the desperation in his voice. 'Then I read the newspapers, and they're describing someone I don't even recognize.'

'That's not unusual,' she told him. 'In fact, the media is famous for it. What they don't know, they make up out of whole cloth.'

He looked at her with anguished eyes. 'But how is the jury going to know which one is the real me?' he asked.

'Okay, I went and saw him,' Joan reported to Dana.

'And?'

The associate shook her head. 'I always thought I was a pretty good judge of character, that I could tell, just by looking at someone, what was what. But this guy, I don't know. I admit, I was absolutely convinced the son of a bitch did it. I was going to go to the jail and meet him, and come back and tell you it was time to get the stardust out of your eyes.'

Dana chuckled. 'And now?'

'Now I'm going to start looking for all the holes I can find in the state's case. Because I have reasonable doubt.'

'I went to the jail the first time, feeling exactly the way you did,' Dana told her. 'I wanted him to be guilty, so of course, in my mind, he *was* guilty. I didn't want this case. I wanted a good reason not to take it. But here I am.'

139

Joan shrugged. 'Two crazy women,' she said.

It suddenly occurred to Dana to wonder whether that might not have been why Paul Cotter had been so willing to put Joan on the case. The client now had two women who might just be crazy enough to believe in him.

'The anonymous tip came by mail,' Al Roberts told Craig Jessup. 'It was typewritten and had a Seattle postmark. It said there was an officer at Bangor whose wife had recently had an abortion at Hill House, and was pretty steamed up about it, and saying some wild things.'

'That's all?' Jessup asked.

'That's all,' Roberts confirmed.

20

'In the prosecution of Corey Latham, we want to send a very strong message,' a spokesperson for the King County Prosecutor's Office told Stone Phillips on *Dateline*.

'What kind of message?' Phillips asked.

'One that says we will not tolerate terrorists in this country, whether they come from the Middle East or the Midwest.'

'Do you think a conviction here will send that message?'

'If not the conviction, then surely the execution.'

'But doesn't terrorism succeed, for the most part, because terrorists are committed to their causes,' Phillips pressed, 'and are apparently ready and willing to die for their acts?'

The spokesperson shrugged. 'Well, I'm a lawyer, not a psychologist. But it seems to me that one dead terrorist means one less terrorist.'

For three months, the Reverend Jonathan Heal had kept Corey Latham in his public prayers. Without ever once having met the young man, the televangelist nevertheless took every opportunity, during his nightly Prayer Hour, to extol his numerous virtues and the unjustness of his circumstances.

It had more than paid off. Slowly at first, but then with gathering momentum, a stream of money had found its way into the good Reverend's Kansas City post office box – coins, bills, checks – from every corner of the country, all with little messages of encouragement and support for the young naval lieutenant. The sheer volume of it had overwhelmed the ministry's two bookkeepers.

'We've had to double our trips to the post office, just to clean out the box to make room for more,' one of them said.

'What do we do with it?' the other one asked.

'How much?' Heal inquired.

'Almost four million dollars, and it's still coming in.'

The Reverend threw back his head and laughed. 'The power of prayer,' he cried.

'We aren't going to keep it all, are we?' the first bookkeeper inquired.

'Certainly not,' Heal asserted. 'You make out a check for, say, two hundred and fifty thousand dollars, and send it along to Seattle. Put the rest into the general fund.'

'Only two hundred and fifty thousand?' the second bookkeeper whispered to the first. 'Is that all he's going to get?'

The first bookkeeper shrugged. 'Who'll ever know?' she replied. 'The lieutenant will be thrilled with his quarter million, and come Christmas, you and I will get an extra big bonus for being such good employees.'

The presidential campaign was in full swing. By the middle of June, the state primaries had all but guaranteed the nominations of the two leading candidates. The Republican convention in July and the Democratic convention in August would do little more than rubber-stamp the already decided.

There would be no surprises, no controversy, no last-minute political maneuverings at either convention; just foregone conclusions. Reporters assigned to the two candidates scrambled to find anything of interest to report.

Pollsters across the country determined that there was little to choose from between the two. They both favored a strong military, better education, improved health care, and less government spending. There was really only one issue on which they totally disagreed: abortion.

'We are supposed to be a civilized country,' Prudence Chaffey declared on CNN's *Larry King Live*. 'What kind of civilization condones murdering innocent infants in the womb, and then condemns murdering their murderers?'

'But it wasn't just people performing abortions who were murdered at Hill House,' King observed.

'That's true, and that's tragic,' the AIM executive conceded. 'And we should do whatever is necessary to prevent such a thing from ever happening again, which is why I support the Republican candidate for president. He has promised us a Constitutional amendment that will guarantee every American the right to be born. And he has pledged to work with Congress toward the criminalization of all abortion.'

'How exactly would you expect him to accomplish that?'

'With relative ease, actually,' the Houston matron replied. 'As we know, the overwhelming majority of the people in this country are opposed to abortion. All they have to do, come November, is vote for those candidates who believe, as they do, that feticide is wrong and must be stopped. As soon as that happens, abortion will be history.'

'The Democratic candidate for president is hardly the irresponsible liberal his opponent would like the American people to think he is,' Priscilla Wales told Larry King several days later. 'He simply doesn't happen to believe that government was ever intended to deprive us of our rights as individuals. Which is why I support him. If we're capable of stepping into an election booth, and casting a vote for the candidate of our choice, why shouldn't we be capable of making every other important decision, as well?'

'There are some who seem to think that the bombing of Hill House was inevitable,' King suggested, 'and that continued support of *Roe v. Wade* will simply escalate the violence.'

The head of FOCUS shrugged. 'Three quarters of the people in this country favor abortion,' she said. 'Now, what are we supposed to do? Honor the majority, as we always have? Or bow to the minority because if you don't give them what they want, they'll go out and make a bomb?'

'How is it that "three quarters" of the population support abortion in this country, while the "overwhelming majority" opposes it?' Dan Rather asked his television audience on the CBS *Evening News*. 'Well, the answer is simple, really. It's all about polls –

who's doing them, and how the results are interpreted. Since polls are frequently something less than scientific, results can be controlled by the specific population samples that are surveyed, and by the language of the questions that are asked. In this case, the two sides of the abortion issue are sampling different populations and slanting their questions to elicit those responses that best support their particular assertions. So the reality of polls is that you can pretty much get them to reflect whatever you want them to.'

The weekly lunch at Al Boccolino had been somewhat less regular since the grand jury indictments against Corey Latham had been handed down, Dana often finding it necessary to work right through lunch.

'It's not a problem, and I understand,' Judith said one Wednesday in late June when Dana forced herself to break away from the office to keep their appointment. 'I only wish I were that busy.'

'Well, it's a mixed blessing, I assure you,' the attorney responded.

In the rush of the case, Dana had not had much time to work on the details of her plan for setting Judith up in an art gallery. It was little more than a week ago that she had finally gotten it thought out enough to sit down with Sam and discuss it. To her delight, he seemed quite receptive to the idea, and even offered to talk to their accountant. She opened her mouth to say something, wanting to share at least the concept with her friend, then closed it again. It wouldn't be right to raise Judith's hopes if nothing came of it.

'How are you doing?' she asked instead.

'Just fine,' Judith replied with a toss of her dark hair. 'I've gotten a couple of small commissions that I'm working on, and I've been talking to a gallery in Bellevue about a show.'

'That's terrific,' Dana said.

'Well, I don't know about terrific,' Judith responded. 'It's very iffy at the moment, but it might pay the bills for a couple of months, anyway.' Not for the world would she tell her friend that her mother was no longer able to help her out financially, or that she was juggling credit cards, or that she and her son, Alex, were living on macaroni and cheese.

'I know this hand-to-mouth business isn't exactly what you'd hoped for,' Dana said. 'But I really do have the feeling that things are going to change for the better for you, and soon, too.'

'Well, soon would be good,' the artist allowed. 'In the meantime, don't worry about me, I'm getting by. So, how's the big case going?'

The attorney shrugged. 'Let's just say,' she said, without going into details, 'that I haven't been getting a whole lot of sleep lately.'

'Are you going to get him off?'

'There's always a chance.'

'Do you want to get him off?'

'If he didn't do it, sure.'

'Didn't he do it?' Judith asked in surprise.

Dana frowned, clearly uncomfortable about discussing an ongoing case. 'If the state can't prove he did it,' she said, 'then he deserves to be acquitted.'

Judith contemplated her friend of thirty years. 'Then no wonder you're not sleeping,' she suggested softly.

Across the restaurant, out of earshot and unnoticed by the two women, a man with a thickening middle, sandy hair, and a five o'clock shadow, wearing khakis and a Seattle Mariners T-shirt, sat eating a bowl of pasta. Tom Kirby had been in Seattle for almost a month, and he had just figured out why he had come.

On arriving, the first thing he did was rent a small apartment in a residence hotel at the foot of Queen Anne, and stock the kitchenette with orange juice and frozen dinners. *Probe* was paying him a healthy per diem that would more than cover a room and three meals a day in a good hotel, but he did not intend to spend any more of it than he absolutely had to. Let his counterparts live high off the hog, if they wished. Lengthy unemployment had taught him to economize.

After settling in, he did some shopping, picking up the T-shirt and a few other items of clothing that would help him blend into the fabric of the city. The last thing he wanted was to be identified as an outsider – a tourist, or even worse, a member of the media.

Then he rented a pickup truck and went exploring, familiarizing himself with the neighborhood surrounding his residence, wandering through the financial, shopping, and international districts, and then poking around the university. He went to a baseball game and cheered for the home team, he learned the bus routes, and he took a ferry back and forth across Puget Sound. Only when he felt reasonably comfortable in his new environment did he turn his attention to the matter that had brought him here.

The Hill House bombing trial was still more than two months off, which gave him plenty of time to look for his angle.

'How will you know where to look?' his publisher asked, a little vague about his reporter's quest.

'Instinct, I guess,' Kirby replied.

He went to the offices of the *Seattle Times* and the *Post-Intelligencer*, and spent days poring over the issues that covered the bombing, requesting more and more until there was a mountain of newsprint on the table in front of him.

In truth, there were dozens of stories in those issues, just waiting to be told, about survivors, about victims, about the families of the victims, about the impact that the loss of the clinic had on the community, but he passed them all over.

'If you could tell me what you're looking for,' a patient clerk suggested after a week, 'maybe I could be of more help.'

'The problem is, I don't know what I'm looking for,' he confessed. 'But I will when I find it.'

He kept looking. He talked to the people he encountered on the streets, the homeless who had depended on Hill House for so much.

'They were good folks up there,' one man told him. 'They understood us, and they cared about us, when no one else in the city did. Now that they're gone, the churches have stepped in. They don't really understand, and they don't really care, but they bring food. The difference is, Hill House did it without making a big fuss. The churches make sure everyone knows.'

There was a good story there, he thought, and not one that the media hotshots who were beginning to fill the city would be likely to go after. But it wasn't the right one.

He turned to the alleged perpetrator. He wondered why such an apparently upstanding young man would go off the deep end like that. It fit his criterion for a Pulitzer. Kirby wanted an interview, but he was told the kid's attorney wasn't letting anyone near him. So instead, the reporter spent a couple of days at Annapolis, and a few more days in Cedar Falls, but didn't come up with very much.

He spoke to people on the fringes of the case, to neighbors, to friends and acquaintances, to potential witnesses. He nosed around the police department and the courthouse, befriending a clerk here, an assistant there, but he knew that Corey Latham's story wasn't the one he was looking for. Nor did it turn out to be the prosecutor or anyone from the investigation team. Finally, on a sunny afternoon in early July, Kirby called his office.

'I don't know about the Pulitzer,' he said, 'but I've got the subject for my story.'

'Who is it?' the publisher of *Probe* asked.

'It's the kid's attorney,' Kirby replied.

'But she won't talk to you,' his boss asserted. 'She isn't talking to anybody.'

'Well, that's the whole point now, isn't it?' the reporter said. 'Why isn't she?'

21

Judith Purcell skidded into the driveway of her Beacon Hill home, relieved that she had managed to make it all the way there, and jumped out, fearing an imminent disaster of some kind. The smoke coming from under the hood of her car was so thick it had almost blinded her the last several blocks.

She couldn't believe it. When the last thing she needed was trouble with the car, this definitely looked like trouble, and she didn't know the first thing about cars. She stood there, frightened and frustrated, and started to cry.

'It would be better if you turned off the engine,' a voice behind her said.

Judith gasped. 'Of course,' she responded. 'I should have thought of that.'

'Let me,' the voice said.

She watched as a man came around the side of the car and proceeded to climb inside, turn off the engine, extract the keys, and pop the hood with calm efficiency. He was not particularly tall, and not particularly trim. His sandy hair was badly in need of cutting, and it looked as though he hadn't shaved for days. He was wearing khakis and a T-shirt, and didn't look familiar.

'If you've got a garden hose handy,' he told her, 'I'll cool this down and take a look for you.'

Judith produced the hose, turned it on at the man's instruction, and watched as he first doused the smoke and then disappeared under the hood.

'Just let me get a screwdriver,' he said a few moments later, trotting over to a pickup parked in the street, and rummaging around in the bed. Returning with a small toolbox, he disappeared under the hood again.

'It's nothing serious,' he declared, perhaps fifteen minutes later. 'A loose radiator hose, that's all. I've tightened it back up, and it should be okay for now. But if it blows again, you might want to take it in to your mechanic and let him check it out.'

'Oh thank you,' she breathed. 'I don't think I could have handled something serious.'

'Modern conveniences,' he said with a grin. 'We can't live with 'em, and we can't live without 'em.'

'Are you from around here?' she asked.

'No,' he replied. 'I've just been doing some work for the people across the street.'

'What kind of work do you do?'

'A little bit of everything, I guess,' he told her. 'I'm your basic handyman.'

'Oh, in that case, please, let me pay you for your time and trouble,' Judith said immediately.

'Not necessary,' he assured her with a broad grin. 'It's always my pleasure to come to the rescue of a damsel in distress.'

The damsel smiled back. 'Do you also tilt at windmills?' she asked.

The man chuckled. 'Whenever possible,' he replied.

He looked to be somewhere in his forties, and while he wasn't especially good-looking, he had a nice face, and he spoke as if he were educated. His eyes were what most drew her attention. It seemed as though they had been looking at the world for at least a hundred years. 'Well then, sir,' she declared, 'you have my undying gratitude.'

'I'll be back over here tomorrow,' he said with a little wave. 'In case the car acts up again.'

She thought about her dripping faucet, her running toilet, her leaking windows, her erratic oven, and her clogged gutters, but not about the fact that she had no money to hire someone to fix them.

'What's your name?' she asked anyway. 'If you're not too busy, I might have some work for you.'

He smiled. 'I'm not too busy,' he said. 'And my name is Tom. Tom Kirby.'

22

With very little fanfare, spring became summer. The days were drier than normal and cooler than expected, but otherwise unremarkable. For Dana, the best part of the season was that daylight lasted until almost ten o'clock.

It had become her habit to take advantage of that, and work late into the evening. She found it easier to do what she referred to as her courtroom planning once the phones had been switched over to the message service, the bustle and chatter of the busy office had subsided, and there were few, if any, interruptions. Corey Latham's trial was scheduled to begin in a matter of weeks, and she had been working sixteen-hour days since the middle of June.

During that time, she had rarely made it home before dark, and only barely made it to Molly's tenth birthday party. She couldn't remember the last time she had cooked a meal for her family, or the last time she and Sam had made love.

Thankfully, he understood. Or if not, at least he accepted it. Perhaps more than she, he had recognized from the start the demands that the Latham case was going to make on her, and on the family. As much as he could, he had filled their scant time together with pleasant evening jaunts around town and happy picnics in the park. Despite his best-laid plans, however, someone from the media usually managed to spot them.

'Tell us your strategy,' they begged from the other side of a street, the next table at a restaurant, a neighboring blanket at Green Lake.

'I'm saving it for the jury,' Dana always replied with a tight little smile that made it clear the inquisitor was to intrude no further. She resented their persistence, and the uncomfortable feeling they gave her of being cornered, like an animal.

The transition from prosecutor to defense attorney had not been an easy one for Dana. Despite her repartee with Brian Ayres over angels and devils, it had always been her intention, after a brief stint in the prosecutor's office, to change sides. After all, she wasn't her father's daughter for nothing. But she had struggled with it for years, perhaps, subconsciously, right up to this very moment.

'How can you defend such scum?' she had asked, the summer between her freshman and sophomore years at Stanford, when her father was in the middle of a gruesome rape trial.

'This is an equal opportunity system,' Jefferson Reid told her. 'Defending him guarantees you and me and everyone else in this country a process that protects all of us.'

'How would it protect the victim to have her rapist go free?' Dana countered.

'I'll tell you how,' her father replied. 'Remote as the possibility may seem to you, what if this "scum," as you call him, didn't do it? What if the evidence against him was flimsy at best, or manufactured at worst, only everyone wanted him to be guilty, so they didn't much care? Now, let's say you were *his* daughter, and he went to prison for fifteen years for a crime he didn't commit. How would you feel?'

'Angry,' she admitted. 'So, is he innocent?'

Reid shrugged. 'I don't know,' he said. 'We'll have to wait for the jury to tell us.'

After fourteen years in practice herself, Dana had come to believe wholeheartedly in the adversarial system as a fundamental part of the judicial process, and she fully understood and agreed with the need to challenge the state to prove its case beyond a reasonable doubt. Still, there was something about the apparent ease with which some defense attorneys could circumvent the rules and manipulate the truth on behalf of a client that upset her sense of moral balance.

After a lifetime of watching her father represent his share of guilty defendants, and marveling at his skill, it always seemed to her that he had a line that he would not cross, which in her eyes, anyway, seemed to justify his actions. She had tried to find that line for herself, despite the pressure she sometimes felt to win at all costs, but she was never quite as comfortable with her position as she had been with her father's. Until now.

Now there was Corey Latham. And she could see clearly all the reasons why it was so important to protect the rights of every defendant. Because unless there was vigorous defense of the guilty, she knew there could be no chance for the exoneration of the innocent.

The transition from defender to champion had taken place so gradually that she had not even been aware of it at first. It had begun with her accepting the case, and assigning the standard presumption of innocence that she applied like a blanket to all her clients, without thinking or judging, simply as a matter of law.

Then, ever so slowly, and without her actually realizing it was happening, that perfunctory presumption gave way to the possibility that Corey Latham really might not be the Hill House bomber after all. His confusion was just too real, his vulnerability too great, his sincerity too obvious, his story too credible, and the evidence far too vague.

'I think I've probably read more books in the past few months than I did in my whole life,' he said with a sheepish grin one day in July. 'I just finished *Les Misérables*, and I have to tell you, I know exactly how Jean Valjean must have felt.'

'He spent almost his whole life as a victim,' Dana replied. 'Hopefully, you won't have to.'

'He made one little mistake, and that started everything. But he wasn't a bad man. I believe he had principles. I believe he was a good man.'

'At one point or another in our lives, many of us become victims of circumstance.'

At that, Corey had sighed. 'Sometimes, at night, you know, when I lie in bed, I listen to the sounds of this place,' he said. 'Men banging around in their cells, whispering to one another in the dark, crying out in their sleep. And I think there's this whole world I never knew anything about before, running parallel with the world I grew up in, and I wonder how we can be so ignorant of each other.'

'This world is not your world, and don't you ever start thinking it is,' she declared, somewhat more vehemently than perhaps was warranted.

He smiled at her then, delight tinged with sadness. 'You know what?' he said mischievously. 'I think you like me.'

'Never mind that,' she said, a bit embarrassed by her outburst. 'Tell me how you're getting along with Dr. Stern.'

'He's okay,' Corey said. 'For a shrink.'

'Do you like him?'

'Yeah, I like him, I guess. He's funny. He makes me laugh sometimes.'

'That's okay,' Dana said. 'I'd just appreciate it if you didn't make him cry.'

'Do you think he'll find me insane?'

She looked at him quizzically. 'Do you want him to?'

'Hell, no. I don't think I'm crazy. But it's like he's got this invisible microscope peering into my brain, and even I don't know everything that's in there.'

She smiled. 'As long as you tell him the truth,' she said, 'I don't think you have anything to worry about.'

Leaving the jail that day, Dana realized she no longer accepted just the possibility of Corey Latham's innocence. In her mind, it was now a probability. And by the end of July, after four months of such conversations in the cramped interview room, after having taken the time, in spite of herself, to get to know the person behind the horrendous indictment, the probability became belief.

Shortly after that conversation, Brian Ayres had begun the process of disclosing the thrust of his case, turning over documentation, analyses, and witness lists to the defense. The material consisted of evidence found in Corey's car and home, a witness who saw what could have been her client's vehicle at Hill House the night before the bombing, and various other witnesses who would testify to Corey's state of mind and actions after he found out about the abortion. Dana spent hours sifting through it all, bouncing ideas off Joan Wills and Craig Jessup, until gradually the shape of a strategy came into focus.

Now she glanced at the chalkboard on the wall beside her desk. On one side, she had diagrammed what was clearly going to be the prosecution's scenario. On the other side, she had drawn her preliminary rebuttal to that scenario. Visualizing an abstract by giving it actual form was a tool that had proven very useful to her over the years. Both she and Joan concluded that the prosecutor's case was even weaker than they had initially thought, and each day Dana grew more convinced that reasonable doubt was going to be well within her reach.

Left unchallenged, the evidence, circumstantial though it was, seemed sufficient to tie the noose around Corey's neck, and Dana could not help but see how the authorities might have come to that conclusion. However, just as she had learned in prosecuting cases that there was no such thing as a coincidence, she had also discovered in defending cases that almost everything could be a coincidence.

Piece by piece, she intended to dispute the state's documentation, analyses, and witnesses, showing the jury how there was easily room for more than one explanation of what, at first glance, might look like convincing fact. Circumstance was always open to interpretation, and offering another plausible interpretation was what created reasonable doubt.

For that, she was counting on Craig Jessup's help. There was no one better at what he did, and if there were anything to find, she knew he would find it. For months, though, he had been digging, and so far, he had not come up with a viable alternative she could shove under the noses of the prosecution and dangle in front of the jury. And time was running out. Still, Dana knew it was there.

'It has to be,' she told him. 'Because Corey Latham didn't do it. And that means there's a mass murderer out there somewhere, walking free, thinking he's gotten away with it. But you and I both know there's no such thing as a perfect crime. He has to have left some kind of trail. I need you to find it.'

Jessup nodded wearily. He had worked on eight cases with

Dana, and he had never before seen her so committed to a defendant. But then, he reasoned, he and Louise weren't all that far behind her.

'All right, I'll take another look,' he promised. 'If there's something there, I'll find it. If it's not, well, hell, I'll find it anyway.'

Whether she realized it or not, Dana had been clinging to those words like a lifeline.

'How's everything going?' Paul Cotter asked from the doorway, startling her out of her ruminations so sharply that she actually jumped.

'Well, as a matter of fact, things aren't nearly as bad as I was expecting them to be,' Dana replied brightly, not about to share her concern with the managing partner.

'Really?'

'Yes,' she said. 'I think we're going to go to trial in pretty decent shape. From what I've seen of the evidence so far, the state's whole case is based on a rather flimsy collection of coincidences that I plan to drive an eighteen-wheeler right through.'

'Really?' Cotter repeated. 'The way I hear it, Brian Ayres and his staff seem to be quite satisfied with what they've got.'

Dana shrugged. 'Oh well, that's only because he's missing a crucial piece of information that I happen to possess,' she said.

'And what's that?' Cotter inquired, looking suddenly interested.

Dana allowed herself a little smile. 'Corey Latham is innocent,' she said.

The managing partner nodded absently, and shifted his gaze to the chalkboard, where he appeared to be trying to decipher Dana's hieroglyphics. 'I'm sure I don't have to remind you that innocence is no defense under the law,' he reminded her.

She leaned back in her chair with confidence. 'No,' she agreed comfortably. 'But it's a great starting point.'

Cotter seemed to study her for a moment, although his eyes were still directed toward the chalkboard. 'I've asked Charles Ramsey to take third chair on this,' he said.

'Oh?' she said. Next to Cotter himself, sixty-six-year-old Charles Ramsey was perhaps the most conservative of the partners. He was possessed of a brilliant mind and an acid tongue. In all her years here, she could not remember him ever taking third chair.

'He won't interfere,' Cotter hastened to assure her. 'He'll be a sort of liaison for the executive committee. You know, someone who can keep us abreast of the case as it progresses, so we won't have to take up too much of your time.'

He didn't fool her for a minute. Even after the documented success of women in the courtroom, and a dozen years of working with her personally, the archconservative could not bring himself to rely on a woman completely. Ramsey was to be the watchdog. But Dana didn't mind. In fact, considering that this was her first capital case, she had to concede it was probably not an altogether illogical move for him to make.

She gave him an enigmatic glance. 'I have no problem with that,' she said.

23

'I've met a man,' Judith blurted out, her eyes shining, unable to keep the news to herself for one more minute.

Dana, who had just stuffed a forkful of linguini marinara into her mouth, could only sit there with raised eyebrows, chewing and staring.

'Now, don't get me wrong,' her best friend continued. 'He's not the man of my dreams or anything like that, but he's nice and he's fun, and he's going through my house like a buzz saw, fixing everything that's ever been wrong with it.'

'You mean, a handyman,' Dana said finally, with some measure of relief. Judith was not particularly known for her judgment of the opposite sex.

'Well, not exactly,' Judith responded with a twinkle in her eye. 'I mean, he started out as a handyman, but, well, he's become more than that.'

Dana repressed a sigh. 'Do tell.'

'First, it was my car,' Judith said. 'That's how we met. Then it was my faucet, and then my gutters, and before I knew it, he was fixing everything. I'm still looking for something he can't do. He's even refinishing my hardwood floors. And on top of it all, Alex just adores him.'

'I know it's none of my business,' Dana said, 'but how can you afford to do all this?'

'Oh, that's the best part, he won't take any money for his work,' the struggling artist told her. 'You see, I'm his damsel in distress, and he's my knight in shining armor.'

'I beg your pardon?'

'Oh, I know it sounds silly, but I think he's lonely, and he's doing all this stuff for me just for the companionship. He's from

Detroit, and he doesn't know many people here. And we really do get on. We talk and we laugh, and I make him wonderful home-cooked dinners. We watch television, we listen to music, we go to movies, we take long walks. We have fun.'

'And?' Dana prodded.

'Okay, okay,' her friend confessed. 'So he's pretty decent in bed, too.'

'I must say, he sounds too good to be true,' Dana murmured.

'He is . . . almost,' Judith said with a happy laugh.

'Then I'm thrilled for you.'

Judith reached across the table and gave Dana's hand a grateful squeeze. 'I knew you would be. And I want you to meet him.'

'I'm sure I'll meet him.'

'No, I mean soon. I know, with the trial coming up and all, you don't have a whole lot of time, but I want you and Sam and Molly to come for dinner. Next Sunday at six o'clock. We'll make it an early evening, and I'll fix something fabulous.'

'I'll have to check my schedule,' Dana responded, surprised by a sudden reluctance. The McAuliffes often dined at Judith's modest Beacon Hill home, and there was no argument that she was a superb cook.

'Oh, come on,' Judith said. 'I know you're busy, but you can't have to work on Sunday. Even God got to rest on Sunday.'

Dana smiled. 'So He did.'

'Besides, it's important to me. I want you to see for yourself that I'm not always such a bad judge of character.'

Once Dana had spoken to Sam about the art gallery, he had gone into action. His loyalties were simple. If Judith Purcell was Dana's friend, then she was his friend also. And friends did whatever they could for one another.

'According to the accountant,' he reported back, 'we don't begin to spend all the money we make. Most of it is sitting in mutual funds. Since we own our home outright, and Molly's education is secure, he sees no problem in our using some of it to make a sound investment.'

'Judith may be a little flighty about some things,' Dana told him, 'but she's got a good head for business, and a great eye for quality art. I think she would be wonderful at running a gallery. I say we pursue it.'

Two days before they were to go to dinner at Judith's, Sam climbed into bed beside his wife.

'The accountant has finally finished tumbling all the numbers,' he told her. 'And he says if we really want to do this, we should probably go all out and buy a building.'

'Buy a whole building?' Dana gasped, sitting upright.

'It's not as scary as it sounds,' he assured her. 'I even have a heads-up on a place that's supposed to be coming on the market soon. It's small. Three stories, less than four thousand square feet, on the edge of Pioneer Square.'

'Judith would be in heaven,' Dana breathed. 'Do you think we could really swing it?'

Sam shrugged. 'I'm still finding out,' he said. 'But it certainly looks possible.'

Tom Kirby's hair was neatly trimmed and his face smooth-shaven. He had traded his khakis and T-shirt for a pair of slacks and a blue oxford shirt. He had even cleaned under his finger-nails. Judith made the introductions, beaming.

He had a firm handshake and a pleasant enough face, Dana decided, although his eyes, which looked directly into hers, seemed much older than his years. He appeared to be totally at ease in his surroundings, and she noticed that he ushered them into the living room as if he were already the man of the house.

'Judith tells me you're a terrific violinist,' he said to Sam. 'I played the violin as a kid, but I have to admit, I wasn't much good at it. I've always envied people who can play it well, though, and I've always thought I'd like to try again someday.'

'Sam gives lessons,' Judith told him. 'Do you teach adults, Sam, or just kids?'

'I teach anyone who wants to learn,' Sam said affably.

'You don't really think there could be hope for me, do you?' Kirby asked.

'It all depends,' Sam replied.

With that, Molly and Alex went off to play, and Judith dragged Dana into the kitchen.

'Well?' she demanded. 'What do you think of him?'

'He seems to be very comfortable here,' Dana said.

'He should be,' Judith said with a laugh. 'He's been in and out of this house almost every day now for weeks. But aside from that, what do you think of *him?*'

'Ask me again after dinner,' Dana replied.

With no great subtlety, Judith seated Kirby next to Dana at the table. The conversation about music continued during the soup.

'Where are you from?' Sam asked over the salad.

'Just about everywhere,' Kirby replied. 'My dad moved around a lot, and took us with him every time but the last time. He left us in Michigan when I was about fifteen. My mother and my sister are still there. But I must have inherited my dad's wanderlust.'

'Have hammer, will travel?'

Kirby smiled. 'It's been something like that,' he said. 'I tried working in an office, but I didn't much care for it. I do better when I'm my own boss, and I can come and go as I please. And I like working with my hands.'

'Well, I for one am glad you do,' Judith said, bringing on the main course.

Dana couldn't help noticing that she placed the pork roast next to Kirby, and handed him the carving utensils as casually as though they had been going through this particular routine for years. She glanced at Sam across the table. He had seen. He looked back at her with a grin and winked.

'How long have you been in Seattle, Tom?' she asked.

'Just a few months, actually,' he replied. 'And it seems I arrived just in time for the good weather.'

'How long are you staying?'

Kirby looked at Judith and smiled. 'Maybe longer than I originally thought.'

'Okay, everyone,' Judith said, both blushing and beaming. 'I invited you for dinner, so dine.'

160

It was a delicious meal, and Judith served it proudly. No one needed to know that it had eaten up her entire food budget for the week.

They fell silent for a few moments, as they obediently focused their attention on the succulent meat and the crisp vegetables and the perfectly seasoned potatoes that went down so nicely when accompanied by the smooth white wine. Then, somewhere between the pork and the pie, Kirby turned to Dana.

'Judith tells me you're an attorney,' he said, casually. 'What kind of law do you practice?'

'I'm primarily a litigator,' Dana replied.

'Yes, but tell him what you're currently litigating,' Judith prompted, getting a sharp glance of rebuke from her friend for her efforts.

'I'm working on the Hill House case.'

Kirby's eyes widened. 'Of course, how stupid of me,' he declared. 'It's been in all the papers. I must have read the name a dozen times. I'm sorry, I just didn't make the connection.'

24

In the middle of final preparations for the Latham trial, when jury selection was less than a week off, Dana did an unheard of thing. She took a day off and drove to Port Townsend. The sky was crystal blue, the sun sparkled off the water, and Mount Baker shimmered like an apparition in the distance, but Dana never noticed.

'There's something about this case that I'm missing,' she told her father.

'What makes you think so?' Jefferson Reid inquired, ushering her into his private office, which was filled with the well-used leather furniture and the well-thumbed law books she remembered from early childhood.

'That's just it,' she replied. 'I don't know. It's just a feeling I have.'

'Well, if it was a strong enough feeling to get you out here, let's take a look at it.'

'Okay, am I crazy? Or is the prosecution's case made up of smoke and mirrors?'

'Well, I can't say as I've been following it that closely, but there may be some of that involved,' he told her. 'I doubt that's all, though. I think they probably have a kernel of truth they're trying to embellish.'

'Then I'm in so far over my head, I don't know up from down,' she admitted. 'Because I'm preparing to defend a case I can't get hold of. I've got our best investigator on the job, and he can't seem to get hold of it, either. Neither can my assistant.'

'Is the state disclosing?'

'Oh, yes, and very promptly. And if you take it all at face

value, Corey Latham is a cold-blooded murderer. But nothing here stands up to serious scrutiny, and Brian Ayres has to know that. So what am I missing?'

'I don't know, maybe nothing,' Reid replied. 'Is it possible this Ayres fellow is holding out?'

Dana shook her head. 'No,' she said. 'Brian is a tough attorney who wants to win, but he won't cheat.' She smiled a little. 'Mostly, it's because he thinks he's too good to have to resort to cheating.'

'Then look into the motivation here,' her father suggested.

'What do you mean?'

'The police needed a suspect, and they needed one fast,' Reid suggested. 'They were being pilloried in the press, made to look like the Keystone Kops. So maybe they went out and manufactured themselves a suspect. They locked on to someone who conveniently had means, motive, and opportunity – which is all they're technically required to do – and closed up shop. Now, right or wrong, the state is stuck with that. For the prosecutor's office even to hesitate, especially on a case of this magnitude, would be ultimately disastrous.'

'You think they would rather risk an acquittal on a shaky case than make sure they had the right guy?'

'Given the circumstances, they may not have had a choice,' Jefferson Reid replied. 'They may be relying on emotion to sway the jury. They may have thought the kid would be going with a public defender. They may really think they've got the right guy.' Then he shrugged. 'In any event, putting the state on trial instead of your client is certainly a defense that's worked well for many over the years.'

25

'Anything I need to know about?' Brian Ayres asked his assistant.

It was the first Monday in August, jury selection for the Latham trial began tomorrow, and the prosecutor did not want any curves thrown at him at the last minute.

'I don't think so,' Mark Hoffman replied. It was the most important case of the young attorney's legal life, and he was not about to blow it. For months, he had hung over the investigators like a shroud, triple-checking everything. Now, the jury consultant was on board, the evidence was all in order, and the witnesses were all prepared. Dozens of motions had been filed and ruled upon. There were no surprises. Well, maybe one. Dana McAuliffe had not asked for a change of venue.

'It wouldn't have done her any good,' Brian assured him. 'This case has had too much exposure to assume an impartial jury anywhere in the state. I think she knew that.'

Mark grinned. 'It couldn't be that happened on purpose, now could it?' he asked.

Brian shrugged. 'When you can, you make the best of what you've got,' he replied. 'Our case isn't all that strong.'

'I don't think we've got a thing to worry about,' Mark declared.

'That's the first mistake you've made so far, ' Brian told him. 'We have everything to worry about. Not the least of which is Dana McAuliffe.'

'Why?' Mark asked. 'Sure, I know her firm has a good reputation and all, but when they palmed this case off on her, instead of putting one of their big guns on it, I figured they were handing us a gift.'

'You think that's what they did?'

'Well, sure. Everyone around here does.'

Brian leaned back in his chair, his head almost touching the wall behind his desk. 'Well, you wouldn't have any way of knowing it,' he informed his young assistant. 'And for that matter, the powers that be over at Cotter Boland may not know it, either – but they *did* put their big gun on this case.'

As usual, Dana was at her desk late into the night. Phase one of the Latham trial, and some would say the most crucial, was about to begin. The evidence was in, the witnesses had been interviewed, the strategy was in place, and the only thing left for her to do was think. Think it all over, from beginning to end, one last time, making sure that she had everything covered, and that there were no loose ends. She had spent the last three hours doing just that. Now she was waiting for a telephone call.

Three weeks ago, the list of prospective jurors had been turned over to Craig Jessup. A week ago, Jessup had passed the list, along with a concise dossier on each person, to jury consultant Lucy Kashahara, a perky thirty-two-year-old that everyone at Cotter Boland swore up and down had to be psychic. So far, in the half-dozen cases for which a specialist had been deemed necessary by the firm, she had not once steered them wrong.

Lucy had taken the information acquired by Jessup and prepared a general, but exquisitely detailed, inquiry: a ten-page, in-depth analysis designed to probe each prospective juror's psyche. All one hundred and twenty who were summoned to the courthouse the previous Friday had been required to fill it out.

'You can ask a question during voir dire,' she explained to Joan Wills. 'But you never really know what kind of an answer you're getting. Depending on his agenda, a person can tell you the absolute truth, or he can tell you what he thinks you want to hear, or he can tell you just what he wants you to know and nothing more. With the questionnaire, we ask the same questions in so many different ways that, in the end, most people can't help but reveal themselves.'

'You don't do that for every case, do you?' Joan asked.

'Only when we think we need an edge,' Dana told her with a wry smile. 'In this case, we're going to need all the edge we can get.'

'And don't forget for a minute that the other side is doing exactly the same thing we're doing,' Lucy added. 'The only hope here is that your consultant is going to be just a little bit better at her job than their consultant is.'

It took all of Friday for the jury pool to complete the questionnaires. They were not turned over until six o'clock that evening. Then Lucy had gone to work, giving up her entire weekend and continuing right through Monday to sift, review, evaluate, compare, and then prepare her recommendations.

The telephone in Dana's office rang just after ten.

'I'm done,' Lucy reported, sounding tired but pleased.

'Good,' Dana replied. 'I'll see you in the morning.'

In eleven hours, Dana thought as she hung up. In eleven hours, she would be walking into court, joined by Jessup, Lucy, Joan, and Charles Ramsey. Among them, they would try to select the twelve jurors and four alternates who would be most likely to decide the fate of Corey Latham in their favor. If they guessed wrong, their client would surely be convicted and sentenced to death. But if they guessed right . . .

Dana pursed her lips. If they guessed right – what? A hung jury? An out-and-out acquittal? Was that too much to expect? Had the fire in the community, ignited by the gruesomeness of the crime itself, been fanned too high and too hot to allow room for rational argument? Had the ongoing presence of spokespersons from the prosecutor's office, airing their case in every tabloid and all over the television newsmagazines, pushed public perspective beyond reasonable doubt? Would people be looking for a neck to hang, no matter whose neck it was?

Not for the first time, Dana found herself wondering whether she had made the right decision not to participate in the media blitz created by the state's efforts to demonize the young naval officer. She had certainly been invited to jump into the fray. From *Newsweek* to the *Seattle P-I* and from *60 Minutes* to *Larry King Live* and everyone in between. She was courted by all of them.

'Don't stoop to the prosecutor's level,' Paul Cotter had advised her. 'Let him try his case in the media. You try yours in the courtroom.'

It seemed sound advice, and dovetailed with her own intuition that told her to stay out of the spotlight where reporters never stopped digging, and so much was so often misinterpreted.

The only deviation from that plan came from Cedar Falls, when Barbara Walters of the ABC newsmagazine *20/20* invited the Lathams to sit down with her for a conversation.

'They're saying such awful things about our son,' Dean explained. 'We just want a chance to set the record straight.'

'Only on the clear understanding, and absolute guarantee, that I'll be given final content approval prior to airing,' the attorney told him.

Amazingly, *20/20* agreed to the demand, but Dana needn't have worried. Walters was a pro, and the living room interview, which filled an entire show at the end of July, was handled with taste and sincerity, and was absent any hint of sensationalism. The Corey Latham who came to life through the words and world of his parents was the Corey Latham that Dana herself had come to know. She hoped fervently that everyone who would wind up on the jury had seen the interview, or if they had not, that she would be able to re-create the essence of it for them in the courtroom.

The telephone call she was waiting for having come, Dana pulled herself out of her chair and left the office, taking the after-hours elevator down to the lobby. Her car was parked just across the street from Smith Tower, ready to take her home, but she ignored it, and instead took the eight-minute walk up to the jail.

'Are you ready?' she asked her client when he was escorted to the interview room.

'I want to get this over with,' he replied. 'I want to go home. I want my life back. Yes, I'm ready.'

'But are you ready if it doesn't go the way you want it to?'

The blue eyes widened slightly. 'Do I have to think about that?'

'There are no guarantees here, Corey,' she cautioned him. 'I'll do the very best I can, but you never really know how a jury will decide until they come back with a verdict.'

'But how could they convict me if I didn't do it?'

Dana sighed. 'I wish I could tell you there were no innocent men in prison,' she said. 'But I know better. In the final analysis, our justice system isn't about truth. It's about the *appearance* of truth. It's about what can be proven, to a reasonable certainty, to twelve specific people, at a given point in time.'

'And I can't prove my innocence?'

'Under the law, you don't have to prove your innocence. On the contrary, the state has to prove your guilt.'

'That's what I don't understand. How can they prove something that isn't true?'

'I don't know,' she had to tell him. 'But sometimes, they do.' More often than they should, she thought to herself, but she would never say it aloud. He was already too fragile.

'Ms. McAuliffe,' he said suddenly. 'I know you're my lawyer, and you're going to do the best you can for me at the trial, but, well, I guess I ought to ask – do you believe me?'

Dana stared at him. There was a routine answer to that question, of course, that had something to do with it not being her business to doubt him, but she knew it wouldn't be adequate just to tell him that.

'I don't normally think about guilt or innocence, Corey,' she said. 'I think about the merits of the case, and whether I can win it. In other words, I assume innocence, which is essential to doing my job. That's why I've never asked you whether you bombed Hill House or not. To be honest, I don't want to know.'

'Why not?'

'Because, if I did ask you, and you told me yes, you had set that bomb and killed all those people, then it would severely handicap my efforts to defend you.'

'How?'

'Well, let's see,' she replied. 'First of all, I could never put you on the stand to testify. It would be called subornation of perjury, and I'm not allowed to do that. I can't knowingly let you lie under oath. I could be disbarred.'

'Are you going to put me on the stand?'

'Absolutely,' she told him. 'You're the best witness we have in this case. And you're going to tell the jury exactly what you told me.'

'But you couldn't do that if you were representing a guilty person?'

'No,' she told him. 'If I knew for a fact that my client was guilty, I would look for mitigating circumstances that I could present to the jury instead, such as diminished capacity.'

'What's that?'

'That's when the defendant admits he did it, but we say he did it under such extreme emotional distress that he didn't fully realize what he was doing at the time. In other words, at the time of the crime, he was not mentally capable of knowing right from wrong. If there's a good enough reason for the distress, and the state is trying him on just one charge – murder one – which means a jury doesn't have the choice of a lesser charge, then they might be inclined to return a verdict of not guilty. The difference is, instead of trying to refute the state's evidence, as we do for a defendant we believe to be innocent, we would try to justify it.'

'You mean, if I really had bombed Hill House, you would tell the jury that they should acquit me since I wasn't in my right mind when I did it because I was so upset about the abortion?'

'Well, maybe something like that,' Dana replied.

'You don't have to worry, Ms. McAuliffe,' he said firmly, his clear blue eyes looking directly into hers. 'I didn't kill those people.'

She smiled a bit. 'That's good,' she said. 'Because I might

have had a pretty hard time convincing a jury that you were still under extreme emotional distress three months after the fact.'

'You do believe me, don't you?' he asked softly.

'Well, since it doesn't really matter to the defense of your case,' Dana replied, 'and I can see how much it matters to you, the answer is, yes, I believe you. I don't think you had anything to do with the bombing of Hill House.'

Corey let out a breath that was so deep and so long that it seemed as though he had been holding it for months. 'Thank you,' he said. 'I'm ready for tomorrow now. I know everything will be all right. God is with me, and you're with me, and if that isn't an unbeatable team, I don't know what is.'

26

The King County Courthouse dominated an entire city block. The massive twelve-story, H-shaped building was separated from the jail by the County Administration Building, but connected to it by a rather ingenious, if unattractive skyway, which was used primarily to shuttle defendants safely back and forth.

Constructed of white brick and granite in Corinthian style, with a columned portico, traditional high ceilings, classic moldings, and elegant marble interiors, the courthouse had opened for business in 1930.

Allison Ackerman had only a passing interest in architectural dinosaurs. It was shortly before eight o'clock on Tuesday as she crossed the building's portico, pushed through one of the revolving doors, surrendered her handbag for a security check, and made her way to the seventh floor.

When the elevator opened into a dramatic oval-shaped lobby, she turned to the left, retracing her steps of four days ago to Room C701, the room where prospective jurors were required to report. She had been told on Friday that one hundred and twenty people, an unheard-of number, had been called in for the Latham trial. It appeared that all but perhaps a handful had returned, and were now trying to cram themselves into a space usually occupied by no more than fifty.

Allison checked in at the desk, giving her name and group identification number. In return, she was handed a white plastic tag that classified her as a juror in big red letters, and assigned a number, 52. She dutifully attached the badge to her jacket before squeezing herself into an empty chair along the wall.

It took a minimal amount of observation for her to conclude

that those assembled came from every social stratum, every educational level, every occupational category, and every age and income bracket that King County had to offer. She saw suits, dresses, housecoats, and blue jeans, along with briefcases, tote bags, and lunch boxes. She wondered which twelve of these people would end up serving on the jury.

A capital case was an interesting process, she decided, and one to observe carefully. When she had arrived at the courthouse the previous Friday, only her fourth visit in nearly a decade, Allison was presented with a clipboard holding two separate questionnaires that she was instructed to complete to the best of her ability. Flipping casually through them, she realized she had never seen anything like this: page after page of repetitive requests for specific information that in some instances, she was sure, bordered on being invasive. It would not have surprised her to find, buried somewhere in the fine print, questions concerning her weight, her sexual preference, and whether she had ever been a member of the communist party. Her curiosity thoroughly piqued, she had done the best she could with it.

It occurred to her now, as she waited for the next step in the process to begin, that she would be required to speak to those responses, and so she sat there and tried to remember exactly what it was she had written, not sure that she could.

Nor was she even sure that she knew what she was doing here. It would have been so easy for her to get out of jury duty. She had been excused three times before, each time for a legitimate reason. But there had been no ready excuse this time, and something had stopped her from manufacturing one. She wondered whether the real reason she was here, and willing to participate in the Latham trial, was because she had a specific interest in its outcome.

The Honorable Abraham Bendali was not, by any stretch of the imagination, what one would call a defendant's judge, but he had a twenty-five-year history of being unerringly fair.

'We couldn't have done better,' Brian Ayres told Mark

Hoffman when the assignment was posted. 'He used to be one of us.'

'We could have done a lot worse,' Dana was quick to assure Joan Wills. 'He may be tough on defendants, but he knows the law better than anyone else on the bench, and he sticks to it.'

A massive man by normal standards, Bendali's six-foot-four-inch frame was reputed to be supporting more than three hundred pounds. It was the result of a childhood of starvation, which he understood intellectually well enough, but could never seem to deal with emotionally. His doctors had long ago given up berating him. His wife had long ago traded their king-sized bed in for twin beds. Out of fear of being crushed in the night, she said.

He was sixty-seven years old, and he had been fortunate to live most of those years in generally good health. The bulk of his diet consisted of fruits, vegetables, and grains, if in gargantuan quantities. He had not touched red meat in over fifteen years, and he regularly measured his cholesterol at a respectable two hundred and twelve. And every dawn, weather notwithstanding, which was no small thing in Seattle, Bendali could be seen propelling his custom-made kayak through the waters of Lake Washington; huge, authoritarian strokes that swept him miles away from the beachfront of his Kirkland home and back again.

Inside the King County Courthouse, he dominated the bench as he dominated the lake, ruling his courtroom with a firm hand and a steely glance, demanding proper conduct and orderly proceedings, and tolerating minimal legal nonsense. It was said that he had once reduced an unprepared attorney to tears by leveling an expectant gaze on him for five full minutes.

Magnified to enormous proportions by thick, gold-rimmed glasses, his deep-set brown eyes missed very little that went on below him. His bushy brows were frequently used as a means of direct, albeit silent, communication. A fringe of gray, which he shaved off as soon as it grew long enough to engage a razor, was all that remained of a once full head of hair. His appearance, added to his reputation for both personal and professional integrity, had earned him the nickname Mr. Clean.

Bendali had not asked for the Latham case, but he had not refused it, either. He knew exactly why it had been assigned to him – so that no hint of impropriety could ever be attached to the trial or its outcome, by either side.

'We've got to keep a tight lid on this,' the presiding judge told him. 'We want it over and done with as quickly as possible. We'll give you all the security you need. We'll take every precaution. We'll back you up on any decision you make.'

Bendali nodded. He had handled his share of high-profile cases over the years, both as a judge and as a King County prosecutor before that. Although nothing else quite rose to the level of Latham, he had a pretty fair idea of the media feeding frenzy that was already in progress, and promised to overwhelm the proceedings, if left unchecked. His first action, therefore, was to exercise his right to bar all cameras from his courtroom.

Members of the broadcast media were furious, trying every legal maneuver they could invent to force him to reverse his decision. Their efforts failed.

'But the people have a right to know,' they protested.

'And so they will,' the five-term Superior Court judge, who over the years had rejected at least a dozen serious political overtures, and several attempts to elevate him to a higher bench, replied. 'The old-fashioned way.'

'But this case has historic merit,' they argued. 'It could set legal precedent well into the next century. The essence of it should not be diluted by secondhand evaluation, but should be accurately documented and preserved.'

'To the best of my knowledge, court documents are reliably accurate and always preserved.'

They tried persuading him with flattery. 'The exposure will make you famous,' they said.

'Who do I look like?' he retorted. 'Lance Ito?'

'You're favoring some over others,' they claimed, resorting to petulance.

'Nonsense,' he declared. 'I don't like any of you.'

'He's biased against the media,' they proclaimed, eventually jumping at any opportunity to discredit him.

'He's using Hitler tactics!' one of the more careless thought it opportune to suggest.

Abraham Bendali, Holocaust survivor, did not bother to respond to that. He designated two rows at the back of his courtroom, which would accommodate approximately forty properly accredited members of the press, to be seated on a first-come-first-served basis, and then turned his attention to other matters.

Brian Ayres was philosophical about the ruling. He knew Bendali well, had appeared before him many times, and had anticipated his decision.

'It would have helped us, of course, to keep emotions running on high,' he told his assistant. 'But it won't hurt us that much.'

Dana McAuliffe was delighted. Since the jury was not going to be sequestered, the less dramatic the recounting of the trial was on every evening newscast, the better it would be for her client.

'Secondhand verbal accounts are far less exploitive than full-color moving pictures of the actual event,' she told Joan Wills. 'This way, the case will have a better chance of being decided by twelve hopefully emotionally stable people than by two hundred and sixty million potential hysterics.'

'Yes, but which twelve people?' Joan wondered aloud.

'Well, idealistically, we're looking for twelve open minds,' Dana said. 'But realistically, the chances of finding them are slim to none. So, absent neutrality, we'll try for as many pro-life supporters as we can get.'

'Which of course means the other side will be going after all the pro-choicers,' Joan observed, wrinkling her nose at the irony.

'In an adversarial system,' Dana conceded, 'that's the way it works.'

Abraham Bendali's courtroom suited him well. A large and airy rectangle located on the ninth floor, it was one of only several to have escaped the major remodeling fervor of the 1970s. It still boasted its original linoleum tile flooring, worn by time and use, and its heavy dark oak woodwork, scarred and stained with age.

The room's walls were hung with portraits of half a dozen of His Honor's formidable predecessors, whose somber expressions spoke legal volumes as they looked silently down upon current proceedings. On more than one occasion, the present occupant had been observed engaging in one-sided conversations with the paintings.

The bench itself was large and impressive, and almost managed to dwarf Bendali, which was no small feat. Three steps below him, his staff buzzed around like a colony of ants. It was said that he had been assigned this courtroom because it was the only one in the building big enough to hold him.

Directly in front of him were two large rectangular tables with captain style chairs drawn up to them. The defendant and his attorneys would occupy the table to Bendali's right, while the prosecution team would sit at the table closest to the jury.

Beyond the tables, and of considerably less interest to the judge, were the spectator seats, which must surely have been designed with repentance in mind. There were six rows of high-backed wooden benches on either side of a center aisle, all uncomfortable in their uprightness.

At eight o'clock on Tuesday morning, the judge was in his courtroom, ensconced in his oversized leather chair, with a coffee mug at his elbow. As he looked out across the empty seats, he was quietly contemplating the beginning of his final trial. He had already made the decision to retire, although no one else knew it yet. And what a trial to go out on, he was thinking, whichever way it went.

Bendali was neither deaf nor blind. He knew what was going on, what had been going on for months now, outside his windows, and it had little to do with the bombing of Hill House. Moreover, he knew it was just a matter of time before it would spill into his courtroom, and he would have to deal with it. Without doubt, the Hill House trial was going to be the most difficult of his career.

He took a long sip of his coffee. After forty years in the legal profession, he knew he wouldn't have wanted it any other way.

At fifteen minutes before nine, Robert Niera quietly entered the courtroom. The thirty-year-old bailiff rather resembled a marmot, with large dark eyes in a pleasant face. He cleared his throat softly, inducing Bendali to look up.

'It's a quarter to, Your Honor,' Robert said.

'Oh, is it already?' the judge murmured. 'Thank you, Robert.' He heaved himself out of his chair, and with a last look around at what had been his home away from home for more than two decades, retreated to his chambers, his bailiff snatching up the coffee mug and following in his wake.

It would not have done for Robert to have his judge in sight when the first comers began to arrive.

Dana entered Abraham Bendali's courtroom and walked down between the rows of spectator seats, her heels clicking along the polished linoleum.

This was the ninth time that she would be appearing before this judge, and there was something about his courtroom that always reminded her of growing up with her father. Something intangible, that spoke of history, and tradition, and old-fashioned integrity. It was a place where she had always felt safe, and confident of finding justice.

As she reached the defense table, she found herself hoping, more than at any other time, on any other occasion in her career, that it was not just an illusion.

'Why do I feel like I should whisper whenever I come in here?' Joan Wills whispered, coming up behind her. 'Like I'm in a church, or something.'

Dana smiled, delighted. 'You feel it, too?' she asked.

'Scared out of my mind? You bet I do,' Joan replied. 'It's like God Himself is going to come down on me just for having the temerity to enter.'

Dana shook her head. 'No, hopeful,' she said. 'I always feel hopeful in here.'

Promptly at nine-thirty, court was called to order.

'All rise,' Robert Niera recited in a rich baritone. 'In the matter of *The People of the State of Washington versus Corey Dean Latham*, Department 65 of the King County Superior Court is now in session, the Honorable Abraham Bendali presiding.'

In addition to the attorneys for both sides and their associates, there was a handful of spectators in the court, mostly reporters. It took less than thirty seconds for them all to scramble to their feet. Then the door to the judge's chambers opened, and with proper ceremony, Bendali took his place on the bench and peered down at those assembled before him.

Representing the defendant was lead counsel Dana McAuliffe, and Bendali was secretly pleased to see her. Corey Latham, standing nervously at her side, was going to need a strong advocate. To the defendant's left was Dana's supporting cast, not the least among them the venerable warhorse Charles Ramsey.

On the other side of the aisle stood Brian Ayres, his young associate, and two other gentlemen, all looking well pressed and confident, which befitted the representatives of the people.

'Be seated,' the judge intoned.

Yesterday, Bendali had dealt with the usual flurry of last-minute motions before turning to the matter of the jury. With Joan Wills and Mark Hoffman in attendance, he had spent the afternoon interviewing the hardship cases; those for whom protracted jury duty would severely impact either their livelihoods or their personal living conditions. Of the one hundred and twenty registered voters summoned to serve, only six had claimed hardship, and after brief examinations, the judge released them all.

Now would begin the actual process of selecting the twelve jurors and four alternates who would hear the case. Bendali turned to his bailiff.

'Let's get started,' he said.

Robert Niera picked up the telephone. Twenty minutes later, the first group of twenty prospective jurors, whose numbers had been randomly selected from a large, rotating drum, was escorted from C701 to the ninth floor, and installed in the adjacent room. One by one, they would be brought into court, asked to take a seat in the jury box, and called upon to answer questions posed by attorneys on both sides.

'Are we ready?' Dana whispered to Lucy Kashahara, seated to her right for this phase of the trial.

'As ready as we're going to get,' Lucy replied.

Craig Jessup leaned forward. 'Don't worry,' he said with a glance at one of the well-pressed gentlemen seated at the prosecutor's table. 'I'm familiar with the opposition. We're going to be fine.'

27

At the end of three weeks, only five members of the jury had been seated by the prosecution and the defense, and the snail's pace was beginning to grate on everyone, especially Abraham Bendali.

'I have reservations at Rosario starting on September 9,' the judge announced. 'That's two weeks with my nearest and dearest. That may not sound like much to you, but I have not had the opportunity to spend two weeks with my family for at least ten years, and I do not intend to miss it.' He glared down at the array of attorneys and consultants before him. 'Do I make myself clear?'

Brian Ayres and Dana McAuliffe glanced at each other across the aisle, and then nodded solemnly to the judge.

The game they played was legal chess, and they were both masters at it, neither of them willing to make a move without first considering every possible countermove. But Bendali had now put them both in check, and they had barely two weeks left to select seven more jurors and four alternates.

At the age of seventy-seven, Rose Gregory was the oldest member of the jury pool. The sprightly, diminutive grandmother, who was referred to as Juror Number 68, had lived in her Queen Anne home for going on sixty years. A lifelong Republican and devout Christian, Rose was morally opposed to abortion. She was also a faithful follower of the Reverend Jonathan Heal, and never missed his nightly Prayer Hour.

'What about other kinds of murder?' Brian Ayres asked her. 'Are you opposed to them as well?'

'Certainly, young man,' Rose replied crisply. 'I believe that only God can take a life.'

'So you would agree that committing a murder in order to somehow prevent a murder is wrong?'

The elderly woman fixed the prosecutor with a sharp eye. 'Murder is always wrong, young man,' she declared.

'Then let me ask you, as this is a capital case, how do you feel about the death penalty?'

At that, Rose sighed. 'I'm not sure,' she replied. 'I understand the government's need to deter certain people from committing violent crimes against others, and I also believe that every man should be held accountable for his deeds. But on the other hand, Romans, Chapter 12, Verse 19, makes it very clear: "Vengeance is mine; I will repay, saith the Lord."'

'Does that mean that you would be unable to sentence the defendant in this case to death, even if you were convinced beyond a reasonable doubt that he had cold-bloodedly murdered one hundred and seventy-six innocent people?'

'No,' Rose conceded after a pause. 'It doesn't mean that. It just means I would have to think about it, and pray on it, very carefully.'

On that note, Brian was finished with the prospective juror.

'Have you formed an opinion about the defendant in this case?' Dana inquired.

'Well, from everything I've read in the newspapers and seen on the television, I gather I'm supposed to think the young man is guilty,' Rose replied. 'But I think I'd rather decide that for myself, if you don't mind.'

A smile tugged at the corner of Dana's mouth. Rose Gregory was an ideal juror for the defense. 'No, I don't mind,' she said. 'I don't mind a bit.'

Juror Number 103 taught history at the McKnight Middle School in Renton. It was not an easy age to motivate, so Stuart Dunn was ecstatic to learn that his jury summons was for the Latham trial. What better civics lesson could he provide his students, he reasoned, than a firsthand account of the justice system in action?

'Would you like to serve on this jury?' Dana asked.

'Oh yes,' the soft-spoken, balding educator replied enthusiastically. 'This is the most exciting legal event to take place here in the twenty-one years I've been teaching.'

'And from what you've read and heard, what do you think about the case so far?'

'As I've cautioned my classes when we've discussed jury trials, we don't know enough about the particulars to think one way or the other, and we won't know until all the evidence comes out.'

'And you think you can keep an open mind until then?'

'Of course,' Stuart said. 'As I tell my students, that's what makes our system work.'

Brian stood up as Dana sat down. 'You're a married man, aren't you, sir?' he asked.

'Yes, I am,' the teacher replied. 'Nineteen happy years and counting.'

'And you have children?'

'I sure do, six of them.'

'That's quite a lot of mouths to feed.'

'Oh, we manage, thank you,' Stuart said with dignity. 'I know you're thinking that teachers don't get paid very much in this state, which unfortunately happens to be the case. But my wife went back to finish up her master's degree in psychology after our youngest started school, and she's working full time now.'

'I'm sorry,' Brian said hastily. 'I didn't mean to imply that you . . . I mean, most of us can't make it on one income these days.'

'How true,' the teacher said.

The prosecutor turned on the charm. 'In my blundering way,' he said a bit sheepishly, 'I was just trying to set up a scenario here, a hypothetical, if you will.'

'Go right ahead.'

'Well, what I was getting to was, let's say your wife became pregnant with number seven. And let's say that for whatever reason – physical, or financial, or psychological – she didn't feel she could handle having another child at that point, and decided to have an abortion without telling you. How would you feel about that?'

'I think I'd feel absolutely terrible,' Stuart replied, playing along. 'Angry and confused, and certainly sick at heart. I admit, having six kids hasn't been easy at times, but my wife and I, we've always rejected the idea of abortion for ourselves.'

'Would you feel an appropriate response to your wife's action would be to bomb the facility where the abortion had been performed, and to kill as many people as possible in the process?'

'No, of course not.'

'Then that leaves me with just one more question. How do you feel about the death penalty?'

'Another thorny issue, and one that's frequently debated in my classroom,' the teacher responded. 'Well, whether we like it or not, it's the law of the land, isn't it? And I suppose, if it should come to it, I'll abide by the law.'

The prosecutor was satisfied. Absent an out-and-out advocate for women's rights, a committed neutral would do.

'What's your position on the subject of abortion?' Brian asked a forty-year-old, divorced real estate agent from Bellevue.

'I think what a woman does with her own body should be up to her,' Karleen McKay, Juror Number 14, responded.

'Have you been following this case?'

The still shapely brunette shrugged. 'How could I not? I'd have to be deaf and blind to avoid it. It's been crammed down our throats for months now.'

'Well then, do you believe that what you've heard has influenced you in any way?'

'Not particularly. Especially when you consider that everything put out there has been pretty much one-sided.'

'So you think you would be able to keep an open mind if you were selected for this jury?'

'Yes.'

Brian gave her an appreciative smile, as much for her appearance as her responses, and took his seat.

'You just said that everything you've heard about this case

so far has been pretty much one-sided,' Dana began. 'May I take that to mean you didn't see the Barbara Walters interview in July?'

'No, as a matter of fact, I did see that,' Karleen replied.

'Well then, compared to everything else you'd been exposed to during the past few months, how did that come across to you?'

'Well, to be honest, it was the first positive thing I'd heard about your client,' the Realtor said. 'Everything else was so negative. And it made it seem like he was very nice, with a good upbringing and good values and all. Of course, it was his parents doing the talking, so it stands to reason they would want to show him in the best possible light.'

'Do you think that the interview in any way tempered some of the other perceptions being circulated about this case?'

'Yes, I think it did. The police and the prosecutors have really gone out of their way to try to demonize the defendant, you know. And don't get me wrong, I can understand that it's their job to do that sort of thing. But the interview with the parents was sort of sweet, and it tried to humanize him. I liked that.'

'I understand that you're pro-choice,' Dana continued, changing direction.

'That's right.'

'Tell me, is that a personal conviction or a political one?'

The Realtor shrugged. 'I'm not sure I understand where the line gets drawn. I believe that the right of free choice is fundamental to freedom. I would hate to think what would happen if we lost that right. Do I believe that abortion should be used as a convenient method of birth control? No, I absolutely don't. Would I campaign to keep abortion legal? Yes, if it came to that, I think I would. But would I get all militant about it, like some people out there do? Probably not.'

'May I ask, have you ever had an abortion?'

'Yes, I have,' Karleen replied, not at all defensively. 'It was some years ago, and I believe it was the right thing for me to do at the time. Would I make the same decision today?' She shrugged. 'I'm not sure. But I certainly wouldn't want anyone telling me I couldn't.'

'Thank you,' Dana said softly, sincerely. 'I appreciate your candor. Now, you told the prosecutor a few moments ago that you felt you could keep an open mind during this trial. Forgive me, but I must ask – do you truly believe you can keep your own personal experience from influencing you?'

The woman sighed. 'Look, I didn't ask to be here,' she replied. 'I was summoned. Okay, I'm here. Frankly, I'd rather be in Tahiti, but I believe in people doing their civic duty. So, I'm willing to serve on this jury, if that's what you want. Or not, if it isn't. Do I believe that abortion should be legal? Yes, I do. Do I think that automatically makes the defendant in this case guilty? No, I don't. That's where I stand. The rest is up to you.'

Lucy Kashahara had developed a code system. A check mark represented those from the jury pool that she believed would be best suited to sit in judgment of Corey Latham. An X was used for those who were to be excluded at all costs. In between, there were circles for those who were likely to be neutral, and a question mark for those who Lucy considered potentially risky. Next to Rose Gregory's name, the consultant had placed a check. Next to Stuart Dunn's, she had put a circle. Beside Karleen McKay's name, Dana could clearly see a question mark.

'You can't be thinking of putting her on, can you?' whispered Joan, as she saw Dana hesitate. 'She's obviously pro-choice. She's going to line right up behind the prosecution.'

'I know, but she's made it clear she doesn't want to be here,' Dana whispered back. 'That means she isn't coming in with a major agenda. I don't think Bendali will accept a dismissal for cause, and we've only got one peremptory challenge left. I'm afraid we might find worse down the line.'

'I'd pass her,' Charles Ramsey said from the other end of the table.

'Do you think McAuliffe will put McKay on?' Mark Hoffman asked Brian.

'Like us, she's only got so many challenges,' Brian replied. 'She'll have to pass on some of the maybes.'

Successful mystery book writer Allison Ackerman turned sixty during the month of jury selection. With peaches-and-cream skin and hardly any gray in her abundant auburn hair, she looked more like forty. For most of the month, she sat in Room C701, where she read, played solitaire, worked jigsaw puzzles, and watched as others came and went. She made it to the ninth floor in the second to last group of twenty.

When it was finally her turn to be summoned to the courtroom, she followed the bailiff down the length of it to the front row of the jury box, settled herself in a black leather chair, and took a deep breath.

The judge was as imposing a figure as any she might have created for her books, a monster of a man who appeared, on the one hand, to be paying scant attention, and on the other, to be in total control of the proceedings he presided over from his perch on the bench. The attorneys, by comparison, looked rather small. Not mean or insignificant in any way, just small. Small in stature, as though, if they weren't careful, they would get lost in the big room.

Finally, the author focused her attention on the accused. He sat quietly at the table farthest away from her, dressed in jeans and a denim shirt, obviously paying attention, listening to the conversations that whirled around him, but making no effort to participate.

Allison was aware that over the past several months the defendant had become a poster boy for the antiabortion movement, and she had to concede it was an engaging image. Corey Latham was wholesome and handsome, and bore no resemblance whatsoever to her concept of how a cold-blooded terrorist should look.

The mystery writer did not particularly believe in the death penalty, even under normal circumstances. But in this case, appealing or not, if there were so much as a chance the defendant was guilty of bombing Hill House, she knew it would not trouble her at all to convict him and sentence him to death.

'Why do you want to serve on this jury?' Brian asked her, the question catching her off-guard.

'I'm sorry,' she replied. 'I wasn't aware that I did.'

'Well, as I understand it, you've opted out of jury duty on three previous occasions.'

'Well, we're talking about a ten-year span here, but as I recall, on two of those occasions, I had manuscript deadlines that simply had to be met,' the author explained smoothly. 'On the third occasion, I believe I had a promotion tour already booked that my publicist was unable to reschedule.'

Brian was polite but persistent. 'And this time, you couldn't get out of it?'

'I didn't try.'

'Do you see this case as material for some future novel? Has your agent already entered negotiations with your publisher?'

Allison was not the least bit intimidated. 'Sorry, but I don't write legal thrillers,' she said with a smile.

'But you do write about murder?'

'Oh, yes. In every conceivable manner.'

'And would you say that years of writing about murder have made you indifferent to it?'

'Hardly,' Allison replied, with just a hint of mockery in her voice. 'As it's my livelihood, I take murder very seriously. At least as seriously as I'm sure you do.'

'And do you think you could be impartial during this trial?'

'Of course.' She lowered her voice a notch. 'I'll tell you a little secret. I never completely decide on my villain until the very end of the story.'

Brian frowned slightly as he took his seat. Here was a woman that he knew was as close to being a perfect ally as he was likely to find in a juror, and she was sparring with him, playing games. He couldn't quite put his finger on what it was exactly, but there was something about her he didn't like. Maybe it was his sense that she carried her feminist agenda like a shield instead of a banner. On the other hand, she was solidly pro-choice, and he was going to need her.

'The consultant says she's a card-carrying member of FOCUS,' Mark whispered in delight.

'I know,' Brian conceded with a sigh. 'But I have this feeling about her.'

'We've only got one peremptory left,' Mark reminded him. 'Do you really want to spend it on her?'

'No.'

'McAuliffe will probably kick her, anyway.'

'Let's hope,' Brian said.

Dana stared at the big black X beside Allison Ackerman's name. Common sense and Lucy Kashahara were both telling her to excuse the author out of hand, but something stopped her, not the least of which was her one remaining challenge.

'You're a women's rights activist, aren't you?' she asked pleasantly.

'Yes, I am,' the author replied without the slightest hesitation.

'And you've been in the thick of the debate right from the beginning, haven't you?'

'Yes, I have. I believe women have been relinquishing their rights to alleviate men's insecurities for far too long. It's the twenty-first century, for god's sake. Isn't it way past time for us to be in control of our lives, our minds, and our bodies?'

'Do you believe in winning at all costs?'

'In what context?'

'I'm asking if you'd be able to separate this case from your cause. Or if you would be willing to convict an innocent man simply to further your feminist agenda.'

Dana thought she saw a flicker of respect in the author's eyes.

'Yes to the first point,' the mystery writer declared. 'And no to the second. At least, not if I truly thought the man might be innocent.'

'Do you believe that Corcy Latham is responsible for the bombing of Hill House?'

Allison shrugged. 'I have no idea,' she said. 'And I don't expect I'd be able to answer that question until I had heard all the evidence both for and against him.'

Dana considered the woman for a long moment. One challenge and three more jurors still to select. She had thought for a moment there that Brian was going to excuse the author, but he hadn't. Maybe he was hedging his bets, relying on her pro-choice position, and hoping to hang on to the last of his challenges, as was she.

Joan shoved the list, with the X beside Ackerman's name in plain sight, under Dana's nose. 'Why are you hesitating?' she whispered. 'You've got to kick this one. She's got agenda written all over her.'

'I wouldn't be so quick to dump her,' Ramsey said.

Dana thought about how thorough and accurate Lucy Kashahara's evaluations always were. Still, there was something about Allison Ackerman that she sensed in person rather than saw in the data that Lucy and Craig Jessup had compiled. The defense attorney bit her lip. She knew Bendali would not excuse the woman for cause, not after two clear declarations of impartiality. If she wanted her off the jury, it was going to cost her the last of her peremptory challenges. Dana leaned back in her chair with resignation. It was for making decisions like this, she knew, that she was being paid the big bucks.

'I believe that abortion is a mortal sin,' Marie Delmonica declared. 'And I believe we must all do everything in our power to put an end to it.'

'Does that include murder?' Brian asked.

'Abortion is murder,' the woman said. 'An eye for an eye, a tooth for a tooth – a death for a death.'

'Excuse for cause, Your Honor,' Brian said.

'Mrs. Delmonica,' Bendali inquired, appearing to lean over the bench, 'given your position on abortion, do you believe you could render an impartial verdict in this case?'

The woman blinked rapidly several times. 'I think I could be as impartial as the next person,' she said. 'Am I sorry the abortionists are dead? No, I most certainly am not. Am I sorry the abortuary is destroyed, so that no more innocent babies can be murdered there? Not for a minute. But that doesn't mean I'd automatically vote to acquit a man if I believed he killed those helpless children in the day care center, not to mention the babies who had just been born, and the triplets who were about to be born, and all those other innocent people I heard about. That's murder, too, isn't it?'

They were running out of potential jurors, and Bendali was running out of patience. 'I see no cause here, Mr. Ayres,' the judge declared.

Brian deliberated. The woman clearly had an agenda. Even if Bendali didn't recognize it, he did. He could feel it, and he could not afford to make a mistake here. He sighed deeply. 'I ask that this juror be excused,' he said.

'Now I bet you're glad you didn't spend the last challenge on Ackerman,' Mark breathed. 'McAuliffe would have passed Delmonica, and we would've had ourselves a hung jury.'

'That's random selection for you,' Brian conceded. 'You never know who'll come up when.'

'Look, I don't care what pretty words you want to put around it,' Geoffrey Walsh declared. 'What that guy did to that building and to those people is inexcusable.'

'Would you be willing to entertain the concept that my client did not set that bomb?' Dana inquired.

'What do you mean?'

'I mean, could you be impartial, could you reserve judgment, could you wait until you heard both sides of the case before you made up your mind about my client's guilt or innocence?'

The transit worker shrugged. 'As far as I'm concerned, lady, if he didn't do it, he wouldn't be going on trial for it.'

'Thank you, Mr. Walsh,' the judge said, before Dana could get the words out. 'You're excused.'

It didn't make any difference to Juror Number 116 whether he was selected to the Latham jury or not. Autumn was going into John Quinn's slow time anyway and there was nothing his crew couldn't handle without him. The independent contractor had taken full advantage of a mini building boom during the past six months to complete two major remodels on Capitol Hill, enlarge a garage in Magnolia, and add a guest house to a waterfront estate on Mercer Island. Fourteen-hour days, seven days a week had been his norm, which hadn't left him with much time for anything more than a quick dinner and five minutes of family time before hitting the sack. But it had been well worth it. His wife calculated that he had already banked more than half again his usual year's income.

'Serving on this jury wouldn't be a hardship for you?' Dana asked.

'No, ma'am, it wouldn't be any hardship,' the beefy, forty-four-year-old Ballard resident replied.

'Then tell me, what do you think about the defendant in this case?'

Quinn peered around her to take a good look at Corey Latham. 'Don't rightly know,' he replied. 'He sure don't look like the kind who could've done what it is they're saying he did. But then looks don't always tell the whole story, do they?'

'In that case, would you be willing to listen to all the evidence presented before coming to any conclusions?'

'Sure. Isn't that how it's done?'

Dana sat down. John Quinn had a circle beside his name. Like Stuart Dunn, he was as neutral a juror as they were likely to find.

'How do you feel about the bombing of Hill House?' Brian inquired.

The contractor shrugged. 'It was an awful thing, no doubt about it – all them people killed,' he said. 'But I can't say as I could tell you much more than that. I haven't really been following the story.'

'Are you a churchgoing man, sir?'

'Yep. Every Sunday, like clockwork. And on Christmas and Easter, too. The wife insists. Thinks it's good for the kids. And she likes to sing in the choir. I suppose it can't hurt any of us too much, so I go quietly.'

'Would you say you were a religious man?'

'If you're asking me if I believe in God, I guess I do. As much as the next man, anyway,' Quinn replied. 'And if you're asking me if I believe in Jesus being the Son of God – well, as I tell the kids, there's nothing wrong with hedging your bets. But if you're asking me if I believe in treating others the way I want myself treated, then I'll give you an unqualified absolutely.'

Brian did his best to suppress a smile. 'Well, as long as we're being right up front here, let me ask you another question – where do you stand on abortion?'

'Don't know that I stand one place or another,' Quinn replied. 'Never came up against it. Me and the wife got two kids, which is all we wanted, and we just either been careful or lucky since then.'

'And what would you say your position was on the death penalty?'

'I guess I'm for it, but only under the right circumstances,' Quinn declared. 'I mean, if you can really prove to me that that guy over there did what you're saying he did, well then, okay, in my book, he deserves whatever he gets.'

'You know, it's weird,' Corey commented when court was adjourned for the afternoon. 'I haven't done anything, day after day, but just sit here – it's been how many weeks now? And in all that time, I never once opened my mouth or even stood up. I just looked and listened. So why do I feel like I've been through the wringer?'

'It's the process,' Dana told him, every bit as weary as he was. 'It drains everyone.'

The weekly lunch at Al Boccolino had temporarily gone by the wayside, but Dana found an evening to have dinner with Judith Purcell. House of Hong, in the International District, was one of their favorites. They both found the crispy Chinese fried chicken to be irresistible.

'I wish we could do this more often,' Dana said as they slid into a front booth and opened their menus, although they already knew what they were going to order.

'Me, too,' Judith agreed, brightly. Not for anything in the

world would the struggling artist tell Dana that she couldn't really afford the meal. After all, she had her pride.

But things were not going well. She had not had a new commission in two months, and even those she did have were not enough to make her anywhere near whole. Her credit cards were just about maxed to the limit, and she didn't know what she was going to do.

'I've been thinking about crispy fried chicken all day,' Dana declared. 'I was standing in court, grilling prospective jurors, and I swear I could smell it, all the way from here to there.'

'How's the case going?' Judith asked.

Dana rolled her eyes. 'If we can ever get a jury seated, and the trial started, I'll let you know.'

'It's still beyond me how you can do this,' Judith said, wagging her head.

'It's my job,' Dana reminded her.

'Nonsense,' her friend said. 'You get to pick and choose your cases. You didn't have to take this one, and don't try to tell me you did. Is it some sort of mislaid Catholic guilt? Is that why?'

'Don't be silly,' the defense attorney retorted, feeling her spine stiffen. 'I happen to believe that Corey Latham did not bomb Hill House. Now what does guilt have to do with that?'

'All right, never mind,' Judith said. 'It's too late now, anyway. So, are you close to getting your jury?'

'Yes, I think so,' Dana said. She was also, she thought with an inward smile, close to putting Judith in an art gallery of her own.

The building Sam had told her about would likely be available in November. The elderly woman who owned it had died, and her heirs were just waiting for her will to pass through probate. Sam had already spoken to them, and they were negotiating a price.

Dana wished she could tell Judith, right here and now, but she knew it wouldn't be fair, just in case there was a glitch, and it all fell through. No, she would wait until the deal was done. Then she and Sam would both tell her, and they would have a celebration. Judith's birthday was in November. What a wonderful gift it would be.

On the first Sunday in September, the *Seattle Times* did a feature story on Corey Latham's lead attorney. It was titled 'Who *Is* Dana McAuliffe?' and it was researched and written without the reporter ever getting past Angeline Wilder at Cotter Boland, or past Sam at the house on 28th Avenue in Magnolia.

'It's your fifteen minutes of fame,' her husband told her, as they spent the afternoon reading the paper and being lazy.

'Oh goody,' Dana replied, without much interest.

'On the eve of one of the most important criminal trials in American history,' the writer began, 'it may seem odd that we know so little about the attorney who has been chosen to head the defense team of the alleged Hill House bomber. But Dana McAuliffe makes a point of being a very private person.'

The profile then ran down all the readily obtainable facts – her background, her education, her experience, added what little information there was available about her personal life, and then appeared to run out of steam.

'After all these words, recounting so many facts,' the piece concluded, 'do we really know any more about Dana McAuliffe than we did before we began? Oddly enough, the answer is – probably not.'

'Would it hurt to talk to some of these people?' Sam asked. 'I should think some publicity might be helpful.'

'This case isn't about me,' Dana replied. 'It's about a terrible tragedy that will have repercussions for decades to come, and a man unjustifiably caught up in the middle of it. I don't want there to be any misunderstanding about that.'

'Maybe that's what you should say.'

Dana shrugged. 'I'd rather do my talking in court,' she said.

28

J ury selection was completed at four o'clock in the afternoon of September 8, twelve good and true individuals having been duly impaneled, plus an additional four who would serve as alternates.

Abraham Bendali scheduled opening arguments to begin on Monday two weeks hence, and then promptly took himself, his beloved wife, Nina, his two sons, their wives, and his three young grandchildren off to the San Juan Islands.

'What's the matter with dad?' his eldest asked. 'He hasn't taken a holiday off for as long as I can remember.'

'I think it has something to do with retirement,' his mother replied. 'He's trying it on.'

So far, Bendali had said nothing to anyone about the impending end of his career. Not even to his wife of forty-three years, although sometimes he had the feeling that she knew more about him than he knew about himself. The only decision he had made was that he would call it retirement. Then, when the time was right, he would sit down quietly with Nina and tell her what the doctors had found.

Dana came home from the jail, where she had gone to spend time with Corey after court was adjourned, stripped off her clothes, and ran hot water into the tub, adding half a bottle of bath salts for emphasis. Her skin turned bright red as she stepped into the tub, but she ignored it, sliding down until the water reached her chin. She could hear Sam downstairs, rattling around in the kitchen, putting dinner together, and she knew that a good wife would get up and go down to help, but she couldn't seem to make herself move. So she stayed where she was, for almost an hour, somewhere between awareness and oblivion, until she felt the stress beginning to float away and the water grow tepid, and then she climbed out and pulled on a thick terry robe.

'The prune is here,' she declared, padding into the kitchen. 'What can I do?'

'Nothing,' Sam replied. 'We're about ready at this end.' He had grown accustomed to cooking over the years, and to his surprise, found he thoroughly enjoyed it. 'So you can just sit right there and let me contemplate your beautiful shriveled self.'

Dana smiled. As independent as she believed herself to be, it never ceased to amaze her how much she had come to depend on Sam to be there for her, with a seemingly inexhaustible reserve of comfort and compassion and support. The irony of it did not escape her. Judith was the one who badly needed a good solid man in her life, but it was Dana who had found him.

'I'll go set the table,' she told him with a happy sigh. 'It's the least I can do.'

Allison Ackerman sat in the breakfast nook of her rambling Maple Valley home. Beyond the windows she could look across her acres of neatly fenced pasture, and watch the horses grazing. It didn't seem to bother them that there was very little grass left to munch on. They had already breakfasted on hay and oats, and were quite content with life.

The mystery writer found herself actually envying them, wishing she could be out there, without a care, without anything more compelling to do than to push her nose around in the soft warm earth.

Pouring her third cup of coffee of the morning, which was something she rarely did, Allison wondered for perhaps the hundredth time what she had gotten herself into. What had possessed her to play word games with those attorneys? It all seemed so absurd to her now.

'What did you do?' her daughter had asked.

'Don't ask,' Allison replied.

'I probably don't have to. You baited them, didn't you?'

The mystery writer sighed. 'Yes,' she admitted. 'I felt sure one of them would kick me off.'

'Couldn't you have just found a way to get out of it, like before?'

While it was true that there was no imminent deadline looming over her, Allison did have a manuscript in the edit phase. She could have used that as an excuse. At the very least, the defense attorney should have let her go. She had made her feminist position perfectly clear. And there was certainly no shortage of people wanting to serve. As she herself had observed, people were falling all over themselves to get on this jury. She had even heard a rumor during her weeks in C701 that someone who had been summoned had actually been offered money to change places with someone who had not.

'Of course,' she told her daughter. She had toyed with the attorneys, skating the edge, challenging both sides to toss her off, quite comfortable, she thought, in the certainty that one of them would. She was at a loss to understand why neither had, and perhaps more important, why she now found herself quite delighted about that. 'But I guess I didn't really want to get out of it.'

Despite her statements to the contrary, Allison began to wonder whether she did indeed have an agenda here. Was it just fun and games, or did she want to serve on this jury, as the defense attorney had suggested, so she could make it a platform for what she so fervently believed in? There was no question that she wanted an end to the subjugation of women. What better statement to make on the subject than to tell the world that despite what the likes of Roger Roark and Jonathan Heal were extolling at every opportunity, the bombing of clinics like Hill House was never justifiable. Even if it meant the conviction and subsequent execution of a clean-cut naval lieutenant from Iowa.

The *20/20* interview with Dean and Barbara Latham had painted a glowing picture of an all-American boy, and Allison had watched every moment of it. To listen to them, their son was the pride of Iowa, an honor student, who cherished life and liberty, believed devoutly in Christian principles, and could not possibly have committed the horrendous crime for which, through some hideous mistake, he was about to stand trial. But what else would parents say?

After twenty years of inventing diabolical characters, the mystery writer had learned to look behind the facade.

Juror Number 103 could hardly contain himself. He had hoped, but never really expected, that he would have a part in the Hill House trial. The only regret Stuart Dunn had was that the school year had started without him, and he would be unable to tell his students the good news. A substitute was teaching in his place, and it would be perhaps months before he could meet his students and share his experiences.

'It's going to be a very controversial trial,' Rose Gregory's grand-daughter told her. 'The press is making the most of it. There are going to be demonstrations and protesters, and crazies running all over the place. Are you sure you want that kind of stress at your age?'

'I didn't ask for this,' Juror Number 68 said in a tone that brooked no argument. 'But I was summoned, and I've been chosen, and I'll do my duty.'

John Quinn was philosophical. 'It was looking like a slow couple of months anyway,' he told his wife.

'We've always lived a quiet life,' she replied. 'I'm just afraid all the publicity is going to be hard on the children.'

Quinn shrugged. 'We'll keep them as clear of it as we can,' he said. 'And there could be an upside here, too, you know. If we get all this publicity, maybe it'll bring some business our way.'

Despite the notoriety that was bound to attach itself to the members of the Hill House jury, Karleen McKay was not partic-ularly overjoyed about being selected.

In addition to the commitment of time, three important clients with whom she had been working would now have to be turned over to another Realtor. Having to split those commissions was going to have a significant impact on her income that the ten-dollar-a-day stipend paid by the state of Washington was not about to cover. Grudgingly, Juror Number 14 spent the time before the trial began getting another agent in her office up to speed.

'Don't ever say I never gave you anything,' the executive assistant of FOCUS said, bursting into Priscilla Wales's private office.

'What?' Priscilla asked.

A big grin spread across the assistant's face. 'They put one of ours on the jury!'

'You mean someone who actually claimed to be pro-choice?'

'No – I mean a bona fide, signed-on-the-dotted-line member of our fine organization. Which means we've got a hung jury at the very least!'

Priscilla couldn't believe it. 'How do you know?'

The assistant shrugged. 'We've got a plant in the AIM operation,' he told her. 'Someone leaked the list and they got hold of it.'

The attorney's mind was whirling. 'Who do we have up in Seattle?'

'No one who could get to this juror.'

'Then find me someone we can put up there who can,' she instructed. 'Someone in the organization who's dedicated enough to go the extra mile, and smart enough to avoid getting caught. Make it a woman.'

'I'll get on it first thing,' the assistant promised.

'And if she does get caught, make sure she understands that she not only doesn't know us, she's never even heard of us.'

The assistant nodded. He knew, perhaps better than anyone else in FOCUS, how much of Priscilla's life was now her work, and how far she would bend the rules if she felt it would give her an advantage. 'You don't really think we could lose the election, do you?' he asked, knowing that was really what this was all about.

Priscilla sighed deeply. 'There's a whole lot of very stupid people in this country,' she replied. 'There's no telling what they might do.'

Elise Latham spent most of her weekends alone, eating TV dinners and watching the shopping channels on television, ordering things she didn't need.

On Sunday the 17th, she went down to the jail for her allotted hour with Corey.

'Happy birthday,' she said with a bright smile. 'How are you?'

'I'm doing just fine,' he lied.

'You're looking good,' she lied in turn, because lying had become second nature to them. Actually, he looked awful. Over the past six months, he had grown gaunt and pale, and now had dark rings under his eyes. And he had developed a persistent cough that the doctors couldn't seem to cure. 'Your mother sent a birthday cake. I gave it to the guard.'

'Who'd have thought we'd be spending my birthday like this?' he said suddenly. 'It was supposed to be so different. I used to think about it all the time on the boat. We would be together in our own home. The two of us, and our baby.'

'Great,' Elise said. 'It's all my fault.'

'I didn't say that,' he protested. 'I just meant, this isn't where I thought we would be.'

She left as soon as the hour was up, managing to duck the reporters who were constantly in her wake, and headed for Belltown, and any bar that was open. She woke up just before dawn, in a filthy bed, beside someone she couldn't remember ever having seen before.

She dragged herself home, surprising the media watch on her front lawn, and locked herself in the bathroom. Three hours later, she emerged, wrapped in a towel, her skin scraped raw from trying to get herself clean.

'Never again,' she muttered to herself as she pulled on a robe and slippers. Then, on impulse, she went to her bureau. Rummaging around at the back of her lingerie drawer, she pulled out an old address book. She sat down on the bed, flipped the book open to a specific page, and stared at one of the entries for a long time. Finally, she got up and went to the telephone.

On another telephone, in a different part of town, Paul Cotter was engaged in a conversation of his own.

'Are you satisfied?' the caller asked.

'For the most part, yes,' Cotter replied. 'Out of the twelve, there are two of possible concern. But I don't think we'll have any problems with the rest of them.'

'What about the two?'

'We'll keep an eye on them. If something comes up, we'll deal with it.'

'If you need anything, you'll let me know?'

'Of course,' Cotter assured the caller. 'Don't I always?'

29

The survivors of the Hill House bombing, along with the families of many of the victims, gathered in the huge presiding judge's courtroom, filling it up.

'I just want you to know that you don't have to do this,' Brian Ayres told them. 'You don't have to be here at all. I can't begin to imagine how painful it would be to have to relive what happened to you. But it *is* your right, and we just wanted to know how many, if any of you, are interested.'

'I'm sure some of us will want to be here,' Frances Stocker responded, and a number of heads bobbed in agreement. The psychologist was walking now, with the aid of a cane, which her doctors thought she was likely going to need for the rest of her life. 'At least, I know I want to.'

'Do we have to commit to the whole trial?' Joyce O'Mara asked. She was still living with her mother in North Bend, still learning to live without a lung and a kidney. 'I'd like to be here some of the time, but I know I can't make it all the time.'

'I can probably be here most of the time,' Carl Gentry said. He was working as a night security guard now, and had his days free. 'I think if our presence is going to help Mr. Ayres win his case, then as many of us as possible should be here.'

'I'd like to come as often as I can,' Ruth Zelkin said. 'On the days my husband can bring me. I'm not too good on the bus yet.' The former day care director was slowly finding her way around in the dark, and had begun learning to use the white cane that offered some measure of independence.

'I can probably make it for most of the trial,' Betsy Toth Umanski said. She reached up and patted the hand that rested on the back of her wheelchair. 'Andy can bring me in the mornings on his way to work, and pick me up after.' Despite her crippling injuries, she and Andy had married, only two months later than they had originally planned, and were already talking about adoption.

'My wife won't be able to come,' Rick Holman told the group. 'But I'll try to be here as often as I can.' Janet Holman had not recovered from the death of her son. In April, she had tried three times to kill herself. After the third attempt, she was admitted to a private hospital. The doctors, so far, had not ventured a prognosis.

'I'll be here,' Joe Romanadis said softly. 'For my wife and my triplets.'

'There's no reason why I can't be here for most of the trial,' Joseph Heradia volunteered. 'I'm not so busy right now that I can't make the time.' Neither a victim nor a survivor exactly, he nevertheless felt a kinship with his co-workers. In addition to that, he had a quarrel with Dana McAuliffe.

'How can you defend that piece of scum?' he demanded when he heard she was representing Corey Latham.

'The same way you can save the life of a man who just murdered a roomful of people and got hurt trying to escape,' she told him.

'It's not the same,' he argued. 'I'll save the man, sure, so he can stand trial for what he did. You're trying to get the guy off for what he did.'

'It is the same,' she assured him. 'Someday I hope you'll see that.'

Well, he intended to put her to the test, he thought, every day, in the courtroom.

A woman stood up at the back of the room, holding a little girl in her arms. 'My name is Shawna Callahan,' she said in a thick brogue. 'My sister Caitlin died in the bombing, and I've come to take my niece home with me. I thank all of you who'll be at the trial, and ask you to keep Caitlin and Chelsea in your prayers.'

'I'm going to be here for my Brenda,' Raymond Kiley said

softly. 'I've already arranged it with my boss. I get as much time off as I need.'

'I'd like to be here, too,' Helen Gamble said. 'I know my twins are still with me, but I want to come for all those, like Brenda and Caitlin, who aren't.'

'Me too,' Marilyn Korba said simply. 'I think my Jeff would want me to bear witness.'

'All right then, I'll tell you what we'll do,' Brian said. 'We'll reserve a block of seats that will be sectioned off and held for you every day until, say, ten o'clock each morning, after which they'll be open to the general public. You can coordinate among yourselves how you want to allot them. Other than that, seating will be on a first-come-first-seated basis. Does that sound reasonable to everyone?'

There was a general murmur of assent.

'I'm willing to be the clearinghouse,' Frances Stocker offered, rising to face the group. 'I can give everyone my telephone number, and you can call and tell me when you want to come, and I'll tell you if there's space available.'

'Wait a minute,' Carl Gentry interrupted. 'What about when the verdict comes in? I think most of us would want to be there for that.'

Everyone nodded, and looked at the prosecutor.

In truth, the value of having survivors sitting in the courtroom every day and reacting to the proceedings, in plain sight of the jurors, was immeasurable, Brian knew. But once the case went to the jury, the impact of having them there virtually disappeared, and every journalist in the country would be vying for a seat when the verdict was announced. Fitting them all into a space that was set up for less than two hundred people would be a major juggling act.

'I don't know,' he admitted. 'But I'll see what I can do, I promise.'

30

There were few cities as beautiful as Seattle at any time of the year. Summer slipping into autumn was no exception. Poised as it was between Puget Sound and Lake Washington, and ringed by breathtaking snow-capped mountains, it was the gem of the Pacific Northwest, and trying to remain one of the country's best-kept secrets.

The last Monday in September dawned bright and clear, the sun rising like a halo over Mount Rainier and bestowing a gentle glow over the city. By eight o'clock in the morning, thermometers were already near sixty.

Abraham Bendali did his usual hour of kayaking across Lake Washington, then showered, dressed, breakfasted on oatmeal and eggs, and kissed his wife goodbye.

'I'll see you in a couple of months,' he said as he departed.

After forty-three years, Nina Bendali knew what that meant. Her husband might come home in the evenings, and be there on weekends, to eat and sleep and read in his study, and he might even carry on conversations with her. But until the end of the Hill House trial, his mind, and yes, she acknowledged, his heart, would be at the courthouse.

Brian Ayres was up by dawn, showered and shaved, and standing in front of the bathroom mirror, practicing his opening statement. He had been working on the statement for weeks, weaving one element of his case smoothly into the next, bridging his transitions, perfecting each paragraph, polishing each sentence, and hammering home his main thesis at every opportunity.

He was lucky to be a quick study. Three or four times through the material, and he had it memorized. It always bothered him to see other prosecutors resort to reading from scripts, unable to make proper eye contact with the jury. It delighted him, however, when he saw defense attorneys doing it.

Once he was satisfied that there was no more he could do, he put the statement aside and took his family off to Lake Quinault for the weekend, forcing himself to clear his mind of everything but the fish. When he returned, he picked up his pages again and read them over, pleased to note that his mind had retained almost everything.

The dress rehearsal in front of his mirror was just icing on the cake.

With the exception of Dana, Elise's scheduled visits, half an hour with his former roommate, Zach Miller, and several Bible sessions with Tom Sheridan, Corey Latham spent the last few days before the trial began alone in his cell. He felt so helpless, so isolated, so depressed, that even the smallest change in routine was a joy. Such as the occasion to shower and dress, and shed his prison garb for the crisp khaki uniform that Dana brought to the jail. He knew what it meant, of course. It meant the trial, finally, and he clung to the belief that when it was over, he would be going home. The alternative was simply too horrific for him to contemplate.

'I want you to promise me something,' he told Dana. 'I want you to promise, if I'm convicted, you won't fight execution.'

'What are you talking about?' she demanded.

'If I'm convicted, it's a given that I'll get the death sentence,' he replied. 'I don't want to go through years of appeals, on the off-chance that maybe I can spend the rest of my life in a place worse than this. If I'm convicted, I want to die – as soon as possible. That's my right, isn't it?'

She didn't have it in her to tell him that he wasn't even in control of his own execution. That a death sentence automatically went to appeal.

Allison Ackerman was up well before dawn, tending to her horses with affection and an extra ration of oats, to make up for what was likely going to be months of neglect.

Even when working, she would find time during every day to go out to the pastures and exercise her prized thoroughbreds, check them over, curry them, scrape their hooves, and serve up special treats of apples or carrots. Along with three dogs of indeterminate breed, they made up her resident family. Her daughter and her three grandchildren, who lived in Pennsylvania, were only occasional visitors.

Allison's husband had died of heart disease over a decade ago, and she had never felt any particular urge to replace him. She had a secure income, a wide circle of good friends, and a full and active life.

And she had a cause. Not only was she successful as the author of a dozen novels whose central character was a strong and independent female, but also she was committed to encouraging women in all circumstances to come out of the shadows. Although she would admit it to no one, Allison Ackerman saw the Hill House trial, with its inevitable national exposure, as a potentially giant step in that direction.

She arrived at the courthouse at eight-thirty, and got caught in a crowd so dense it was almost claustrophobic. Media people from across the country vied for street space with pro-choice advocates and pro-life demonstrators. Television cameras, barred from the courtroom, set up shop outside to cover the show. A battalion of police did their best to keep them all at bay, and to prevent some of them from coming to blows.

'The fun hasn't even started yet, and tempers are already short,' Allison commented to a burly officer who made a path for her.

'Yes, ma'am,' he said with a sigh. 'I'm hoping for early rain.'

Safely inside, Allison made her way to the ninth floor, to the jury room at the rear of Judge Bendali's court, and was surprised to find she was the first to arrive.

It was not an overly large space, but it was large enough for a rectangular oak table that had twelve chairs drawn up around it and a row of half a dozen more chairs positioned against the long wall. Two small bathrooms were located in an alcove on the other side, next to several vending machines. The room's biggest drawback was that the windows that ran along the short wall at the far end were too high to look out of.

Allison got herself a cup of coffee, sat down in one of the chairs along the wall, and waited as, one by one, the other jurors filtered in.

It was an interesting group, the inveterate people-observer decided. Although they had presented themselves in every conceivable kind of getup during the preliminary phases of jury selection, today all the men appeared in suits and ties, crisply ironed shirts, and polished shoes. Similarly, all the female jurors had decked themselves out in dresses or stylish suits, with nylon stockings, high heels, and full makeup. For herself, Allison had chosen a pantsuit.

'I guess we're going to be spending a fair amount of time together,' Stuart Dunn observed as they milled around the room a bit self-consciously. 'Maybe we should get to know one another.'

'Should we introduce ourselves by name or by number?' a twenty-three-year-old cosmetologist asked with a nervous giggle.

It was a good question. 'Why don't we start with first names,' Allison suggested, 'and maintain an illusion of anonymity?'

Everyone looked around at everyone else, and then at the county official whose job it apparently was to baby-sit them. The man shrugged.

'Sounds good to me,' a fifty-two-year-old barber said. 'The name's Ralph.'

'Well then, I'm Kitty,' said the cosmetologist.

The ice was broken, as each in turn produced a name, and then went on to expand upon that initial identification by volunteering an occupation, which resulted in further conversation.

'The name's Eliot,' a fifty-eight-year-old gentleman said. 'I'm a pilot.'

'I'm Bill,' said a thirty-five-year-old airplane mechanic. 'I've been on the line at Boeing for twelve years now, and you'd never get me up in one of those things.'

'What kind of writing do you do?' Allison asked a twenty-nine-year-old Asian-American woman.

'Computer manuals,' the woman, who had identified herself as Elizabeth, replied.

'Really?' a twenty-six-year-old named David chimed in. 'I'm a programmer.'

'What do you teach, Stuart?' a soft-spoken, forty-eight-year-old African-American man asked.

'Middle school history,' Stuart Dunn replied with pride.

The man smiled and nodded. 'I'm Aaron, and I teach philosophy at Bellevue Community College,' he said.

By the time Abraham Bendali's court was called to order, the jurors were already well on their way to getting comfortable with one another.

With Joan Wills in tow, Dana McAuliffe made her way to Abraham Bendali's courtroom. The two of them had walked up from Smith Tower together, Charles Ramsey preferring to make his own way there, and battled through the mess out front. It therefore came as no particular surprise to Dana, when they exited the elevator on the ninth floor, to find half a dozen camera crews camped out in both the lobby and the hallway.

'Get used to it,' she murmured to Joan, knowing they would likely run this gauntlet every single day of the trial.

It was barely nine o'clock, yet the spectator section was already packed, every uncomfortable seat occupied, strangers agreeing to squeeze themselves together in pews that properly sat five to make room for six. Even so, scores of others had been turned away at the door.

Dana took several moments to sort through the mass of files she and Joan had lugged from the office before turning around. She was pleased to note that in addition to Elise Latham, looking cool and composed in a soft green dress, about a dozen of Corey's friends and family members were seated in the first row behind the defense table. Dean and Barbara Latham had flown in late last night, and were there along with Zach Miller and two other naval officers from Bangor, Evelyn Biggs, Tom Sheridan, and several people who identified themselves as members of Corey's support group.

209

Corey had asked his minister to look out for Elise, and so the man had, picking her up at her front door and bringing her downtown, running interference for her both outside and inside the courthouse, and now sitting protectively at her side.

'I've taken a one-month leave from work, so I can be here every day,' she told Dana, her voice sounding somewhat defensive. 'After that, I don't know. I can't afford to lose my job.'

Dana nodded her appreciation. It was important for Corey's wife to be in the courtroom, visibly behind her husband. But the attorney had to acknowledge that the young woman, without benefit of assistance from her family, had to earn a living.

'Well, we aren't going to worry about that now,' Sheridan said, gently patting her hand. 'God has a way of providing.'

'Thank you,' Dana murmured, and then turned to smile at her client's parents. 'It'll mean the world to Corey to have you here,' she said.

'I'm here for the duration,' Barbara said, 'but Dean will have to go back.'

Although Dana knew that Elise had invited her in-laws to stay at the house on West Dravus, they had instead chosen to stay at a hotel within walking distance of the courthouse. Sheridan had arranged it, and secured a special rate for them, as well.

'It gives us twenty-four-hour room service, if we need it, and a lot less public exposure,' Dean explained, looking at her from eyes that were very like his son's.

Worry lines had creased the man's face, etching themselves deep into his skin, aging him well past his years. The kind of worry lines that, no matter the outcome of this trial, would never go away.

Across the aisle from the defendant's supporters sat a large contingent of what Dana would come to regard as the Hill House people, that poignant mixture of survivors and relatives of those who had not survived. Even eight months after the tragedy, she still saw canes and braces and wheelchairs. What was not so visible were the broken lives that would never be repaired.

It was unavoidable, she knew. They had every right to be here, however prejudicial their impact on the jury, and Dana knew enough to know it would be considerable. It was a futile effort to file a motion to have them excluded, and Bendali rejected it outright, as she knew he would. But she was obligated to do it on behalf of her client.

On the heels of that thought, Corey Latham entered the courtroom. The khaki officer's uniform was intended to make him look clean-cut and upstanding, but the effect was all but overshadowed by the shackles on his hands and the escorts at his side.

A sudden hush fell as Corey walked slowly down the aisle, past the reporters in the back rows, past the general public, past the survivors' section, and past his own contingent of family and friends, to the table where Dana was waiting. At her nod, the escorts removed the shackles and retreated.

Despite Corey's prison pallor, his face lit up when he saw his parents, and he practically fell into their arms. Barbara couldn't help herself. Tears ran as freely down her cheeks as they did her son's. Even Dean made no effort to hold them back.

For perhaps five minutes, the people who loved and believed in Corey Latham embraced him, something they had not been allowed to do since his arrest, as the people of Hill House looked silently on. Dana had no idea what was going through the minds of those who saw, but she hoped that it was a scene they would remember, down the road, when it was time for the real healing to begin.

At exactly nine-thirty, Robert Niera called the court to order and everyone stood as Abraham Bendali appeared. The judge made his way to the bench, taking a moment to adjust himself in his chair, and then peered down at those assembled.

'Be seated,' he directed, in his most magisterial tone, and waited until the scraping and scuffling in the gallery subsided. Then he glanced at his bailiff. 'All right,' he said with a nod, 'let's have the jury in.'

Robert walked to the back of the room and through the door

in the rear wall. A moment later, he returned, escorting sixteen people down the aisle, and directing them into the jury box. They took their seats according to the sequence of their selection. Allison Ackerman, selected ninth, sat in the third chair in the second row, with Karleen McKay to her right, and John Quinn to her left. The four alternates were then seated in the last two chairs of each row.

It was the first opportunity for most of those in the courtroom to see the jury. The reporters hoped they would be expressive, the Hill House people hoped they would be resolute, and the defendant's supporters hoped they would be fair.

Abraham Bendali contemplated the packed house before him. All the players were present and accounted for, he determined, and the audience was in place. For the last time – for him anyway – the show was about to begin. He raised his gavel.

Tom Sheridan, holding Elise's hand on his right, and Barbara's on his left, closed his eyes and said a prayer. The gavel came down sharply. The trial of Corey Latham was under way.

PART TWO

'Justice and judgment lie often a world apart.'
– Emmeline Pankhurst

PART TWO

I

Brian Ayres rose to his feet and faced the jury. 'Good morning, ladies and gentlemen, and thank you for being here,' he said in his best courtroom voice.

In response, sixteen people mumbled a self-conscious 'Good morning.'

The prosecutor smiled. 'When I tell you how grateful I am that you are here, because the system wouldn't work without you, I'm not trying to flatter you, or gain an advantage of any kind. I'm simply telling you the truth. You represent the protection that is guaranteed to every American under the Constitution. Without you, doing what you're about to do, none of us is safe, and that's the truth. And that's what this trial is all about, too – the truth. And your ability to hear it, and recognize it, and act on it.'

He paused for a moment, and Dana smiled to herself. She had to admit he was not only brilliant, but in his element. This was his theater, he had already taken center stage, and he had hooked the jury with his very first lines. And as if that weren't enough, he looked terrific in his gray suit and blue shirt. Dana watched the jurors closely. As expected, the women were leaning just a little bit forward, while the men were sitting just a little bit taller, and both were listening just a little bit harder.

'I know I don't have to tell any of you what happened at Hill House on the first Tuesday in February,' Brian continued smoothly. 'The details have been in all the newspapers and news-magazines and on every television channel in the country, if not the world. You would have to have been off the planet to miss it. So, the primary focus of this trial isn't going to be on the devastation of Hill House. It's going to be on the person who caused that devastation. It's going to be about the state of Washington, represented by me, proving to you, beyond a reasonable doubt, maybe even beyond any doubt, that the man sitting at that table over there,' and here he pointed directly at the defendant, 'planted the bomb that blew up Hill House, and killed one hundred and seventy-six men, women, and children.'

As if on cue, it seemed that everyone in the courtroom exhaled. Brian took the opportunity to walk slowly over to his table and pick up a sheet of paper. When he turned back to the jury, the conversational tone of before was gone.

'Susan Marie Abbott, twenty-eight,' he read from the paper. 'Jean Arnold, forty-four. Melanie Kay Aronson, thirty. Eleanor Nash Barrington, fifty-three. Richard Bucklin, twenty-two months . . .'

'Oh, my God,' Corey gasped, when he realized what the prosecutor was doing.

Dana reached over and put her hand on his arm, squeezing as hard as she dared, to steady him as best she could, while Brian Ayres slowly read aloud into the record the litany of the dead.

The prosecutor's opening statement leapfrogged the lunch hour and lasted into the afternoon. By the time he had finished laying out the evidence he planned to present in the coming weeks, it was past three o'clock, and time for the afternoon break.

Half an hour later, Abraham Bendali looked at Dana.

'Do you wish to proceed at this time?' he asked her. 'Or would you prefer we adjourn until tomorrow?'

'If it's all right with the court, I'd prefer to proceed, Your Honor,' she replied.

The judge nodded, and Dana stood up. She had chosen a tailored burgundy gabardine suit for her first appearance before the jury, and added small gold hoop earrings and a thin gold necklace. Her skirt was not too short and her heels were not too high. She referred to her choice of outfit as dressing down, and she would continue to dress down for the entire trial. While it was important to look professional in the courtroom, Dana knew it was just as important not to keep reminding everyone of the high-priced attorney that she was.

'Good afternoon, ladies and gentlemen,' she began, in a voice that was soft but modulated to carry clearly to the back of the courtroom. 'Contrary to popular opinion, I am not here to get my client off at all costs. That's not what I do. Our courts are based on an adversarial system, which means the right of a defendant to compel the state to prove its case beyond a reasonable doubt. Mr. Ayres and I are the adversaries in this case.' She paused for a moment to point an index finger at the prosecutor. 'I'm the one who keeps him honest,' she said. '*That's* what I do. And in doing that, I protect not only my client, I protect each and every one of us against undue persecution and prosecution.'

'I see she memorizes, too,' Mark Hoffman whispered to Brian.

'Taught her everything she knows,' Brian whispered back.

'It's my job to question, on your behalf, every single piece of evidence the state presents,' Dana continued. 'It's my obligation to kick it, stomp on it, discredit it if I can, try to tear it to shreds, and then see if it can still stand up and walk. If enough of it does, then it's your job to convict my client of the crime for which he stands accused. But if it doesn't, then it will be your duty to tell the state it's got the wrong man.'

At that, some of the jurors blinked.

'Now, in this case, I realize that won't be an easy thing for you to do,' Dana told them. 'The death of one hundred and seventy-six people can't be readily discounted. The presence here in this courtroom of some of those who survived can't be casually dismissed. What's more, you're an unsequestered jury, which means the pressure on you from the media and from the advocacy groups that are congregating right outside the courthouse door will be enormous, and difficult, if not impossible, to ignore.'

To her surprise, Allison Ackerman discovered there was something about the defense attorney that she liked, even if, unfortunately, it wasn't her client. It was a kind of in-your-face determination to tell it as she saw it, good or bad, and hang the consequences. It made her appear rather vulnerable, and Allison had always had a soft spot in her heart for under-dogs.

'If you think you wouldn't want to be standing in my shoes, you might be right,' Dana continued. 'I'm probably not going to be very popular in this town for a while. But then, I'm not so sure I'd be happy standing in *your* shoes, either. The world wants a resolution here, a fitting end for the victims, closure for the survivors, relief for the rest of us. We all want someone to pay for Hill House. The question is – how much do you care whether that someone is the right one?'

At that, several jurors stirred in their seats.

'Does that make you uncomfortable?' Dana asked. 'It should. I can assure you it makes my client uncomfortable. Because it's his life you've got in your hands. And the wrong decision here isn't going to make up for those who were lost. Not one of them.'

Allison sighed. Impartial as she was going to do her best to be in this matter, the prosecution's presentation had struck a chord in her. With his opening statement, Brian Ayres had begun making the case that she had been anticipating, one that was meticulously prepared, logical, credible, and inescapable. What the defense attorney was now saying was not what she wanted to hear.

'As you listen to the state's case,' Dana said, looking straight at the mystery writer as though she had read her mind, 'I'd like you to do something, if you can. I'd like each of you to put yourself in Corey Latham's shoes. Walk around in them for a while. Decide whether you'd be willing to be convicted of this crime, based solely on the evidence that the prosecution is going to present. I believe you'll find the answer is no. I believe you'll come to the same conclusion I have – that Corey Latham is innocent.'

With that, Dana turned to go back to her table and take her seat, pausing just long enough to glance up at the bench. 'We can adjourn now, Your Honor,' she said with a little smile.

The point was not lost on Bendali. The defense did not intend the jurors, or the media for that matter, to sleep on the prosecutor's unrebutted remarks. After admonishing the jury not to discuss the case among themselves, or with anyone else, he recessed his court until ten o'clock the following morning.

The day had gone pretty much as the defense team had thought it would. Brian Ayres had spoken for four hours. Dana McAuliffe had spoken for four minutes.

2

'You may call your first witness, counsel.'

With those words from Judge Bendali, the second day of the Hill House bombing trial began. Brian Ayres, wearing a navy blue suit and beige shirt, rose from his seat and faced the jury.

'Good morning,' he said with a comfortable smile, and every juror smiled back at him, and murmured 'good morning' in response. Then he turned to the bench. 'The people call Howard Metzger, Your Honor.'

A burly man, about fifty years old, was ushered into the courtroom and directed to the witness box. As he passed between the rows of spectators, many craned their necks to get a good look. The court clerk administered the oath and asked the witness to state his name for the record. Then Metzger, who had been called to testify at some three dozen trials in his twenty-three-year career, sat down and looked calmly at the prosecutor.

'Mr. Metzger,' Brian began, 'will you please tell the jury who you work for.'

'I work for the Federal Bureau of Investigation,' Metzger replied, with the barest hint of a southern accent.

'And what do you do for the FBI, sir?'

'I investigate bombings.'

'Were you called to the site of the Seattle Family Services Center last February?'

'Yes, I was.'

'What did you find?'

'I found a building that had been destroyed by fire.'

'And what determination, if any, did you make about the cause of the fire?'

'I determined that the fire had been caused by the detonation of a bomb.'

'Were you and your team able to collect any residue or particles from that bomb?'

'We were.'

'Did you then transport these materials, without any incident of contamination, to your laboratories for extended analysis?'

'We did.'

'And as a result of these analyses, have you been able to ascertain the nature of that bomb?'

'Yes, I have. It was what's known in the business as an aspirin bomb.'

'Will you explain that?'

'It's a plastique form of explosive that combines common household aspirin with methyl alcohol, garden-variety fertilizer, and battery acid.'

'Can you tell the jury, Mr. Metzger, how difficult is it to make a bomb?'

The FBI man shrugged. 'It can range anywhere from simple enough for a precocious child, to so technical or intricate that it would require an expert.'

'How difficult is it to make an aspirin bomb?'

'It would take some knowledge and great care, but it wouldn't require an expert.'

'Would someone who was, say, trained in military weaponry be able to construct it?'

'Yes, certainly.'

'Does such a bomb need to be made under laboratory conditions?'

'No,' Metzger replied. 'It could be made in any well-ventilated area, with very basic equipment.'

'Like a garage?'

'A garage would do nicely.'

'Did you find anything else of significance in the residual material you gathered?'

The expert nodded. 'We collected a number of fibers that we were able to identify as having come from a fabric used to make duffel bags. We think it likely that the bomb was transported in such a manner.'

'Were you able to identify the duffel bags?'

'Yes. We determined that they were standard military issue.'

A slight murmur rippled through the Hill House section of the spectator gallery.

'That's getting right down to it,' Helen Gamble whispered to Raymond Kiley.

Over the next several hours, Brian had the FBI agent go over the specific aspects of creating the kind of bomb that had blown up Hill House, and he was pleased to note that the jury appeared to be paying close attention. He kept asking questions until several of the jurors visibly began to tire of the topic. At that point, almost the end of the day, he was ready to turn his witness over to the defense.

Dana, dressed in soft gray, stood up. 'I realize the hour is late, but if you'll bear with me, I have just a few questions,' she said pleasantly, as much to the jury as to the witness. 'Now, Mr. Metzger, you said earlier, did you not, that someone trained in military weaponry would be qualified to produce the kind of aspirin bomb that blew up Hill House?'

'Yes, I said that.'

'Did you mean to imply that producing an aspirin bomb would *require* that level of expertise?'

'No, I didn't,' the FBI agent replied.

'Who else then?'

'Well, I guess anyone with a basic knowledge of high school chemistry would probably be qualified.'

'But how would the average high school chemist learn to make such a bomb?'

'Unfortunately, it's a lot easier than you think,' the FBI agent said. 'Aside from books and pamphlets that are available through the mail, just for the asking, you can get instructions for making a variety of bombs right off the Internet.'

'No special expertise necessary?'

'No.'

'No military weaponry training required?'

'No.'

'Just anyone with the intent, and access to the Internet?'

'Yes.'

Dana nodded thoughtfully. 'All right now, let's turn to the duffel bag fibers,' she went on smoothly. 'You say they came from a standard military issue duffel bag, is that right?'

'Yes.'

'How did you determine that?'

'We compared the fibers to a number of fabrics until we found a match.'

'And the duffel bag that matched, the standard military issue one you identified, where did you get the sample to verify your test?'

'I guess it came from a surplus store.'

'You mean, you didn't have to go to the military?'

'No.'

'You didn't have to borrow a bag from someone currently serving in the armed forces?'

'No.'

'Someone in your department simply went to a retail surplus store, like the one right down on First Avenue, and bought it? Just like anyone else could?'

'I guess so.'

'I see,' Dana said.

A rustle fluttered through the Hill House section.

'I guess maybe it isn't going to be as easy as I thought,' Helen Gamble murmured.

'All right then, Mr. Metzger,' Dana concluded, 'to summarize your testimony: You collected a quantity of residual material from the bomb site, which you then put through an extensive and intensive examination, calling in all the best minds in the FBI to consult with you. Is that correct?'

'Pretty much.'

'Then please tell us, other than requiring a rudimentary knowledge of chemistry and the computer, did anything in this exhaustive analysis tell you, with any degree of certainty, anything definitive about the person who made the bomb?'

The expert blinked. 'No,' he replied.

'Thank you, sir,' Dana said. 'No further questions.'

A whole day, Allison Ackerman thought, as she made her way home to Maple Valley. A whole day getting a cram course on how to make a bomb, only to find the expert couldn't tie the damn thing to the defendant. And Dana McAuliffe knew he couldn't. Allison chuckled to herself. She was smart, that one. And cool, too. There was no way she was going to argue that a bomb hadn't destroyed Hill House. All she could do was try to separate the bomb from her client.

So, what had the day been all about? Laying the ground-work for future testimony, she decided, putting the best possible spin on it. But she couldn't help feeling a pang of resentment. It wasn't that her time had been wasted, exactly, but it had certainly been a letdown.

To Joan Wills, the one thing that set Dana McAuliffe head and shoulders above the rest was that she never forgot she was a woman, and she never let anyone else forget it, either. As a female who had made the grade in a traditionally male-dominated arena, she had perfected a combination of softness and directness that gave her the advantage of a one-two punch on an unsuspecting opponent. It also didn't hurt that she was a lot smarter than most of the men in the business.

'You nailed the FBI guy,' Joan said exultantly as they sat around Dana's office after court.

'Not really,' Dana responded. 'He was neutral. He was just testifying to the results of his investigation. All I did was let the jury know that those results didn't have to point only in the direction the prosecution wanted them to.'

'And you did it so agreeably.'

Dana shrugged. 'There's rarely any need to get nasty with a witness. And as my mother used to tell me, honey almost always gets you more than vinegar.'

'You'd think some of the guys would figure that out.'

'Well, let's not tell them,' Dana said with a chuckle. 'We need all the advantage we can get.'

'She undercut us pretty good, don't you think?' Mark Hoffman observed.

'Not at all,' Brian assured him. 'We're not in there trying to say each and every piece of evidence has only one interpretation. We're just going to pile up enough pieces of evidence to convince the jury that there's only one reasonable interpretation.'

'You have to admit, though, she's smooth.'

Brian smiled. 'Yep. I'll give her that. But being smooth isn't always the same as being right.'

'I thought things went well today,' Elise Latham ventured to tell her husband during visiting hours. 'Ms. McAuliffe certainly made mincemeat out of that FBI guy's testimony, anyway.'

'I hope so,' Corey replied. 'It's hard to tell about the jury, though. I watch them sit there and listen, but I can't tell what they're thinking. They don't give up very much.'

Elise stole a quick glance at her watch. 'Look, your folks are downstairs, waiting to see you,' she said. 'So, I'm going to cut my visit short, and let them have the rest of the time. But I'll see you tomorrow in court, okay?'

Without waiting for an answer, she blew him a kiss through the Plexiglas wall and made her exit. Leaving the jail, she walked quickly up James Street and turned left at Sixth Avenue. A black BMW was parked halfway down the block. After looking around to make sure that no one was following her, she slipped into the front seat. Immediately, the big car gunned its engine and pulled away from the curb.

'I'm afraid you're famous again,' Sam McAuliffe informed his wife when she got home.

'What did I do this time?' Dana asked.

'You made the cover of *Newsweek*,' he replied.

'*Newsweek?*' She was plainly incredulous. 'What on earth for?'

225

'I guess they seem to think you're newsworthy.'

She wagged her head. 'I'm just doing my job,' she said with a sigh. 'If it's newsworthy that somebody's doing her job, this world is in a sad state.'

'Don't you even want to know what they said about you?'

'Is it libelous?' she asked.

'I don't think so,' Sam replied.

'Then I don't care what they said.'

'They said you were an enigma,' he told her anyway. 'A gifted mystery woman keeping to the shadows.'

'I can't say much for their reporting ability,' she observed. 'I'm hardly in the shadows.'

'They said, even in the direct glare of the spotlight, you seemed to be in the shadows. And they wondered why.'

'If they ask you,' Dana said, dismissing the implication with a chuckle, 'you can tell them it's because I'm shy. '

3

Next on the stand for the prosecution was the head of the King County bomb squad, a lean and weathered man, somewhere in his forties, named Henderson. And after greeting the jury in the same friendly fashion as the day before, Brian turned to his witness.

'Will you please tell the court when you arrived on the scene?' Brian asked.

'My unit was called to Hill House at four o'clock in the afternoon,' Henderson replied. 'Approximately two hours after the explosion.'

'And what did you find?'

'We found a mess,' the man said. 'By the time we got there, the fire was almost under control and many of the bodies had been removed, but the place was just one giant hazard. Beams hanging, parts of the second floor suspended in midair, pieces of heavy equipment teetering. Everything was soaked, and every few minutes something would give way and the whole place would start to shift. It was very dangerous and very slow going.'

Seated on an aisle in the survivors' section, Joyce O'Mara reached out and grasped Betsy Toth Umanski's hand. 'Let me know if this gets too hard to hear,' she whispered. 'I can take you out for a while.' The two women, who had been together when the bomb exploded, had become friends.

'As a result of your investigation,' Brian inquired, 'what do you believe caused the destruction of Hill House?'

'We found the remains of a bombing device,' Henderson replied, 'and we believe that to have been the cause.'

'What sort of remains?'

'Mostly traces of various chemicals and a number of fibers,

227

which we immediately turned over to the FBI for analysis. And we also found parts of a small timing mechanism, which we believe was attached to the bomb, and used to fix the time of detonation.'

'Where did you find these remains?'

'In the basement of the building.'

'What, if anything, did you determine about that?'

'We determined that was where the bomb had been placed.'

'Could you determine how the basement would have been accessed?'

'According to the building plans, access was through an outside trapdoor. Easy for anyone to find.'

Over the next two days, Brian took the bomb expert through the particulars of the crime scene, what he had seen, what he had found. Henderson brought models into the courtroom to demonstrate, step by step and in excruciating detail, exactly what the bomb had done to Hill House and how. At times, it proved too much for some of the survivors, several of whom left the courtroom in tears. It was Friday afternoon before Brian was ready to bring his direct examination to a close.

'To do the kind of damage that this bomb did,' he asked his witness, 'would you say the basement was where it should have been placed?'

The weary expert nodded. 'To insure maximum effectiveness, the thing couldn't have been positioned better,' he declared. 'And mind you, it wasn't just left in the basement. All indications are, it was placed right at the structural center of the building.'

'In your experience, is that something the average person would know, where to set a bomb?'

'In my experience, most people don't have a clue,' Henderson replied. 'They think as long as they get it in the general vicinity, it'll do the job. That's why a lot of bombs fortunately do only minimal damage. This guy, on the other hand, knew exactly what he was doing.'

Brian nodded and turned toward the defense table. 'Your witness,' he said.

'What sort of expertise would it take for someone to know exactly where to plant a bomb?' Dana asked.

'Well, a structural engineer would know, of course,' Henderson responded. 'And an architect, I suppose. A building contractor, probably. And someone trained in, or familiar with, demolition work. There's a big difference between leaving a bomb next to a wall, and placing it at the structural center of a building.'

'But how about just some ordinary person who wanted to find out? For example, what if I had in mind to plant a bomb in this courthouse. I'm not an engineer or an architect or a demolitions expert. Let's say I'm just an anarchist. How would I find out where the structural center of the building was?'

Henderson shrugged. 'Well, I guess you could go to the planning department at city hall and look up the building plans,' he said. 'Or I suppose you could go to a library and look it up in a reference book.'

'That simple? Just go to a library and look up how to find structural centers in a reference book?'

'Pretty much. If you were that interested.'

'Okay,' Dana said. 'What about dumb luck?'

'I don't understand.'

'What about the average person, who knows nothing about the proper placement of a bomb and doesn't think of going to city hall or a library, who just leaves it at the right spot by luck?'

'That's not been my experience, but I suppose there's always that chance,' Henderson conceded.

Dana smiled to let him, and the jury, know she did not consider him the enemy. 'Let me ask you something else,' she said easily. 'The part of the timing device you recovered from the debris, how big a part was that?'

'There were several parts, actually. The biggest was, oh, maybe an inch by an inch and a quarter.'

'An inch . . . that's a pretty big piece. Were there any identifiable fingerprints on it?'

'No.'

'Any kind of fingerprints at all?'

'No. Not even a smudge.'

'I see. Well then, can you tell me, were you able to determine, either from the parts of the timing device, or anything else in your investigation, when the bomb was set?'

Henderson looked puzzled. 'How could I tell that?' he asked.

'Is that a no?'

'Of course. There's no way to tell that from my investigation. All I know is it was set sometime before two o'clock in the afternoon. How long before, I don't have any way of knowing.'

'Well, was there anything to tell you *who* set it?'

'No.'

'So, let me get this straight. You're saying that in addition to not knowing when the bomb was set or who set it, there was nothing in any of what you found in your thorough investigation that could in any way be linked to the defendant over there. Is that correct?'

'I guess so.'

'No fingerprints, no clothing fibers, no hair, no DNA, not even a military issue footprint?'

Henderson shrugged. 'No.'

'Thank you,' Dana said. 'No further questions.'

It was just before four o'clock, more than enough time for the prosecution to call another witness. But the bomb expert's testimony had been grueling, both for the jurors and many of the spectators, and Abraham Bendali took advantage of the break to adjourn his court for the weekend.

Big Dug sat under the Alaskan Way viaduct and fretted. He had been fretting for some months now, ever since Joshua had told him about the delivery man. While Joshua might not appreciate the importance of what he had seen, Big Dug certainly did.

The kindly giant had spent the evening at a favorite bar, nursing a beer as long as he could, watching the newscasts and listening to the television analysts discussing the trial. Then he went in search of Joshua, but couldn't find him. So he sat with his back up against a concrete pillar and tried not to doze as he waited for his friend to come along. It was after eleven o'clock before he finally saw him.

Joshua was sauntering down the street, singing a happy little tune.

'Where you been?' Big Dug asked.

'I been down to Ivar's,' Joshua told him. 'I was over to Colman Dock, and this couple come off the nine-ten ferry, all dressed up nice and clean like, and asks me if I'm hungry. Well, I was, so I said yes. And the next thing I know, they take me to Ivar's and sit me down at a table with a real napkin, and tell me to order anything I want. I sure wish you'd been there.'

'What did you order?'

Joshua's eyes shone. 'I had a big bowl of chowder and then I had two orders of fish and chips, and a root beer. And then I had ice cream. And the waiter said it was all paid for.' He rummaged around in the pocket of his coat. 'It's probably not too hot anymore, but I got extra so I could bring it to you.' He offered his friend a pile of limp potatoes and three pieces of fried fish wrapped in a red napkin.

Big Dug ate the food gratefully. The beer he had drunk earlier had been his only dinner. 'We need to talk,' he said when he was done.

'About what?' Joshua asked.

'About the delivery man,' Big Dug told him.

'Oh that,' Joshua said. 'I don't want to talk about that.'

'I know you don't, but you got to.'

'Why?'

'Because it might be important,' Big Dug said.

'Why?'

'It's the trial, you see, the trial of that guy they say bombed Hill House.'

'What's a trial?' Joshua asked.

'It's like a public hearing that they hold up at the courthouse,' Big Dug said patiently, 'when the people who say that someone did something very bad and the people who say that he didn't

231

get together to try to convince this other group of people that they're right.'

'What about it?'

'Well, what you saw could make a difference in how the whole thing ends up. If this guy did bomb Hill House the way the prosecutor says he did, then there should be a conviction.'

'What's a conviction?'

'It's when this other group of people, called a jury, all agree that someone broke the law and did something very bad.'

Joshua frowned. 'Like me, because I slept at Hill House?'

'No, not like you,' Big Dug assured him. 'You didn't start the fire. You didn't break the law. You didn't do anything bad, I told you that. But the thing is, you see, as it turns out, by being there that night, you may have done something good.'

'How?'

'You may be an eyewitness.'

'What's an eyewitness?'

'That's someone who saw what happened.'

'But I didn't see what happened,' Joshua protested. 'I just saw the delivery man.'

'That's the whole point,' Big Dug said. 'I think that delivery man might just be the guy who planted the bomb.'

Joshua's eyes opened wide. 'How do you know?'

'Well, I don't know for sure. That's why I think we should go to the police, and tell them. They'll know.'

'What would I have to do?'

'They'll probably ask if you can identify the man you saw.'

'But I can't,' Joshua said. 'I didn't see him very good, I told you that. I couldn't even tell if it was that guy they showed on the television.'

'Then that's what you tell them.'

'Are you sure I won't get in trouble?'

'I promise,' Big Dug said. 'You're not going to get in trouble. The police are just going to want to talk to you, that's all. Look, if it'll make you feel better, I'll go there with you, just to make sure they treat you right.'

Joshua thought about it for a long moment, about how safe

232

and good his life was with Big Dug looking after him, and about how he didn't want any of that to change. 'I don't know,' he said finally. 'It's kinda scary.'

'I know,' his friend told him gently. 'But I think it's something you gotta do.'

'Can I study on it for a while?'

Big Dug shrugged. 'I guess so, sure,' he said. He didn't have to push. He knew, sooner or later, Joshua would come around.

Roger Roark, the executive director of the Coalition for Conservative Causes, met with a few of his inner circle advisors.

'McAuliffe is already doing a better job than I expected,' he declared. 'I thought she was supposed to be weak in capital cases.'

'Inexperienced, perhaps,' someone suggested, 'but not weak. My understanding is that she's as sharp as they come.'

'Then we have work to do,' Roark said. 'Our position here is quite simple: Latham has to be convicted.'

'What for?' a bulky man with a crooked nose inquired. 'For acting on our beliefs? I thought this sort of thing was exactly what we want to encourage.'

'Normally, it would be,' Roark conceded. 'But we've got an election coming up, and our candidate wants an all-American symbol he can ram down the throats of the opposition. An acquittal is of no use to us. Not when we've got a golden opportunity to create a martyr.'

'Good God, we can't go public with that,' an elderly gentleman exclaimed.

'Who said anything about going public?' Roark retorted. 'I simply want it understood within our own organization: Whatever it takes, whatever it costs, we get a conviction.'

4

The King County medical examiner was called to the stand first thing Monday morning. Arthur Pruitt was a rotund little man of fifty-two, with a bristling mustache and receding hairline. His one outstanding feature was a pair of enormous hands. They were so large, in fact, that they had prompted one young assistant of some years ago to suggest that a football would easily disappear in just one of them, and another to wonder how he could perform his anatomical work with such precision.

As soon as the doctor had taken the oath, given his name, and settled his bulk in the witness box, Brian Ayres stood up and greeted the jury. Then he nodded to the judge.

Abraham Bendali cleared his throat. 'Good morning, ladies and gentlemen,' he said, addressing the spectators in the packed courtroom, particularly those in the survivors' section. 'This witness is going to be testifying at some length about those who died in the Hill House bombing. It's likely that it will be very graphic and disturbing testimony, and I want to warn you of that in advance, should any of you feel you might not want to be here during it.'

There was a general rearrangement among the spectators as a handful rose and exited the room, not one of them a survivor.

'I don't think anything could be more graphic or more disturbing than what I lived through every day for two weeks with my Jeffrey before he died,' Marilyn Korba was heard to murmur, as she stayed where she was.

Across the aisle, Dana smiled wryly to herself. Brian was going to play every card he had, even if it meant using the survivors. She didn't blame him. In his position, she would have done the same.

'Cheap shot,' Joan Wills whispered.

'The cheaper the shot, the weaker the case,' Dana whispered back.

Once the preliminaries were out of the way, and Pruitt had detailed the credentials that qualified him as an expert witness, he proceeded to pluck a file, as if by random, from one of two large boxes that had accompanied him into court, and spread it open across his lap.

'Case Number KCME00-087,' he recited. 'A forty-six-year-old Caucasian woman, medium frame, five feet six inches in height, weighing one hundred and sixty-five pounds. Presented with crushed skull, severed spinal cord, and multiple other lesser fractures and lacerations.'

'Were you able to determine the cause of death?' Brian inquired.

'It could have been either of the two main injuries,' the medical examiner replied, 'which occurred within milliseconds of one another. They were both potentially fatal.'

'And do you have an opinion as to what might have caused those injuries?'

'I found them to be consistent with a sudden fall of some distance, with the victim landing on her back.'

'Were you able to establish the time of death?'

'I determined that death was instantaneous,' Pruitt declared, 'and according to the wristwatch the victim was wearing on her left arm at the moment of impact, probably occurred shortly after two o'clock on the afternoon in question.'

In preparation for this testimony, a slide projector and a large light board had been brought into the courtroom. The medical examiner removed a stack of slides from the file and passed them to Brian, who in turn passed them to his assistant. Mark Hoffman slipped the stack into the projector and brought the first one into focus on the accompanying screen.

Brian glanced at the jurors. 'I'm sorry,' he said, as he saw several of them visibly wince. Then he turned to Pruitt. 'Will you be good enough, doctor, to describe for the court what we're looking at.'

'We're looking at a postmortem view of the deceased,' the medical examiner replied. 'However, the slides tell only part of the story. The other part is the X-rays, which, as you will see, define each of the two potentially fatal injuries.' With that, he pulled a number of films from the file. 'If I can have the light board now, I think I'll be able to make things quite clear.'

With a nod from the judge, Robert Niera wheeled the cumbersome device to the front of the courtroom. As soon as the bailiff had it plugged in, Pruitt stepped down from the witness stand and proceeded to clip the X-rays onto the board, in full view of the jury. Using a pointer, he then went back and forth from the clinical films on the board to the grim slides on the screen to delineate each of the victim's primary injuries. And at every step, he endeavored to be as explicit as possible about how and why, in his opinion, the injury was consistent with the detonation of a bomb.

'If you look at this area here,' he said, indicating one of the X-rays, 'it corresponds to the upper section of the spinal cord, known as the brain stem.' He pointed at the screen, which showed a slide of a female corpse laid out on a table, her hair covering her face, her back exposed. 'The shaded part you see in the X-ray indicates a hyperflexion/hyperextension injury to the cervical spine that was so severe it severed the spinal cord at the first cervical vertebra. In effect, this separated the brain from the nervous system, resulting in death.'

'What did you determine was the cause of this kind of injury?' Brian asked.

'A violent contact between the body and another, harder object, in this instance, a floor,' he replied. 'A contact that was so abrupt and so uncompromising that the more pliant of the two objects, the falling body, had no choice but to give way.'

'Is this the kind of injury that could occur in the aftermath of an explosion?'

The medical examiner nodded. 'Absolutely. If you think about an explosion that's strong enough to take out a building, causing a person to fall from a height, as all indications are this woman did, the falling body would incur what is called, in layman's terms, a whiplash. A severe snapping action of the head and neck, backward, then forward, and then back again, which crushed the skull and severed the spine. She didn't have a chance.'

Even in the back row of the jury box, Allison Ackerman, who made her living by depicting the grisliest of murders, felt her stomach turn. It was one thing to fantasize about death, she concluded, and quite another to come face-to-face with the reality.

When the demonstration was over, Pruitt reclaimed the witness stand. After giving the jury a moment to catch its collective breath, Brian turned to the medical examiner.

'Were you able to identify the victim?' he asked softly.

Pruitt consulted his file. 'Yes, I was,' he replied. 'Brenda Kiley.'

In the third row of the survivors' section, Raymond Kiley was unable to stifle a sob. Beside him, Helen Gamble grasped his hand in both of hers. At the defense table, Corey Latham winced. None of it was lost on the jurors.

'The miracle here,' the medical examiner concluded, 'is that I understand she was holding two babies in her arms at the time of the explosion. They both survived with minimal injuries.'

During Arthur Pruitt's four days of testimony, the Kiley evaluation was more or less repeated one hundred and seventy-five times. And each time was as disturbing as the first, especially when it came to the children who had been in the day care center, and the newborns who had not even lived long enough to have their names recorded.

With his never-ending supply of photographs, X-rays, and uncompromising details, the medical examiner chronicled the injuries that every victim had sustained, and wherever possible, linked the primary injury to the victim's death, and the cause of injury to the results of an explosion. By the time he finished, there was no doubt in anyone's mind that the one hundred and seventy-six people who died as a result of being at Hill House on the first Tuesday in February had met their end by the detonation of a bomb.

It was also apparent that by the end of the four days, jurors

237

and spectators alike were emotionally exhausted, and some, perhaps, even growing a little resentful of the siege. Over half of the Hill House people had not made it through the entire testimony.

'Thank you, Dr. Pruitt,' Brian said as he sank into his chair. It was obvious that he, too, was feeling the effects. And in showing that, the jurors found themselves able to separate the prosecution's presentation, which they loathed, from the prosecutor himself, whom they liked.

Across the aisle, Dana glanced at her client. Corey Latham sat with his head down, gray-faced and withdrawn, gone inside himself for protection.

'I have only one question of this witness,' she informed the bench, incurring a look of gratitude and relief from the jurors, because they liked her, too.

'Was there anything in your determinations, Dr. Pruitt, that indicated who set the bomb that killed these people?'

'No,' the medical examiner replied.

'Thank you,' Dana said, true to her word. 'That's all.'

It was barely three o'clock, but Abraham Bendali didn't care. He knew when enough was enough, and he had certainly had enough. Without preamble, other than to admonish the jury about discussing the case, he banged his gavel.

'We're adjourned,' he said.

'Was the prosecution right to get the blood and gore over and done with so early?' Joan Wills asked over a yogurt in the Cotter Boland lunchroom. 'This could be a long trial. Don't they run the risk of having the impact diluted by the end of it?'

Dana shrugged. 'I think Brian wanted to start with what he thought would have the biggest impact. Sometimes, if you set the scene well enough, you can blind the jury to the actual weakness of your case.'

'But four days of it? I hate to say it, because I really hurt for the victims and their families, but after the second day, all those corpses, and pieces of corpses, stopped being real to me, and started looking like mannequins.'

238

'I don't know,' Dana said. 'I'm not sure I'll ever forget the pictures of some of those babies. They looked very real to me.'

'Well, yes, I guess that part got pretty bad,' Joan conceded. 'Maybe I'm just reacting like a defense attorney, and Brian was right. Sow the seeds and reap the verdict.'

'We were never going to be able to deny that all those people died,' Dana told her associate. 'Or that they died because of a bomb. That was going to be established, no matter what.'

'But where does that leave us?'

'Our position hasn't changed. What happened was horrendous, it should never have happened. There's no possible justification for it, and the person who planted that bomb and killed all those people deserves to hang. It just wasn't our client. And that's the bottom line, even if Brian is hoping that after this no one is going to give a damn whether Corey did it or not.'

Jonathan Heal swept into Seattle's Alexis Hotel, his considerable entourage in his wake, and was immediately shown to an opulent suite on one of the two floors he had reserved. He had scheduled a week of prayer meetings, to be broadcast across the country, conveniently coinciding with the advent of the Hill House trial. It was the first time the televangelist had made a pilgrimage to Seattle, and he had booked the bulk of the convention center for the occasion. All performances, including a thousand-dollar-a-head gala on Saturday, were sold out in the first twelve hours after the event was announced.

Special invitations for the gala had been issued to a select few that Reverend Heal was quick to explain were supporters who had been especially devoted down through the years. He announced that they would sit at the head table on Saturday night, and be recognized for their loyalty. Among those who were to be so honored was, to her astonishment, Rose Gregory.

'Oh my goodness, I'm so excited,' Rose told her granddaughter. 'To be singled out by that dear man.'

'Grandma, you deserve it more than anyone I know,' the granddaughter said.

'But to sit at the head table, with all those really important people, and Reverend Heal, too? Surely, I don't deserve that.'

'Why not? You've supported him and his ministry for as long as I can remember. You should be rewarded.' There was little doubt in the young woman's mind that the amount of money her grandmother had contributed to Jonathan Heal's coffers over the past two decades easily added up to thousands.

'Well I dare say, it'll be a sight more pleasant to think about than this terrible trial I'm involved in,' Rose declared. She squared her shoulders as a little smile, the first in days, brightened her eyes. 'I think I'll wear my lilac lace.'

All Allison Ackerman wanted to do was go home and take a long, hot bath. Her knees were wobbly and her brain felt like mush, and she longed for the peace and quiet of her farm. But at the last moment, she thought of her pantry, and forced herself to stop at the market. She didn't notice the van that drove into the lot right behind her, not even when it pulled into the parking space beside her, not even when she walked right past it on her way into the store.

'Allison? Allison, is that you?' a woman of about her own age called, climbing out of the van.

The mystery writer turned. The person approaching her was dressed in jeans and riding boots, had her predominantly gray hair pulled back in a ponytail, and appeared to be wearing little if any makeup. Allison hadn't the faintest idea who she was.

'Yes?' she responded politely.

'I thought that was you,' the woman bubbled. 'It's Julia, Julia Campbell. We met last year, at the FOCUS convention in San Francisco.'

'Of course,' Allison said, recognizing the board member's name, but recalling a widow, like herself, in smart business suits, with upswept hair and perfect makeup. 'I'm sorry for not remembering you. I'm afraid my brain isn't functioning very well at the moment. How are you? What are you doing here?'

Julia smiled. 'I'm fine,' she replied. 'And I'm here because of you.'

'Me?' Allison responded with clear and immediate caution.

Because of her widespread reputation as an author, she was routinely bombarded by promoters soliciting her endorsement of everything from politically sanctioned murder to pantyhose.

'Yes, you told me so many wonderful things about Maple Valley, I had to come see for myself. So I came, and I saw, and I live here now.'

'Well, for goodness sake,' Allison said, relief evident in her voice.

'Oh yes, and I have to tell you, I love it. It was time for a change. California was getting so bad. And I was looking for more acreage than I could afford there, anyway. I have Arabians, you know, and judging by the way they've been kicking up their heels lately, I think they're pretty happy, too.'

'How long have you been here?'

'Just since last month.'

'You should have called me,' Allison said, automatically warming to another horse person. 'There was no need to wait until we just happened to bump into one another.'

'Well, you're busy. I didn't want to bother you.'

'Nonsense,' the mystery writer declared. 'Now that you're here, we'll have to get together, and at least celebrate your arrival.'

'I'd like that,' Julia said.

'Oh dear,' Allison said, remembering. 'I'm afraid it might have to wait awhile, though.'

'Of course. You have deadlines.'

Allison chuckled. 'Actually, what I've got right now is jury duty.'

Julia's eyes widened. 'You must be kidding. How excruciating.'

'It's my own fault,' the author said with a shrug. 'I was just too arrogant to get out of it.'

'Then I hope at least you got on an interesting case,' Julia declared.

'Well, I'm really not allowed to discuss it, but I think you could say it's interesting,' Allison said. 'I just didn't want you to think I was putting you off.'

'No, I understand.'

'And I promise, we *will* get together, just as soon as it's over, and give you a proper welcome.'

'I'll look forward to it,' Julia said with a bright smile.

5

Each morning before court, Dana and Joan met at Smith Tower to discuss the progress of the trial before walking up to the courthouse together, leaving Charles Ramsey, who did not bother to sit in on these conversations, to make his own way there. There was comfort in having a comrade to help negotiate the journey across Third Avenue.

'It looks like there are more of them every day,' Joan remarked on the morning after the medical examiner had completed his testimony, as they tried to slip between the lines of protesters, gawkers, and cameramen. 'It's getting harder to tell the players, even *with* a scorecard. Or a placard, as the case may be.'

Dana shrugged. 'Like it or not, that's what a free country is all about,' she said.

'What?' Joan declared. 'Free speech or mob mentality? Look at those cameramen. They're like ghouls, hanging around, *hoping* for something to happen that they can record and replay umpteen times on the nightly news. Look at the platform they're willing to give these crazies. Never mind the impact it'll have, they don't give a damn about that. They just need to justify their existence. Mark my words, there's going to be trouble before this trial is over.'

As if to underscore her words, a heavyset woman with bleached blond hair was suddenly in front of them, barring their way. 'How can you do this? How can you defend the butcher who murdered those poor defenseless babies?' she screeched at Dana, her spittle spraying the attorney's face. 'You want to set him free to murder other innocent children?'

From the corner of her eye, Dana saw the cameras swinging around to focus their lenses on the little scene. She opened her mouth to make as benign a response as she knew how, but before she could find the appropriate words, Joan stepped between them.

'Madam,' the associate said to the blonde, in a voice made of satin, 'I sincerely hope that neither you nor any of your loved ones ever know the pain and anguish of being accused of a crime you did not commit. And I can think of two you're committing right now – harassment and assault.'

'Huh?' the woman retorted.

'And if those policemen over there should see fit to arrest you, I hope your attorney will fight to protect your rights as vigorously as Mrs. McAuliffe is fighting to protect Lieutenant Latham's.'

With that, she turned her back on the startled protester and the cameras, and propelled her partner ahead of her into the courthouse.

'Oh my God,' Dana gasped. 'I can't believe you did that. Harassment? Assault?'

'Hey, why not? She did assault you, didn't she? With her saliva.'

'You're too much,' Dana said.

Jesse Montero took the stand first thing Friday morning, walking slowly down the aisle to the witness box, nodding to people in the survivors' section, who in turn gave him encouraging smiles as he passed.

Brian approached his witness. 'Mr. Montero, please tell the court what you were doing for a living last February,' he instructed.

'I worked then as head custodian at Hill House,' he replied. 'I mean, the Seattle Family Services Center.'

'In that capacity, you knew the building very well, did you not?'

'I knew every inch of her.'

'On the evening before the bombing, what time did you leave work?'

'At nine o'clock, same as always,' Jesse replied. 'Building

closes at six, cleaning staff works, then I make sure everything's done right.'

'Were you usually the last to leave the building?'

The former custodian nodded. 'I come in last, sometimes, at noon. I leave last. I lock up.'

'And what time did the clinic open in the morning?'

'People come in at eight.'

'So that's eleven hours that the building was unoccupied?'

'Except if there was an emergency, or if someone just delivered,' Jesse clarified. 'Then people, they could be there all night.'

'Was there any emergency that night? Or a new mother staying over?'

'No.'

'How many doors were there to Hill House?'

'Three. Front door, side door, back door.'

'And you locked up all three every night?'

Jesse shook his head. 'Side door was always locked, never open,' he said. 'I locked front door and back door.'

'What about the basement?'

'I check, but I don't lock.'

'Why not?'

'No lock to lock. Nothing's ever kept in that basement. I go down every night, make sure there are no rats. That's all.'

'When you went to the basement, Mr. Montero, how did you get there?'

'From the outside,' he said. 'Around the path to the trapdoor.'

'Not from inside?'

'No way down there from the inside,' Jesse told him. 'Only from the outside.'

'Where is the trapdoor?'

'Around the side of the building, toward the back.'

'In plain sight of anyone who might be looking for it?'

Jesse nodded. 'Through the side gate and up a little ways.'

'Could anyone have gained access to that basement?'

'Sure,' the custodian said with a shrug. 'Whoever want to. No lock. Anyone could get in.'

'All right then, you left Hill House at nine o'clock that night, having locked the front and back doors to the building, and checked in the basement?'

'Yes.'

'At that time, did you see anything that wasn't there the night before?'

'No. There was nothing.'

'Nothing that caught your eye, nothing that looked suspicious?'

'Nothing at all. I tell you, nothing was ever kept in that basement.'

'Then you're positive, absolutely positive,' Brian persisted, 'that at nine o'clock on the night before the bombing, that basement was empty. There was nothing in it that looked like a bomb, or looked like it might have held a bomb, like duffel bags, maybe, or big sacks, anywhere at all?'

Jesse shook his head. 'I tell you, I would've seen something if it was there,' he declared. 'I saw nothing. No bags, no bombs, no rats.'

The last witness of the week was seventy-two-year-old Milton Auerbach. He was an innocuous little man with wispy gray hair, rimless spectacles, and a mouthful of gold teeth. As he walked to the stand and took the oath, his eyes darted from the judge to the jury to the attorneys, and as he perched on the edge of his chair, he looked, to Allison at least, like a bird in a cage.

'State your name and address,' the clerk directed.

'Milton Auerbach,' he said in a reedy voice. 'I live at 2212 Summit Avenue in Seattle.'

Brian greeted him with a warm smile. 'Good afternoon, Mr. Auerbach,' he said.

'Good afternoon,' the little man replied.

'Thank you for coming in today.'

'You're welcome.'

'Can you tell us, sir, how long have you lived on Summit Avenue?'

'Going on forty-two years now,' Auerbach replied. 'But I think it's time for me to move.'

'Forty-two years?' Brian echoed. 'That's a long time to live in one place. You must know the neighborhood quite well.'

'As well as anyone, I suppose.'

'Do you do much walking around in the area? In the daytime, that is?'

'Of course. No need to take out the car when you have two good legs.'

'I expect you've seen a lot of changes in all those years.'

Auerbach snorted a little. 'Used to be a nice, quiet neighborhood. People knew one another. Kids could play outside. No one ever even thought to lock a door. Now you hardly know anyone. There've been three burglaries in my building in just the past year. You take your life in your hands every time you cross a street, and in broad daylight, too.'

'What about at night?'

'Night? Now, that's different. After eleven o'clock, things get pretty quiet. It's the hospitals, you know. After the night shift comes on, businesses shut down. Even McDonald's closes up. Although, with the food they serve, the hospitals should pay them to stay open. Keep the heart attacks coming.'

A little titter floated through the courtroom and Auerbach looked up, surprised that anyone would find humor in his words.

'Sir,' Brian said, suppressing his own chuckle, 'where were you on the night before the bombing of Hill House?'

'Where I was every night, with my wife, my Emma.'

'And where was she?'

'In the hospital,' he replied.

'What hospital was that, sir?'

'Harborview Medical Center.'

'You said you were with your wife every night last winter,' Brian said gently. 'Will you tell us why?'

'She had a stroke the Sunday after Thanksgiving, right in the middle of breakfast. I remember we were having waffles. Emma didn't fix waffles very often. The doctor said they weren't good for us. She was in the hospital for three months.'

'And it was your custom to spend a good part of each day and evening with her?'

'Of course. Where else would I be? My Emma had never been alone. I was there from when she woke up in the morning, until she fell off to sleep at night.'

'And on the night in question, what time did you leave the hospital?'

'As soon as she went to sleep. It was a little after midnight.'

'Did you usually stay that late?'

Auerbach shook his head. 'No. Usually she drifted off around ten, and I left then.'

'But not that night?'

'No. That night it was midnight.'

'It was more than seven months ago. How are you so sure?'

'Because that night was our fiftieth wedding anniversary,' the little man said with a catch in his voice. 'I had a special dinner brought into the hospital, and the doctors were very nice and let her have some champagne. And then I gave her a diamond anniversary band. She always wanted a diamond anniversary band. She was so excited, it took her a long time to get to sleep that night.'

'So you're positive, there's no doubt in your mind, that it was a little past midnight when you left your wife at Harborview Medical Center?'

'Yes, I'm positive.'

'And where did you go when you left the hospital?'

'I went home,' Auerbach said. 'Where else would I go at midnight?'

'How did you get home?'

'I walked, like always.'

'You weren't afraid to walk alone in the neighborhood at night?'

'Afraid of what? I'm an old man. Is someone going to mug me? I have no money. I fall, I get hurt, there are hospitals all around to take care of me. I sat with my Emma all day, I liked to walk home at night.'

With a nod from Brian, Mark Hoffman rolled a bulletin

248

board up in front of the jury. Pinned to it was an enlarged map of part of the First Hill section of Seattle, with street names and little boxes identifying the Harborview Medical Center, the Seattle Family Services Center, and the apartment building on Summit Avenue where Milton Auerbach lived clearly marked on it. The prosecutor picked up a black marker.

'Please tell us, sir, what route you took to get to your home that night,' he instructed.

'Same route I always took,' Auerbach replied. 'I came out of the hospital on Ninth Avenue, and walked along Ninth until I got to Jefferson Street. I took Jefferson up to Boren. Then I walked down Boren until I got to Madison, and there I crossed the street, on the corner where Hill House used to be, and turned right.' He spoke slowly, and Brian used the pen to mark the old man's path on the map. 'I walked up Madison until I got to Summit. Then I turned left on Summit, and walked to my apartment house, which is the third apartment building on the right-hand side.'

'That's Ninth to Jefferson to Boren to Madison to Summit,' Brian repeated slowly. 'Is that what you said, sir?'

Auerbach nodded. 'That's what I said.'

'And that's the route that you took home from the hospital on the night of your fiftieth wedding anniversary?'

'Yes.'

'Can you tell me if, during your walk home that night, there was anything that caught your attention?'

'Yes, there was something.'

'And what was that?'

'I saw a car parked on the north side of Madison Street, maybe halfway between Boren and Minor.'

'A parked car?'

'Yes.'

'On the north side of Madison?'

'Yes.'

'Facing west?'

'Yes, west. I kind of cut the corner on Boren a little, so I walked right in front of the car.'

249

Brian drew a small rectangle on the map, where Auerbach had indicated the car had been parked. 'Would you say the car you saw was right about here?'

The old man peered at the spot and nodded. 'Yes, I would say right about there.'

Brian put the letters CAR in the middle of the rectangle. 'All right, you noticed a parked car,' he said. 'Now you have to admit that it doesn't seem terribly unusual to see a car parked on a city street. So can you tell us why you happened to notice that particular vehicle?'

'To begin with, I noticed because it was the only car parked on the street. The graveyard shift at the hospitals comes on at eleven. After that, there isn't much traffic in the area at night.'

'I see,' Brian acknowledged. 'All right, what kind of car was it?'

'It was one of those four-wheel-drive things you see so many of these days.'

'A sport utility vehicle?'

'Yes. One of those.'

'Did you happen to notice the make of the vehicle? Or the model?'

'No, I'm sorry, I didn't,' the witness confessed. 'I don't know that much about automobiles.'

'What about the color?'

Auerbach shrugged. 'The streetlights up there do funny things to color, so I'm not sure what color the car was, but I know it was dark. Maybe black or gray.'

'Could it have been green?'

'Dark green, sure, or brown, or navy. All I know is it was something dark.'

'Well then,' Brian inquired, 'was there anything about this particular vehicle, other than its simply being there, that called it to your attention?'

'Yes,' the witness replied. 'It had a military sticker on the windshield.'

'A military sticker?'

'Yes. That's really why I noticed it.'

'And why is that?'

'Because my sister's boy was in the Navy, and he had a sticker on his windshield, just like the one I saw on that car that night. And I recognized it as I went by.'

'Can you describe this sticker?'

'Well, it was maybe three or four inches long by maybe an inch high, and it was white, and it had some numbers and letters on it, and a round Department of Defense logo,' Auerbach said. 'And then there was a tab attached to the bottom of it.'

'Could you tell what color the tab was?'

The witness shook his head. 'No. Because of the streetlights, again. They make red look like blue, and blue look like green. So, I couldn't tell you for sure. Just like I couldn't tell you for sure about the color of the car.'

'Well, were there any words printed on the tab?'

'Yes, I'm pretty sure there were,' Auerbach admitted. 'Those tabs are used for base designations. But I didn't look close enough to read it. I didn't realize it would be important. It just registered on me that the sticker was like the one my nephew had.'

'And at what base here in Washington did your nephew serve, sir?'

'He worked on the submarines,' the little man replied with pride. 'And he was assigned to Bangor.'

At that, Mark Hoffman handed Brian a posterboard, perhaps two feet by three feet in size, and in full view of the jury, the prosecutor showed it to the witness. 'Did the sticker you saw, the one you say was just like the one your nephew had, look like this, sir?'

On the poster was an enlarged version of the Department of Defense decal that was used on military bases for vehicle and occupant identification. The round logo was clear against the white background, and along the bottom was a bright blue tab with the words 'SUBASE BANGOR' printed in thick black capital letters.

Dana was out of her seat in a flash. 'Objection,' she exclaimed.

'Approach,' Bendali instructed, pushing his microphone to

the side. 'Yes, Ms. McAuliffe?' he inquired as the two attorneys reached the bench.

'Your Honor,' the defense attorney declared, 'this witness was unable to testify as to either the color of the sticker tab, or any words that may have been printed on it. I resent counsel's attempt to implicate my client unfairly by allowing the jury to see an enlarged version of the precise sticker that he has on his vehicle.'

The judge glared down at Brian. 'What are you doing, Mr. Ayres?'

'It's an exhibit that I planned to bring in a little later in the trial, Your Honor,' Brian said ingenuously. 'In the interests of economy, I was using it at this time only as an example, for clarification, not implication.'

'Not in my courtroom,' Bendali retorted, staring him down. 'And don't make me have to repeat myself. Now, step back.'

'Nice try,' Dana murmured, as they retreated.

'Just earning a living,' Brian murmured in response.

'The witness is instructed not to answer the last question,' the judge declared, adjusting his microphone. 'And the jury is instructed to disregard the last exhibit.' He glowered one more time at the prosecutor, and then gave him a curt nod.

'I apologize to the court, if I misled anyone in any way, and I apologize to you, Mr. Auerbach,' Brian said, with just the right amount of contrition in his voice. 'Now, if we may, let's return to the dark-colored sport utility vehicle with the military sticker on the windshield. Do you recall ever having seen that vehicle before that night?'

'No.'

'Are you certain?'

The little man shrugged. 'As certain as I can be.'

'And have you seen that vehicle since?'

'No.'

'Do you still walk around the neighborhood during the day?'

'Yes.'

'Do you still walk home from Harborview Medical Center in the evening?'

252

'No,' Auerbach answered.

'Why not, sir?' Brian asked gently.

The little man blinked several times before he answered. 'My Emma died,' he said.

A murmur of sympathy ricocheted around the courtroom, as Brian thanked the witness and took his seat.

'Great,' Dana muttered under her breath, sending a reproachful glance in the prosecutor's direction. 'First, he tries to ambush me, and now I get to beat up on an old man who lost his wife.' With a sigh, she stood up. 'I'm very sorry about your wife, Mr. Auerbach,' she said to the witness, and the sincerity in her voice was unmistakable.

'Thank you,' he replied.

'Would you like to take a moment?' He shook his head. 'Would you like a glass of water?'

'Maybe, yes, please,' he replied, and Joan had a glass filled by the time the words were out of his mouth.

'Thank you,' Auerbach said, as he accepted the glass and took several gulps.

'Just take your time, sir.'

'I'm all right now,' he said.

Dana smiled kindly. 'Well then, I have just a few questions for you.'

'All right,' he said.

'You say you really noticed the parked car because of the sticker on the windshield, is that correct?'

'No. First, I noticed it because it was the only one on the street. Second, I noticed it because of the sticker.'

'Right,' she conceded. 'And you also said you couldn't be sure what the exact color of the vehicle was, only that it was dark? Maybe black or gray, you said.'

'That's right.'

'And you know it was a military sticker, but you couldn't be sure what color the tab was?'

'No, I couldn't be sure,' he allowed. 'Not with those lights.'

'And you don't have a clear idea of what was printed on the tab, is that also correct?'

'That's correct.'

'By the way,' Dana said casually, 'what did your nephew do on the submarines?'

'He was a communications technician,' the little man said. 'He owns an electronics shop now.'

Dana walked to the defense table, and took an exhibit from Joan. It was a posterboard, measuring approximately two feet by three feet in size, and displaying a Department of Defense sticker with a bright red tab affixed to the bottom of it. Across the tab, printed in thick black letters, were the words 'NAS FALLON.'

'In general, Mr. Auerbach, did the sticker you remember seeing on the windshield of that parked car in any way resemble this one?' she asked, holding the exhibit up for both the witness and the jury to see.

The little man nodded. 'Yes, that could've been it,' he said.

'Let the record show, Your Honor, that the sticker just identified by the witness as generally resembling the one he saw on the night in question is a photocopy of a sticker used at the Fallon Naval Air Station in Fallon, Nevada.'

'So noted,' Bendali said, as a buzz rippled through the courtroom.

From the corner of her eye, the defense attorney caught a grudging glance of respect from the prosecutor.

'Now, Mr. Auerbach,' she continued, 'did you happen to notice the license plate on the vehicle you saw?'

The witness paused for a moment. 'No, not really,' he said. 'Not to remember it, anyway.'

'Please think hard, sir,' Dana prompted. 'It would have been the front plate, and you've already testified that the car was facing toward you, and that you passed directly in front of it.'

'Yes I did,' the little man acknowledged. 'I think the plate must have been there, because I don't have the impression it was missing. But I just don't remember seeing it.'

'Well, was it your impression, at least, that it was a Washington State license plate?'

Auerbach had to think again. 'I'm sorry,' he said. 'I couldn't even be sure of that.'

'All right,' Dana continued, 'you testified earlier that you walked from Ninth to Jefferson to Boren, and then crossed at Madison, and walked up Madison to Summit, is that correct?'

The little man nodded. 'That's correct.'

'Did you always follow the same route every time you walked home from the hospital?'

'Sure.'

'I mean exactly, sir. I mean, is it possible that you usually crossed at Boren, but maybe sometimes you walked up Madison and crossed at Minor?'

'Well, yes, I crossed at Minor some of the time, if the light was against me at Boren,' he explained. 'But mostly I crossed at Boren.'

'But you're pretty sure that on that night, you crossed at Boren.'

'Well, I think so. Of course, it was quite a long time ago.'

'Just one more thing, then, sir,' Dana continued. 'When did you go to the police to report having seen the car? Was it immediately after the bombing, or did you wait a period of time?'

'I didn't go to them,' Auerbach corrected her. 'They came to me.'

'Oh? How was that?'

The witness shrugged. 'They were out on the street for several days, asking people in the neighborhood if they'd seen or heard anything around the time of the bombing. I was walking to the market. One of them stopped me and asked, so I told him about the car.'

'Do you remember approximately when that was?'

'I believe it was around the first of March,' he said.

'About a month after the bombing?'

'Yes, I would say so.'

'So, you didn't think seeing the car was all that important, did you, until the police approached you?'

The witness blinked. 'Why should I?' he said. 'It was just a car, like a lot of others.'

In the survivors' section, Carl Gentry shook his head in disgust. 'What good is that?' he muttered to no one in particular.

Dana smiled again. 'Thank you, Mr. Auerbach. That's all I have.'

The little man stepped down from the stand, and walked up the aisle and out of the courtroom. Allison watched him go. He was totally neutral, she decided, with no ax to grind, no position to protect. What he saw was what he saw, nothing more.

'Dirty pool,' Dana said to Brian, as Bendali adjourned for the day.

'Good comeback,' the prosecutor acknowledged.

'You gave me no choice.'

'It was my own fault then, Punk,' Brian conceded. 'I should have remembered.'

'Remembered what?' Dana asked.

He grinned. 'That you're as good as I am.'

Sam greeted her at the door with a big kiss. 'I hope you had a good day,' he said.

'Why?' she asked, instantly suspicious.

He plucked a tabloid off the kitchen counter. 'Saw it at the market this afternoon.'

Smeared across the front page was a picture of Dana, apparently taken one day as she was leaving the courthouse, side by side with a picture of her ex-husband.

'MY EX-WIFE WAS A BIGAMIST,' the headline screamed. The piece then went on to recount all the sleazy details of a failed marriage that the writer could either elicit or invent.

'My ex-wife was a bigamist,' the petulant San Francisco divorce attorney declared at the very end of the interview. 'All the time she was married to me, she was really married to her career.'

Dana shook her head when she was finished reading. She was seething inside, furious that the spineless worm would air his petty insecurities in public. But all she said was, 'Let's try not to let Molly see this.'

'I don't particularly like the way things are looking,' Prudence Chaffey confided to an AIM board member, having spent the evening getting up to date on the proceedings in Abraham Bendali's courtroom. 'I thought we could count on Ms. Mc-Auliffe to argue a case for justifiable homicide. But so far, she's just trying to refute the state's evidence.'

'And making mincemeat out of it,' the board member observed.

'Granted we want an acquittal,' Prudence said. 'But this is all about the election, and we need an acquittal for the right reasons. Isn't there something we can do?'

'We're already on it,' the board member told her.

6

At exactly six o'clock on Saturday evening, a sleek silver limousine pulled up in front of Rose Gregory's modest Queen Anne cottage, and a man in gray livery stepped out and walked smartly up the path to ring the doorbell.

'Oh, my goodness,' Rose exclaimed. 'I get to ride in a limousine?'

The only other time Rose had ridden in such luxury was twenty-two years ago, to her husband's funeral, and the two occasions could not be compared.

'You have yourself a wonderful time tonight,' her granddaughter said, hugging the tiny woman in lilac lace.

'I'm going to do my best to remember every detail, so I can tell you all about it when I get home,' Rose whispered as she swept out the door on the arm of the chauffeur.

The inside of the limousine was every bit as elegant as the outside, with plush gray upholstery, polished wood paneling, a full bar with cut crystal decanters, and even a television set.

'If you want to turn on the TV, just push the button on the left,' the chauffeur told her, as he guided the big automobile away from the curb, and slipped expertly into traffic.

Giggling just a bit, Rose leaned forward and pushed the button. Immediately, the set lit up, and the Reverend Jonathan Heal came onscreen by way of a prerecorded tape, dressed in his familiar white tuxedo, ruffled shirt, and bow tie.

'Hello, Rose,' he said in his liquid golden voice. 'I can't tell you how happy it makes me to know that you'll be joining us tonight. I've been looking forward to meeting you, in person, for a long time now. It will be the highlight of my evening.'

'Oh my,' Rose said to the television image. 'I'm so happy you invited me.' She lowered her voice. 'You know, I could never have afforded to come on my own.'

'Leroy is bringing you directly to us,' Heal continued over her confession, 'so you just sit back and relax, and enjoy the ride.'

The trip to the Seattle Convention Center didn't last nearly long enough for Rose. She had to go all the way back to her courtship days to recall being treated like such royalty.

As the limousine came to a halt, the door flew open and a young man with a broad smile and an enormous bouquet of red roses offered her his hand.

'On behalf of the Reverend Heal, welcome, Rose,' he said, helping her out of the car, and escorting her right through the crowd and into the building.

'Oh my,' Rose murmured.

'You are one of our very special guests tonight,' the young man told her, 'and I'm instructed to take you right to the Reverend.'

It was a small room, set apart from the area where the banquet was to be held, and the first thing Rose noticed was that it was filled with white flowers.

'To be honest, it reminded me of a funeral,' she told her granddaughter later.

'Just make yourself at home, Rose,' the young man said, taking her coat and disappearing. 'Help yourself to anything you like.'

A large table set up in the middle of the room sagged with platter after platter of elegant hors d'oeuvres. Rose wondered who was going to eat it all.

'That food would have fed us for a whole month,' she told her granddaughter afterward.

Five minutes later, Jonathan Heal swept in, his aide in tow, looking exactly as he had on the television set in the limousine.

'My dear Rose,' he said, grasping her hand, and she watched as it disappeared into his. 'You don't mind that I call you Rose, do you?'

'Certainly not,' Rose replied breathlessly, thinking it was a little late for her to object now.

'I am so happy you could be with us tonight,' he went on. 'One of the best parts of taking my ministry across the country like this is that I get to meet so many of the wonderful people who fill my life with light, and make the journey worthwhile. People like you, Rose. Your support and your generosity over the years have kept me going, like a beacon, through good times and bad. Knowing you were there has made all the difference.'

'My goodness, Reverend,' Rose said, overwhelmed. 'I do what I can, but I'm sure I'm just one of the little people.'

'There are no little people, Rose,' he told her. 'Not in the Kingdom of God.'

'He made me feel like I was the most important person in the whole world,' Rose reported to her granddaughter.

'Would you like some champagne?' Heal invited.

'Well, maybe just a little would be all right,' Rose said shyly.

An aide immediately popped the cork on a bottle of Dom Perignon that was cooling in an ice bucket judiciously placed off to the side. 'Let's toast to our finally meeting, and to the wonderful future I know is ahead of us when it includes someone as devoted to the cause as you.'

Rose was not much of a drinker, and the champagne tickled her nose on the way down. 'Oh my,' she said with a little giggle. 'This is such fun.'

Heal gestured to his aide and a platter of caviar was suddenly at Rose's elbow. She carefully spread some on a small cracker, and swallowed it in one bite.

'Now I do feel special,' she said.

'You have no idea how special you are, dear lady,' Heal told her, signaling his aide to refill her glass. 'You alone have the opportunity to do something great for humankind.'

'I do?' she responded.

'Oh yes,' he assured her. 'You alone are in a position to give voice to the millions of voiceless ones who perish every year. You alone can champion the sanctity of life.'

'My word, how can I do that?' she cried. After his effusive compliments, and two glasses of champagne, she was floating.

'By telling the world that everyone has the right to be born,' he replied. 'By using your good heart to persuade others that a plea for the preborn is a plea to be cheered, not jeered. And that an act for the preborn is an act to be commended, not condemned.'

'What are you saying, Reverend?'

'I'm saying it's up to you, Rose. There's no one else. You must speak for all those who have no voice.'

'But I've always supported the fight against abortion. You know I have.'

'So you have. But now, our Lord has given you a unique moment, the chance for a perfect union with Him. When that moment comes, Rose, grab it. Face your peers with righteousness as your sword. You are one of His precious children, and He waits on you. He has spoken to me, and through me, He speaks to you. Here, Rose, take my hand. Feel Him, feel His love, His courage, His strength, His commitment to holy life, as He says to you that you must not convict Corey Latham for acting in His name.'

Sunday, Allison Ackerman slept in, not awakening until a shaft of autumn sunlight slanted across her pillow.

It was a long weekend, due to Columbus Day, and it was such a relief to have three days away from the courtroom to clear the dreadful proceedings from her consciousness. Like a series of doors shutting behind her down the long hallway of her mind, she moved further and further away from the agony of what she was being forced to witness. That distance, she knew, was the only thing that would enable her to return to the courthouse on Tuesday morning.

But today was still Sunday, and Allison stretched lazily. Two of the dogs were curled up at the foot of her bed, snoring softly, encouraging her to linger on a lazy morning. She glanced at the clock on the nightstand. Ten minutes past ten, practically the middle of the day. She rolled over to look out the window. The horses seemed content to nibble at the ground, and would probably not mind waiting a bit longer for their morning ration of hay and oats and attention.

She fell back against the pillows, and almost immediately an unbidden image of an eighteen-month-old corpse blinded her. The little girl had been squashed like a bug by a falling beam. According to the medical examiner's testimony, there wasn't an intact bone left in her body. Of all the images of the past week, that one had stayed with Allison.

It was ironic, really, for a woman who earned her living writing about the goriest details of murder her imagination could conjure, that she would be having so much difficulty dealing with the real thing. True, the Hill House bombing was infinitely more horrendous than any scenario she had so far invented. But more than that, there was a significant difference between the portrayal of murder for the purposes of entertainment and enjoyment, and the actual murder of an eighteen-month-old infant for the furtherance of some twisted ideological belief.

For the first time, Allison found herself wondering whether her portrayals of frivolous murder were an insult to victims of the real thing. To a woman with a signed contract for two more books in place, it was not a welcome thought.

In the middle of a deep sigh, the doorbell rang. By the time Allison had scrambled into a robe and hurried down the stairs, a tan sedan was disappearing up the drive. She opened the front door for a better look, and a large manila envelope that had apparently been propped against the door fell into the hallway.

Allison picked it up. Her name was written on it, but nothing else. She closed the door, took the envelope with her into the kitchen, and dropped it on the table. Only after she had started the coffeemaker, poured a glass of orange juice, and popped an English muffin into the toaster did she turn to it, slitting the top open with a bread knife.

Inside was a sheaf of some three dozen flagrantly inflammatory photographs, eight-by-ten glossy prints of butchered fetuses that Allison was apparently supposed to assume had been sucked and scraped out of uteruses during abortion procedures.

A note accompanying the photographs begged the author to consider the alternative. 'Are one hundred and seventy-six lives, albeit innocent, really too high a price to pay for the chance to save the million and a half lives each year that without a second thought are cut short of taking that first breath?'

The images were truly horrible to look at, and the note had a point. But they meant little if anything to Allison. Her personal definition of life began and ended with the viability of a fetus's survival outside the mother's womb. Even carrying her own daughter for nine months, feeling her kicking and turning and growing inside her, had not changed that.

The doorbell at Stuart Dunn's Renton home rang shortly after noon.

'I'll get it,' his eleven-year-old son shouted, bounding down the stairs. A moment later, the youngster skidded into the kitchen, carrying a thick manila envelope.

'Who was it?' Stuart asked, his eyes teary from chopping onions as he helped his wife prepare lunch.

'Nobody,' the boy replied. 'Just this.'

He handed the envelope to his father, and dashed out.

'What's that?' Stuart's wife asked.

'Haven't a clue,' the teacher said, wiping away the tears.

The envelope had his name scrawled across the front, no address, no return. He ripped it open, and pulled a stack of photographs from inside. They were identical to the ones Allison Ackerman had received. Affixed to the stack was a note that read: 'What you saw in court was indeed hideous, but was it more hideous than what happened to these poor souls, and the millions like them? Please, remember the voiceless. They have only you to speak for them now.'

'Oh my God,' Stuart murmured.

'What?' his wife asked, alarmed because his face had suddenly gone white.

Stuart shook his head slowly, and pushed the photos across the counter for her to see.

'But why would anyone send these to us?' she said, perplexed and angry by the intrusion of such wretchedness into her kitchen. 'We don't endorse abortion. We've never endorsed abortion.'

'What I want to know is how they found out.'

'Who? What?'

'No one was supposed to know who was on the jury,' Stuart told her. 'It was supposed to be kept confidential. But someone knows. Whoever sent me these knows.'

The light of understanding came into his wife's eyes. 'Of course,' she breathed, oddly relieved. 'What are you going to do about it?'

'I think I have to tell the judge,' the history teacher said.

'Will they take you off the jury, if you do?'

Stuart thought about that for a moment. 'It's possible, I guess. Maybe even probable. But it doesn't matter. I still have to tell.'

'But is it right that someone can manipulate the system like this?'

'No, it isn't right.'

'Then why should you pay? You're an honest man, and you would have rendered a fair and impartial verdict.'

'I know,' Stuart said with a sigh. 'But sometimes, that doesn't matter.' There was no way to hide his disappointment from his wife; she knew him far too well for that. He shrugged. 'Either way,' he reasoned, 'I guess my students are going to learn an important lesson about how our legal system really works.'

At two o'clock, barely minutes after the dinner dishes had been cleared away, a similar envelope was delivered to John Quinn's Ballard home.

'What the hell?' he demanded, when he saw the contents.

'What's the matter, dad?' his thirteen-year-old daughter asked. 'What's in there?'

'Nothing,' the contractor replied, quickly shoving the photographs under the bulk of the Sunday newspaper. 'Just junk mail.'

'What is it?' his wife asked, as soon as the girl left the room.

Quinn pulled the photographs out and handed them to her. 'They're pretty awful,' he warned.

'Good gracious,' she said, wincing as she glanced through them. 'These are sick. Why would anyone send them to you?'

'It must be about the trial,' he told her.

She took a second, longer look at the gruesome images. 'You mean, those antiabortion people found out you're on the Hill House jury? But how could they? Information about jurors is supposed to be kept confidential, isn't it?'

'Yes,' he said, 'but it's all I can think of.'

Fear crept into her eyes. 'These people are really crazy, you know,' she said. 'I've heard about some of the things they do to get their point across. If they went to all the trouble of finding out who you are, and where you live – who knows what they'd try to do to us? And who's going to protect us?'

Quinn nodded. The same thought had occurred to him. Trial or no trial, his first responsibility was to take care of his family.

Karleen McKay was showing property. The client was a fresh-faced young couple from South Carolina. In the first five minutes of meeting, Karleen learned that he was being transferred, and that she was pregnant, and that their marriage had almost ended six months after it began.

'We just didn't know each other very well,' the woman confided. 'And we probably got married for all the wrong reasons. It was just through the blessings of Jesus that we made it through the bad time.'

'How was that?' Karleen asked politely.

'I got pregnant,' the woman said. 'As unbelievable as it seems, it was the answer to my prayers. But I must say, it's an awesome responsibility. Just thinking about bringing another life into this world scares me.'

'Yes, it can be a life-altering experience,' Karleen said.

'I didn't know whether I was ready for children, but the minute I found out I was pregnant, well, everything changed. Do you have children?'

'No, I don't,' Karleen told her.

'Well, when you do, you'll know what I mean. It's like finding out what your real purpose is on earth.'

'I'm sure,' Karleen murmured.

'No, it's true,' the woman insisted. 'To tell you the truth, when my husband came home and told me we were being transferred to Seattle, well, I didn't want to come. I'd heard about that terrible bombing, and about how that nice naval lieutenant who's accused of doing it is probably going to be executed for it. And I told my husband, those must be godless people in Seattle. We can't take our unborn child there.'

'Oh, I don't think people here are much different than people anywhere,' Karleen suggested.

'Well, that's just what my minister back home told me,' the woman said. 'That there were good people everywhere. It just takes some of them longer to realize it. He said not to judge too harshly. He said God works in mysterious ways, and that before everything was said and done, the jury on that trial would do the right thing. Wasn't that wonderful of him to say that? Just to cheer me up?'

'Oh yes,' Karleen assured her.

'I mean, everyone has a right to be born, don't they?' she continued. 'Life is God's gift, and I think I know that as well as anyone. I mean, how would you have felt if you had never been born?'

'I rather think I would never have known the difference,' Karleen replied.

'Oh no, I don't believe that,' the woman exclaimed. 'I believe our souls precede us into this world. I believe we would know if someone sucked us out of our mother's nurturing womb before we had a chance to know full life.'

'I think the next house on the list is going to be perfect for you,' Karleen said.

'Yes, of course,' the woman responded. 'But I'm not giving up on you.'

'On me?' Karleen asked. 'What do you mean?'

'I mean I'm going to be praying,' the woman said fervently, 'just as hard as I can, that you and the rest of your jury will celebrate that young man's bravery, not profane it.'

Tom Kirby had taken to stopping by Judith Purcell's Beacon Hill home on Friday evening, and staying until Monday morning. He came in grimy work clothes, purported to have become grimy from crawling around other people's houses, and occasionally from odd jobs he did for her neighbors. Judith happily laundered his clothes for him.

She cooked dinners for him on Fridays, nothing fancy, casseroles mostly. She was relieved to learn that he actually liked macaroni and cheese. The rest of the time, they went out to restaurants, the three of them, and he paid. It was a small thing, but it helped.

After the first weekend that Kirby had come and stayed, she had a long conversation with Alex. The twelve-year-old had been surprisingly adult.

'Hey, mom, if this guy is someone you want to hang around with, I'm okay with it,' the boy said. 'I know how much you like it when he's here. I like him okay, too. He's pretty neat.' Alex kicked his shoe at the floor. 'Anyway, it's kinda nice, having another guy around the house, you know, someone to do guy things with. But if you just want me to get lost sometimes, I can go hang with friends.'

She hugged him hard. 'This is your home,' she said firmly. 'You're never in the way here, and no one wants you to get lost, not for anything, ever. It's just that I wouldn't like it if you felt, you know, uncomfortable. And I'd want you to tell me about it.'

Alex grinned. 'Hey, I'm a big kid,' he said, hugging her back. 'I know all about that stuff. You taught me, remember?'

'I'm not sure he'd ever admit it, but I think Alex really likes you,' she told Kirby on Sunday evening. 'Of course, I'm not exactly surprised. You're so good with him.'

The three of them had spent the day at Seattle Center, and then stopped at Burger King for dinner. Now Alex was asleep in the room down the hall, and she and Kirby were getting ready for bed.

'He's a good kid,' Kirby said. 'The kind I'd like to think I would have had, if I'd had a son. You've done a great job with him.'

Judith sighed. 'The way he hangs on your every word, I think he misses having a father.'

Kirby climbed into the four-poster and plumped up the pillows. 'I'm not sure I can tell you what I think you want to hear,' he said with a sigh.

'You've already told me,' she said. 'No strings. I know that.'

'I've got too many issues of my own to deal with,' he said, 'before I can take on anyone else's. I'm not real reliable. I don't stay in one place longer than it takes to start feeling too comfortable, if you know what I mean. And I'm starting to feel like I've already stayed here longer than I should.' It took him by surprise to realize he was actually telling her part of the truth, but he didn't think it would do any harm, and it might even help. 'I tried to be up front with you about all that.'

'Oh you were,' she said lightly, slipping into bed beside him. 'But you know us women. We always think, with enough good home cooking, we can change a man's mind about anything.'

He pulled her against him. 'I wish I had it all together, so I could be what you want,' he murmured into her hair. 'I wish I was as secure as you.'

She let out a laugh. 'Me, secure? Whatever gave you that idea?'

'Oh, I don't know. Just the way you act, I guess,' he said. 'You're so confident and sure of yourself. You and your friend both. I think you're two of the most self-sufficient women I ever met.'

'You mean Dana?'

'Yeah,' he replied.

'Well, you're right about her, but you're way off about me,' Judith said with a little chuckle. 'The last thing I am is self-sufficient. You should know that by now. I'm a definite leaner. Always have been, probably always will be.'

'Really? You could've fooled me. Why do you think Dana is so much more secure than you?'

Judith shrugged. 'I don't know. She just always seems to have everything going right for her, you know what I mean? It's been that way as long as I've known her. It's like she took control of her life the day she was born and never let go of it. She knows exactly what she wants and exactly how to get it. I don't

268

know how, but she does it. Even if something goes wrong, she's always been able to get past it, and just keep on going.'

'I doubt anything serious has ever gone wrong for her. She seems so . . . complete.'

'Well, she's been my best friend since grade school,' Judith said with a yawn, 'so I could tell you a thing or two. But of course, I can't.'

'Heavy private stuff, huh?' he asked, feeling the hair on the back of his neck begin to tingle.

'Oh yes,' Judith murmured, snuggling up against his chest. 'Very heavy.'

7

At twenty minutes past nine on Tuesday morning, Robert Niera knocked lightly on Abraham Bendali's door.

'Yes, Robert, come in,' the judge invited.

'I think we may have a little problem, Your Honor,' the bailiff said.

'What is it?' Bendali responded.

'A juror has just approached me with this,' he said, handing a manila envelope to the judge.

Bendali saw Stuart Dunn's name written on the envelope. He opened it, and extracted the contents, spreading the photographs out across his desk.

'Isn't this something,' he murmured. He picked up the note that had accompanied the photographs, and the expression on his face darkened. 'Just one?' he asked his bailiff.

'Actually, five spoke to me,' Robert replied. 'But I think more were contacted. Three of them got envelopes like this, two said they had been approached by other people.'

The judge wagged his head back and forth. 'Get opposing counsel in here,' he said.

'All right, Ms. McAuliffe, what do you know about this?' Bendali barked as soon as the prosecution and defense teams had assembled in his chambers.

'Absolutely nothing, Your Honor,' Dana replied, scanning the photographs. 'I assure you, I've never seen these before, I don't deal with people who promote this kind of politicking, and I'm as outraged about it as you are.'

Bendali fixed her with a stony stare and a raised eyebrow. 'Are you certain?'

Not in the least intimidated, Dana glared right back at him. 'Are you accusing me of jury tampering?' she asked.

'Should I be?'

'Hardly,' she said evenly. 'Like any decent attorney, I like to win, and I'll push the envelope as far as it can go in the interests of my client. But I never break the rules. If you don't know me well enough to know that, perhaps Mr. Ayres would be good enough to vouch for my integrity.'

Brian nodded. 'I can, and I do, Your Honor,' he said. 'I've known and worked with Ms. McAuliffe for well over a decade.'

'Then it seems we have a leak proportionate to that of the *Titanic*,' Bendali declared. 'What are we going to do about it?'

The attorneys glanced at each other.

'I guess we could call for a mistrial,' Brian said without much enthusiasm, because he was happy with the way his case was going, he liked the jury he had, and he really didn't want to start over.

'That would be an option,' Bendali said, and looked at Dana. 'Ms. McAuliffe?'

'Well, naturally, a mistrial isn't what we're looking for,' she said with a sigh, because she, too, liked the jury as seated. 'My client's been in jail for almost seven months now. Any further delay in clearing his name would be to his disadvantage. Obviously, he had no hand in this. And to penalize him for someone else's misdeed doesn't seem entirely fair. But, Mr. Ayres is within his rights.'

Bendali looked thoughtfully at both attorneys. 'I can't see that sequestering the jury at this point would help any,' he said. 'The damage, whatever it may be, is already done.'

Joan Wills had been studying the photographs. 'Excuse me, Your Honor,' she said now. 'May I say something?'

'Go right ahead.'

'Well, sir, I'm one of the defense attorneys here, and even so, I find myself offended, not impassioned, by these pictures. I think I would resent having them sent to me. Is it possible some of the jurors might feel that way, too? And if so, then maybe no serious damage has really been done, and we don't have to go to a mistrial.'

The judge scratched his jaw. 'Mr. Ayres, shall we have the jury in and find out, before I make a final decision?'

Brian nodded. 'By all means, Your Honor,' he said.

With Robert Niera leading the way, the twelve jurors and four alternates filed into the courtroom and took their seats. To their surprise, not only was the courtroom empty of spectators, but the judge in his voluminous black robe was not seated on the bench; he was standing in the well, conferring with counsel.

'Ladies and gentlemen,' Bendali began. 'Something has come to the attention of the court that we have to deal with. I understand that some of you have already spoken to the bailiff, but I now want to ask all of you a very important question.' The sixteen people sitting in the jury box glanced at one another. 'Over the past few days,' the judge continued, 'have any of you been approached, either indirectly or in person, by someone who appeared to have knowledge of your status as a juror in this proceeding, and attempted to influence you?'

Almost immediately, seven hands went up, and soon after, another six were raised. With a chart in his hand, Bendali surveyed the group.

'Juror Number 76,' he said. 'You didn't raise your hand. Does that mean you received nothing, and spoke to no one about this case over the weekend?'

'No,' cosmetologist Kitty Dodson replied, looking a bit embarrassed. 'But I went out with a friend Friday night, and I haven't been back to my place yet. Why? What did I miss?'

A giggle rippled through the jurors. Bendali smiled. 'Hopefully, nothing of any great importance,' he said. He checked his chart again. 'Juror Number 7, were you home for the weekend?'

'No, I wasn't, as a matter of fact,' Eliot Wickstine, the pilot, replied. 'Since we were off for three days, the wife and I went up to our cabin in Birch Bay. After that medical examiner's testimony, I needed a break.'

'I can relate to that,' the judge conceded, checking his chart a third time. 'And how about you, Juror Number 94?'

'I was home, safe and snug,' David Reminger, the computer programmer, reported. 'I was online most of the time, catching up. I had no unsolicited phone calls, no unexpected deliveries, no unfamiliar e-mails. But I'm unlisted. I have a privacy thing, and I make it a point to be unreachable, except by post office box, which I haven't checked yet today.'

Bendali nodded. 'All right,' he said to the group. 'Other than those who were not contacted, how do the rest of you feel about what happened?'

'I was surprised,' Elizabeth Kwan, the technical writer, said. 'I thought information about jurors was supposed to be kept confidential.'

'So it is,' the judge agreed. 'However, as you can see, sometimes things happen.'

'Well, I'm a barber,' Ralph Bergquist said. 'And I snuck in a little work on Saturday. And this guy comes in, and he's not one of my regulars, or anything. In fact, I'd never seen him before. But he sits himself down in my chair, and as soon as the towel is around his neck, he starts preaching at me, all about my moral duty to the preborn. So finally, I told him if I wanted preaching, I'd go to church, and then I kicked him out with only half his hair cut off. Served him right.'

'My wife's worried,' John Quinn admitted. 'Which means, I gotta worry. She thinks some of these people are lunatics and might try to harm us.'

At that, several jurors looked worried.

'Right now, I'm fairly confident that persuasion is what this is about,' Bendali reassured them all, 'not intimidation.'

'If that's the case, then I have bad news for whoever's doing it,' Karleen McKay declared. 'Because it had the opposite effect on me. I wasted my whole Sunday showing houses to a woman who may or may not be moving here from South Carolina, but who obviously was only interested in telling me how hard she was going to pray for my enlightenment.'

'I'm with you,' Bill Jorgenson, the Boeing employee, said. 'I might not have liked sitting through the medical examiner's testimony a whole lot, but I know why we had to do it. Those photographs I got were something else altogether. It wasn't fair. I needed the weekend to kick back, watch some baseball, relax a bit – not be put on overload.'

'I think people are entitled to their opinions,' Rose Gregory said. 'I watch Reverend Heal's Prayer Hour every day, and he's always been outspoken about his opposition to abortion, and about his support of the defendant in this case. But I don't mind telling you, I was very disappointed when I realized his inviting me to his gala on Saturday night was just an opportunity for him to try to convince me to vote to acquit. I think I have a right to make up my own mind.'

Bendali smiled. 'Not just a right,' he told her, 'but a duty.' He turned to the rest. 'If all of you feel the way Juror Number 68 has just said she feels, then perhaps we don't have a problem.'

'I came in here thinking I was the only one who got those photographs,' Stuart Dunn said. 'I thought, when I told, it would mean I would be removed from the jury, and I was angry about that. Once I realized most of us were approached, one way or another, I thought the only option would be a mistrial, and that made me even angrier, because it would mean those people had won. Well, I don't think we ought to send that message.'

'If I were to decide not to declare a mistrial,' Bendali said, 'are there any of you who would feel uncomfortable about continuing to serve on this jury?'

A number of jurors shook their heads, while several others simply shrugged.

'My wife,' John Quinn said with a sigh. 'It's no problem to me, but she worries. We got two kids. We got a dog.'

'Do you wish to be excused, Juror Number 116?' the judge asked.

'Don't do it, John,' Karleen McKay said. 'Stuart's right. Don't let them win.'

There was instant agreement from the rest of the group. The trial was just two weeks along, but Dana could not help noticing that the jurors had already bonded.

'Is there a way to protect us?' Quinn asked. 'I mean, protect our families and our homes?'

'If it came to that, yes,' Bendali declared unequivocally.

'Okay then, I'm not going to be a quitter,' the contractor said. 'I'll stick.'

The other jurors nodded their approval.

'One last question, then,' the judge concluded. 'In light of what's happened, do each and every one of you still believe you can come to a fair and impartial verdict in this case?'

All sixteen people in the jury box thought about that for a moment, and then nodded.

'Thank you for your input,' Bendali said. 'I'm going to recess court for today. You'll have my decision tomorrow.'

'Am I right to assume that the other side has the list as well?' Aaron Sapp, the philosophy instructor, asked.

The judge shrugged. 'Good question,' he said. 'At this point, it's not known. Why do you ask?'

'Well, it seems to me, if they do, and we get pressure from them down the road, then neither side will have the advantage,' he reasoned. 'They'll just cancel each other out.'

8

Abraham Bendali did not declare a mistrial, and Brian Ayres did not protest the decision. To be honest, the prosecutor couldn't be certain that the backlash from the incident hadn't actually worked in his favor.

Dana came away with the same impression, and it left her both irritated and intrigued. 'It's probably an impossible task,' she told Craig Jessup. 'But see if you can find out who leaked that jury list.'

'Leave it to me,' the private investigator said with a casual shrug. 'You know the old saying – the impossible just takes a little longer.'

'Do you really think he'll come up with anything?' Charles Ramsey asked. 'Sounds like a wild goose chase to me. And at his prices, a rather expensive one, at that.'

'He's the best in the business,' Dana reminded him. 'If the information's out there to find, you know he'll find it.' She looked at the senior partner. 'We've spared no expense on this case so far. If I'm supposed to start counting the pennies now, no one's told me.'

'Oh no, it's nothing like that,' Ramsey hastened to assure her. 'I just meant there must be some better use we could make of Jessup's time.'

Detective Dale Tinker had been on the job for twenty-eight years, having graduated fourth in his class from the police academy. He was a beat cop for the first three years of his career, then worked vice for five years before requesting a transfer to homicide, where he had been ever since. He held just about every commendation the Seattle police department had to offer, and he had earned the respect of his peers. They called him the Iron Man.

His hair was now almost totally gray, and the laugh lines around his eyes and mouth were permanently etched into his face. He tried to keep himself fit, but he liked beer too much, and a paunch had developed around his middle. He had just turned forty-nine, but he looked closer to sixty.

He had passed the advancement exam, and there had been talk, on and off, of moving him up, but nothing had come of it. A few glitches in his record, perhaps, some said. Lack of opportunities, others insisted; there was not a lot of room at the top. Something about domestic violence kept cropping up.

Tinker had worked close to six hundred homicides in his career, clearing an impressive eighty-two percent of them. But he had never worked one that meant as much to him as this one did. He thought he had seen everything. He thought he was tough, seasoned, beyond shock. Then he caught the call to Hill House, and for the first time in his twenty-eight years, he threw up at a crime scene. Like a rookie. Nobody in his squad teased him. It just made him more human, they thought. If anything, they respected him more.

He had handled this case from the beginning, tirelessly, relentlessly, waiting for the breaks to come his way, putting the pieces together, honing the ragged edges into a snug fit. He was not stupid, he knew this was his ticket to promotion, probably his last chance at it. When he took the witness stand on Wednesday morning, it was with confidence and determination.

'Detective Tinker,' Brian began, as soon as the oath had been administered and the police officer's credentials had been detailed, 'you were in charge of the Hill House investigation, is that correct?'

'I was in charge of the information-gathering phase of the investigation, yes,' Tinker replied.

'And what did this phase consist of?'

'Basically, it consisted of talking to survivors, talking to witnesses, evaluating witness statements, developing additional witnesses, linking information received from witnesses to possible suspects, interviewing possible suspects, and gathering potential evidence. In essence, following up on all the leads that eventually led to the apprehension of the defendant over there, the person we believe bombed Hill House.'

'Connecting all the dots, so to speak?'

'Yes, you could say that,' the police officer agreed amiably, taking his lead from the prosecutor. 'Connecting all the dots.'

'Then let's start at the beginning, Detective,' Brian suggested. 'And see exactly how the dots led you to Corey Latham.'

During his two days of direct testimony, Dale Tinker described the procedure he had followed in the Hill House investigation. 'We did everything by the book,' he assured the court. 'We knew how important this was, and we didn't want any of it coming back on us because of sloppy work or stupid mistakes.'

'It took you some six weeks to make an arrest,' the prosecutor said at one point. 'On average, is that a long time?'

'It depends on the case,' Tinker replied. 'Some solve quick, some take longer. Six weeks is a relatively short time for a major crime, really, but it probably seemed to the public like it took forever.'

'When, during that time, did you get your first concrete lead?'

'Well, we were collecting evidence right along, of course, but the big break came about a month into the investigation.'

'What break was that?'

'A sport utility vehicle with a military sticker was reported having been seen on Madison Street the night before the bombing.'

'What did you do as a result of that information?' Brian prompted.

'First we identified everyone connected with the seven military bases in the Puget Sound area who drove a dark-colored SUV,' Tinker declared. 'Then we visited the bases, and interviewed all those personnel we had previously identified. With permission from the owners, we also did a cursory inspection of those vehicles.'

'Then what?'

'We narrowed the list down, using some additional information we received, and then reinterviewed five naval officers at the Bangor Submarine Base. Based on those interviews, we determined the defendant to be a person of interest.'

'What was that additional information?' the prosecutor prompted.

'We received information that the wife of one of the officers at Bangor had an abortion at Hill House a couple months before the bombing, and that her husband was pretty steamed up about it.'

'What did you learn from speaking to the five officers at Bangor?'

'Our interviews confirmed that only one of the five had recently been in that situation: the defendant, Corey Latham.'

'What did you do then?'

'We obtained a search warrant.'

'And when you conducted the search of the defendant's home and vehicle,' Brian inquired, 'what, if anything, did you find?'

'First, we examined the defendant's sport utility vehicle, and collected what were later determined to be traces of chemicals and fibers that the FBI labs confirmed were consistent with those used to make the bomb that blew up Hill House. Then we performed a search of the home. Trace materials found in the defendant's garage produced the same results as those found in the vehicle.'

'Detective Tinker, why did you reach the conclusion that this crime was abortion-related?'

'We considered a number of alternatives, naturally, including international terrorism, the possibility of a disgruntled ex-employee, and the targeting of a particular current employee. We even considered random sabotage. But after our preliminary investigation, we settled on the abortion attack for one specific, and we think, valid reason.'

'And what was that reason?'

'When we interviewed the survivors, we learned something about the group of antiabortion protesters that had taken over the corner of Boren and Madison.'

'What about them?' Brian asked.

279

'They were always there,' Tinker said. 'Rain or shine. They came every day the clinic was open, half a dozen to a dozen of them.'

'Yes?'

'On the day of the bombing, they didn't show up,' the police officer said. 'Not one of them.'

In the Hill House section, Carl Gentry nodded, having been the one who supplied that bit of information to the police.

Craig Jessup called Dana at home at ten o'clock Thursday night.

'Sorry to be calling so late,' he said, 'but I wanted to be sure and catch you before you headed off to court tomorrow.'

'You found out already?' she asked.

'No, it's not about the jury list,' Jessup replied. 'I've got something else for you.'

'What?'

'A guy by the name of Pauley, Jack Pauley.'

'What about him?'

'How does means, motive, and opportunity sound?' the investigator replied.

'You have what appears to be a very impressive record,' Dana said to Dale Tinker, when the police officer returned to the stand on Friday morning.

'I just try to do my job the best I can, ma'am,' the detective said modestly.

'Yes, you claim an eighty-two percent arrest rate. I'd say that speaks for itself. But tell me, do you offhand know how many of your arrests result in convictions?'

Tinker shifted in his seat. 'No, I couldn't say.'

'Well, I could, Detective,' Dana said smoothly. 'But that's because I checked. It's only forty-eight percent. How would you explain that?'

The police officer shrugged. 'I'm not responsible for how prosecutors try their cases, or how juries come to a verdict,' he said. 'I give them the goods, I testify, and that's all I can do.'

In the second row of the jury box, Allison Ackerman smiled

to herself. While the evidence so far clearly tilted toward the defendant's guilt, she was coming to respect the defendant's attorney a little bit more each day. Here, in barely two minutes, McAuliffe had taken an upstanding police officer, who in direct testimony had come across as a shining protector of the people, and made him appear ever so slightly shoddy.

'Well, let's talk a little about those "goods," shall we, Detective?' Dana invited pleasantly. 'You've testified that once you received Mr. Auerbach's description of the vehicle parked on Madison Street the night before the bombing, you identified all local military personnel who drove such vehicles, is that correct?'

'Yes.'

'So you made two assumptions, did you not?'

'I'm sorry, I don't follow.'

'Well, first you assumed that this vehicle was somehow connected to the bombing.'

'Oh, I see what you mean. Well, we thought it was possible, yes.'

'And second, you assumed that this vehicle came from one of the local military bases.'

'Well, sure. It made more sense than to assume that someone from somewhere else had a reason to blow up a building in Seattle. And we couldn't very well investigate every military base in the country.'

Dana walked over to the defense table and picked up the poster she had shown to Milton Auerbach. 'I'd like you to take a look at this sticker, Detective, which was identified by the previous witness as looking like the one he saw that night.'

Tinker looked. 'Yes?' he said.

'It's a sticker from a United States military base, not here in Washington, but in Nevada.'

'I can see that. So what?'

'So, what kind of vehicle did you say the defendant drives?'

'He drives a dark green 1995 GMC Jimmy.'

'A 1995 Jimmy,' Dana echoed.

'That's right.'

'Well, tell me, Detective Tinker, what if I told you that this particular sticker came from the windshield of a 1996 charcoal gray Toyota 4Runner, and that it was parked on Madison Street between Minor and Summit on the very same night?'

There was a startled murmur in the courtroom, and the judge had to rap his gavel several times to restore order. Brian glanced sharply at Mark Hoffman, but the associate shook his head in response. Dale Tinker glared at Brian, who shrugged.

'Objection, Your Honor,' Brian said uneasily. 'Does defense counsel have some evidence of this other vehicle to introduce?'

'If it becomes necessary,' Dana replied.

'Objection overruled,' Bendali ruled. 'Proceed.'

'Detective Tinker?' Dana prompted.

'Mr. Auerbach said the car he saw was parked between Minor and Boren,' the police officer insisted.

'Yes, I know,' Dana responded. 'But it was late at night, it was his fiftieth wedding anniversary, his wife was dying, and he had just had champagne. Couldn't he be forgiven for making one small mistake?'

'I don't know that he made a mistake,' Tinker said defensively.

'That's true,' Dana conceded. 'Well then, let's move on to that additional piece of information you received about the naval officer whose wife had had an abortion at Hill House. Where exactly did that information come from?'

'It was a tip.'

'Yes, of course. I understand that. But what sort of tip was it?'

'What do you mean?'

'Well, we all know that the police get tips from informants all the time. I'm simply asking if this particular tip came from one of your regular, reliable sources, or from someone else.'

'Someone else,' he mumbled.

'And who was that?'

'We don't reveal the names of our informants,' Tinker said.

'I do realize that,' Dana acknowledged. 'So let me put it another way. Was anyone in your department acquainted with the person who provided you with this particular information?'

There was a long pause. 'No,' the detective said finally. 'It was an anonymous tip.'

'Anonymous?'

'Yes,' Tinker admitted.

'Did you record the call? Were you able to trace it?'

The detective scowled. 'It wasn't a call, so we couldn't trace it. It was an anonymous letter.'

A buzz rose among the spectators, and several members of the jury, including Allison Ackerman, blinked.

'But that doesn't make it any less reliable,' Tinker argued. 'It turned out to be true, didn't it?'

'Did you make any effort to find out who sent this anonymous letter?' Dana inquired, choosing to ignore his last remark.

He shrugged carelessly. 'Sure we tried, but we didn't get anywhere.'

'I see.'

'Look, we had the old man's ID on the car, and we had a tip about an abortion,' Tinker declared. 'We put it together, and took it where it led us, which was right to the door of your client.'

'So it was,' Dana murmured. 'Now, let's take a look at all this incriminating evidence you claim to have found when you searched my client's premises. You say there was aspirin residue in the Jimmy, is that correct?'

'Yes, all over it, front and back, and we found it in the garage, too.'

'Was it a particular kind of aspirin? A special brand, perhaps? Or some exceptionally high dosage used specifically for bomb making?'

'No, it was just ordinary aspirin, which according to the FBI is exactly what would be used for bomb making.'

'You say there were traces of sulfuric acid, as well, is that also correct?'

'Yes, both in the car and in the garage.'

'What is sulfuric acid most commonly associated with, Detective?'

'Well, it's something you'd find in car batteries, if that's what you're asking,' Tinker replied.

'Yes, that's exactly what I was asking,' Dana confirmed. 'And how about the fertilizer you found in the car and in the garage? Was this some rare variety of fertilizer, one that would have to be purchased for the specific purpose of making a bomb?'

'No, it was common garden fertilizer.'

'Common garden fertilizer? You mean the kind someone would use to, say, fertilize a bed of roses?'

Tinker shrugged. 'I suppose. But you don't need any special fertilizer to make a bomb, just one that has a high enough concentrate of sodium nitrate.'

'All right,' Dana continued. 'Now, you say you found fibers consistent with the material used to make duffel bags, is that correct?'

'Yes,' he replied. 'Once again, in the vehicle and in the garage.'

'What kind of duffel bags?'

'Military duffel bags.'

'Detective Tinker, relying on your expertise, gained from twenty-eight long years as a police officer, would you say that it would be unusual to find fibers from a military duffel bag in the vehicle and in the home of a military man?'

'Of course not,' Tinker replied. 'That was the whole point. We came to it from the other direction, you see. Fibers from a military duffel bag were found at the crime scene.'

'Yes,' Dana agreed. 'And we've already heard testimony about the easy availability of military duffel bags to the general public. So let me ask you, did you find any methyl alcohol in your search of Mr. Latham's premises?'

'No.'

'How about Vaseline?'

'No.'

'Nothing as common as Vaseline was found anywhere in the house?'

'No.'

'How about wax?'

'No,' Tinker said.

'According to the FBI expert, whose testimony the court heard, those ingredients were necessary parts of the bomb, too. How do you explain not finding any traces of them in Corey Latham's car or home?'

'I can't,' Tinker admitted. 'Look, a case doesn't always get handed to us, all wrapped up nice and neat, the way we might like it to be. If it did, then we'd have everything we needed to make it airtight. We don't. But we did find enough concrete evidence to arrest your client with confidence. That's our job, and we did it. He had the means, the military know-how to make a bomb. He had the motive; his wife had an abortion and he was steamed about it. And he had the opportunity; we found what could have been bomb-making materials right there on his premises. On top of that, his alibi could not be reliably confirmed, and his vehicle was seen at the scene.'

Dana turned on him sharply. '*His* vehicle, Detective?' she challenged.

'Well, a vehicle that was identified as being consistent with his,' Tinker amended.

'You said, "consistent with." That simply means the vehicle might have looked something like the one he drives, doesn't it, not that the vehicle seen at the scene *was* his?'

'Yes.'

'That vehicle was never identified by anyone as a 1995 GMC Jimmy, was it?'

'No,' he conceded.

'So what we have is a man who was understandably upset because his wife had an abortion,' Dana summarized thoughtfully. 'A man who uses military duffel bags because he's in the military. A man who was undeniably in possession of lethal products like aspirin, fertilizer, and battery acid. And a man who is unlucky enough to drive a car that might or might not resemble one that might or might not have been seen at the scene the night before the bombing. Do I have it all straight now?'

'Yes,' Tinker said grudgingly.

'And on the basis of that – what did you call it – concrete

evidence? – you stopped looking for anyone else, didn't you?'

'Yes.'

'Why?'

'Because we were sure we had the right guy.'

'The *right* guy, Detective Tinker, or after six weeks of extraordinary pressure – *any* guy?'

He sighed. 'You can see it your way,' he said. 'We see it ours. Whether you like it or not, every bit of evidence we were able to gather pointed directly at only one person, your client, and no one else.'

'How would you know?'

'I beg your pardon?'

'You latched on to the defendant, and stopped looking at anyone else, didn't you?'

'Let me remind you that we were out there "looking," as you call it, for a month before we got to him. We found nothing.'

'Couldn't that simply mean that the real perpetrator was better at what he did than you were at what you did?'

'In my experience, that's rarely the case.'

'Granted, it's rarely the case,' Dana conceded. 'But is it possible?'

Tinker shrugged dismissively. 'Anything's possible, I guess.'

Brian Ayres stirred in his seat. He had a feeling he wasn't going to like where this was headed.

'Then isn't it also possible, Detective,' Dana pressed, 'that someone else planted the bomb at some other time between nine in the evening and eight in the morning, and therefore wasn't noticed by Mr. Auerbach, or anyone else who has yet come forward? Which is why you haven't caught him?'

'Again, Ms. McAuliffe, if you're going to insist on the hypothetical, anything's possible.'

'Detective Tinker, who is Jack Pauley?'

'I have no idea,' he replied, doing his best to control his irritation.

In the Hill House section, Frances Stocker's head shot up. The detective might not know who Jack Pauley was, but the psychologist did. She still saw his wife in her nightmares, a limp doll with her head attached by a thread to her neck.

'What if I told you that Jack Pauley works in construction, and is considered a demolitions expert? What if I also told you that he's a drunk and a wife abuser? What if I further told you that his wife had an appointment with a therapist at Hill House on the very day of the bombing, and that he ran a real risk of exposure? Would that jog your recollection any?'

'I remember the name now,' Tinker said, pulling a small notebook out of his jacket pocket, and thumbing quickly through it to refresh his memory. 'Let's see, wasn't his wife killed in the bombing?'

'Yes,' Dana corroborated. 'As a matter of fact, she was.'

'There were two young kids,' he said, finding the page. 'We talked to the guy. He said he was out with some friends the night before the bombing.'

'Did you check?'

'Yes, of course we checked,' Tinker retorted. 'We're not amateurs, Ms. McAuliffe. We confirmed he was at the bar he said he was at until about one o'clock in the morning. And we also confirmed that he drives a red Dodge pickup.'

'Where did he go after he left his friends?'

'He went home, I guess.'

'You guess?'

'Well, we couldn't prove otherwise.'

'I see,' the defense attorney declared. 'So, here we have someone else with means, motive, and opportunity. He's a demolitions expert. His wife was seeking therapy at Hill House after years of physical abuse, and might well have ended up leaving him, if not pressing criminal charges against him. And no one can vouch for his whereabouts after he left his friends. Don't you think he deserved a second look, Detective?'

'We didn't know about the abuse,' Tinker admitted. 'There was no insurance policy or anything like that. We checked. The guy seemed all broken up over his wife's death, so we didn't see that there was any motive.'

'You mean, he didn't fit your profile, don't you?' Dana suggested. 'His wife hadn't had an abortion, he didn't own an

SUV with a military sticker, and he had an alibi for Milton Auerbach's narrow window of time shortly after midnight.'

'That's right,' the detective snapped, finally unable to keep the hostility from his voice.

'Thank you,' Dana said, sensing the moment. 'I have nothing more.'

With the wisdom that comes from decades on the bench, Abraham Bendali ordered a recess, and no sooner had judge and jury filed out than the courtroom erupted. Angry spectators began to toss heated words at one another. The group from Hill House turned to Frances Stocker, seeking confirmation of the defense's charge. Reporters dashed out to file new leads for their stories.

Brian Ayres, clearly caught off guard, turned to Dana. 'Where did you get that information?' he demanded.

'What information?' Dana asked innocently.

'Don't play games with me,' he barked, seeing his case suddenly in shambles. 'How did you get that stuff on Pauley?'

'The same way you would have if your police department had been doing its job,' she retorted.

'And what about the other thing? Where did that Nevada sticker come from? Was there really a 4Runner parked between Summit and Minor that night?'

At that, Dana shrugged. 'Whether it was there that night or some other night, it doesn't matter,' she said. 'What matters is that your Detective Tinker should have made it his business to find out.'

'Dammit,' he said under his breath.

'I warned you, Dink,' she reminded him. 'Rush to judgment, remember? You know me. You should've listened.'

9

Dinner at the Dunn house was always a boisterous affair, with eight people clamoring for food and attention at the same time. Oblivious to it all on this night, however, Stuart was playing with his food, pushing a stack of fish sticks around a mound of potatoes on his plate, first into a square, then a triangle, and finally being brave enough to try a circle.

'What's the matter?' his wife asked. 'I thought you liked fish sticks and mashed potatoes.'

'It's the trial,' he mumbled, glancing around the table. Seven pairs of eyes were focused on him. He stuffed a fish stick in his mouth, followed by a bite of potatoes, embarrassed at being caught. 'I guess it's put me a little off my feed.'

His wife nodded. 'Not as much fun as you thought it would be?'

Stuart shrugged. 'I feel like a piece of taffy, you know. First the prosecutor pulls you in one direction and then, just when you think you're on firm ground, the defense comes on and pulls you back in the other direction. It's only three weeks, and I'm already worn out. What a process.'

'It could be worse, dad,' his eleven-year-old said with all the angst of a sixth-grader. 'You could be back in school.'

Elise Latham reached Dana at home late on Saturday. 'The police came back,' she said.

'What did they want?' the attorney asked.

'I don't know, they didn't tell me. They just went to the closet, and took Corey's seaman's cap and his windbreaker.'

'That's all?'

'That's all.'

'Thank you for calling,' Dana said. She hung up the telephone with a puzzled frown on her face.

'What's the matter?' Sam asked.

'I'm not sure,' she replied.

Elise hung up the telephone and put on her coat. Then she slipped out the back door, cut through to the alley behind the house, and made her way to the waiting BMW.

'Allison, it's Julia Campbell,' the voice at the other end of the telephone said.

'Hello,' Allison replied breathlessly. It was a little after eleven o'clock on Sunday morning, and she had just that moment come in from the pasture.

'Well, I know we were supposed to wait until you were finished with your jury duty thing before we got together, but I find myself in need of some advice, and I was hoping you wouldn't mind my jumping the gun a bit, and calling you now.'

'Not at all. What can I do for you?'

'Well, I'm assuming that you know a good horse vet,' Julia said with a little sigh.

'Sure,' Allison responded. 'At least, I think the one I use is pretty good. Why? What's wrong?'

'I don't know. One of my mares is acting funny.'

'Well, his name is Bill Barrett, and he's in the book, but I don't know where you'll be able to reach him today.'

'Oh, that's right, it's Sunday. I forgot. Why is it our animals always seem to have a crisis on weekends?'

'He has an emergency number. I can give it to you if you think it's that serious.'

'That's just it, I don't know. She seems fine, and then I saddle her up, and she starts tearing the place apart.' There was a pause. 'I don't suppose you'd be willing to come take a look at her, would you? Maybe an objective eye would tell me if it's serious.'

The last thing Allison wanted to do was go out on the one day of the week she reserved for her animals. With a sigh, she reached for a pad and pen on the nightstand. 'Sure,' she said. 'Tell me where you are.'

An hour later, the two women sat in Julia Campbell's warm, cheerful kitchen, drinking coffee.

'You probably think I'm a ninny,' Julia said. 'Not to think of something so simple as having a burr in the cinch.'

Allison shrugged. 'As you said, sometimes it takes an objective eye.'

'Well, I thank you, and the mare thanks you.' Julia got up and poured more coffee. Then she pulled a tin of muffins, a spinach omelet, and a platter of sausages from the oven, and put them on the table.

'Oh, I shouldn't,' Allison said.

'But I insist,' her hostess declared. 'I drag you out on a Sunday, you save me a veterinarian bill, not to mention keeping me from making a complete fool of myself. The least I can do is feed you.'

'In that case,' the author said, 'you twisted my arm.'

'So,' Julia said casually, as the food was being devoured, 'how's your trial going?'

Allison rolled her eyes. 'Let's just say, I'd like to be somewhere else. Anywhere else, actually.'

'That bad?'

'Well, that grisly, anyway.'

'Oh my, are you on a murder case?'

'A murder case to end all murder cases, I'm afraid.'

Suddenly, Julia's eyes popped. 'Oh no,' she said. 'Don't tell me you're on the jury in that terrible bombing case.'

'That's the one,' Allison said.

'Well, you have my deepest sympathy,' Julia declared. 'I can imagine, just from the little I've been seeing on television and reading in the newspapers, how horrendous it must be.'

'Some of it *has* been pretty bad,' Allison admitted. 'A lot worse than I anticipated.'

'I know you can't talk about the trial itself, but I'm really surprised you even got on the jury,' Julia said. 'I thought that McAuliffe woman was supposed to be so smart. You'd think she would have excused you right off the bat. I don't know what she could have been thinking. But you sure found a way to fool her.'

'I did?'

'Well, I mean, I know you. I know what you believe in. And in spite of that, you figured out how to get on that jury.'

'To be honest, I never expected to get on,' Allison said. 'I gave both sides plenty of opportunity to kick me off. I was certain one of them would. And I'm as surprised as you are that neither did.'

'Amazing,' Julia murmured. 'With all the research they do on prospective jurors these days, and all those high-priced consultants they're using, I can't believe McAuliffe didn't know.'

'Know what?'

'Well, know that with you on the jury, she would never get an acquittal.'

'Why is that?' Allison asked.

Julia looked puzzled. 'I guess I just assumed,' she said. 'I mean, of course you'll vote to convict, won't you? How could you not? He's guilty, isn't he?'

'I don't know yet,' Allison replied carefully. 'Do you?'

'Oh come on,' Julia exclaimed. 'From everything we're hearing about the case, it's obvious he's guilty as sin. You can't have any doubt about that, despite his attorney's bag of tricks. Besides, you don't want to send the wrong message, do you?'

'What message is that?' The author knew she was not supposed to discuss anything about the case, but she was intrigued.

'You don't want people to think that the continued suppression of women is acceptable, do you?' Julia demanded, then dismissed the idea. 'No, of course you don't. You couldn't possibly. You're one of us.'

'If by that you mean a committed member of FOCUS, yes I am,' Allison granted.

'Sure you are. And I don't have to tell you that we're fighting for our very existence here, and the future of our daughters and our granddaughters. That's what this election is all about, for

292

heaven's sake. Making sure we get the proper people into office. People who will make women's rights a Constitutional protection. But of course, you know that.'

'Yes, I know that,' Allison said. 'But what does it have to do with this trial?'

'It's because you're *somebody*,' Julia declared. 'And when a somebody speaks, people listen. You've just been given the most visible platform in the country, my girl. You have to use it to promote our position. And what could support our position more than the conviction of a terrorist like Corey Latham? Landing on this jury might have been a fluke, but now that you've done it, let's be practical – you've got to take advantage of it.'

10

'They've added a witness,' Joan Wills told Dana the next morning.

'Who?'

'Someone named Joshua Clune.'

'Who is he?' Dana inquired.

'Haven't a clue,' Joan replied with a shrug. 'But they're putting him up first thing.'

'Get Craig Jessup on it immediately,' Dana said, already out the door.

Joshua had never been so scared in his whole life. Not even when that car had plowed into him all those years ago in Wisconsin, and he had been in the hospital for so long, and had ended up with the scar on his face. In fact, he felt a little like that now, like he could see something awful coming, and he couldn't do anything about it.

He had thought over what Big Dug said about talking to the police for almost a week before he agreed to go. Then he took Big Dug up on his offer to go with him.

'They aren't going to put me in jail, are they?' he kept asking.

'No, they're not,' Big Dug assured him. 'They're just going to talk to you, and then take down what you say, that's all. And it might not end up being important at all.'

So Joshua talked to the police, to a man with gray hair named Tinker. He told him that he had seen the delivery man, but couldn't identify him.

'He was tall, and he had on a jacket and one of those soft caps.'

'Do you know what time it was that you saw the – uh – the delivery man?' Tinker had asked.

'Well, I know it was after McDonald's closed,' Joshua remembered. 'That's at eleven.'

'How soon after?'

Joshua shrugged. 'I don't think I know that. I was asleep. I woke up. I don't have a watch.'

They talked for a little more than two hours before Tinker thanked him for coming in and told him he didn't think it would be necessary for him to testify.

'What's testify?' he asked Big Dug when they were on their way back down to the waterfront.

'It's when you have to go into the courtroom, and swear to tell the truth, and sit in a chair in front of a whole bunch of people, and you get asked a lot of questions,' his friend told him.

'But then, everyone would know what I did,' Joshua cried, aghast. 'They would know I slept at Hill House when I wasn't supposed to.'

'Well, I don't think you have to worry about that,' Big Dug said. 'Didn't the policeman say you wouldn't have to testify?'

He had, but then he had apparently changed his mind, because first thing Saturday morning, two uniformed officers had come looking for him. Without Big Dug there to protect him, they had driven him to the police station, put him in a cell, and left him there for a long time. Finally, he was taken to a room with a table and some chairs and a big mirror in it, and the gray-haired policeman.

'Joshua, we're going to have to go over your statement again,' Tinker told him.

And they had, for the rest of Saturday, and on into Sunday. They talked endlessly, and they showed him pictures, and then they talked some more, and showed him more pictures, until Joshua wasn't sure any longer what he had really seen that night at Hill House, or what they told him he had seen.

On Monday morning, they let him shower, and gave him a pair of clean jeans and a shirt to put on, and then took him to the courthouse, and told him to wait. Then a different man had come in and asked him questions, and Joshua answered as best he could remember, but his head began to hurt. The only good thing about the whole weekend, if he could say anything about it was good, was that they brought him whatever he wanted to eat, and there was a bed in the cell where he slept.

But now he was alone and frightened and very confused. He didn't want to go into the courtroom place they told him about, in front of strange people, and answer any more questions. He wanted to go back to the waterfront and find Big Dug. His friend was sure to be worried about him by now, he'd been gone for such a long time. Joshua wondered suddenly if anyone would think maybe he wasn't coming back, and take his box and his blanket.

Big Dug had been wrong. The police *had* put Joshua in jail, after all. They had simply waited until his friend wasn't there to stop them. And he was worried that they were going to keep him there because now they knew for certain that he had slept at Hill House.

'I'm not sandbagging you,' Brian assured Dana when the defense attorney stormed into his office. 'I got word of this witness's availability exactly five minutes before I sent word to you through Joan. And if you want a continuance before you cross, I won't oppose it.'

'What's his testimony?' Dana asked.

'He's an eyewitness.'

'An eyewitness to what?'

'He can place the defendant at the scene, at the time we believe the bomb was set.'

'If there's anything,' Dana implored her client just before court was due to convene, 'anything at all that, for whatever reason, you didn't feel able to disclose before, now's the time to tell me.'

'About what?' Corey asked.

'They're putting a witness on the stand this morning who

can corroborate Milton Auerbach's testimony. He can put you at Hill House the night before the bombing.'

There was a pause while Corey looked at her with an empty expression in his eyes. 'There's nothing to tell,' he said finally. 'I guess I can't believe, after all these months, that you don't know that.'

Dana sighed. 'I had to ask, I had to hear you say it,' she told him. 'All right then, let's go hear what this mystery witness has to say, and hope to hell I've got a miracle or two tucked away in some pocket I've forgotten about.'

Joshua shuffled to the stand with the aid of a deputy, who placed his left hand on the Bible, and showed him what to do with his right hand. The clerk read the oath, and the deputy nodded.

'I do,' Joshua said, as he had been rehearsed.

Then the deputy sat him down and retreated. Joshua smiled at him, and gave a little wave as the man took a seat at the rear of the courtroom.

'Please state your name and address,' the clerk instructed.

'Joshua Clune,' the witness recited. 'I live in Seattle, under the viaduct.'

A murmur rippled through the spectator section, and Dana blinked in surprise.

'A homeless man?' Joan whispered.

'Brian must really be panicking,' Dana whispered back, knowing, as far as most juries were concerned, that homeless people rarely made credible witnesses.

'Joshua,' the prosecutor said kindly, 'how long have you lived under the viaduct?'

'As long as I been here,' Joshua replied, smiling broadly. 'It's real nice. I have my own box and my own blanket. That is, I do if someone didn't take them by now because I been gone so long. And I have good friends, like Big Dug.'

'You said, as long as you've been here. How long is that?'

'Well, let's see,' Joshua replied, scratching a bit at his freshly washed hair. 'It must be close on a year now. I think I came in

October.' He paused for a moment and then nodded. 'It must have been October, 'cause I remember it wasn't raining yet. It didn't rain until November.'

Dana quickly scribbled down the words 'Big Doug,' and looked up to see that several members of the jury were beginning to smile. She had to admit, with a sinking heart, it was easy to like the young man.

'All right, Joshua,' Brian continued, 'tell us about when you got sick.'

'I got sick in the end of January,' Joshua replied. 'I had a cough and a fever, and my throat hurt real bad.'

'And what did you do?'

'Big Dug took me to Hill House, to see the doctor.'

'And what did the doctor do?'

'He examined me real good, and then he told me to come back the next day for medicine.'

'And did you?'

Joshua looked down. 'Uh-huh,' he mumbled.

'I'm sorry,' Brian prompted him, 'but you'll have to speak up.'

'I went back to Hill House,' Joshua said in a louder voice.

'The next day, like the doctor told you?'

The witness looked as though he might cry. 'No,' he said, almost whispering. 'I went the night before.'

'Why did you do that?' Brian asked gently.

'Because I forget, sometimes,' Joshua said. 'And I didn't want to forget the doctor, and not get my medicine.'

'What did you do at Hill House when you went there?'

'I found a little place toward the back, where it was nice and cozy, and I went to sleep.'

'What time did you go to sleep, Joshua, do you remember?'

'I went to sleep around ten and then I woke up. When I woke up it was around eleven-thirty.'

'How do you know what time it was?'

'Because McDonald's had just closed and the people who work there were going home. That's what woke me up.'

'And what happened when you woke up?'

298

'Not much for a while. Then the delivery man came.'

'What do you mean, the delivery man?'

'A man came to the clinic. He had packages and he took them down the basement.'

'How much later?'

'I don't know . . . about half an hour. Maybe a little more.'

'So sometime around midnight, a man came to Hill House and took packages down into the basement?'

'Uh-huh.'

'Did you see the man clearly?'

Joshua shrugged. 'It was dark, but I could see him.'

'What can you tell us about him?'

'He had on a jacket.'

'What kind of jacket?'

'It was dark and it had a zipper.'

Brian picked up a navy windbreaker. 'You mean, like this?'

'Yes, that's it.'

'Anything else?'

'He had on a cap.'

'What kind of cap? Like a baseball cap?'

Joshua shook his head. 'No, like a winter cap.'

Brian picked up a navy blue seaman's cap, and showed it to the witness. 'Like this?'

'Yes,' Joshua said. 'Just like that.'

'Were you able to see the man himself, what he looked like?'

Joshua nodded solemnly. 'It was dark, but I could see pretty good,' he said, looking at Corey Latham. 'It was him.'

11

It was early afternoon before Brian finished his examination of Joshua Clune, and the judge advised the jury that the trial would not resume until Wednesday. 'If you need more time,' he told Dana, 'just let my clerk know.'

'What do we do now?' Joan asked as the two attorneys left the courthouse.

'We wait for Craig Jessup to come up with something,' Dana replied. 'And we pray.'

The jurors were delighted to have a day off. In twos and threes, they filed out of the courthouse, into the autumn sunlight, threading their way through the crowds that threatened to block Third Avenue completely, and had already slowed traffic to a crawl. Since the start of the trial, the number of people converging on the area had increased dramatically, from a few dozen during jury selection to what was now estimated to be close to a thousand. They brandished their banners and their posters, shouted their messages, sold their trinkets, prayed, and sang. Aside from a few minor skirmishes, however, the demonstrations had been peaceful. A full complement of police was on hand each day to try to keep it that way.

'Look at them all,' Karleen McKay commented to Allison Ackerman, as the two women exited together. 'Don't any of them have jobs to go to?'

'For a lot of them, I think this *is* their job,' the author replied.

'Protect the preborn,' a short, slender man with inch-thick eyeglasses beseeched the two jurors, trying to stuff his pamphlets into their hands. 'Celebrate life.'

'Protect free choice,' a short, heavyset woman with facial hair pleaded with them, trying to press her flyers into their hands. 'Without it, we're no better than slaves.'

'I'm dizzy,' Karleen said, as they got to James Street and turned left.

'I'm nauseated,' Allison said.

They parted company at the parking garage on the corner of James and Second. It was on the tip of Allison's tongue to ask Karleen if she'd like to go for coffee, but it would have been awkward. The trial was what they had in common, and they were not allowed to discuss it.

The mystery writer drove home to Maple Valley instead, fixed herself a peanut butter and jelly sandwich, and poured herself a glass of milk. 'Comfort food' her mother called it, when Allison was a child and worrying over something. It had always worked, and she had done the same with her own daughter.

Allison sat at the kitchen table while she ate, and watched the horses frolicking in the pasture. Joshua Clune was on her mind. Homeless he might be, and developmentally delayed, as well, but he was also believable. He had no reason to lie. And his identification of Corey Latham was the first piece of evidence in the three-week-long trial that tied the defendant directly to the crime. It was a while coming, she thought, but could not have been more welcome.

'I'm getting real worried about Joshua,' Big Dug told the nondescript man who had casually sought him out Tuesday morning. 'He disappeared on Saturday. I'm starting to think something awful might have happened to him.'

'I guess it depends on how you look at it,' Craig Jessup said with a shrug. 'He appears to be in police custody.'

'The cops got Joshua?' Big Dug looked puzzled. 'Why? What did he do?'

'I don't know that he did anything,' Jessup replied. 'All I know is they had him in court this morning, testifying at a trial.'

'The Hill House trial?' Big Dug asked.

'Why would you think that?' the investigator asked.

'Because he was there that night, at Hill House,' the behemoth replied. 'The night before the bomb went off. I think he saw the guy who planted it.'

Jessup's stomach fell. 'Is that so?'

'But when the police interviewed him a couple weeks ago, they said he wouldn't have to testify.'

'Why was that?'

'Because he couldn't identify the guy,' Big Dug said. 'All he really saw was a shadow. He couldn't be positive it was that fellow they arrested. The best he could do was say it might be him.'

'Are you sure?' Jessup inquired.

'Sure I'm sure. I showed him the defendant's picture in the newspaper, and even took him to a bar so he could see the guy on television. Joshua couldn't identify him, not for certain.'

The investigator frowned. 'I see,' he said.

'What're the police gonna do with Joshua?'

'Don't worry, I don't think they'll do anything bad to him,' Jessup said. 'They're probably just keeping track of him until his testimony is over. I expect you'll see him back here very soon.'

'It's my fault, you know,' Big Dug admitted. 'I'm the one made him go to the police in the first place. He didn't want to go. I promised him they wouldn't put him in jail. But that's what they did, isn't it? They put him in jail. After I promised him they wouldn't.'

'I think so,' Jessup said.

'The poor kid, he must be scared to death. And he'll probably never trust me again, after this. Look, mister, you seem to be in the know. Do you think you could maybe make sure he's doing okay? He's a little slow in the head, you see. He needs looking after.'

'I'll do what I can,' the investigator promised, already knowing what he had to do.

Judith Purcell didn't remember driving home. She didn't remember getting out of her car, or going into the house. When

Tom Kirby found her, she was sitting on the stairs, in the dark, still in her coat.

'What's the matter?' he asked in alarm.

She shook her head, as if to clear it. 'What time is it?'

'It's almost six,' he told her. 'Where's Alex?'

'What day is this?'

'What do you mean, what day is this? It's Tuesday.'

'Then Alex's at basketball practice. What are you doing here?'

'I left my blue shirt.'

'Oh,' she said. 'I didn't wash it.'

'Don't worry about it. Just tell me what's wrong.'

What's wrong, she thought, is my whole life is about to collapse. The vice president of the bank had been very kind, but what could he do?

'I'm sorry, Ms. Purcell,' he had said, 'but your mortgage payments, well, they haven't been made in months. We notified you, repeatedly. We tried to help. We warned you this might happen. We have no choice.'

'It's nothing,' she told Tom. What was the point in crying on his shoulder? He couldn't help her. She didn't know how he made ends meet, as it was. Whatever it was, when her husband had died so unexpectedly, when her second marriage had fallen apart, no matter, Judith had always somehow managed to land on her feet. Only this time, she knew there was nothing but quicksand beneath her.

'Well, if this is nothing,' he said, 'I'd hate to see you when it's something. Talk to me.'

She looked up at him then and sighed. 'I'm going to lose my house,' she said.

'What do you mean, lose your house? Why?'

'Because I haven't been able to pay the mortgage for a while, and the bank's going to foreclose.'

'How long haven't you paid the mortgage?'

She shrugged. 'Six months.'

'Why didn't you tell me?' he demanded.

'What for?' she replied. 'It's my problem, not yours. Besides, I didn't think you were in a position to help me.'

303

'Well, you should have told me anyway,' he insisted. 'Who knows? I might have been able to come up with something.'

She smiled wistfully. 'For someone who doesn't want to get too serious, you're sounding awfully serious, all of a sudden.'

'Look, maybe I don't have the kind of money you need, but there has to be an answer here,' he said. 'Do you own anything of value that you could take a loan on?'

'Anything of value I might have had is long gone,' she told him.

'What about your friend Dana? She must earn a good living. Couldn't she lend you some money?'

'She's been buying my work at twice its market value for years now. I can't ask her for any more.'

'Well, how about your family?'

'My mother's done all she can, too,' Judith said, biting her lip to keep it from quivering. 'I'm really at the end this time. And it's not that I mind for me so much, but I mind so terribly for Alex. Having a useless mother isn't his fault, and he shouldn't have to pay for it.'

'What will you do?' he asked.

She shrugged. 'I don't know. Try to get some kind of job, I guess, although God knows what I'm equipped for. Find a cheap apartment for us to live in, if I can. I kept thinking, my big commission is right around the corner, you know,' she said with a catch in her voice. 'The one that'll make my name, and put me over the top.' Tears finally began to roll down her cheeks. 'I'm good at what I do, I really am,' she sobbed. 'It isn't fair.'

'There may be a way,' he said.

'There isn't,' she said through her tears. 'Believe me, there's nowhere else I can go. I've tapped out everyone I know, and practically put my mother in the poorhouse in the process. I haven't just robbed Peter, I've robbed Paul, too, and now it's all caught up with me.'

'There may be a way,' he repeated, a little more emphatically than before, because he could still hear his editor's voice over the telephone this morning, telling him enough was enough and it was time to fish or cut bait.

'What?' she asked with a sigh.

'If you had, say, information of some kind that had value to someone else, maybe that someone else might be willing to pay you for it.'

'Information? What do you mean, information?' she asked, clearly perplexed. 'I don't have any information that anyone would want to pay me for.'

'Are you sure?'

Judith frowned. 'Of course I'm sure. What is it you think I know?'

'I don't know,' he said with a shrug and then his eyes widened. 'Wait a minute. What about the trial?'

'What trial? You mean the Hill House trial?'

'Yes.'

'What about it?'

'Well, you've got to know that the tabloids are tripping all over themselves to get the inside scoop on it, and you just happen to know the lead defense attorney, don't you? Maybe Dana's told you something juicy you could offer to sell to them.'

'I don't think you understand,' she said. 'Dana doesn't discuss her cases with me. She doesn't discuss her cases with anyone. Not even with Sam.'

'She hasn't told you even a little something?'

'I assure you, not even a little something.'

'Well then, what about Dana herself?' he suggested. 'She hasn't exactly gone out and promoted herself, when you'd think that's exactly what a defense attorney ought to do in this situation.'

'Well, there's a reason for that,' Judith said, without thinking.

He was instantly alert. 'If that's the case, and the reason is juicy enough,' he suggested smoothly, 'I bet one of those tabloids would pay really big money to hear it.'

'Don't be silly, I couldn't do that,' Judith declared. 'She's my best friend. I couldn't rat out my best friend.'

'Hey, you're the one with money problems,' he said. 'I'm just trying to help here.'

'I know, I'm sorry, but no,' she told him.

'It's too bad,' he said. 'Some of those papers would probably pay a hundred thousand for the right story.'

'Do you mean a hundred thousand dollars?' Judith asked, incredulous.

'At least,' he said. 'Maybe even a hundred and fifty. For the right information, of course.'

'I had no idea,' she murmured.

He shrugged. 'That's why I thought, well, you said you'd been friends forever, so it stands to reason you'd know something about her that would make a good story,' he prompted. 'And with that much money, you could probably clean up your debt, and keep the house for Alex, and maybe even be able to stick with your art a while longer.'

Judith shook her head. 'It wouldn't be right,' she said.

'Okay,' Kirby said, choosing a different strategy and taking her in his arms. 'What time does Alex get home?' he murmured into her hair.

Judith giggled in spite of herself and her predicament. 'Any moment now,' she told him. 'Can you wait until after dinner?'

Kirby waited, although he knew he was as close to getting what he wanted as he would ever be, and wasn't about to let it slip out of his grasp. He dutifully ate the macaroni and cheese, which he had come to loathe, and managed, without much resistance, to get three glasses of wine into Judith.

When dinner was finally over, she came to him eagerly, and it pleased him that he was able to oblige, because sex was the last thing on his mind.

'I'm sorry about your money problems,' he said as they lay together afterward. 'I didn't mean to imply that you should betray a confidence. I was just trying to help.'

'I know,' she murmured dreamily. 'And I appreciate your caring so much. God knows, I could use the money. And if it were anyone but Dana, I might be tempted. But we go back too far.'

'Jeez, now you've got *me* curious,' he said with a casual chuckle.

'Well, it's not that big a deal, really,' she told him. 'It's mostly just the irony of it.'

He yawned as if it didn't mean everything in the world to him. 'What irony?'

'Why, taking this case, of course,' she said. 'Dana just plain should never have taken this case.'

'Why not?'

'Well, when I tell you, you'll understand,' Judith confided with a little giggle, knowing she could trust him without question.

He spent half an hour coaxing all the details out of her, and as soon as he had everything he had come for, he made his escape, inventing an early job in the morning. Then he was out the door and in his pickup. He forced himself to drive a safe distance away before he brought the vehicle to a halt and allowed himself a howl of pure animal pleasure.

'Tracking me down on Tuesday night, when I was going to see you on Thursday, anyway?' Al Roberts said, opening the door of his West Seattle home. 'It must be pretty important.'

'If it wasn't, I wouldn't be here,' Craig Jessup declared.

The telephone in Paul Cotter's private office, the one that bypassed the main switchboard, rang at nine.

'Glad you're still there,' said the voice at the other end of the line.

'I was waiting,' Cotter responded. 'I had a feeling you'd call tonight.'

'It looks like things are going well.'

'Yes,' the attorney agreed cautiously.

'What?' asked the caller, suddenly alert. 'Do you foresee a problem you haven't told me about?'

'No,' Cotter replied. 'But I never like to start the celebration too soon.'

The caller chuckled. 'That's why you're so good at what you do.'

'I just hope we've got everything covered,' Cotter declared.

'Don't you think you do?'

There was a pause. 'Yes,' the attorney said. 'But then, you

307

never know when something unexpected will jump up and bite you.'

It was well past midnight before the telephone in the McAuliffes' cozy Magnolia house rang. Dana was waiting, grabbing the receiver on the first ring, hoping it hadn't awakened Sam.

'It's all right,' Craig Jessup told her. 'I've got everything we need. You can go to bed now, and sleep like a baby.'

12

'Mr. Clune, I have just a few questions,' Dana began pleasantly, when court resumed on Wednesday morning.

'Joshua,' the witness corrected her, with a trusting smile.

'I beg your pardon?'

'I'm not Mr. Clune,' he said. 'I'm just Joshua.'

'Oh, I see, I'm sorry,' Dana said, smiling back. 'All right then, Joshua, who was the first person you told about seeing the delivery man at Hill House?'

'Big Dug,' he replied. 'I told Big Dug.'

'Who is Big Dug?'

'He's my friend.'

'And when you told your friend, what did he say?'

'He didn't say anything. Not right then, anyway.'

'When *did* he say something?'

'It was weeks past that, after that man got hisself arrested,' Joshua replied, nodding at the defendant.

'What did Big Dug say then?'

'He showed me a picture in the newspaper, and asked me if that was the delivery man I saw.'

'What did you say?'

'I said I didn't know.'

'Why did you say that?'

Joshua shrugged. 'Because it wasn't a very good picture.'

'Then what did Big Dug do?'

'He took me to the bar where we go sometimes, 'cause they let us sit all night and drink one beer, if we want, and he showed me the man's picture on the TV.'

'What did you say then?'

'I said I didn't know again.'

'Do you mean you couldn't recognize the defendant on the television, just like you couldn't recognize him from the newspaper?'

'Yes,' Joshua said.

'But you went to the police anyway, didn't you?'

'Much later, after Big Dug said it was the right thing to do.'

'And when you talked to the detectives, were you able to identify the man you saw at Hill House?'

Joshua shook his head. 'No. I told them it was dark, and he was too far away.'

'And what did the detectives say after you talked to them?'

'They said I wouldn't have to come here and tell in front of people.'

'Was that because you couldn't identify the man you saw at Hill House?'

'I guess so,' Joshua said.

Over at the prosecution table, Brian Ayres began to shift uncomfortably in his chair.

'Then what happened last Saturday?' Dana asked.

'The police came and put me in jail,' the witness testified. 'Big Dug said they wouldn't, but they did.'

'And have you been at the police station ever since?'

Joshua nodded. 'Yes, but I don't want to stay there. I want to go home. I didn't mean to sleep at Hill House. I told them I was sorry. But Big Dug said I didn't make the fire happen. If I didn't make the fire happen, do I have to stay in jail?'

'No,' Dana said gently. 'You won't have to stay in jail. We'll see to it that you get to go home.'

A big smile spread across his face. 'That's good,' he said. ''Cause I really miss my friends.'

'Joshua, tell me, what happened after the police came and got you on Saturday?'

'You mean after they put me in jail?'

'Yes.'

'They talked to me, first one and then another, all day. I got hungry, and I was sleepy, too, and after a while, I didn't know what they were saying. Then they gave me food, and let me sleep on a bed. The next day, they talked to me again, like before, all day.'

'When they talked to you, what did they say?'

'They talked to me about the delivery man. About how bad a man he was, and how he deserved to be punished for what he did.'

'What else?'

'They showed me pictures.'

'Pictures of what?'

'Of Hill House when it was burned down. And of people lying on the ground.'

'And they told you the man who did that should be punished?'

'Yes. Then they showed me pictures of different men, lots of pictures, until I finally remembered the man I saw.'

Brian scribbled something on a piece of paper and passed it to Mark Hoffman.

'Okay, Joshua, one last question, to put this all together,' Dana said. 'Until the police talked to you over the weekend, and showed you all those pictures, you couldn't identify the defendant as the man you saw at Hill House the night before the bombing, could you?'

Joshua thought for a moment. 'No,' he said finally. 'I guess I wasn't sure about him before that.' Then he smiled brightly, wanting to please. 'But I am now.'

Mark Hoffman did Brian's bidding and summoned Dale Tinker to the courthouse.

'Do you want us to lose this case, Tinker?' Brian charged the detective. 'Is that what this is all about?'

'I don't know what you're talking about,' the police officer retorted.

'What you gave us was marginal at best. Did you have to compound it by coercing a witness?'

'The retard identified the guy, didn't he?' Tinker replied. 'And he stuck to it in court. What do you want from me?'

'Yeah, he identified him all right, but was it before or after you locked him up for two days and scared the piss out of him?'

The detective looked at his shoes. 'I don't know how she found out about that,' he mumbled.

'She's not the problem, Tinker, *you* are,' Brian said. 'And I'm starting to wonder whether you got any of it right.'

'You want my badge? Is that what you want?'

'I want a conviction,' the prosecutor declared. 'That's what I want.'

'We don't have the wrong guy,' Tinker insisted. 'That son of a bitch did it. I can smell it on him. And I've been in this business long enough to know.'

'I don't care what you can smell,' Brian told him. 'I care what you can prove.'

'I'm proud of you,' Jefferson Reid declared over the telephone. 'I'm proud that you're my daughter.'

'Thanks, dad,' Dana said. They had spoken at least once a week since the trial had begun, she seeking him out for guidance and support. But this was the first time he had called her.

'What you did with that eyewitness was brilliant,' he told her. 'You're taking full advantage of every opportunity they give you.'

'It's because I believe in Corey,' she said simply. 'I believe the police either stumbled on him, or were led to him, couldn't believe their good luck, and just held on to him for dear life, to the exclusion of everyone else.'

'All you need is to establish reasonable doubt,' he told her. 'You've discredited their eyewitness and you've given the jury another person with means, motive, and opportunity to look at.'

'Jack Pauley had every bit as much reason to bomb the place as Corey did, and no alibi,' she said in disgust. 'The police hardly looked at him.'

'There's one thing that still niggles at me, though,' he said.

'I know, the anonymous letter,' she said. 'Not so much who sent it, as why. My investigator's working on it. But he's also working on half a dozen other things that are just as important, and he's a one-man operation.'

'I keep thinking this may be as complicated as a conspiracy,' he mused, 'or as simple as someone who really knows something, but didn't want to come forward personally.'

'I just don't think there's anything to know here,' she told him. 'I'm a pretty good judge of character. I know I am. And I couldn't be so wrong about Corey. I just couldn't.'

'If nothing else, I admire your loyalty,' her father said with a gentle chuckle. 'If I were ever on trial for my life, you're the one I'd choose to represent me.'

Those words meant more to her than anything.

The event was a Seattle institution, the annual black tie dinner of the Coalition for Conservative Causes. Some five hundred people filled the ballroom at the Olympic Four Seasons Hotel, and for a mere twenty-five hundred dollars, dined on lobster bisque and roast squab.

Each year, someone who exemplified the ideals of the organization was invited as an honored guest. On the dais this year was the Republican nominee for president of the United States, in the middle of a ten-city fund-raising tour.

It was during the cocktail hour, when the champagne was flowing, and three kinds of caviar were being passed around, that Roger Roark, the executive director, happened upon an acquaintance.

'Why, Paul Cotter, you old reprobate,' he exclaimed with a friendly slap on the back. 'I don't think we've seen you around here in years.'

'Roger,' the attorney acknowledged, as the rather sizable group surrounding them turned to observe.

'Come to hobnob with some of the old crowd?' Roark asked.

'Come to see the nominee in person,' Cotter replied. 'If he's going to be our next president, I wouldn't say no to an introduction.'

'It would be my pleasure,' Roark said. 'By the way, I hear your firm is involved in that Hill House trial.'

'We are.'

Roark shook his head. 'Sad case,' he remarked. 'In my opinion,

313

it's a no-win situation, any way you look at it. All those people dead, that poor young man caught in the middle.'

'Sometimes,' Cotter suggested, with an eye on those listening, 'we do things because we have to, not because we want to.'

'Of course, we do,' the executive director said, slapping the attorney on the back. 'Just get the poor slob exonerated, my man. Isn't that right, everyone?'

The surrounding group vigorously nodded their agreement.

13

Judith Purcell sat on the floor of her bathroom with her head hanging over the toilet. She could not stop vomiting. The nausea had hit her yesterday, when she called Tom Kirby to tell him his shirt was laundered, and the residence hotel operator told her he had checked out.

'What do you mean, checked out?' she demanded.

'I mean he's no longer staying here,' the operator said. 'He's gone back to Los Angeles.'

'Did you say Los Angeles?' Judith asked, knowing it had to be a mistake. Kirby told her he had come from Detroit.

'Yes, Los Angeles,' the woman confirmed.

'Did he leave a forwarding address, or a telephone number?'

'No, he didn't.'

'Thank you,' Judith said automatically, and hung up. She didn't have a clue what was going on, but perhaps it wasn't such a big mystery after all, the operator had just gotten it wrong and he was *going* to Los Angeles, not returning there. It made no sense that he would have lied to her about where he came from. What reason would he have had?

And then the first wave of nausea hit, because she realized that it didn't matter where he came from or where he was. What mattered was that he was gone, without so much as a word.

The next witness for the prosecution was an expert from the United States Navy. He spent Thursday morning testifying, in as great detail as possible without breaching military security, about Corey Latham's training in weaponry, his undergraduate work in engineering, his acumen with firearms, and his understanding of the fundamentals of precision bombing and warfare.

Dana's questions of the expert were few and mostly perfunctory. Corey's military training was not in dispute, and there was little to be gained by a lengthy cross-examination.

On Thursday afternoon, Elise Latham's sister, Ronna Keough, was called to the stand. She wore an ill-fitting navy blue suit and high heels that made her appear taller than she was but pinched her feet.

'Mrs. Keough, will you please tell the court where you were on the afternoon of September 14 of last year?' Brian inquired.

'I was with my sister Elise,' Ronna said, clearly uncomfortable with her situation.

'Exactly where were you and your sister?'

'We were at Hill House.'

'Will you tell the court why you and your sister were at Hill House on that particular day?'

Ronna glared at the prosecutor, then glanced helplessly at Elise, seated in the first row behind the defense table. 'We went to Hill House to have an abortion,' she replied, reluctantly. 'It was a terrible thing Elise was doing, and she didn't want to go through it alone.'

'And you stayed with her at Hill House while she had this procedure?'

'Yes. I wasn't in the room, of course. But I waited for her out in the lounge.'

'And you took her home afterward?'

'Yes,' Ronna replied. 'She was in some discomfort, and pretty emotional about the whole thing.'

'What sort of discomfort?'

Ronna sighed. 'Mostly, she had cramps, and she was bleeding a bit. The doctor said she might.'

'The doctor who performed the abortion?'

'Yes. He gave her some pills to take, and he said she shouldn't be left alone. So I took her home, made her some soup, gave her the pills, talked to her for a while, and then put her to bed. She was exhausted. She fell right asleep.'

Suddenly, a woman rose from her seat in the middle of the spectator gallery. 'She sleeps the sleep of the devil,' the woman exclaimed. 'Her soul will burn in hell for taking that life. And yours, too, for helping her!'

At that, a second woman jumped up. 'Deny a woman's right to choose,' she cried, 'and you deny her the right to exist!'

Abraham Bendali banged his gavel sharply.

'Abortion is neither a right nor a choice,' someone else shouted. 'Not in God's eyes!'

The judge banged his gavel again. 'That will be enough,' he ordered, in a voice that in twenty years on the bench had never brooked an argument.

'If you can't trust me with a choice,' a woman chanted, ignoring him, 'how can you trust me with a child?'

'I wouldn't trust you with either,' a man shouted back at her.

Bendali banged his gavel a third time, and kept on banging it, to no avail. The courtroom erupted. All the restraint of the past month vanished, as emotions burst like water over a dam.

Allison Ackerman couldn't believe it. The spectators were ignoring the judge and practically spitting at one another, hurling insults as fast as they could think them up. Not even in her wildest mystery novels had she conceived of such a thing happening. Around her, the other jurors sat wide-eyed.

Dana was astonished. She had never witnessed a scene like this, not in fourteen years of practice. 'This is something that might happen in the movies,' she murmured to Joan Wills, 'but not in a real courtroom.'

'Please don't obscure the issue here,' Raymond Kiley rose from his seat in the Hill House section to implore. 'This isn't about abortion. It's about a bombing.'

'That's right,' Joe Romanadis said in support. 'It's about a man on trial for murder.'

'Yes, murder,' another person cried. 'The murder of all those innocent people. May he burn in hell!'

'The murder of murderers is no crime!'

'That's not what the Supreme Court says,' someone declared.

'Conception is holy. The hell with the Supreme Court,' another shouted.

With that, a woman threw something that hit Elise in the

back of the head. Then several people began hurling things at her, and at her sister. Corey leaped from his chair and tried to cover his wife with his own body. One of the jailhouse guards pulled him away, while the other grabbed Elise and pulled her to the floor.

'Abortion is legal in this country,' someone shouted.

'Legalized murder is still murder,' someone else retorted.

'Safeguard women's rights!'

'Save the preborn!'

'Protect free choice. It's all that stands between us and slavery!'

'Kill the killers!'

It was only a matter of seconds before the invective turned into violence – shouting, punching, kicking, hair-pulling, clothes-tearing, and what was later revealed to be spitball-throwing violence. The two deputies stationed at the door to the courtroom jumped into the fray, with little effectiveness.

Almost immediately, people began looking around for anything that could be used as a weapon. Handbags started swinging. Frances Stocker's cane was snatched from her side by a man who promptly began wielding it like a baseball bat.

Betsy Toth Umanski was seated in the first row aisle, where, unable to turn, she could hear, but not see, what was happening behind her.

'What's going on?' she asked her husband. It was a rare day when he was able to stay with her. But before he could reply, she was abruptly and unceremoniously dumped from her wheel-chair. As the culprit made off with what he intended to use as a battering ram, Andy Umanski leaped on top of him. After that, it didn't matter what ideology one espoused, the madness engulfed everyone. The crowd had become a mob.

From the very beginning of the trial, Abraham Bendali had been anticipating something like this. When he motioned to Robert Niera, it was barely an instant before the bailiff was escorting the jury out of the room, through the front, to the judge's own chamber. Just as quickly, Corey's guards removed the defendant, his wife, his mother, his former landlady, and his sister-in-law to another location, with Charles Ramsey, Joan Wills, and Mark Hoffman scurrying after them.

Just before exiting with the remaining court personnel, the clerk picked up a telephone and called for help. But the judge, not knowing exactly what he was dealing with, and not about to take any chances, had already pressed the alarm button positioned beneath his right hand.

Within minutes, half a dozen deputies descended on the scene. In the ninth-floor corridor, network cameramen saw the officers rush by, and caught a glimpse of the commotion as the courtroom doors opened and closed. But they were obliged to stay where they were, helpless and frustrated, while inside, reporters scribbled furiously, and the court sketch artist tried his best to capture at least the essence of what was taking place.

Two of the six deputies pushed their way down the center aisle, and turned to face the gallery, their primary mission to protect the court. They withdrew their service revolvers, grasped them in both hands, released the safety catches, extended their arms in firing position, and froze. It was clear that they would fire, if they had to, but only if they had to. With batons and handcuffs ready, the remaining deputies tackled the crowd.

For some reason that neither of them would later be able to explain, except to say that they felt it their duty to bear witness, Dana McAuliffe and Brian Ayres remained in the courtroom, alternately fascinated and appalled.

It took almost half an hour and another dozen deputies to quash the brawl and return some semblance of order to the courtroom. Before it was over, there were seven arrests, two concussions, a broken arm, some cracked ribs, a fractured wrist, a dislocated shoulder, and numerous cuts and bruises. Joe Romanadis sustained a black eye, Raymond Kiley had a deep cut on his right cheek, and Andy Umanski had suffered a broken nose. Those arrested went directly to jail. Those with minor injuries were treated on the scene by a paramedic team, and those who were more seriously injured were taken to Harborview Medical Center.

And during it all, a stony-faced Abraham Bendali sat on the

bench and watched. When order was finally restored, he cleared his throat, and fixed a steely eye on those who remained in the courtroom.

'I trust that we have this all out of our systems now, and will not have to suffer anything that even remotely resembles a repeat episode,' he said. 'To this end, and I might add, at significant cost to the taxpayers, I will request that a contingent of armed deputies be on hand for the remainder of the trial.'

As if to emphasize his words, four deputies took up positions at various points around the room. As soon as they were in place, Bendali peered down at the two attorneys with a heavy sigh. 'Would either side object to an adjournment until tomorrow?' he inquired of them.

'No objection, Your Honor,' Brian said with relief.

'No objection,' Dana echoed weakly.

The judge reconvened his court, apologizing as best he could to the jury and the witness, to the defendant and the defendant's wife, and to the contingent of Hill House survivors, after which he recessed the trial until the following morning.

Dana had always considered herself a seasoned professional, in control, and able to handle just about any situation. She had no idea how frightened she was until it was over, and the rush of adrenaline had subsided, and she tried to stand up, and found her knees buckling beneath her.

'What just happened?' she asked, wondering how long it would be before her legs would be willing to work again.

'A bit of anarchy,' Brian replied. 'Are you all right?'

He was looking pretty shaky himself, Dana thought as she gave him a weak smile. 'Ask me again after a few stiff drinks,' she said, 'and I'll let you know.'

Abraham Bendali went into his chamber and pulled a bottle of scotch from his desk drawer. Taking a glass from the tray on his credenza, he half filled it, and then downed it in one gulp.

'Are you all right, Your Honor?' his bailiff asked, standing in the doorway.

'Yes, of course, Robert,' he replied. 'Come in, come in.' He plucked a second glass from the tray and poured another portion of scotch. 'Here,' he said, holding it out to the young man. 'I can't believe you don't need this every bit as much as I do.'

Robert took the glass with a shaking hand. 'Thank you, sir,' he said, sipping at it.

Bendali helped himself to a second drink, and sat contemplating it for a moment. 'Just how close do you think we came, Robert?' he asked.

'I'm not sure, sir,' the bailiff replied. 'And to be perfectly honest with you, I'm not sure I want to know, either.'

'Do you think I did the right thing, calling in the artillery?'

'Absolutely,' Robert said without hesitation. 'I can't see as you had any choice about that.'

The judge wagged his head in disgust. 'Spitballs,' he muttered.

'They knew nothing else was going to get through the metal detectors,' the bailiff said.

'That's just the point. I summoned an army to fight spitballs.'

'Yes, but you didn't know that's all they had at the time. You couldn't take the chance that they hadn't found some way to sneak in a gun or two. And anyway, some of those spitballs weren't just paper, you know. There were stones in the middle of them.'

Bendali downed his second scotch and placed the glass on the desk. 'I can't remember the last time a case drove me to drink,' he said. 'I think I'm getting too old for this.'

'You, sir?' the bailiff declared, emboldened by the liquor. 'You've got the best mind on the bench, and everyone around here knows it.'

'Thank you, Robert,' Bendali said, genuinely moved. He wondered when the time would be right to tell the young man that this was his final trial.

14

Under the eyes of armed deputies, Ronna Keough returned to the witness stand on Friday.

'I have just a few more questions,' Brian assured her. 'Was there an occasion in November of last year when you received a telephone call from the defendant?'

'Yes.'

'Will you please tell the court the substance of that conversation?'

'He told me that Elise had refused to talk about the miscarriage, and he wanted to know if I knew what had caused it.'

'The miscarriage?'

'Yes. I guess Elise told him she'd had a miscarriage, not an abortion.'

'What did you say?'

'Well, I didn't know Elise was going to lie to him. She made me swear not to tell our parents about it, but she didn't tell me not to say anything to Corey. I guess it never occurred to her that he'd call me. Anyway, at the time, I just thought he'd gotten it wrong. So I told him that she was probably just feeling guilty.'

'What did he say?'

'He wanted to know what she would have to feel guilty about.'

'What did you say?'

Ronna sighed. 'I told him maybe the reason she was feeling guilty was because abortion was a mortal sin.'

'So you were the one who told the defendant that his wife had had an abortion, not a miscarriage?'

'I didn't mean to, but yes, I guess so.'

'What was his reaction?'

'The telephone went silent,' Ronna replied. 'He never said another word. After maybe a minute or two, he hung up.'

'Thank you, Mrs. Keough,' the prosecutor said. 'That's all I have.'

Dana contemplated the witness. While the state could not compel the defendant's wife to testify against her husband, no such privilege extended to the wife's sister. Brian had done a clever end run in getting Elise Latham's abortion into evidence, as well as the lie. It went a long way toward providing Corey Latham with a motive for bombing Hill House. The damage was done, and could not be undone. It would be foolish even to try.

'We have no questions for this witness, Your Honor,' the defense attorney said.

Elise Latham did not return to the courtroom on Friday, and would not return until she was called to testify. Her month's leave of absence from her job was up, and she was expected back at work. That and the fear of another public assault gave her a convenient reason to move quietly out of the picture.

Dean Latham had returned to Iowa, and Corey's Navy buddies, who had taken precious vacation time to be at the courthouse for the first weeks of trial, had gone back on duty. That left Barbara Latham, Evelyn Biggs, and two or three rotating members of Corey's support group holding the banner on the defense side of the aisle. Occasionally, Tom Sheridan made an appearance. Fortunately, today was one of those occasions, and from the corner of her eye, Dana saw the minister put his arm comfortingly around Barbara.

The prosecutor's last witness of the week was Alan Neff, the doctor from Hill House who had performed Elise Latham's abortion. By a sheer stroke of luck on his part, Dr. Neff had been sick with the flu the week of the bombing, recuperating at his home in Lake Forest Park.

'I want to make it perfectly clear to you,' the physician had told the prosecutor, when he was subpoenaed to testify, 'I am bound by the terms of doctor-patient confidentiality. I cannot and I will not discuss Mrs. Latham's care or treatment.'

'I have no intention of asking you about your interaction with Mrs. Latham,' Brian assured him. 'I'm going to ask you about your interaction with Mrs. Latham's husband.'

There was a pause. 'How do you know I had any interaction with her husband?' Neff inquired.

'Lucky guess, maybe,' Brian replied with a shrug. 'And telephone records.'

The doctor sighed. 'All right,' he said. 'Tell me what you want.'

'Thank you for coming in today, Dr. Neff,' Brian said, as the physician settled himself in the witness box, four months to the day after their conversation. 'I would like to begin by asking if you know Corey Dean Latham.'

'I know who he is,' Neff replied, 'but we've never met, face-to-face.'

'When you say you know who he is, what do you mean?'

'I mean, I know he's the defendant in this trial,' the witness said. 'And I also know he's the husband of one of my patients.'

'Doctor, you said you never met the defendant, face-to-face. Did you have another kind of contact with him?'

'Yes.'

'Will you explain for the court?'

'There were a whole lot of telephone calls, perhaps as many as two dozen of them in the period of a week. Calls made to my office, and to my home.'

'What was the nature of these calls?'

Neff paused. 'Demanding,' he said finally.

'Demanding, how?' Brian asked.

'He wanted to discuss something I was not at liberty to discuss with him.'

'Did this something concern his wife?'

'Yes.'

'What happened when you told him you couldn't discuss it?'

'He became . . . frustrated,' the doctor replied. 'And then the harassment started. At first, he would call me at the clinic. After a few days of trying to reason with him, I just refused to come

324

to the phone, so then he began calling me at home, at all hours of the night, demanding that I talk to him about his wife. I tried to tell him that the discussion he needed to have was with his wife, not with me, but that just made him angry. So finally I had to tell him that if he didn't stop calling, I would call the police.'

'So, by the time you told him to stop calling, he was angry?'

'Yes, I'd say so. Very angry.'

'And to the best of your recollection, when did these telephone calls take place?'

'Last November,' Neff replied.

'Now, without going into detail, or abrogating any doctor-patient confidentiality, did you have occasion to see the defendant's wife on a medical matter, prior to these telephone calls? Say, in September of last year?'

'Yes, I did.'

Brian turned to the bench. 'I'd like these telephone logs entered into evidence, Your Honor,' he said.

Bendali nodded. 'So ordered.'

'Thank you,' the prosecutor said to his witness. 'That's all I have.'

'These telephone calls that annoyed you so much, Dr. Neff,' Dana said, rising as Brian sat. 'When you told my client you felt he was harassing you, did they stop?'

'Yes.'

'You didn't have to call the police, or try to dissuade him further?'

'No.'

'So my client may have been desperate for help and begging for information, but he wasn't irrational, or intimidating, or anything like that, was he?'

'Well, he was angry.'

'So you said. Did he threaten you? Did he threaten to harm your family?'

'No.'

'And after that week in November, did my client ever attempt to telephone you again?'

'No.'

Dana contemplated the witness for a moment. 'Do you think he held you personally responsible for something in connection with his wife?'

'I think, by his actions, he made that perfectly clear,' the physician replied.

'Your house wasn't bombed, was it?'

'No, of course it wasn't. But Hill House certainly was.'

'Yes, two and a half months later,' Dana acknowledged. 'And if I remember correctly, you weren't at the clinic that day, were you?'

'No, as a matter of fact, I wasn't.'

'That's right. You were at home. As a matter of fact, you were at home all that week, with a bad case of the flu, isn't that so?'

'Yes, well, maybe your client didn't know that,' Neff suggested.

'All it would have taken was one phone call to find out, wouldn't it?'

'I suppose.'

'You suppose?' Dana fingered a piece of paper. 'Doctor, are you acquainted with a woman by the name of Maureen O'Connor?'

'Yes, I am,' he replied with a puzzled frown. 'She's a patient of mine.'

'Well, Mrs. O'Connor is willing to come here and testify, if necessary, that on the Monday before the bombing, she called the clinic to speak to you, and was told that you were out with the flu, and had canceled all your appointments for the rest of the week. Now, let me ask you again, would it have taken anything more than one phone call to determine that you were not at Hill House?'

'No, I guess not,' he conceded.

'And yet, Dr. Neff,' the attorney continued, 'you were perfectly willing to let this jury believe that it was my client's anger at you that prompted the bombing of Hill House, weren't you?'

326

'What the jury believes is up to the prosecutor,' the physician declared. 'All I said was the defendant was very angry.'

'Yes, you did say that,' Dana granted, thoughtfully. 'You lost a lot of good friends that day at Hill House, didn't you?'

'Yes, I did,' he replied.

'And you'd like to believe that the police did their job, the way police are supposed to do it, and caught the right man, wouldn't you?'

'Sure I would.'

'It wouldn't bring your friends back, of course, but it would mean at least some kind of closure, wouldn't it?'

'Yes.'

'And those of you who are left could start putting the whole tragedy behind you, and begin getting on with your lives, couldn't you?'

Neff blinked several times. 'Yes,' he said.

'Doctor, do you blame yourself for the bombing of Hill House?'

He sighed. 'Maybe, a little,' he said, his voice catching a bit.

'Enough to want to help hang an innocent man?'

'No, of course not,' he said. 'I would never want to do that.'

'All right then, after the telephone calls ended, did you have any further contact with my client?'

'I did,' he replied after a slight pause.

'Can you tell us what that contact consisted of?'

'About two weeks later, I got a letter from him.'

Brian shot a look at Mark Hoffman, who shrugged in response.

'Will you please tell the court what the gist of that letter was?'

'As I remember, it said that he and his wife had finally been able to talk, that they had gotten into counseling, and that he had faith things would work out. He apologized for his harassment, hoped I understood, and thanked me for not reporting him to the police.'

'Did this letter sound like someone who was so consumed with anger that he was going to go right out and plant a bomb?'

'No, I guess it didn't,' he answered.

'Or did it sound like someone who had suffered a severe shock, but was trying to come to grips with it in as adult a manner as he could?'

'Well, yes,' he said, with a nod. 'I'd have to say that it did sound a little like that.'

'Thank you,' Dana said. 'I have nothing further.'

'Why didn't we know about that letter?' Brian barked at his associate.

'He never said anything about it,' Mark replied. 'And we never asked.'

'Ayres sets them up, and McAuliffe knocks them down,' Paul Cotter's caller observed.

'Well, that's what a defense attorney does,' Cotter responded.

'Yes, and she does it very well, doesn't she?' the caller said. 'Perhaps even better than any of us realized.'

'I have good news,' Sam declared at the dinner table that night. 'We've come to terms on the Pioneer Square building.'

Dana's eyes widened. 'Really?' she gasped. 'It's ours?'

'As soon as all the paperwork is done.'

'Oh how wonderful! How scary! We have to tell Judith. I can't believe this! Let's invite her to dinner on Sunday, and just drop it on her then.'

At ten o'clock on Friday evening, Tom Kirby knocked at Judith's door.

'Oh my God, where have you been?' she cried. 'They said you'd checked out. I've been going crazy.'

'Sorry,' he said. 'It was a last-minute thing. I didn't have a chance to call.'

He looked different. His hair was neatly cut, he was clean-shaven, he was dressed in a jacket and tie, and his shoes were polished. But Judith hardly noticed.

'Where were you?'

'I was in Los Angeles,' he told her. 'I was down there lining up a job.'

'You took a job . . . in Los Angeles?' she asked blankly.

He sighed. 'Look, I told you it was only a matter of time before I moved on,' he said. 'Well, it's time. Truth is, if it weren't for you, I would've been gone long ago, and this job, well, it's too good to pass up.'

'Oh.'

'Come on, don't say it like that. It's who I am. You knew that. I was always up front about it. And we had some good times together.'

'When do you go?'

'Well, that's the hard part,' he said. 'I'm getting back on a plane tonight, in a couple of hours as a matter of fact. I have a cab waiting.'

'Tonight?' she gasped. 'Well, I mean, I suppose that's wonderful for you, if it's what you want. But what about us? What am I going to do when you're gone?'

'Oh, well, that's part of why I'm here,' he said, pulling an envelope from his jacket pocket. 'I'm sorry things didn't work out the way you wanted between us, but here's something that should make it a little easier.'

Inside the envelope was a check for one hundred and fifty thousand dollars. His publisher had been ecstatic over the story, standing over Kirby's shoulder and reading as the reporter wrote. He had not balked at the price.

'What's this for?' she whispered, although with a sickening jolt, she realized she already knew.

'For your story,' he said.

'You didn't, you couldn't have,' she cried. 'I told you that in confidence.' But she knew it was futile, because she could see it all now, the whole three months, and what it had really been about.

'Don't worry,' he said. 'From what you've told me, I don't think Dana will mind helping you out. It's not as if she did anything illegal. It's a good story. It makes her more human. It'll be out in the next issue of *Probe* magazine.'

'I see,' she said. It was as though someone had shot her through the heart, only instead of falling down dead, she was standing up dead.

He put his arms around her and pulled her against him. 'Where's Alex?' he asked.

'He's spending the weekend with a friend,' she said automatically.

'Tell him I said goodbye.' Then he kissed her hair, and was gone.

Judith stood alone in the foyer, hearing his footsteps fade down the front path, and stared, unseeing, at the check in her hands.

15

Judith pleaded illness on Sunday, declining the invitation to dinner at the McAuliffe house, flat out refusing to allow Dana to come over with chicken soup, and intimating it was too much for her even to talk on the telephone.

'It must be one of those flu bugs,' she told her best friend of more than thirty years. 'And I won't have you catching it. You have to be in court every day, with all your wits about you.'

'Well, I have something to tell you,' Dana said. 'Something very exciting that I know you'll want to hear.'

'That's nice,' Judith replied weakly.

'No, I mean something really important,' Dana said. 'And I don't know how much longer I can keep it to myself. So promise you're going to get over this soon.'

'Sure, I promise.'

They agreed that they would get together as soon as Judith was feeling up to it. By then, Judith reasoned, the latest issue of *Probe* would be on the newsstands, the dinner invitation would likely be withdrawn, and the friendship would be damaged beyond repair. Part of her wanted to speak up, to warn Dana about what was coming. But another, bigger part of her was in denial.

'You can invite your friend Tom if you like,' Dana suggested.

'No,' Judith said dully. 'He won't be around. He's . . . well, he's gone out of town . . . for a while.'

On Monday, the prosecution put Zach Miller on the stand. He was an attractive young man, Allison Ackerman noted, in the mold of military officers, and his uniform was freshly pressed.

'What is your relationship with the defendant, Lieutenant Miller?' Brian asked.

'We're friends,' Zach replied. 'We used to be roommates.'

'Did this friendship continue past the time of the defendant's marriage?'

'Yes.'

'At the beginning of November, last year, did you have a series of conversations with the defendant concerning his wife?'

'I'm afraid you're going to have to be a little more specific than that,' Zach replied. 'Corey and I have had a lot of conversations about his wife, since before she was his wife.'

'All right, Lieutenant,' Brian replied, easily. 'Did you have occasion to discuss Mrs. Latham's abortion with the defendant?'

'Yes, I believe we did.'

'Will you please tell the court the substance of those conversations?'

Zach sighed. 'A couple of days after he got back from his last patrol, Corey told me that Elise had had a miscarriage while he was gone.'

'Did he indicate to you how he felt about that?'

'Yes. He said he was sick at heart. And he looked it, too.'

'And subsequently?'

'About a week after that, he told me that Elise didn't have a miscarriage, after all. She had an abortion.'

'And what was his reaction to that?'

'He was understandably upset.'

'What do you mean when you say upset?'

'I mean upset. He had tears in his eyes and he seemed to be distracted and depressed.'

'Is that all?'

Zach shrugged. 'Isn't that enough?'

'Lieutenant, did you not tell Detective Tinker that Corey Latham was angry when he found out about the abortion?'

'I may have used that word at the time, I don't remember.'

'Well, let's see if we can jog your memory a little. Was he angry?'

'Angry. Upset. What difference does it make? His wife not

only lied to him, she killed his baby,' Zach replied. 'Wouldn't that put you just a little bit off center?'

'Yes,' Brian replied, 'it would. In fact, it would make me pretty angry.'

'All right then, if you like that word better, he was angry.'

'How long would you say his anger lasted?'

'I don't know. For a while, I guess.'

'Longer than two weeks?'

'Maybe.'

'Longer than a month?'

'Look, I didn't count the days, and I don't really remember. In any case, it was his wife he was upset with, not the clinic.'

'Thank you, Lieutenant.'

'Here we go with angry again,' Dana said with a sigh as she rose from her seat. 'Tell me, Lieutenant Miller, did the defendant rant and rave about what had happened?'

'No.'

'Did he make any threats?'

'Not that I heard.'

'Did he say he was going to go make a bomb and blow up Hill House?'

'Of course not.'

'What did he say?'

'Not much of anything. He just got real quiet. That's how he is when something's bothering him. He just gets real quiet and chews on it until he works it out in his mind.'

'Was there anything about his state of mind during that time that gave you any indication he was plotting violence?'

'Absolutely not,' Zach assured her. 'Corey isn't like that. He's the coolest guy I know. He wouldn't hurt a flea.'

'Thank you,' Dana said.

'Redirect, Your Honor,' Brian said.

The judge nodded.

'Were you saying just now, Lieutenant Miller, that Corey Latham is incapable of hurting anyone?'

'No, not incapable, just not likely to.'

'You mean, if some enemy stormed our shore, and killed

333

Americans, Lieutenant Latham would not be likely to respond?'

'No, I don't mean that,' Zach replied. 'He's a naval officer. Of course he'd respond. I just meant we're trained to defend, not initiate. We aren't trained to be the aggressor, to go out and attack someone, unprovoked.'

'Oh, so you're saying he *would* fight if provoked, that he *would* defend against an enemy that had stormed our shore and killed Americans?'

'Yes.'

Brian leveled a long look at the defendant before turning back to the defendant's friend. 'Are you telling this court, sir, that Corey Latham would go out and defend dead Americans he probably never knew, but he wouldn't go out and defend his own aborted baby?'

Zach blinked.

'Objection,' Dana declared. 'Calls for a conclusion.'

'Withdrawn,' Brian said, before the judge could rule, or the witness could respond.

Craig Jessup slipped into the courtroom just after the lunch recess.

'We have to talk,' he whispered in Dana's ear.

The attorney nodded. 'Okay, let's meet at the office around six,' she suggested. 'I'll arrange it with Joan and Charles.'

That was normally how they did it; having everyone in on the initial discussion saved time later. But Jessup shook his head.

'No, not at your office,' he said.

Dana frowned. 'What's the matter?'

'Not now,' he replied. 'How about coming up to my place?'

In all their years of working together, he had never invited her to his home. 'All right,' she said. 'Your place.'

If Dana thought Jessup's behavior odd, she had no time to dwell on it as a tall spare man with a big space between his front teeth, who identified himself as Henry Lott, took the stand.

'Can you tell us where you work, Mr. Lott?' Brian asked.

'I work at Bay Auto Supply in Bremerton,' he replied.

'And how long have you worked there?'

'Let's see . . . I been with them going on twelve years now.'

'To the best of your recollection, were you working there last December 15?'

'Yes, I was.'

'How do you come to be so certain?'

'Last March, when the police come asking, I checked my time card.'

'Do you know the defendant?'

'Sure do,' the witness said.

'How do you know him?'

'The lieutenant used to come in the store at least a couple times a month, getting stuff for his Jimmy.'

'Do you recall seeing the defendant on December 15?'

'Yes, I do,' Lott confirmed. 'He come in around four-thirty in the afternoon.'

'You're pretty sure of the time?'

'Yep. That's always when he came in. After work, you know, before he gets on the ferry.'

'When he came in that day, what did he want?'

'He wanted a new battery.'

'Did you sell him one?'

'Sure did.'

'What did he say he wanted the battery for?'

Lott looked perplexed. 'For his Jimmy, of course,' he replied. 'The one he had was going on two years old, you see, and he thought it was starting up kind of sluggish in the mornings sometimes, so he decided it was time to replace it. He took care of that car like it was living and breathing.'

'And you're sure that it was on December 15 that the defendant entered your store to purchase a new battery?'

'Sure I'm sure.'

Brian approached the witness, and handed him a slip of paper. 'Will you tell the court what this is?' he requested.

Lott looked at the paper. 'It's a credit card receipt,' he said, 'for sixty-five dollars and thirty-two cents.'

'What does it say the receipt is for?'

'A battery.'

'Whose credit card was used for the purchase?'

'The lieutenant's.'

'And the date on the receipt?'

'December 15.'

'Thank you, sir. That's all.'

Dana sat forward in her seat. 'No questions, Your Honor,' she said.

Bendali nodded. 'You may call your next witness, Mr. Ayres.'

'The prosecution calls Carney Toland,' Brian declared.

Carney Toland, a small wizened man of about forty, with greasy hair and dirty fingernails, took the stand.

'Where do you work, Mr. Toland?' Brian inquired of him.

'I have an auto parts shop – B&T Auto Parts – up on Aurora Avenue,' he replied.

'Were you working at your shop the week before Christmas of last year, specifically on the third Sunday of the month?'

'I was,' Toland replied.

'It was a long time ago, how can you be so certain?'

The man shrugged. 'Because I'm at the shop every Sunday. My partner works Saturdays. I work Sundays.'

'And do you recall having a customer that day who purchased a battery from you?'

'Well, I probably had half a dozen,' the witness said, 'but only one who looked like him.' He nodded in the direction of the defendant.

'Out of half a dozen, why would you remember him?' Brian asked.

'He was a clean-cut, good-looking kid, very polite, very friendly-like, and he made an impression on me. So I remembered him.'

'Did he say anything about why he wanted the battery?'

'He said the one in his vehicle was two years old and was starting up kind of slow in the mornings, so he figured it was time to replace it. He seemed real knowledgeable about cars.'

'We have heard previous testimony that the defendant purchased a battery for his SUV on December 15. So I must

336

ask you, sir, are you absolutely certain that it was just a few days later that the defendant came into your shop and purchased a similar battery?'

'As certain as I can be,' Toland declared.

'Thank you,' Brian said.

Dana rose from her seat. 'Mr. Toland, when exactly did you remember that my client came into your shop to purchase a battery?'

'When I saw his picture in the newspapers.'

'And when was that?'

'Sometime in March or April, I guess.'

'So, two months after the bombing, you saw my client's picture in the paper and suddenly remembered you had seen him in your shop, purchasing a battery, is that correct?'

'Yeah, pretty much.'

'Now, Mr. Toland, you said you sold as many as half a dozen batteries that day, didn't you?'

'At least,' he amended. 'It may have been closer to a dozen.'

'So it was pretty busy in your shop, is that right?'

He nodded. 'Oh, yeah. The place really hops on the weekends.'

'Do you remember everyone who purchased a battery from you that day?'

'Well, maybe not everyone. But anyone who used it to make a bomb, I guess I'd remember.'

'I see,' Dana said. 'So, if Corey Latham hadn't been accused of making a bomb, you wouldn't have remembered him, is that your testimony?'

'No, no, I know my customers,' Toland quickly assured her. 'And I remember him from the shop.'

Dana glanced across the spectator gallery. 'Mr. Vaughan, will you stand up please.' In one of the middle rows, a medium-sized man of about thirty scrambled to his feet. Dana turned back to the witness. 'Do you recognize the man standing, sir?'

Toland squinted at the man. 'He looks a little familiar,' he said. 'But no, I can't say as I recognize him exactly.'

'What if I told you that he was in your shop on the very

337

same Sunday in December, and purchased a battery for his car. Would you remember him then?'

. The auto parts dealer blinked. 'Was he?'

'You don't know, do you?' Dana pressed. 'You don't remember him, do you?'

There was a pause. 'No, I don't,' Toland said with a sigh.

'Thank you, Mr. Vaughan,' Dana said. As the man sat back down, Dana picked up several slips of paper and approached the witness. 'Do you recognize this?' she asked, handing him one.

. Toland looked at the slip. 'It's from my shop,' he said. 'It's a credit card receipt for a battery.'

'Whose name is on the receipt?'

'Lester Vaughan,' the witness read.

'On what date was the receipt issued?'

'On December 19.'

'So, on December 19, Lester Vaughan was in your shop to buy a battery for his car, but you don't remember him.' She handed him the remaining slips. 'Will you please tell the court what these slips are?'

'They're also credit card receipts.'

'Yes, for items purchased from your shop by Lester Vaughan over a two-year period. But you don't remember him. And yet you want this court to believe that Corey Latham walked into your shop once, and you're able to positively pick him out of a newspaper?'

'He was there,' the auto parts dealer insisted. 'I remember him.'

'Do you have any credit card receipts for my client,' Dana inquired, 'for December 19 – or any other date, for that matter?'

Toland shook his head. 'No, I don't. But he could have paid cash. Lots of people pay cash. Three of the batteries I sold that day, I sold for cash. I have the register receipts. He could've been one of them.'

Dana shrugged. 'But we'll never really know, will we?' she said, finished with the witness.

'Mr. Toland,' Brian said on redirect, 'when you saw the

defendant's picture in the newspaper, did you tell the police that you recognized him as someone who had bought a battery at your shop on December 19 of last year?'

'Yes, I did,' the auto parts dealer said firmly. 'I thought it was him. I don't know, I still think it was him.'

A heavyset, platinum-haired man by the name of Carl Thorson was the next witness to take the stand.

'Mr. Thorson,' Brian began, 'will you please tell the court where you live?'

'I live on Queen Anne Hill,' the man replied, 'next door to Corey and Elise Latham.'

'Do you know the defendant?'

'Yes. He and his wife moved in a little over a year ago. We would talk occasionally, over the fence, you know, like neighbors do.'

'Do you recall seeing the defendant any time during the first week in November of last year?'

'Yes.'

'Will you tell the court under what circumstances?'

'It was about ten o'clock on a Tuesday night,' Thorson related. 'I work at a bakery, and have to get up at three in the morning, so I usually go to sleep around eight. On that Tuesday, I'd been asleep for about two hours, when I got waked up by loud shouting.'

'Could you tell where the shouting was coming from?'

'My bedroom windows face out on the Lathams' house. The shouting was coming from there.'

'What did you do?'

'The first time, I called them on the telephone. Elise answered, and I asked her please to keep the noise down.'

'Did they?'

'For a while. Then just as I was getting back to sleep, it started again. Well, then I got a little mad. So I got up, got dressed, and went over there. It's a good thing, too, because Corey looked like he was about to start smacking her around.'

'Objection,' Dana declared.

'Sustained,' Bendali said. 'The jury will disregard the last remark.' He turned to the witness. 'Mr. Thorson, please listen carefully to the questions as they are asked,' he advised, 'and just tell us what you saw and what you heard, not what you think.'

'Okay, I saw that Elise was crying, and that Corey was stomping around the house, all red in the face, and mean-eyed. And he was yelling about something, calling her a bitch and a murderer. He didn't seem to care that I heard him, either. Tell you the truth, I'm not sure he even knew I was there.'

'He called his wife a bitch and a murderer?'

'Yes, he did,' Thorson confirmed. 'At least twice that I heard.'

'Did you say anything?'

'I asked Elise if she was all right. My wife was still awake, so I asked if she wanted to come back with me to my house for a while.'

'You thought that Elise Latham might actually be in imminent physical danger from her husband?'

'Well, I don't know,' he replied, 'but it sure looked that way to me.'

'Thank you,' Brian said.

'Mr. Thorson, do you and your wife ever argue?' Dana inquired.

'Everyone argues sometimes,' he replied. 'I suppose we do our share.'

'When you argue, do you shout?'

'Yeah, sure.'

'And do you ever say things, or in the heat of anger, call your wife names you later regretted?'

'I guess so,' he conceded.

'Have you ever had an argument with your wife that was so heated that you went out and bombed a building over it?'

'No, of course not.'

'All right, Mr. Thorson, let's go back for a minute to the night you went over to the Lathams. You testified that you thought Elise Latham was in such physical danger that you asked her to leave her house with you, is that correct?'

'Yes.'

'When you suggested that, what did she say?'

'She thanked me, and said it wouldn't be necessary.'

Dana looked surprised. 'You mean she declined the opportunity to remove herself from imminent physical danger?'

He shrugged. 'I guess she didn't see it as serious as I did.'

'Do you think that can be the case sometimes, that what we think we see, looking in from the outside, may not be what's really happening on the inside?'

'I can only tell you what I heard and what I saw,' he said. 'I can't tell you what it means.'

Dana smiled. 'Thank you for your time, Mr. Thorson,' she said.

Brian had no redirect. 'Your Honor,' he said, 'the prosecution has one more witness to call, but due to a scheduling conflict, he won't be available until tomorrow afternoon. May I beg the court's indulgence, and request a recess until then?'

Bendali peered over at the defense table. 'Ms. McAuliffe?'

'The defense has no objection, Your Honor,' Dana replied.

'All right then, ladies and gentlemen, you get a rare morning off,' the judge said to the jury. 'We'll see you all back here tomorrow at one o'clock, ready to go. Is that right, Mr. Ayres?'

'Yes, Your Honor,' Brian assured him.

At six o'clock, Dana made her way up Capitol Hill to Craig Jessup's house. Louise Jessup opened the door. She had pale hair that was brushed to gleaming, bright eyes that took in everything, a few extra pounds that went unnoticed by most, and a bubbly personality that was a perfect complement to her husband's quiet demeanor.

'Come on in,' she said with a welcoming smile. 'Would it be all right if I called you Dana? I've heard so much about you over the years, I feel as if I know you.'

Dana smiled. 'Dana it is, and you took the words right out of my mouth.'

'Craig's in his office,' Louise said, beaming. 'He said to bring you right up.'

Jessup's small, second-floor office seemed filled to overflowing by a scarred old desk that sagged under an avalanche of books and papers and files, a bookcase stuffed with all manner of texts, and a battered recliner. He gestured her to his prized recliner.

'I'm sorry we had to do it this way,' he said. 'But I think you'll understand why in a moment.'

'Well,' she responded cautiously, 'you certainly got my attention.'

'I followed the jury list leak,' he told her, getting right to the point. 'I know where it came from.'

Dana frowned. 'Why do I think I'm not going to want to hear this?' she murmured.

'I've had a contact inside the AIM organization for a number of years now,' he explained. 'It took me a while to warm him up, but eventually, he put me on to someone, who put me on to someone else, who finally put me in touch with another person who was in a position to know, and he confirmed to me that AIM had the list two days after the jury was sworn in.'

'Two days after?'

He nodded. 'Once I knew that, all I had to do was track backward.'

At that moment, Louise came in with two steaming mugs of coffee. She placed one of the mugs on the desk in front of her husband, and handed the other to Dana. 'I think you're going to need this,' she murmured.

Dana sighed. Given the backlash the fetal photograph campaign had generated, she had already concluded that the leak had most likely come from the prosecutor's office, and after fourteen years of friendship, she didn't want to hear the name.

'Who?' she asked dully.

Jessup plucked a piece of paper from a file on the desk, although he didn't have to read from it. 'Charles Ramsey,' he said.

'Who?' she said again, positive she had heard him incorrectly.

'Charles Ramsey,' the investigator repeated clearly.

Dana blinked. Jessup was telling her that her third chair, the venerable senior partner of Cotter Boland and Grace, had not only breached legal ethics, but had leaked a document that could very well result in the conviction of their client. It didn't make any sense.

'That's not possible,' she said.

'That's exactly what *I* thought,' Jessup acknowledged. 'So I double-checked, and then I triple-checked. I'm afraid it came up the same way all three times.'

'But he'd have to be crazy to pull a stunt like that.'

The investigator shrugged. 'Or senile.'

Dana sagged into the recliner, unsure what to think or what to feel. Craig Jessup was both meticulous and cautious, she knew, and he was never wrong.

16

Dana was curled into a corner of the living room sofa, contemplating her dilemma. It was approaching three o'clock in the morning. Both Sam and Molly had been in bed for hours, but it would have been useless for Dana to try to sleep. Not until she had figured out what to do.

The obvious move was to go to Paul Cotter immediately. Armed with Craig Jessup's information, he would of course have no choice but to remove Ramsey from the case. But was that all they were obligated to do? Did they not have an ethical duty, as officers of the court, to report jury tampering?

Charles Ramsey had been practicing law for as long as Dana was old, and to the best of her knowledge, he had an unblemished record. Other than a desire to win a case that he believed was unfairly stacked against them, she could not understand what had prompted him to do this. And while she might applaud his determination, she was appalled at his method.

He had committed a crime that was punishable by imprisonment and she knew she should report him. But how could she ruin his career, when it was clear at least his heart had been in the right place? And more important, once she did report him, where did that leave her?

Exposing Ramsey was almost certain to cause a mistrial and that was her biggest problem. On the whole, she was quite happy with the way things were going in court. She truly believed they had mitigated a great deal of the state's case, and she was not at all sure that a mistrial would be in the best interests of her client.

On the other hand, if she didn't go to Cotter, if she allowed the matter to slide for a while, and her client was convicted, could she then blow the whistle and have the verdict set aside? Where was her obligation? Where was her loyalty?

Her head began to ache and without thinking, she reached for the telephone on the table beside her.

'I'm sorry,' she said when Jefferson Reid answered, 'but I need your help.'

'Just give me a moment,' he responded, and she heard a click, and knew he had put her on hold while he made his way out of the bedroom and into his study. 'All right,' he said, coming back on the line, 'what is it that has you worrying at this ungodly hour?'

She told him what she had learned. When she finished, it was several minutes before he replied.

'You believe in Corey Latham, don't you?' he said, not really asking.

'Yes, I do,' she replied. 'Absolutely.'

'Then I'm afraid that puts you between a rock and a hard place,' he told her. 'Because your first obligation here is not to your client, it's to the law. It's always to the law. Jury tampering is not just a felony, it's an automatic mistrial.'

'But we've been down that road,' she said, 'and the judge declined to call it.'

'Because he didn't have all the facts,' Reid suggested. 'In any case, your third chair is facing disbarment, maybe even jail time. And you can't sit on it. Believe me, you don't want to. Things like this have a way of coming back to bite you. And your instincts are correct. It's probably going to work against your client.'

'What's the matter?' Louise Jessup asked her husband, finding him in his office. She had awakened at seven o'clock to discover he had not come to bed at all.

'There's something I'm trying to get hold of,' he told her, rubbing his eyes. 'But it's just out of reach.'

'What? Something about the jury leak?'

'Yes,' he said with a sigh. 'But I can't quite grasp what it is.'

* * *

345

Dana was at Smith Tower by eight-thirty, although she knew that Paul Cotter rarely arrived before nine.

'Jeez, you look like someone got you with a gavel,' Angeline Wilder told her as soon as she entered the office.

'Thanks for the compliment,' Dana replied, thinking the receptionist had come closer than she knew to hitting the mark.

She went into the bathroom and surveyed her face. There were dark circles under her eyes, and her skin had a definite grayish cast to it. She reached for her handbag. If Angeline had noticed, so would the rest of the world. Her usual modicum of makeup was not going to be sufficient today.

At twenty minutes past nine, Angeline buzzed her. 'Mr. Cotter just came in,' she announced.

At nine-thirty, Dana was knocking at the managing partner's door.

'Come in, come in,' he invited, when he saw her.

'I'm afraid we might have a problem,' she said, closing the door behind her.

'With the case?' he asked.

'No, not exactly.' She handed him the report Craig Jessup had given her.

'This could be serious,' he said, when he had scanned the contents.

'Yes,' she agreed. 'I don't mind telling you, I didn't get a whole lot of sleep last night. I was trying to find a good way out. I couldn't.'

'Well, how do you want to proceed?'

Dana shrugged. 'He's off the case, of course. Past that, we're bound to report him.'

'Do we have to be so hasty?' he asked.

'Do we have a choice?' she countered.

He sighed. 'Look, all we have are some damaging but so far unverified allegations. Don't you think, before we go off half-cocked, and maybe ruin a good man's life and reputation, we should confirm the facts?'

'How?'

'Why not let me look into it,' Cotter suggested. 'You have

346

the trial to worry about. Let me worry about this.'

'What about the third chair?'

'Yes, there's that,' he mused, drumming his fingers on his desk. 'Well, we can't very well take him off the case, without raising a lot of awkward questions. So, why don't we just let it lie for the time being, until we get everything sorted out?'

'All right,' Dana said, with an inward sigh of relief. She had put the problem into the managing partner's very capable hands, and it was now his to deal with. She was off the hook, so to speak, which was just fine with her. As he had said, she had other things to worry about.

Half an hour later, Paul Cotter was engaged on his private line.

'What the hell is going on?' the voice at the other end demanded.

'I'm not sure,' Cotter replied.

'Are you as out of control as you sound?'

'This has just been brought to my attention,' the attorney declared defensively. 'It hardly means I'm out of control.'

'Well, you're going to have to do something, aren't you?'

'Of course I am,' Cotter snapped. 'It's just going to take a little time to figure out what.'

The final witness for the prosecution was Omar Ram.

A short, dark man, Ram lived with his wife and six children in a small house on the back side of Queen Anne Hill.

'Do you know the defendant?' Brian asked.

'I most certainly do,' the man replied with a smile. 'He lives right across the street, and is always very polite to me and to my family.'

'Tell me, sir, were you at home around midnight on the night before the Hill House bombing?'

'I was.'

'Will you please tell the court specifically where you were?'

'At that hour, I was in my bed.'

'Can you recall whether anything unusual happened on that particular night?'

'Yes, indeed,' Ram said in his clipped voice. 'Ours is a very quiet neighborhood, you see. So much so that I am usually able to sleep soundly with my window open. But on that night, I was restless and not sleeping, and I remember distinctly hearing the sound of an automobile engine being started.'

'Can you tell us what time that was?'

'Oh yes,' the witness replied. 'It was at fourteen minutes past midnight.'

'How can you be so sure?' Brian pressed.

'When I heard the vehicle, I looked immediately at the clock beside my bed.'

'Why?'

'In our neighborhood, automobiles are usually in bed, as are their owners, at that hour,' Ram declared. 'And I worried that someone might be ill.'

'Could you tell, sir, where the vehicle you heard was when the engine started?'

'Oh yes,' the man said. 'It was directly across the street.'

'Thank you,' Brian said.

'Mr. Ram,' Dana inquired on cross-examination, 'when did you report that you had heard a car start up that particular night?'

'A policeman came to my door in the middle of March,' he replied. 'It was then that I reported it.'

'That was about six weeks after the bombing, is that correct?'

'Yes, it was.'

'That's a pretty long time to remember something as unimportant as hearing a car engine, isn't it?'

'As it turned out, it was not so unimportant.'

'Yes, but you didn't know that at the time, did you?'

'No, this is true. I did not.'

'And yet you are absolutely positive that you heard the car engine start up on that specific night?'

'Oh yes. You see, my memory is quite good.'

'I'm sure it is. Tell me, where were you, say, the night before?'

'On the Sunday? I think I was at home.'

'You think? You aren't positive?'

348

'I am positive,' Ram corrected himself. 'I was at home.'

'Did you hear a car engine start up late that night?'

'No, I do not recall hearing one,' the witness said. 'I must have been sleeping.'

'On the night you say you heard the engine start up, did you get out of bed and look to see who it was?'

'No, I am sorry to say I did not.'

'Could you see out the window from where you were?'

'No, I could not.'

'So you heard an automobile engine being started, but you cannot testify that the one you heard belonged to my client?'

'No, I cannot say that with any certainty.'

'And am I to assume that also means you did not see who was driving the vehicle?'

'No, I did not,' he said.

'So,' Dana summarized, 'your testimony here today, sir, is that you claim to have heard an automobile start up around midnight, but you cannot positively identify it. You cannot identify the person who was driving it, and you can tell us only that you believe it came from directly across the street. Is that correct?'

'That is correct.'

'And you're certain that it was the night before the bombing?'

'I am certain.'

'It couldn't have been the night before, or even the night after?'

'No,' the witness declared. 'I have said it was that night.'

'Thank you. I have nothing further.'

'Mr. Ram,' Brian asked on redirect, 'although you can't positively identify the vehicle you heard for the court, what makes you think it came from the house directly across the street?'

'Because the engine was that of an automobile,' Ram replied confidently. 'You see, there are only four houses at our end of the street. Mine, Lieutenant Latham's, and two others. The occupants of the other two houses both drive trucks, each of which has been fitted with a low-cost dual exhaust system. Such engines have a much louder sound than that of a regular automobile, or a sport utility vehicle.'

'Thank you,' Brian said, turning away, and then turning back again. 'By the way, Mr. Ram, will you tell the jury what you do for a living?'

'I am an automobile mechanic,' he replied.

There were no further questions. The witness was excused.

Brian watched him leave the courtroom before he turned and addressed the bench. 'The prosecution rests, Your Honor.'

The judge peered down at Dana. 'Will you be prepared to present your first witness tomorrow morning, counsel?' he inquired.

'Yes, we will, Your Honor,' Dana assured him.

Bendali rapped his gavel. 'Court will be adjourned until ten o'clock tomorrow morning.' He turned to the jury for his daily reminder. 'I remind the members of the jury that you are not to discuss this case among yourselves, or with anyone else, or to allow anyone to try to influence you about this matter in any way.'

'It's so hard,' Karleen McKay said, as she and Allison Ackerman traveled down in the elevator together.

'What is?' Allison inquired.

'Well, it's all a jumble in my head, everything we've seen and heard, and I want to talk about it. I need to talk about it. I have to sort it all out, so I'm sure I've got it straight. Only we're not allowed.'

'I know,' the author responded. 'That's why I go home every day after court and have conversations with my computer.'

'What do you mean?'

'I'm keeping a kind of journal, dumping everything I can remember from each day into my computer, and then I try to look at it from different perspectives.'

'Spoken like a true writer,' Karleen declared. 'Does it work?'

'Well, I think so,' Allison replied. 'However, it's a bit like watching a tennis match. First the ball's in one court, and then it's in the other.'

Karleen chuckled. 'I know exactly what you mean,' she said. And that was as far as either of them would go in discussing the trial.

Since the riot in the courtroom, the crowds outside had grown increasingly restless. Several skirmishes had prompted police to set up barricades along Third Avenue between James and Jefferson to protect the courthouse and reduce traffic to one lane. The demonstrators, essentially pushed away from the building entrance, and out of camera range, began to mill around both cross streets, waving their placards and shouting their slogans.

'Abortion is murder!'

'Freedom is choice!'

Karleen and Allison exited the building, walked to the corner of James, and headed for the garage on Second Avenue where both their cars were parked. Suddenly, a man was blocking their way. He wore a huge button on his lapel that depicted a mutilated fetus and proclaimed the preborn's right to life.

'You're on that jury, aren't you?' he charged.

As the author and the Realtor glanced at each other, both realized, too late, that Karleen had forgotten to remove the juror identification badge from her jacket.

'Excuse us, please,' Allison said, trying to push past.

But the man let out a yell. 'Here's two of them!' he cried. 'We got two of them!'

In an instant, the women were surrounded, as some two dozen impassioned protesters looked to vent their frustration.

'Are you going to convict Corey Latham?' someone asked.

'Are you going to take his life for trying to save others?'

'Let us through,' Allison demanded, but no one was listening.

'He's a saint, not a sinner,' a woman cried.

'He's a savior,' another claimed.

Suddenly, the mob was two mobs, as a dozen others quickly sized up the situation and descended on the scene, ready and eager to shout and taunt and shove.

'He's a murderer,' one of them declared.

'Speak for the victims, who no longer have a voice,' someone else entreated.

'Convict the bastard!' another demanded.

Afterward no one could say for sure which side threw the

first punch, but that was all it took for the opposing groups to be at each other's throats. And the two jurors were caught right in the middle of the pushing and punching.

Someone lunged forward at someone else, and a fist caught Allison in the ribs. An instant later, someone else inadvertently rammed an elbow into her kidneys with such force that it knocked her to the ground. She heard Karleen shouting something from above, but she was helpless to respond, as feet began stumbling every which way over her. She tried to crawl, but couldn't move. She tried to cry out, but could barely breathe. She managed to get her arms up around her head, but that left her body exposed. She counted seventeen stomps before she lost consciousness.

17

Abraham Bendali was as angry as Robert Niera could ever remember seeing him. One look at Allison Ackerman's battered body was all it took, as he sat in his chambers on Wednesday morning with the mystery writer and the attorneys. Court was in recess, the other jurors notified to stay at home.

In the aftermath of the street fight, Allison was removed to Harborview Medical Center, where she was obliged to spend an uncomfortable night. In addition to a concussion, her left arm was in a sling, the result of a sprained shoulder. Three stitches had to be taken just above her left eye. There was an ugly bruise across the small of her back, along with numerous lacerations on her arms and legs, and she had sustained four cracked ribs. A night in the hospital had been deemed necessary to evaluate the concussion and monitor her kidney function.

'Do you wish to be removed from the jury, Mrs. Ackerman?' Bendali asked her. 'I want you to know I wouldn't blame you, if you did.'

Allison glared at him. 'No, I do not,' she said firmly. 'I've gone too far with this to quit now, just because of a bunch of thugs. If my injuries won't be a distraction to anyone, Your Honor, I would very much prefer to stay.'

Bendali sighed. 'This whole thing has gotten totally out of control,' he acknowledged, his irritation obvious in the tone of his voice. 'I could order the jury sequestered for the remainder of the trial. How would that be?'

'Inconvenient,' Allison replied. 'For me as well as everyone else, I suspect. Besides, I don't think I was a target out there. They were looking for any excuse to fight each other. I just got in the way.'

The judge considered his options for a long moment. 'All right,' he said finally. 'If you want to stay, and you don't want to be sequestered, I'll arrange for you to have an escort both to and from your home. As a matter of fact, I'll arrange escorts for everyone. From now on, no member of this jury – no one connected with this trial – is going to be put at risk.'

'Thank you,' Allison said. 'I think we'll all appreciate that.' She was thinking of Karleen McKay, who had endured her own share of cuts and bruises. The Realtor had been with her at the hospital, and had been kind enough to stay until Allison was moved to a private room.

'We're in recess until tomorrow morning,' Bendali informed the attorneys, and then peered at the juror. 'That is, if you think you'll feel well enough by then,' he added. 'If not, we'll damn well stay in recess until you do.'

'I'll be well enough,' Allison declared. She had no desire to prolong this ordeal any longer than necessary.

'Tell me the truth,' Corey urged. 'How do you think it's going?'

Dana had gone to the jail to let him know there would be no court today, and they had been allowed to meet in the purple interview room.

'I think we're doing as well as can be expected,' she told him, preferring to be cautious.

'You sound like a doctor trying not to tell a patient that he's dying,' Corey said with a grimace.

'The whole thrust of the prosecution's case was to link together a string of coincidences that on the surface look like they lead only to you,' she said. 'I'd be lying to you if I said that Brian Ayres hadn't done a pretty good job of it. But that's only half the picture. In our presentation, we're going to show the other half. We're going to break some of those links, offer plausible alternatives, and show those coincidences to be just that – nothing but coincidences.'

'I want to get on that stand,' he declared. 'I want to get up there and tell the jury I could never have killed all those people.'

'You'll have your chance,' she assured him.

'I just hope they'll believe me.'

Dana reached over and squeezed his hand. 'So do I,' she said; because she had never made him any promises, she had always been honest.

He looked down at her hand covering his. 'That woman who got hurt,' he asked, 'she'll be all right, won't she?'

'Yes, I think so.'

Corey let out a long sigh. 'I want this to be over,' he murmured. 'I don't want anyone else getting hurt because of me.'

'I'm concerned,' Roger Roark confided to his select group of advisors. 'My read on this Hill House thing is that McAuliffe has negated enough of the state's case to end up with a hung jury, if not an out-and-out acquittal. She's coming up to bat now, and we've got to figure out a way to strike her out.'

'What do you have in mind?' someone asked.

'I haven't a clue. You're my think tank. I need you to figure it out.'

'I want to say something first,' the bulky man with the crooked nose said. 'I've been following the case pretty closely, and I have to tell you that I'm not so sure any more that this Corey Latham is guilty.'

'So what?' Roark inquired.

'So maybe we should leave McAuliffe alone. Let her do her job. Why should we want to convict the kid if he's innocent?'

'You've been a member of this group for a long time now,' Roark replied patiently. 'Certainly long enough to understand that it's the cause that matters – not the individual. It's always the cause.'

It was midnight before Dana could unwind enough to get into bed. She tried to be quiet, but Sam woke up anyway. Or perhaps he'd just been lying there, waiting for her. In either case, he reached over and put his arms around her.

'I know it's not the same, because there are no lives at stake,' he murmured into her hair. 'But I always have this precipitous feeling before a concert, like someone in the audience will discover I'm a fraud, that I can't really play the violin, and Benaroya Hall will come crashing down. I think they call it stage fright.'

In the darkness, Dana smiled and snuggled against him. 'Here, I've always thought of you as my rock,' she said. 'And it turns out you're really a jellyfish.'

He chuckled. 'Just trying to help,' he said.

'You always do,' she told him.

'Are you ready for tomorrow?'

'I can't remember a case I've been more ready for,' she said. 'And yet, I'm not ready at all.'

'It's because you care,' he suggested. 'Maybe more than you're willing to admit, more than you ever have before.'

'I believe in him,' she said. 'I really do. I don't think he had anything to do with that bombing.' She sighed. 'It's hard for me to explain.'

'Try,' he urged.

'The truth is, ninety-nine percent of our job as defense attorneys is to find a loophole for the client to slither through, whether he's guilty or innocent. Don't ask, don't tell – we don't care. But this time, it's different. This time, I do care. And I'm so scared that if I make just one tiny mistake, it could cost Corey Latham his life.'

'I think it's an awesome responsibility, to do what you do,' Sam said. 'But it seems to me, with you behind him, he's already way ahead of the game.'

Dana considered his words for a long moment. 'In law school,' she said, 'we were taught that it was dangerous to get emotionally involved in a case because it could cloud the judgment.'

'Speaking strictly from personal experience, of course,' Sam said, nuzzling her neck, 'I'd have to say that getting emotionally involved can also clarify the judgment.'

She sighed with a mixture of despair and relief. 'Without you, I couldn't do it, you know,' she told him.

'I know.'

'That interview my ex gave to the tabloids – painful as it is for me to admit, there was some truth in it.'

'I know that, too.'

'And you're still here?'

'Uh-huh.'

'Why?'

He shrugged. 'I guess, because here is exactly where I want to be.'

She wrapped her arms around him. 'I was right the first time,' she said. 'You *are* a rock.'

'Yes, indeed,' he said with a deep chuckle. 'And at the moment, I just happen to be able to prove it to you.'

His hands began to reach under her nightgown.

'Oh my,' she said with a nervous giggle, because she couldn't recall the last time they had made love. 'I've been so preoccupied with other things, I'm afraid I might have forgotten how.'

'Hmmm,' he replied, as he followed his hands with his lips. 'Well, if you have, it will be my unadulterated pleasure to refresh your memory.'

357

18

'Ms. McAuliffe, you may call your first witness,' Abraham Bendali declared at ten o'clock on Thursday morning.

Dana rose from her chair, dressed in a beige suit and pumps, with a simple gold chain around her neck. She looked expensive but not extravagant.

'The defense calls Dr. Ronald Stern,' she said.

The fifty-six-year-old Harvard-educated psychiatrist made his way slowly to the witness stand, dragging a shriveled right leg. A victim of polio, he was dependent on both a leg brace and a forearm crutch to support him.

Without realizing it, those in the courtroom held their collective breath as he maneuvered himself onto the stand, and then awkwardly shifted both his crutch and his weight so he could use his hands to take the oath. They watched as he twisted his body into the chair. And then they listened, fascinated, as he detailed his professional history.

Among other things, he was a professor emeritus from his alma mater, and he was preeminent in the field of criminal behavior, specializing, over the last two decades, in the psychology of terrorism.

During the past six months, he had been to Cedar Falls, Annapolis, Orlando, Charleston, and Groton, and had made fifteen separate trips to Seattle.

'Dr. Stern,' the defense attorney began, when he had been accepted as an expert witness, 'how much are we paying you for your testimony here today?'

Several of the jurors blinked, and Brian Ayres, seated at the prosecution table, smiled wryly to himself. Although he knew exactly how good Dana Reid McAuliffe was, every once in a while, she still managed to surprise him.

'You're not paying me anything,' Stern replied.

'I beg your pardon?' Dana questioned.

'I provided my services to your firm, free of charge.'

'I see. Well, we're at least paying all your traveling expenses, are we not?'

Stern shook his head. 'No,' he said. 'The United States government is.'

'Well, far be it from me to look a gift horse in the mouth, but may I ask why?'

'It's part of an ongoing program, designed to study various acts of terrorism, both past and present, in an effort to formulate reliable psychological profiles of known terrorists. It's hoped that these profiles will give us a reasonably accurate way to identify potential terrorists in the future.'

'What are some of the specifics you look for?'

'Specifically, we are looking for recognizable aberrant behavior patterns stemming from early childhood,' Stern replied. 'To that end, and wherever possible, we investigate family background and conduct. We also examine the nature of relationships that are outside the family unit. We look at the level of education and research the educational experience, interviewing teachers, students, and administrators. We perform exhaustive psychological testing. We're particularly interested in evaluating communication skills. And in those cases where it is appropriate, we analyze job history.'

'Will you tell the court some of the incidents you've investigated?'

'We did a detailed analysis of the recent school shootings – Mississippi, Kentucky, Tennessee, Oregon, Colorado, California. We studied various aspects of the World Trade Center bombing, the Oklahoma City bombing, the embassy bombings in Kenya and Tanzania, and the Lockerbie incident. Of course, in some of those cases, we weren't able to interview the subjects.'

'In those instances where you *were* able to interview the subjects, did you find that their psychological characteristics consistently fit the criteria of your profiles?'

'Yes,' the psychiatrist replied without hesitation. 'I'm pleased to report that they did, with almost textbook accuracy.'

'Was there any particular characteristic you can point to that was consistent among those you studied?'

'Yes, an obvious one, really,' he said. 'But one that did need to be proven.'

'And what was that?'

'We realized that, while motives and methods might vary, terrorists have one thing in common: a deep-rooted anger manifesting itself in the need to cause destruction.'

'As part of your study, Dr. Stern, you interviewed a great many people connected to my client, Corey Latham, did you not?'

'Yes, I did. All told, I spoke with close to a hundred people.'

'And you also interviewed the defendant, didn't you?'

'Yes, I did.'

'In total, how many hours do you estimate you spent with him?'

'Over a period of six months, I'd say I spent upward of ninety hours with Lieutenant Latham.'

'Doing what?'

'We did a lot of talking,' he said. 'And a fair amount of testing.'

'And Dr. Stern, on the basis of those ninety hours of talking and testing, what if any conclusions did you draw?'

'I found your client to be an anomaly in our study.'

'An anomaly?'

'Yes.'

'Why was that, sir?'

The psychiatrist shrugged. 'He didn't fit any of the standard psychological criteria we had developed for terrorists.'

'Did I hear you correctly?' Dana pressed. 'Are you saying this alleged monster, this alleged butcher, this animal accused of bombing a building and killing almost two hundred people *isn't* a terrorist?'

'What I'm saying is, he doesn't fit any of our profiles.'

'Just so that I'm clear about this, doctor, and more important, so that the jury is clear about it, I'd like to go over the specifics of your thesis.'

As Dana was eliciting the pertinent details behind Ronald Stern's expert opinion, Craig Jessup was sorting through the morning mail. There was the usual number of bills, credit card applications, and catalogues, and at the bottom of the pile, an envelope bearing the elegant gold letterhead of Cotter Boland and Grace.

Jessup was surprised. He had long since tendered his September invoice and been paid in full. It was rare for him to receive written communication from the firm between statements. He ripped open the envelope, and extracted a single, typewritten page.

'This is to inform you,' it read, *'that no additional services will be required regarding the Latham case. If there is any amount still owing, please submit a final invoice, at your earliest convenience, so that we may reimburse you.*

'We thank you for your excellent effort on behalf of this matter, and look forward to working with you again in the near future.'

Paul Cotter, himself, had signed the letter.

Jessup did not particularly appreciate being cut off like this, in the middle of trial, without any warning. Especially now, when he was working on a new angle that was just beginning to come into focus. He laid the letter on his desk and sat there, elbow on armrest, rubbing his chin. He wondered why Dana hadn't mentioned it to him.

The defense finished its direct examination of Ronald Stern in the late afternoon.

'Doctor, based on your extensive work in the field of terrorist psychology, the number of hours you spent with my client, and the results of your profiling, do you have an opinion as to whether my client has the predisposition of a terrorist?'

'In my opinion,' Stern said flatly, 'he does not.'

'Thank you, sir.'

At that, there was a slight but audible sound of exhaling by

361

a number of jurors. Dana sat down, well satisfied. She had argued endlessly with Paul Cotter about using Stern as a witness, about the effectiveness of putting a Harvard type in front of a Seattle jury. But he had been able to take the most complex psychological theories and reduce them to easily understandable concepts, and he had done it as though he were sitting around a kitchen table with his audience, engaging in a conversation over a cup of coffee.

'I don't understand the problem,' she had told the managing partner. 'We need the best and he is the best. And besides, it isn't going to cost us a dime.'

She had won her argument, and in the wake of the psychiatrist's testimony, and the jury's reaction to it, she felt totally vindicated.

The jury's reaction was not lost on Brian, either. Stern was a powerful witness, his work praiseworthy, his credentials above reproach, his infirmity giving him an extra measure of credibility. He was what was known as a sympathetic witness, and the prosecutor knew the jurors would not take kindly to seeing him battered by cross-examination.

'Dr. Stern,' he inquired pleasantly, 'relying on all the expertise you've gained in the field of terrorism, can you state unequivocally that Corey Latham did not bomb Hill House?'

The psychiatrist contemplated the question for a long moment. 'My research is based on probabilities, not absolutes,' he replied finally. 'My examination of the defendant did not reveal the psychological characteristics associated with having committed this crime. But no, I can't state unequivocally that he did not.'

'So, even though he doesn't fit the profile, and doesn't fall within the parameters of your study, that man over there,' Brian said, pointing at the defendant, 'could still have gone out and bought aspirin, and sulfuric acid, and fertilizer, and made a bomb, stuffed it into a duffel bag, and planted it at Hill House, couldn't he?'

'I don't think it's probable,' Stern conceded, 'but it's possible he could have done that.'

'Thank you, doctor,' the prosecutor said. 'That's all I have.'

'Do you think Brian undermined Stern's testimony?' Joan Wills asked on the way back to Smith Tower.

'Not a lot,' Dana replied. 'When you're dealing with reasonable doubt, possibilities don't usually carry enough weight.'

The two attorneys were now being accompanied, door to door, by King County sheriff's deputies, as were the prosecutors and the jurors, by order of Abraham Bendali. The officers, Guff and Marty, guided them through the ninth-floor camera gauntlet and the milling crowds outside the courthouse like an oar slicing through water, accompanied them into the elevator at Smith Tower, and deposited them safely on the seventeenth floor.

'What time in the morning, ma'am?' Guff inquired of Dana.

'Uh, nine o'clock, I guess,' she said, '. . . thank you.'

'Will you be together?' Marty asked.

The attorneys nodded. The deputies touched their hats and were gone.

Dana sighed uncomfortably. She was used to keeping a low profile, and while she appreciated Bendali's good intentions, she felt exposed. 'It's so conspicuous,' she said to Joan.

'Maybe so,' the associate responded. 'But I don't mind telling you, after what happened to those two jurors, I feel a lot safer with them in front of us.'

Elise Latham stretched out on the bed like a cat, her body glistening in the glow of the lamp.

'I really should go home,' she said.

'What for?' the man beside her asked.

'Because I have to be at the courthouse bright and early tomorrow,' she told him. 'I'm testifying.'

'So?'

'So, there's a deputy who's going to arrive at my house at eight o'clock in the morning, courtesy of King County. How do you think it would look, me showing up from Mercer Island instead?'

Steven Bonner chuckled. 'You mean, it wouldn't look very wifely?'

Elise sighed. 'I'm afraid there's not much I've done in the past month that would look very wifely,' she said.

'I know,' he agreed. 'That's why it's been such fun.'

'Fun for you,' she retorted. 'Absolutely necessary for me.'

'You know, I think I like you better now than before,' he told her. 'You're a lot less uptight than when we were engaged.'

She looked at him archly. 'I was only uptight because you were playing me for a fool.'

'I didn't mean to,' he said. 'I guess I just wasn't ready to settle down back then.'

She laughed. 'What are you trying to tell me, that you are now, when it's too late?'

'I'm trying to tell you that I'm sorry, and that I know I blew it.'

Elise blinked. 'In that case, you're forgiven.'

'I think I may have let happiness get away, and now the best I can hope for is a little excitement in my life,' he said, sounding strangely sincere.

She poked him in the ribs. 'Like getting it on with the wife of a terrorist?'

He chuckled. 'I don't suppose it could get much more exciting than that, could it?'

'Whatever turns you on, sweetie.'

'*You* turn me on,' he said. 'So, what are you going to testify to in court tomorrow?'

'The truth,' she said with a shrug. 'Whatever that is.'

'The truth and nothing but the truth,' he recited, trailing an index finger down the length of her body. 'Does that include telling the jury where you've been spending your nights recently?'

'Maybe I should,' she said, quivering beneath his touch. 'Maybe they would feel so sorry for Corey, they'd acquit him, just because I'm such a bad wife.'

'Is that what you want,' he murmured, beginning to suck at her nipples, 'for Corey to be acquitted?'

She shivered deliciously. 'It depends on my options,' she said. 'Maybe I should tell them that the reason I fled to another man's bed is because my husband is guilty, and I can't stay with him, knowing that.'

'And will you also tell them how irresistible that other man finds you?' he whispered, slipping his hand between her legs. 'How insatiable.'

Elise groaned. 'Come any closer and I'll show you just how insatiable I can be,' she dared him. 'And then I really do have to go home.'

The wife of the accused walked to the stand with her head up and her eyes straight ahead, looking neither right nor left. Her mauve dress had long sleeves and a high collar, and fell well below her knees. A matching bow held her sleek blond hair securely at the nape of her neck. Her makeup was soft. Corey looked at her longingly as she passed.

Dana rose from her seat and took several steps toward the witness. 'Elise,' she began, conversationally, 'when did you and Corey first meet?'

'It'll be two years in November,' she replied.

'When did you become engaged?'

'Six weeks later.'

'And you were married four months after that?'

'Yes.'

'Between the day you met and the day he came back from his last patrol, how much time would you say you and Corey actually spent together?'

Elise shrugged. 'All told, about five months.'

'Was that time enough for the two of you to get to know each other pretty well?'

'No, it wasn't,' the young wife admitted. 'I think, knowing what we know now, we should probably have waited at least a year before we got married. But we were in love, and that was all we could think about.'

At the defense table, Corey smiled.

'There has been testimony during this trial that, in September of last year, you had an abortion,' Dana said gently. 'Is it true?'

'I'm not very proud of it,' the witness replied with a heavy sigh, 'but yes, it's true. I did have an abortion.'

'Will you tell the court why?'

'I was scared,' Elise said simply. 'Here I was, all by myself and married to a man I hardly knew. I didn't know whether it was the right time to bring a child into the world. I couldn't see the future. All I could see was where I was, right then and there, and I was scared.'

'Scared of what?'

'Scared of being a mother, of not being able to cope. Scared of what it would do to our marriage, to have a baby so soon. Scared that Corey wouldn't be there when we needed him.'

'And he couldn't help you work it through?'

'That's just the point, he wasn't here. Only it wasn't like he was on some business trip or something, and I could talk to him on a telephone if I had to. No, he was out on a boat, in the middle of an ocean for three months. And it wasn't just that I couldn't talk to him. I couldn't even write to him about it. The stupid Navy didn't allow it.'

'The Navy wouldn't let you talk to your husband, or write to him that you were pregnant and needed his help?'

'No,' Elise said flatly, 'they wouldn't.'

'So you had to make the decision?'

The young woman nodded. 'Maybe it was the wrong decision, I don't know,' she said. 'All I know is I had to make it on my own.'

'What happened when Corey found out?'

'He was furious. And I made it worse by lying to him. I don't know why I did that. I just thought it would be easier.'

'Did you know how Corey felt about abortion before this happened?'

Elise shook her head. 'I don't think it ever came up. We talked about having kids someday, sure, but we never talked about *not* having kids.'

'All right, so Corey was furious when he found out you'd had the abortion,' Dana prompted. 'Can you tell us what he did?'

'In the beginning, he just couldn't see it from my side,' Elise said. 'All he could focus on was that I'd killed his baby, that

I'd taken a life. He screamed at me, he stormed around the house, he smashed things. But mostly, he cried. And that was the worst part, hearing him cry like that.'

At that, Corey blinked rapidly a few times, and swiped a hand across his eyes.

'How long did this go on?'

'For maybe two weeks.'

'Then what?'

'Then I guess the anger began to go away, and we started to talk. Sometimes, we'd stay up all night talking.'

'About what?'

'About how we were going to get through this,' Elise said. 'About whether or not our marriage was going to survive.'

'Did you get any outside help?'

She nodded. 'Yes, we did. That was Corey's suggestion. We joined a church when we moved to Queen Anne, so we went to the minister there for counseling. Then he got Corey into this support group, and after that, things got better.'

'What kind of support group?'

'It was for people who had lost a child,' Elise said. 'At first, he went almost every night. After that, it was maybe once or twice a week. I guess it helped, because by the end of November, he was pretty much his same old self again.'

'So, as the person closest to him, would you say that it took Corey about a month to work through everything, and come to terms with it?'

'Yes. About that.'

'We've heard testimony from one of your neighbors, Carl Thorson, who said he came in on the middle of an argument between you and Corey one night, and believed it was about to turn violent. Is this true?'

'Did he come over one night when we were arguing? Yes, he did,' Elise conceded. 'Did it turn violent? No, it didn't.'

'Then let me ask you this, during the entire month between the time Corey found out about the abortion, to the time when you believe he became reconciled to it, did he ever turn violent toward you?'

'No, never,' Elise said emphatically. 'Not before, not during, not after, not ever.'

'Thank you,' Dana said. 'Now, will you tell us a little bit about your house?'

'Well, it's not very big. It has a little living room with a dining area, a small kitchen, two bedrooms, a bath, and a detached garage.'

'Is Corey handy around the house?'

'Oh yes, he can do lots of things.'

'Does he have a workshop area?'

'He works out in the garage, sometimes,' Elise said. 'We park the car in the driveway.'

'Do you ever go in the garage?'

'Sure, I do. There's not much storage space in the house, so we keep extra canned goods and supplies and stuff in the garage. I probably go out there for something several times a week.'

'So you're pretty familiar with what belongs in the garage, and what doesn't?'

'Sure.'

'If there was something there you didn't recognize, like, say, a dozen car batteries, would you have noticed?'

'A dozen car batteries?' Elise echoed. 'Of course I would've noticed. Who wouldn't?'

'Do you think, if Corey had been building a bomb in your garage, you would have known it?'

'Of course I would've known. I was in and out of the garage all the time. My God, how could I not have known if my husband was building a bomb?'

'All right then, let's move on to the night before the bombing. Where were you?'

'I was out for the evening,' she replied. 'It was a co-worker's birthday. A bunch of us from the office took her to dinner.'

'What time did you get home?'

'A little before ten o'clock.'

'Was Corey home when you got there?'

'Sure. He was watching television – *3rd Rock from the Sun*.

369

It's his favorite show. I watched the last ten minutes of it with him.'

'What did you do then?'

'We did what we always did. We watched the news, had our cocoa, and went to bed.'

'What then?'

Elise glanced at the jury, embarrassed. 'Well, we got it on a little,' she mumbled, blushing. 'And then we went to sleep.'

'Are you a heavy sleeper, Elise?' Dana asked.

'No,' the young woman replied. 'As a matter of fact, I've always been a very light sleeper. It's why I like our neighborhood, because it's quiet. If so much as a car goes by, it wakes me up.'

'Taking that into consideration, if Corey had gotten out of bed for any reason during the night, would you have known it?'

'Yes, I would've,' she said without hesitation. 'He used to get up sometimes to go to the bathroom. I always woke up. Sometimes, it would wake me up if he just turned over in the bed.'

'Did Corey get up on the night before the bombing?'

'No, he didn't.'

'Let's be very clear here. Are you as certain as you can be that on that night Corey did not get out of the bed you share, he did not put on his clothes, he did not leave the house, and he did not get in his car, start the engine, and drive away?'

'No, he didn't do any of those things,' Elise said. 'I'm as certain of it as I can be.'

'We've heard testimony here from your neighbor across the street, Omar Ram, who said he heard a car engine start up shortly after midnight. He further said he believed the car was your husband's.'

'I know Mr. Ram,' Elise said. 'He's a nice man, but I think he got his nights mixed up.'

'What do you mean?'

'I mean that the day before, which would have been Sunday, my brother and his wife came over for dinner. They didn't leave

370

until around, well, it must have been twelve-fifteen. I think that may have been the car starting up that Mr. Ram heard.'

The judge took the noon recess as soon as Dana completed her direct examination of Elise Latham. Some forty reporters hurried out of the courtroom to file their stories. Those in the Hill House section sat as if dazed, not sure what to think about what they had just heard.

Stuart Dunn felt sorry for Elise. She was so clearly caught in a no-win situation. It wasn't that her testimony wasn't believable, exactly, it was that a wife wasn't always the most reliable witness when it came to her husband. After lunch, it would be up to the prosecutor to discredit her, and to his surprise, Stuart found himself uncomfortable with the idea. Elise seemed so fragile, somehow, and the history teacher didn't want to see her hurt or humiliated.

There was something about Elise Latham that Allison Ackerman didn't quite like or, perhaps, trust. A chilliness, she thought, beneath the soft dress. Or it might have been that her answers seemed just a shade too rehearsed. Allison was well aware that witnesses were primed before their testimony, but she would have expected just a little more emotion from a wife whose husband was accused of such an unspeakable crime. And there was something else, too, that the mystery writer had noticed. During her entire testimony, Elise Latham had never once looked at the defendant.

While Joan Wills dashed out of the building to pick up sandwiches, Dana took Elise in tow, settling her in an available room just outside Judge Bendali's chambers. The young woman was shivering, and, it seemed, close to coming apart.

'You did just fine,' the attorney reassured her.

'Sure,' Elise said with a shrug. 'But that was the easy part. After lunch comes the hatchet job, right?'

'Just keep your composure, and you'll get through it.'

'What composure? I feel like a train is about to run right over me.'

'Then use that feeling,' Dana advised. 'It'll make you just

that much more sympathetic to the jury. And remember, wait three seconds after each question before you respond.'

'I know,' Elise said. 'In case you want to object.'

'Answer only the question that's asked of you, and keep your answer brief. Don't offer any additional information.'

'I know,' Elise repeated, with an edge of irritation. 'You've told me a zillion times already.'

At that moment, Joan poked her head in the door. 'May I see you a moment?' she said to her partner, an unreadable expression on her face.

'Sure,' Dana said, and followed Joan out into the hallway. 'What's up?'

'I think maybe you'd better take a look at this,' Joan said, handing her the latest issue of *Probe*. 'It was at the deli.'

Dana glanced at it. A color photo of herself, wearing the very same gray gabardine suit she was wearing today, and carrying a briefcase, stared back at her, beneath a black headline that screamed, *'Hill House Defense Attorney Had Abortion There!'* Below, the lead paragraph read: 'Attorney Dana McAuliffe, who is defending the man accused of bombing Hill House because his wife had an abortion there, apparently had an abortion there herself. According to reliable sources, McAuliffe had the abortion about five years ago.'

'What on earth . . . ?' she muttered.

'I checked three other places,' Joan told her. 'It's everywhere. I know these tabloid types are notorious for making things up out of whole cloth, but I can't believe they'd be so stupid as to think they could get away with something like this. The way I look at it, they've just bought themselves a multimillion-dollar libel suit.'

'No,' Dana said, her head beginning to throb, and her knees suddenly so weak that she had to lean against the wall for support. 'I don't want a lawsuit.'

'But you can't just turn the other cheek,' Joan declared indignantly. 'It's out there, in black and white, for everyone to see. You can't let them get away with that.'

'Please,' Dana said wearily, 'just let it go.'

'But that's what slime like this counts on, that you won't fight back.'

'Just let it go,' Dana repeated, angry and numb at the same time.

'Look,' Joan persisted, 'I know how focused you are on the trial right now, and I can understand that you don't want anything to interfere with that, but the firm can handle this. You don't have to be involved.'

Dana turned on her. 'Tell me,' she snapped, 'what is it about the word "no" that you can't seem to comprehend?'

Joan stared at her mentor, taken aback, and then her mouth dropped. 'Oh my God,' she whispered. 'It's true, isn't it?'

Dana closed her eyes, and let out a long breath. 'So, now you know,' she said in a leaden voice. 'Now the whole world knows.'

'I don't know what to say,' Joan murmured.

'I'm sorry, I shouldn't have barked at you like that,' Dana told her. 'But as you now see, I wouldn't have much of a case for libel.'

'No, it's all my fault,' Joan asserted. 'I shouldn't have pushed. I can be pretty obtuse sometimes.'

Dana pressed her fingers against her temples. 'I tried so hard to keep my personal life out of this,' she said tightly. 'I guess I should have known I couldn't.'

'Does it matter?' Joan asked. 'What does it change, really? So you won't be the darling of the pro-life people anymore. Does that bother you terribly much?'

'Hardly.'

'And the last time I looked, abortion was still legal in this country. Which turns it all into a big so what!'

'You think so?'

Joan shrugged. 'As far as I'm concerned, it's business as usual. And right now, that means lunch. It just so happens, I'm starving.'

'You go on,' Dana told her with a weak attempt at a smile. 'I have something I have to take care of first. I'll be there in a minute.'

Dana found a temporarily unoccupied office with a telephone, and quickly dialed a number. It took four rings before Craig Jessup answered.

'Oh good,' she said. 'I'm glad you're there. I need you to change gears for me, if you could.'

There was an awkward pause. 'What do you mean?' Jessup asked finally.

'Well, I know you're working on the anonymous letter, but I was hoping I could get you to squeeze in something else that's just come up,' she explained.

'I guess I'm a little confused,' he said. 'I'm not working on your case anymore.'

Now it was Dana's turn to be confused. 'Why on earth would you quit in the middle of trial?' she asked.

'I didn't quit,' he replied. 'I got a letter telling me you were terminating my services.'

'Terminating your – What are you talking about? What letter?'

'You didn't know?'

'Know what?' she demanded.

'I got a letter from the firm,' Jessup explained. 'It came yesterday, saying that my services were no longer required. Cotter signed it.'

'That's absurd,' she told him. 'It must be some kind of mistake, a clerical error or something. Don't worry, I'll take care of it. Meanwhile, consider yourself back on the job. And please tell me you haven't gotten involved in something else already, because I have no idea how I would get through the rest of this trial without you.'

'No, I'm still available,' he said. 'I guess I should have called you when the letter came, but I assumed you knew about it.'

'Well, I assure you I didn't,' she declared. 'But it doesn't matter. As far as I'm concerned, it never happened. So, can you help me?'

'What do you need?' he asked.

She steeled herself. 'In case you haven't seen it yet, there's a story out today in a sleaze magazine called *Probe* that says I

374

had an abortion at Hill House,' she said, as matter-of-factly as she could. 'My guess is it was leaked by someone from the clinic, in an effort to scuttle my case, and secure a conviction. I want to know who.'

There was a momentary silence at the other end of the line, and Dana held her breath for what seemed forever, until she heard his voice again.

'I'll get on it immediately,' he said softly.

Jessup stared pensively at the telephone, long after he had hung it up, his mind already at work. He had stumbled across something a couple of days ago, before he'd gotten the letter, that had struck him as odd – a piece in a puzzle whose shape he couldn't quite grasp. It had nothing to do with Dana, directly, but he wondered if there could be a connection.

He thought about the magazine article. Finding out where the information had come from would be relatively easy. What might be difficult, he knew from experience, was telling the client.

20

Somehow, Dana managed to swallow some of her sandwich, managed to finish coaching Elise Latham in the complexities of cross-examination, and managed to return to the courtroom for the afternoon session with her head high. Despite her outward demeanor, however, she was certain she could feel every eye in the room fastened on her. At one point, she couldn't resist stealing a quick, questioning glance behind her. Finding nothing out of the ordinary, she sighed so audibly that Joan overheard.

The associate was concerned. For some reason he neglected to share with them, Charles Ramsey had not returned to court after lunch, and Joan worried whether Dana would be able to get through the afternoon session. Although, technically, he was the third chair, it would have been comforting to have the senior partner there for backup.

She needn't have worried. Dana knew how to separate her personal life from her professional one. This was not the time to think about the harm done by the tabloid article, or even to think about Sam. Oh God, Sam! No, now she had to focus every ounce of her attention on the proceedings at hand. She owed that to Corey. Later, when she was out of the courtroom, she would take stock, assess the fallout, and consider her options. And deal with other matters.

Brian's cross-examination of Elise Latham took up a good part of the afternoon. He poked and prodded, but as far as some of the jurors were concerned, Stuart Dunn and Allison Ackerman among them, he didn't seem to make much headway. Until just after four o'clock.

'Mrs. Latham,' he said, 'you testified earlier that your normal habit on weeknights was to watch the ten o'clock news, have your cocoa, and go to bed. Is that correct?'

'Yes.'

'Who made the cocoa?'

Elise shrugged. 'Sometimes I did, sometimes Corey did.' She gave him a direct look. 'For the past seven months, I have.'

'On the night in question, who made the cocoa?'

'I don't really remember,' Elise replied. 'Does it matter?'

At the defense table, Dana's eyes narrowed ever so slightly. She knew exactly where Brian was going.

'It may matter a great deal,' Brian said smoothly. 'So why don't you take a moment to think about it.'

The witness glanced over at Dana, but the attorney could not give her anything but an imperceptible shrug.

'All right, I think Corey made the cocoa that night,' she said.

'The defendant made the cocoa, and after drinking it, you slept soundly all night. Is that correct?'

'What are you trying to say, that he drugged my cocoa?' Elise demanded.

'Objection,' Dana interrupted. 'May I ask where the prosecutor is going with this line of questioning?'

'Mr. Ayres?' the judge inquired.

'Your Honor, assuming, as the prosecution does, that the defendant did get out of bed that night,' Brian explained, 'I'm just trying to determine if there could be a reason why a light sleeper like Mrs. Latham might not have awakened.'

'It sounds like a fishing trip to me, Your Honor,' Dana suggested, 'based on the grossest speculation. Does the prosecutor have anything to back up his hypothesis? He certainly made no mention of it in his own case. Is there new evidence that I haven't been made aware of?'

Bendali fixed a steely eye on the prosecutor. 'Do you have evidence you're planning to introduce here, counsel?'

Brian sighed. 'Not at this time, Your Honor,' he admitted.

'Objection is sustained,' the judge declared. 'The jury will disregard counsel's fishing expedition.'

In the second row of the jury box, Allison smiled to herself.

Dirty trick or not, Brian Ayres had executed it well. He had no proof of it, but he wanted the jurors to consider the possibility that Corey Latham might have doctored his wife's cocoa to make her sleep through the night. Despite the judge's admonition to disregard, that thought would rattle around twelve minds for some time to come.

'I have no further questions,' Brian declared, his job done.

'Redirect, Ms. McAuliffe?' Bendali inquired.

Dana sighed. The damage was already done. Anything she could do now would only make it worse. 'No, Your Honor,' she said.

'Then we're adjourned until ten o'clock Monday morning,' he declared.

The moment the gavel sounded, and both the defendant and the jury had been escorted out of the courtroom, some forty reporters descended on the defense attorney, and Dana readied herself to try to discredit the notion of drugged cocoa.

'Is it true, Ms. McAuliffe?' several exclaimed. 'Did you really have an abortion?'

She was stunned. In the heat of battle, she had actually managed to put the tabloid article out of her mind. She opened her mouth, and closed it again.

'Ms. McAuliffe has no comment at this time,' she heard Joan saying. And then she felt the associate grasp her by the arm, and with Robert Niera's help, propel her to the front of the courtroom and through the door that led to the judge's chambers.

Robert had been out during the lunch break. He had seen the latest issue of *Probe*. Making a quick decision, he put the two women in his own office. 'I'll get the deputies,' he said.

'I was afraid something like that might happen,' Joan murmured.

'To tell you the truth, I'd forgotten all about it,' Dana said, with a touch of irony. 'I was too busy envisioning every five o'clock news lead in the country warning mothers about the potential dangers of hot chocolate.'

'I say we get back to the office and come up with some kind of statement,' Joan suggested. 'On both issues.'

Before Dana could respond, Guff and Marty, the two deputies, appeared in the doorway.

'Are you ladies ready?' Guff asked.

'We certainly are,' Joan replied.

Questions began firing at them the moment they entered the corridor outside the courtroom. Ignoring them, the two officers marched the attorneys through the swarm of media people, physically clearing the way when necessary, and hurried them into a waiting elevator. Three reporters appeared out of nowhere at the last minute, and tried to jump aboard before the doors closed. They were unceremoniously shoved aside.

'Whew!' Joan exclaimed. 'It's like dodging real bullets.'

'I think we're in the clear now,' Guff said.

Dana set her jaw. Joan was right, of course. She was going to have to come up with a statement about the article, or risk having her personal life disrupt the trial. But it would have to be carefully thought out.

By the time the elevator doors opened on the main floor, she had settled on a gracious but firm, 'No comment for now.' That would stop them for today. By tomorrow, she would be prepared.

To her great relief, there were no reporters waiting to accost her in the lobby. She was safe for the time being, knowing that outside the courthouse, they could blend into the crush of people, and likely be gone before anyone had a chance to recognize her.

One by one, they pushed through the revolving door, made their way out from under the portico, and turned left toward Jefferson. The demonstrators, grown now from hundreds into thousands, were alternately singing and shouting at one another. But the moment they saw Dana, they began to surge toward her, threatening to break through the police barricade.

The first projectile hit just as they were crossing Third Avenue. The overripe tomato caught Dana full in the chest and oozed its way down the front of her coat.

'Baby killer!' someone shouted.

'Murderer!'

379

'May you rot in hell!'

Before anyone quite realized what was happening, tomatoes were pelting her from all directions, followed by raw eggs, and finally, animal feces, some of it spilling over onto Joan.

'Abortion makes you the mother of a dead baby!' a woman hissed in her face.

Guff and Marty sprang into action. Grabbing the two women, they pulled them back from the corner and into a handy doorway. Guff then barked into his two-way radio, and almost immediately, half a dozen additional deputies were on the scene. Using locked arms, they managed to drive back the crowd enough to get a police car through. The attorneys and their guards quickly climbed inside and were driven off.

'No more of this walking stuff. From now on, we drive you wherever you need to go,' Marty told them, and neither Dana nor Joan were of any mind to argue.

'My God, what happened to you two?' Angeline Wilder exclaimed after the deputies deposited the attorneys in the Cotter Boland reception area some ten minutes later. She wrinkled her nose. 'You smell like a barn.'

'We just ran into a few unpleasant people, that's all,' Joan told her.

'I can guess why,' Angeline said archly, a copy of *Probe* in plain view on her desk. She lowered her voice. 'I think you'd better go clean up a bit. Mr. Cotter said I was to tell him the moment you came in. He'll probably be looking for you.'

'No kidding,' Joan said sardonically. She took Dana by the arm and steered her into her office. 'Coat,' she said, and waited until Dana undid the buttons. Then she peeled the filthy garment off her partner, and tossed it aside. The gray suit was untouched. 'Come on,' she said.

'Where?' Dana asked.

'To the bathroom, of course. We have to wash that stuff out of your hair.'

Dana allowed herself to be propelled down the hall and into the bathroom, and did not protest when Joan stuck her head under the faucet and ran water and then soap all over it.

Angeline purloined a towel from Paul Cotter's private bathroom, and Dana permitted Joan to dry her hair. The two attorneys were back in Dana's office for less than a minute before the intercom buzzed.

'May I see you in my office, please,' the managing partner said, in a manner that required no response other than dispatch.

Dana rolled her eyes at Joan. 'I think I feel just like the lamb does who's heading off to the slaughter,' she said.

Straightening her shoulders, she marched down the corridor, and knocked on the solid mahogany door at the far end. There was no visible copy of *Probe* in Paul Cotter's office, he was far too sophisticated for that, but Dana knew it was there, somewhere.

'Charles tells me the trial is going well,' he said as soon as she was seated across the desk from him.

'I would say it's going as well as we expected,' she concurred.

'He also tells me you and Latham appear to have become especially close.'

'We've become professionally close, yes,' she amended.

'That might make things a bit awkward.'

'What things?'

He looked at her thoughtfully for a moment. 'Look, I'm not going to beat around the bush with you on this,' he said. 'I've seen the tabloid that came out today. I assume you know what I'm talking about?'

'I do.'

'Well, my personal feelings about the matter aside, I'm very much afraid this . . . revelation, whether there is any truth to it or not, may present a major roadblock to your continuing to first-chair this trial.'

'Why is that?'

'I think it should be obvious,' he suggested. 'If the media frenzy over you is even half what I believe it's going to be, just the distraction alone could considerably lessen your effectiveness, and I think you'd have to agree that would not be in the best interests of the client.'

'Not saying whether I agree with you or not at the moment,

what do you see as an option?' Dana inquired, wondering whether Joan would be able to handle Corey on the witness stand.

'I think there may be a reasonably uncomplicated solution,' Cotter replied. 'We could simply slide Charles up to first chair, allow you to stay on in second chair, so there's at least the appearance of continuity, and move Ms. Wills down to third.'

Dana blinked in surprise. 'You want to put Charles Ramsey in charge of the defense, knowing what you know about him, about what he did?'

The managing partner shrugged. 'What do we know about him?' he asked. 'Other than some off-the-wall allegation I can't seem to find anyone able to corroborate, all I know is that he's been a first-rate attorney, with a spotless reputation, since before you were born.'

'Is that why Craig Jessup got a letter terminating his services?' she asked. 'Because he stumbled onto something that could tarnish Ramsey's image, and by proxy, this firm's?'

'Jessup acted irresponsibly,' Cotter barked. 'He was retained to investigate certain matters pertaining to the trial itself, and he chose to go far afield of that. I will not have employees overstepping their bounds.'

'He didn't overstep, he was acting on my instructions,' Dana informed the managing partner. 'I asked him to look into the jury list issue. When it backfired on us, I thought it might be relevant down the road.'

'Well, I may have overreacted,' Cotter conceded.

'I'm glad you feel that way,' she said, 'because I've already rehired him.'

He frowned. 'Perhaps we should leave that decision to Charles,' he suggested.

'Oh?' Dana said. 'I thought we were just talking possibilities here. Are you saying a decision's already been made?'

'Well, I naturally assumed, under the circumstances, that is, that you . . .'

Defer to him as the head of her firm, she would. Give up without a fight, she would not. 'You assumed what?' she asked, her voice neutral. 'That I'd just roll over and relinquish the reins? Why would I do that? As you may recall, you begged me to take this case, when I made it perfectly clear I didn't want it. But now it's mine, and frankly, I think I'm doing a damn good job of it.'

'This is not a commentary on the quality of your work,' he reminded her. 'It's not your competence that's at issue here.'

'My current personal discomfort notwithstanding, I have no reason to think I can't continue to do a good job,' she told him. 'Furthermore, the key to this case is going to be, and always has been, Corey's own testimony. And I have serious reservations about Charles's ability to handle him effectively on the stand. He doesn't know him. He's barely said two words to him in court. He's never even bothered to go up to the jail and meet with him. On top of that, he hasn't sat in on so much as one of the preparation sessions. On the other hand, Joan has done all these things. So if you're really serious about replacing me, she's the one you should consider.'

Cotter scowled at her. 'May I remind you that you're speaking about a respected senior partner in this firm,' he said. 'And while I appreciate your loyalty to Ms. Wills, I happen to be confident that Charles would handle the defendant's testimony without the slightest difficulty, and is the proper choice.'

'And you're prepared to make that decision right here and now?'

'Is there any reason not to?'

'Well, don't you think you might be jumping the gun just a little bit?' Dana wondered.

'What do you mean?'

'I mean, wouldn't it be more appropriate to wait and see whether the media influence becomes the distraction you envision,' she suggested, 'before you leap to the conclusion that it's going to be, and pull me off the case, perhaps prematurely?'

Cotter cleared his throat. 'Well, yes, I see your point,' he allowed. 'All right, I'll get in touch with the executive committee, and we'll all plan to meet here on Sunday, say at two o'clock, and assess the situation then.'

Dana smiled with a lot more sanguinity than she felt. 'That sounds reasonable to me,' she said.

Over the past several weeks, Rose Gregory had grown so fond of Dana McAuliffe, and her valiant efforts to defend that nice naval lieutenant, that when she saw the tabloid at the checkout counter in the Queen Anne Safeway, she just didn't know what to think.

'The woman never claimed to be a paragon of virtue,' her granddaughter tried to tell her.

'She never came out and said she wasn't, either,' Rose countered.

'Did she have to?' her granddaughter argued. 'She was hired to do a job, to defend Corey Latham, whatever her personal beliefs were. Well, that's exactly what she's doing, and I have to tell you, I admire her for it.'

'But she seemed such a fine young woman,' Rose said. 'I trusted her. She seemed to have the right moral values.'

'She's exactly the same person you liked this morning.'

'Maybe,' Rose said with a sigh. 'But now I'm so disappointed, I just don't know what I'm going to do. I certainly hope this isn't going to affect the way I feel about the defendant.'

Although she never dared admit it to anyone, Allison Ackerman got some of her best story ideas from the tabloids. The murders were always depicted as being so gory, and the circumstances, real or imagined, were so bizarre. During the trial, she had studiously avoided looking at any newspaper, or at any television newscast or commentary that concerned itself with the case. It wasn't only because the judge had admonished the jury not to, although that was reason enough. It was more that she really wanted to make up her own mind, without any outside influence.

But the latest issue of *Probe* changed all that. It stared at her from across the counter in the pharmacy, and Allison grabbed up a copy without a second thought, stuffing it into her handbag after she had paid for it, so the deputy who accompanied her wouldn't see it.

Once safely inside her house, she pulled the tabloid out and proceeded to read the article about Dana McAuliffe, word for word, without even taking off her coat.

'Well, I'll be damned,' she muttered when she got to the end, a big smile spreading across her face. 'I knew I liked that lady.'

It was true. During the course of the trial, Allison had come to admire the defense attorney for her competence, her conduct, and her quiet confidence as a woman in what was still considered a man's profession. Now, she admired her even more.

21

Dana drove home automatically, her mind not on the road. It had taken four associates to get her through the media mob outside Smith Tower, and safely into her car.

She had been so immersed in the trial that it never occurred to her that there would be members of the media who were so desperate for something to report that it didn't matter whether it was about the Hill House bombing or not.

She was certain the whole thing would blow over in a few days, as all things tended to do, but she wasn't so certain that it would be soon enough for Paul Cotter.

'That son of a bitch,' Joan had muttered, when Dana relayed the gist of the conversation with the managing partner. 'If he takes you off the case now, it's as good as a conviction.'

'You don't have confidence in Charles?' Dana inquired.

Joan gave her a look that said it all.

'Are you upset because he skipped over you?'

'I'm upset because I want an acquittal here,' Joan replied. 'And I don't think Charles Ramsey has a prayer of getting it.'

'Why would you say that?'

Joan shrugged. 'I don't know. It's a feeling I get. I'm not saying he's senile or anything like that. It's just that he doesn't really seem to care about the case. He's not on top of it like you are. You know, he's never once looked at the files.'

Dana nodded slowly. 'So, what do you suggest I do?'

'Put a statement together,' Joan replied. 'Shrug the whole thing off, flat out deny it, fall on your sword, do whatever you like. But get it over with. And as quickly as possible. Tonight, if you can, because you've got the weekend for it to blow over. In any case, the sooner you deal with it, the sooner it'll be behind you, and the better your chances of getting Cotter off your back.'

Although Dana would have preferred never having to deal with the issue at all, she had to agree that Joan had a point, and the two attorneys spent the next several hours preparing just such a statement.

Now, as she turned the corner onto 28th Avenue, and saw the swarm of humanity trampling across her lawn, Dana was even more convinced that Joan was right.

She climbed out of her car, walked resolutely up the front steps to her house, and turned to face the crowd. Immediately, a dozen lights blinded her.

'Ms. McAuliffe, do you have any comment to make about the article that came out in *Probe* today?' someone up at the front asked.

'Did you have an abortion?' someone shouted from the back.

Dana took a deep breath. 'I happen to feel that one's private life ought to be just that – private, and that it should have no bearing on the conduct of one's professional life,' she said in a soft voice. 'But clearly, there are those of you who have no respect for others, or their privacy. Those of you whose only interest is in a headline that will sell more copies than the competition, or a lead story that will earn a higher rating than the other networks. Obviously, it's my turn to provide that grist for your mills.' Here, she paused for perhaps two beats. 'The article that appeared in the tabloid is essentially correct,' she continued. 'Five years ago, I did indeed terminate a pregnancy at Hill House. I believe it was the proper decision for me to have made at the time, and I made it for what I felt were valid reasons. In any case, it was a deeply personal decision that, right or wrong, I have lived with ever since.'

Not waiting for the barrage of questions that were bound to follow, she nodded once, and then stepped quickly out of the glare and through the front door, locking it securely behind her.

The house was dark and silent. Only one dim light shone from the kitchen. No ten-year-old came rushing into her arms. A chill ran down Dana's spine that was so gripping that she gasped. During the past eight hours, the only thing she had thought about was the impact the disclosure of her abortion would have on the trial. She hadn't allowed herself to think of the impact it would have on her husband and daughter.

Dropping her briefcase, she stumbled toward the kitchen, hoping for a note that would tell her where they had gone. Instead, she found Sam sitting quietly on a stool, his eyes cast down, his hands folded on the counter in front of him.

'You *are* here,' she gasped in relief. 'There were no lights. I thought you were out somewhere. Where's Molly?'

'I took her to Port Townsend this afternoon,' he said, his voice dead. 'She's with your parents.'

Dana was surprised for a moment, and then the wisdom of his action sank in. 'That's probably best,' she said, and searched her brain for something else she could say. 'Have you had dinner?'

'I wasn't hungry.'

'Do you want me to fix you something?'

'. . . no.'

'Sam . . . ?' she began. But he wouldn't look at her. He just sat there, with his head down, everything gone out of him. She shut her eyes. 'I'm sorry,' she whispered. 'I am so . . . sorry.'

And then he did look at her and she wished he hadn't, because his eyes were as dead as his voice. 'That's just not good enough,' he said.

'They were about to offer me a partnership,' she tried to explain. 'I know that firm. If there'd been a baby, they would never have given it to me. I'd have been shunted aside, and the offer would have gone to some guy who wasn't half as good as I am. I would still be an associate – still second chair, five years later. I worked hard. I deserved that partnership.'

'And what did I deserve?' he asked.

'I thought you understood,' she said. 'About me, about my work.'

'Is that all our marriage is about,' he wondered, 'under-standing you?'

Dana blinked. 'You've always supported me, in whatever I

388

did,' she said slowly. 'I guess I just came to expect it.'

'But you see, I wasn't just supporting you, Dana,' he told her. 'I was supporting *us*, our marriage, our family. At least, I thought I was.'

'But you were, Sam,' she said, wondering why it suddenly felt like she was standing on quicksand. 'The only reason it worked at all was because of you.'

He shrugged. 'Well, it doesn't matter now,' he said.

'What do you mean?' she asked, alarmed. 'Of course, it matters. We need to fix this. *I* need to fix it.'

'No,' he said. 'I wanted to wait until you got here, but I'm going now.'

He got up from the stool and started out of the kitchen. Dana felt her heart stop.

'Going? Going where?' she managed to ask.

'I'm not sure,' he said over his shoulder. 'I'll have to find a place. I'll let you know when I'm settled.'

He walked out to the foyer, and she watched as he picked up a suitcase by the front door she hadn't noticed on her way in.

'Sam, oh God, Sam, don't leave,' she cried. 'We can work this out. I know we can. I've said I'm sorry. I am sorry. So terribly, terribly sorry.'

His hand was on the doorknob. He stopped and looked back at her. 'Yes, I believe you are,' he said, his voice weary and full of pain. 'But ask yourself why you're sorry, Dana. Is it because you killed our baby . . . or because I found out about it?'

And then he was gone.

22

It was as though a thousand pounds had been lifted from Elise Latham's fragile shoulders. Her testimony was over, she had done what she could for Corey, and now she was free. When a taxi dropped her two blocks from Steven Bonner's Mercer Island house on Friday night, it was as though she were entering a new life.

'I'm a new woman,' she announced. 'The old Elise is history. From now on, I do what I want.'

'Then let's celebrate,' he said.

'How?' she asked breathlessly.

'Let's hop down to Cabo for the weekend.'

'Really?' she squealed, her eyes opening wide. 'Cabo San Lucas? Like in Mexico?'

'It's the only Cabo I know,' he said.

'Tell me you're not kidding. Tell me we could really go there.'

'Why not? I'm free. You're free. What's stopping us?'

'Absolutely nothing. All I have to do is go home and pack something.'

'That's your old life,' he said. 'There's a plane leaving at nine o'clock. Whatever we need, we'll buy when we get there.'

It was at the airport that she first saw the news, and heard the statement that Dana McAuliffe gave to the media.

'Well, I'll be damned,' she said.

'Probably,' Steve told her with a chuckle.

'No, it's the hotshot who's defending my husband.'

'What about her?'

'She had an abortion. Just like I did. I knew there was something about her. I just didn't figure on that.'

* * *

Through the long hours of the night, Dana alternately stared out the window and lay across the bed, wanting sleep, but not wanting to get undressed and crawl under the sheets, because Sam wasn't there to hold her, and warm her, and protect her from the world.

The telephone rang repeatedly, and thinking each time it might be Sam, she answered. It wasn't. It was only a string of awful people, who didn't give a damn about the time or about what she was going through, but just wanted her to know how they felt.

'Murderer!' they screeched.

'Baby killer!'

She hung up on them. After a while, she took the receiver off the hook. There was something about the calls that seemed vaguely familiar to her, but she couldn't quite grasp what it was, and it was too much trouble to try. Instead, she wrapped herself in the cold comfort of silence. She had never felt so alone. When it grew light outside, she took a shower, got dressed, and went to Port Townsend.

Molly seemed surprised to see her. 'You haven't come to take me home, have you?' she asked anxiously. 'Daddy said I could stay all weekend, and I've made plans.'

'Stay you may,' Dana assured her. 'Are you having fun?'

'Oh yes,' the ten-year-old replied, her eyes shining. 'There's just so much to do.' And she was off with her cousins.

'Thanks, mom,' Dana said, when the girl was gone.

'We're not entirely cut off here, you know,' her mother told her. 'We're aware of what's going on in the big city. I don't know how long we can pretend that nothing's happened.'

Dana sighed. 'I'm sorry,' she said. 'We'll leave, if that would make things easier for you.'

'No need for that,' her mother said. 'You raise your children the best you can, but once they're grown and gone, you no longer have control over what they do.'

'I know I've disappointed you,' Dana said. 'I've probably disappointed everybody. But I did what I thought I was supposed to do.'

'God knows we're not all perfect,' her mother reflected. 'Which is why He teaches us as much from our failures as from our successes. What's done is done. It's how you live with it that counts.'

Dana nodded. 'That's what I have to figure out,' she said.

Her mother glanced at the clock on the kitchen wall. 'Then I expect you'll want to see your father. He's still down at the office.'

There was no resentment in her voice that her husband would routinely go to work on the weekend, only acceptance of how things were.

Dana found Jefferson Reid at his desk, poring over legal tomes, searching out precedents.

'A few more years of this, and I'll be blind,' he grumbled when he saw her. 'They keep printing this stuff smaller and smaller.'

'That's because there's more and more of it,' she suggested. 'If they made the print large enough to be readable, you wouldn't be able to lift the book.'

He pushed the tomes aside. 'I guess I don't have to ask you what you're doing here,' he said.

She dropped into one of his deep leather chairs. 'Why?' she asked. 'Because I always come running to you when I'm in trouble?'

'Is your case in trouble?' he asked immediately.

'No, I don't think so,' she said. 'Cotter is making a few noises about moving me out of first chair, but I can't believe he's really serious about doing it. Other than that, all things considered, I think we're in pretty good shape.'

'Can you handle the distraction?'

'I don't see why not,' she said. 'I made a brief statement last night, and I'm going to wait to see how that plays out before I decide whether I need to do anything more.'

'Well, if you're worried about us, your mother's the religious one in the family, but she's also a realist. Mind you, it'll stick in her craw for a while, but she'll work through it.'

'I know.'

He peered at her. 'Then what's the problem?'

'Sam's gone,' Dana said.

'What do you mean, gone?' he asked.

'He left me last night.'

Jefferson Reid contemplated his daughter for a long moment. 'You didn't tell him, did you?'

She shut her eyes and shook her head. 'I wanted to,' she said. 'But I knew how much he wanted a child of his own, and I didn't know how to tell him that a partnership in my law firm was more important at the time. I thought I'd take a couple of years, get established, and then have a baby. But I was always working so hard, I guess the right time never really came.' She sighed. 'I didn't want him to know that I'd killed his only chance.'

Reid rubbed his chin thoughtfully. 'Did you tell your mother about this?'

'No,' Dana admitted. 'But I was thinking maybe, if it was okay with both of you, that Molly could stay here for a while. Well, at least until the trial is over. It would make things a lot easier, and she wouldn't miss that much school. We're only talking a few more days.'

'I'll talk to your mother,' he said. 'That won't be a problem.'

'Thanks, dad,' she said, pulling herself out of the chair. 'I guess I'll get going then.'

'Aren't you going to stay the weekend?' he asked. 'I'm almost through here. We could talk some more.'

'No,' she replied. 'I have to get back, and see what kind of hell has broken loose. I have a meeting with Cotter tomorrow afternoon, and I've got to see Corey. Right now, he's my top priority: getting through the rest of this trial, and getting him acquitted, if I can. I have to make sure none of my personal stuff touches him in any way.'

Reid stood up and took her in his arms. 'I know you,' he said. 'You'll tough it out.'

She was halfway out the door when she stopped. 'I don't get it,' she said. 'You've always made the decisions for the family, done what you thought was right, and mom never questioned

393

it. You raised me to be just like you, to follow my dream, to go for the career, to make the hard choices. But then I try to do what I think is right, and look what happens.'

'I guess that's my fault,' Jefferson Reid said, shaking his head. 'I did raise you to be like me, but I forgot to tell you that being a woman in a man's world doesn't make you a man.'

Craig Jessup felt a little silly, walking through Volunteer Park on a Saturday morning, counting off benches until he found the one his caller had specified. Clandestine operations were not exactly his thing. But the man had been insistent, and Jessup complied. He figured if the information the caller had hinted at was as promised, it would be a small price to pay.

He sat down at one end of the designated bench, opened the required newspaper, and began to wait.

At exactly ten minutes before eleven, a bulky man with a crooked nose sat down at the other end of the bench and pulled out a newspaper of his own.

'Nice day we're having, isn't it?' the man inquired casually.

'If you like October,' Jessup replied, as he had been instructed. 'Myself, I prefer May.'

The opening gambit had been played. The bulky man nodded as if satisfied. 'Please keep your newspaper up while we talk,' he said.

'Can't I take notes?' Jessup asked. 'I don't work too well from memory.'

The man seemed to think about that. 'I'd prefer if you didn't,' he said after a moment. 'And I won't give you my name. I'm in enough danger, just meeting with you. But I felt I had to do it.'

'Why?' Jessup asked. 'Are you a plant or a traitor?'

'Neither,' the man replied. 'I'm just a moral man, who believes that the ends don't always justify the means. We'll talk, and when we're finished, I'll leave my newspaper on the bench. Be sure to take it with you.'

Behind his copy of yesterday's *Times*, Jessup rolled his eyes. This had better be good, he thought to himself.

*   *   *

Sam McAuliffe spent the night watching CNN from a hotel room near the Space Needle, torturing himself over endless replays of the statement Dana had given.

'Proper decision,' she had said, made for 'valid reasons.' For almost seven years now, he had eaten breakfast with her every morning, and slept beside her every night. He thought he knew everything important there was to know about her. As far as he could tell, they had a perfect marriage. He didn't understand how she could have lived the past five years of it with that awful lie between them. He began to wonder if, in fact, he really even knew her at all.

Could a law partnership have meant so much more to her than her marriage? He understood her career was important, and that it would always come first. It was impossible not to recognize that. But to the exclusion of anything else? He had known her as intimately as a man could know a woman, and the thought that her family might mean nothing to her had never occurred to him, even when it was staring him in the face. Still, he couldn't quite bring himself to accept that the last seven years had been nothing more than an act.

Sam hugged himself as hard as he could to stop the tears, but they came anyway, long, shuddering rivulets of them. He rocked back and forth on the bed, a grown man crying like a lost child. He had never been lonelier or more miserable than he was at that moment.

In the morning, he went out and rented a small, furnished apartment in Magnolia by the week, because he wanted to be close to Molly. He was the only father she had any real memory of, and he would not do to her what the other one had done. Then he went by the house, both relieved and disappointed to find that Dana wasn't home, packed up a few more of his things, and left.

It was just past three when Dana returned, pushing her way past a rude gaggle of press people at her front door. Safely inside, she saw that her message machine was blinking at her.

Dropping her coat and handbag on the floor, she ran to the telephone, hoping for a message from Sam. There wasn't one. However, there were four messages from Craig Jessup and one from Joseph Heradia. With a sigh, she returned Heradia's call first.

'I just wanted you to know, in case you were wondering,' he said, 'I had nothing to do with that article.'

'I was pretty sure of that,' she was quick to assure him. 'Doctor-patient confidentiality works the same as attorney-client privilege.'

'And I also wanted you to know,' he added, 'that I don't blame you now for taking this case. I gave you a pretty hard time about it at first. I was that upset. But I've been sitting in the courtroom, listening to the testimony, and well, I have to tell you, I'm not so sure any more that the police got the right guy. And if they didn't, well then, I don't see why you shouldn't get him off.'

'Thank you,' Dana said, feeling her heart lurch inside her chest. 'Thank you very much.' If someone with an understandable bias against her client could come to that conclusion, she wondered how far behind the jury might be.

She dialed Jessup's number next, and he picked up on the first ring.

'I was afraid you might have taken off for the weekend,' he said with obvious relief.

'Well, as a matter of fact, I did go out to Port Townsend,' she told him, 'but only for a couple of hours. Why? What's wrong?'

'I think you'd better come over here,' he replied.

She was ringing his doorbell twenty minutes later.

Louise Jessup ushered her in, rolling her eyes. 'He's been in a tizzy for hours,' she confided. 'Ever since he came back from the park.'

'The park?' Dana echoed.

But Louise put her finger to her lips. 'Let's let him tell you,' she whispered.

They found Jessup in his office, reading over some pages. He gestured to the recliner. 'Please sit,' he said.

'Would you two like some tea or some coffee?' Louise inquired.

Her husband shook his head. 'This time, I think you'd just better bring the scotch,' he said.

Dana blinked. 'Okay, what's this all about?' she asked.

'I kept bumping into things in this case that just didn't make sense to me,' he began. 'And I don't like it when that happens. I'm the kind of guy who needs to see the whole picture. Anyway, I have a detective friend down at the department. We've known each other for almost thirty years, and I'd trust him with my life. So when things started turning funny, I went to him, and to make a long story short, I now have reason to believe that some members of your firm may be into something they shouldn't be.'

'You mean Cotter Boland?' she said, startled.

He nodded. 'I had a conversation today with someone who is very much in the inner circle of the Coalition for Conservative Causes.'

'That's Roger Roark's group, isn't it?'

'Yes,' he said. 'Did you know that they're footing the bill for Corey's defense?'

Dana stared at him. 'No, I didn't,' she replied. 'Cotter said we were taking the case as a favor to a friend. He didn't say who the friend was.'

'Well, it's Roark,' Jessup confirmed. 'Aside from two hundred and fifty thousand dollars contributed by some televangelist, the rest has come right from the CCC – well over a million dollars, so far.'

'I knew Cotter Boland was conservative, but I didn't realize it reached that level.'

'There's more,' Jessup said. He leaned over his desk and picked up a handful of microcassette tapes. 'These recordings were made of a number of inner-circle CCC meetings by the fellow I talked to today. Publicly, Roark's group has been pretty clear on the subject of Corey Latham, deploring the act, but

397

applauding the actor, so to speak. Privately, however, it appears they intend to see him convicted.'

'Your contact told you that?'

'Yes.'

'The CCC wants Corey convicted?'

'Yes.'

'But why? They're staunchly pro-life.'

'Yes, but Roark's in bed with the Republican nominee for president, and the race is too close to call. The nominee has as good as promised Roark an antiabortion amendment if he's elected. And Corey is the fall guy. The clean-cut All-American who single-handedly took on the evils of abortion. An acquittal won't do it. The nominee wants a martyr.'

Dana frowned uncomfortably. 'Is this heading where I think it is?' she asked.

'I'm sorry,' he said, hating to have to tell her. 'According to these tapes, you were expendable.'

She wanted to scream at him that it wasn't true, that taking the case had been her decision. But there was enough in what Jessup was saying that made sense to her. 'Well, I'll be damned,' she murmured. 'The jury list – it was leaked deliberately, wasn't it? The backfire was intentional.'

He nodded. 'More than likely, Ramsey was acting on Cotter's instructions.'

'That's why Cotter put him in third chair. He probably hadn't sat third chair in thirty years. He wasn't a watchdog, he was a spy. And it's why Cotter put me off when I told him about the leak. And why they terminated you.'

'Probably.'

At that, Dana sat up just a little straighter in the recliner. 'Well, I'm afraid they miscalculated,' she said. 'Roark, Cotter, Ramsey, and all the rest of them, whoever they are.'

'How is that?' he asked.

'Because I intend to win this case,' she told him.

Jessup smiled and, reaching for a piece of paper on his desk, tore it in half, and threw it into the wastepaper can. 'Paid in full,' he said.

'What do you mean?'

'That was my final bill. I doubt that Cotter Boland would have paid it, under the circumstances. But you just did.'

23

Dana was at the jail at eleven o'clock on Sunday morning. While she waited for Corey, she thought over what she was going to say to him, and how she was going to say it. How would she tell a man on trial for his life because his wife had an abortion that his attorney had had one, too? How would she explain to a man who held all life sacred that she had taken a life because it interfered with a career step?

Or would she have the opportunity to tell him anything at all? If he had already heard about the article in *Probe*, or if he had been allowed to see any of the Sunday morning news shows on which she was being prominently featured, would he reject her out of hand?

It was simple really, she decided. If he gave her the chance, she would tell him the truth, straight up, whatever the result. It was only fair, and it was how she preferred to deal with clients anyway.

Corey entered the interview room then, shuffling in his shackles, and Dana's heart sank. His face was drawn, his expression ragged.

'What's going on?' he asked in an agitated voice, as soon as he saw her.

'Well, it's a bit of a long story,' she began.

'She never showed up for visiting hour, and she didn't call,' he declared. 'Is she sick? Did something happen to her?'

Dana blinked. 'Back up,' she told him. 'Who? When? Where?'

'Elise, of course,' he said. 'She didn't come for the visit yesterday. My mother was here. They usually split the hour, but Elise never came. Have you seen her? Have you talked to her? My mother said she'd try to find out, but I won't see her again until tonight. Do you know what's going on?'

'No,' Dana had to tell him. 'I haven't seen or talked to Elise since court adjourned on Friday.'

'Something awful's happened to her, I just know it,' he said.

'I'll find out,' Dana promised. 'But don't worry, I know you would have heard if it was anything serious. I'm sure she'll be here tonight, right on schedule.'

'I hope so,' he said.

'Friday was an extremely traumatic day for her, you know. Maybe she just needed to take some time for herself.'

'You think that was it?'

'I certainly think it's possible,' she told him.

'I don't know,' he said. 'The last few weeks, she's been acting a little funny.'

'Stress,' Dana suggested. 'We've all been under a lot of stress.'

'Yeah,' he allowed. 'I guess that could be it.'

Dana took a deep breath. 'Corey, I know you're worried about Elise, but we have to talk about something else now.'

'What?' he asked, suddenly alert. 'Is it something about the trial? Has something gone wrong?'

'The trial is going just fine,' she replied, 'but we have to talk about me. That is, about me staying on as your attorney.'

'What are you saying?' he asked in alarm. 'Are you saying you want to quit on me?'

'No, of course not,' she assured him. 'But there was a story concerning me that came out in one of the tabloids yesterday, and it has to do with—'

'I know about that,' he said, interrupting.

'And I know how you feel about abortion.'

'So?'

'So, if you're uncomfortable being represented by me, now that you know, I'd understand.'

'I'm not uncomfortable,' he said. 'We never talked about it, but I always figured you were pro-choice, being so career-minded and all.'

'And that doesn't bother you?'

He shrugged. 'If you can be pro-choice, and still believe that I'm innocent, why should it bother me?'

'And you're absolutely certain you want me to stay on as your attorney?'

'Of course,' he said. 'You're my attorney. I don't want any other. I won't accept any other.'

'And what if the people who are paying your bills want it otherwise?'

'Do they?' he asked.

'It's possible,' she said carefully. 'They're pretty conservative, and what with the publicity from the article and all, they might be motivated to remove me.'

'Well, they may be paying my bills – and don't get me wrong, I do appreciate that – but they're not sitting in my seat,' he reasoned. 'When they are, then they can pick whatever attorney they want.'

At exactly two o'clock, Dana walked into Paul Cotter's office. Charles Ramsey was there, as she had expected, but absent from the room was the third member of the executive committee, Elton Grace.

'Why don't we get started,' Cotter suggested, as he and Charles took two of the chairs around the Oriental coffee table, and he gestured her to another.

'Aren't we waiting for Elton?' Dana inquired.

'No,' the managing partner replied. 'I'm afraid he wasn't able to join us today. He hoped you'd understand.'

'I see,' she said, thinking that she understood much better than he realized.

'However,' Cotter continued, 'Charles and I have discussed the entire situation at length, and we are both of the opinion that we should go ahead and make the changes that you and I discussed on Friday.'

'You think that would be in the best interests of the client, do you?' she asked politely.

'Yes, we do,' he confirmed in a fatherly tone. 'We also happen to think it would be in your best interests, as well, my dear. Removing you from the limelight should make the media far less intrusive on your life.'

402

'I see,' Dana said again.

'I know you wanted to see this case through to the bitter end, but believe me when I say this is not any kind of failure on your part. Your work has been exemplary. Charles has said so repeatedly. And we know you did not intend your personal life to interfere with your professional responsibilities.'

'No, I didn't,' she said. 'And I don't believe it has – or that it would.'

'I know you're disappointed,' Cotter said, 'but you'll just have to trust that the old fogies know best on this one.'

Dana looked the managing partner directly in the eye. 'I'm afraid not, Paul,' she said. 'I'm afraid I can't trust you on this one at all.'

'I beg your pardon?' Cotter was clearly taken aback. 'I'm not sure I heard you correctly.'

'You heard me,' she said. 'I don't believe you are acting in the best interests of the client.'

'Come now, you're hardly in a position to—'

'Who's paying for Corey Latham's defense?' she asked, cutting him off.

'I don't see as that's particularly relevant to this conversation,' he replied.

'Back in March, you said we were taking the case as a favor to a friend,' she said calmly. 'I'm the attorney of record, and as such, I think I have a right to know who the friend is who's paying for the defense of my client.'

'Actually, the money is coming from various places,' Cotter said. 'A good part of it came from the Reverend Jonathan Heal, through his national congregation.'

'That was only a quarter of a million. What about the rest?'

The two men exchanged glances. 'How did you know the amount?' Ramsey asked.

'Oh, I know all kinds of things, Charles,' she replied. She turned back to Cotter. 'Where's the big money coming from?'

'Well, if you really must know, a sizable amount of it is being donated by the Coalition for Conservative Causes.'

'That's Roger Roark's group, isn't it?'

'Yes.'

'And is he the friend you mentioned?'

'We've known each other for a long time.'

'And was there any condition attached to his checkbook that gave him any special influence, either over you, or over the outcome of the case?'

'Certainly not.'

With a sigh, Dana opened her briefcase, took out a micro-cassette player, set it on the coffee table, and pushed the button.

'Okay, we're going to shell out at least a million bucks for this Latham kid's defense. How are you going to guarantee us a conviction?' a voice on the tape asked. *'Are you going to fix the jury?'*

'No, but something almost as good,' Cotter's own voice replied. *'I'm going to put a green attorney in charge, a female junior partner with limited capital crime experience. And I'll have Charles keeping an eye on her, ready to step in, just in case.'*

Dana hit the button, stopping the tape. 'Would you like to reconsider your answer?' she suggested.

Cotter's face went white. 'Where did you get that?' he demanded.

'Is that what really matters here, where I got it?' Dana asked. 'It seems to me that what matters is the two of you, knee-deep in ethical violations, perhaps even criminal acts.'

'Oh, come now,' Ramsey declared.

'If I were you,' Dana continued, ignoring him, 'what I'd be worrying about is what would happen if the bar association ever got hold of this tape. I'd worry about Craig Jessup's report on your little attempt at jury tampering. I'd worry about the repercussions if your colossal conflict of interest ever ended up in the newspapers. In fact, the only thing I wouldn't worry about, if I were you, is the Hill House bombing trial, because Joan Wills and I have that very well in hand.' She returned the tape player to her briefcase and stood up. 'By the way, there are three complete copies of this information, all in safe hands,' she added. 'And instructions for what to do should

404

any unforeseen accident befall either me or Craig Jessup. Have I made myself clear?'

Ramsey just glared at her.

'You've made yourself perfectly clear,' Cotter told her, unable to keep a hint of admiration from his voice. 'Go ahead, finish your trial. If Latham is convicted, all of this will have been for naught. This firm will not be handling his appeal. If he's acquitted, we'll have a rather irate benefactor in Roger Roark, but then he'll hardly be in a position to argue. Do we understand each other?'

Paul Cotter was smooth indeed. Dana nodded. 'We do,' she said.

Starting at seven o'clock, after Corey reported that Elise had not shown up at the jail for the second straight day, Dana began to call the Lathams' number every hour on the hour, each time getting no answer. Finally, at eleven o'clock, she climbed into her Camry and drove over to West Dravus. There was always a chance, she supposed, that the young woman was in some kind of trouble.

The house was dark, and the front yard was deserted, the small contingent of media people that still camped in her rosebushes having called it a night.

Dana parked across the street and sat for a moment, contemplating whether to get out, in case Elise might be inside, sick or injured or in need of some kind of assistance. She had just decided, as long as she had come all the way over here, to go knock on the door, when a black BMW pulled up to the curb.

A man climbed out and walked around to the passenger side. Elise slid out of the car with a small suitcase, and Dana watched as the two walked up the path to the front door. In the glow of the streetlight, there was no mistaking the long embrace. Then Elise went inside, and the man got back in the BMW and drove away. Dana wished she were anywhere but in her car, on this street, seeing what she had just seen. The question was, what was she going to tell Corey?

She needn't have worried. He seemed much relieved when she called him the next morning.

'About Elise,' Dana began, not yet sure of the words she would use.

'I know,' he said with a chuckle. 'I just talked to her. I should have remembered. She gets PMS real bad, sometimes, and when she does, she can't even get out of bed. It can last for days. I don't know how she can stand it, myself.'

'Well, I'm glad you got it all straightened out,' Dana murmured, keeping her voice carefully neutral. After all, who was she to pass judgment on anyone else's actions?

24

Dozens of freshly painted posters and hundreds of angry protesters, demanding her removal from the Latham case, greeted Dana's arrival at the courthouse.

'Traitor,' they screamed from behind the barricades.

'Satan's servant!'

'Baby butcher!'

News networks, anticipating the moment, turned their cameras full on her and thrust their microphones in her face.

'Tell us about the abortion, Ms. McAuliffe,' they demanded.

'Are you going to resign from the case?'

'Just ignore them, ma'am,' Guff suggested, as he escorted her from the police car to the portico. 'Ignore them all.'

Dana gritted her teeth, and looked straight ahead. All she had to do was get through the rest of the trial, she told herself, and secure an acquittal for Corey. If she could just concentrate on the trial, everything else would somehow take care of itself.

The captain of Corey's submarine was the first to take the stand on Monday. His testimony was brief and essentially uncontested, his purpose to establish the mood of the defendant during the months following his return from sea.

'For the first few weeks after Lieutenant Latham returned to shore, he seemed to be depressed and distracted and frequently short-tempered,' the officer testified. 'It was necessary for me to speak to him several times about his performance.'

'How long did this last?' Dana inquired.

'I'd say it was somewhere around the end of November when I noticed that he seemed to have regained his composure and settled down. I assumed he had come to terms with whatever matter had set him off.'

Tom Sheridan came next.

'Can you tell us how long you've known the defendant?' Dana asked during the course of his testimony.

'Let me see now, I met Corey and Elise shortly after they were married,' the pastor of the Puget Sound Methodist Church replied in his resonant pulpit voice. 'Which I suppose means I've known him almost a year and a half.'

'And how often would you say you saw Corey during that year and a half?'

'During the time when he was home from sea, I saw him at least several times a week.'

'What, if any, opinion did you form about the kind of person he was?'

'I found him to be a thoughtful, caring, deeply committed human being,' Sheridan said.

'Committed to what, sir?' Dana inquired.

'Committed to people,' the pastor replied. 'He was a regular participant in our program to feed the homeless. Whenever he wasn't on duty at the base, he was available to anyone in the congregation who needed assistance, in everything from carpentry to transportation. People sought him out, just to talk, because he was always willing to listen. He helped organize a volunteer care program for children during church services. And if anyone were ill, he'd go fetch medicine or bring soup or run errands. Anything he could do to help.'

'In November of last year, did you have occasion to meet with Corey and Elise Latham?'

'Yes, I did,' the minister verified. 'We met on a number of occasions.'

'And will you tell the court about the nature of those meetings?'

'The Lathams requested counseling to deal with the loss of a child. We met twice a week for the better part of a month.'

'The loss of a child, Reverend Sheridan?' Dana questioned.

'Yes,' he said. 'While Corey was at sea, Elise had opted to abort their baby. They were both having a difficult time dealing with the emotional consequences of that act, especially Corey.'

'Can you describe for the jury his demeanor at that time?'

'He was distraught, he was despondent, he was angry, he felt betrayed. All the normal things one would feel under the circumstances.'

'Objection, Your Honor,' Brian said. 'The witness is offering a conclusion by characterizing the behavior of the defendant as normal.'

'Sustained,' Bendali said.

'Let me rephrase the question,' Dana said. 'Reverend Sheridan, have you ever counseled any other people who were in a situation similar to that of Corey and Elise Latham?'

'Yes, I have,' the minister replied. 'Over the past twenty-five years, I'd say I've counseled somewhere between fifteen and twenty couples.'

'And based on your experience as a counselor, can you point to any common behavioral characteristics among people who have lost a child?'

'Yes, I can,' he said. 'They all went through periods of being distraught, despondent, and angry. And depending on the particular circumstances, some of them felt betrayed.'

'So when you characterized Corey Latham's behavior as normal, what you meant was that it was consistent with the behavior of other people you have counseled who have lost a child, is that correct?'

'Yes.'

'All right, Reverend,' Dana continued smoothly, 'did you ever detect a characteristic in any of the people you counseled that could be described as a tendency toward violence?'

'I would have to say no.'

'Would you know how to identify such a tendency?'

'Yes.'

'May I ask how you would know?'

'For five years, early in my career, I was a prison chaplain at the state penitentiary in Walla Walla. I know what violence

409

is, what signs to look for, and how to identify them.'

'So, if I were to ask whether you saw any indication that Corey Latham was so distressed by his wife's abortion and subsequent deception that he would have resorted to blowing apart a building full of people, what would you say?'

'I saw no such indication,' Sheridan declared. 'In fact, I would say the opposite.'

'Will you explain that?'

'Instead of seeing Corey take his anger out on others, I saw him take it inside himself. I think he blamed himself for the abortion. There was nothing in anything he said or did that indicated that he blamed either Elise or the clinic.'

'But there has been testimony in this court that Corey did in fact have at least one loud, potentially physical argument with his wife.'

'People argue, Ms. McAuliffe,' the minister said. 'Sometimes, they even shout and throw things. In my experience, that's just venting frustration. In many cases, it's necessary for the health and well-being of a relationship. But it's a far cry from premeditated violence.'

'In the course of your counseling the Lathams, did you have occasion to recommend to Corey that he join a support group?'

'I did. It's not an official church group, but several members of our congregation belong to it. It's specifically for people who are grieving the loss of a child. I think they do good work, so I'm happy to make referrals.'

'And you referred Corey Latham to this group?'

'Yes, I did,' the minister confirmed. 'I thought he would benefit from the opportunity to verbalize his feelings among people who would understand what he was going through and be able to help him adjust.'

'And to your knowledge, did he attend any of the group's meetings?'

'To my knowledge, he was going to the meetings at least once each week, right up until the time he was arrested.'

'Thank you,' Dana said. 'That's all I have.'

'Reverend Sheridan,' Brian inquired, 'is the fact that you saw

410

no indication of violence in the defendant a guarantee that he did not bomb Hill House?'

'Well, no, it's not a guarantee. It's simply an evaluation.'

'And, sir, isn't the real reason you referred the defendant to the support group because you were unable to help him reconcile his anger in counseling?'

'No,' Sheridan said. 'He was making great strides in counseling. I referred him to the support group because he was ready to take the next step.'

'Not because he was having so much trouble dealing with his anger that he was taking it out on his wife?'

'No,' the minister said. 'There was no evidence of that. As I said, in times of stress, Corey seemed to me to turn inward, not outward.'

'And you're an expert on behavior?'

'No, Mr. Ayres,' Tom Sheridan suggested mildly, 'just an observer.'

'Where's Charles?' Joan Wills inquired as Brian finished his cross-examination, and the judge announced the lunch break.

'He isn't going to be with us anymore,' Dana said smoothly. 'Cotter said something about another case that required his attention.'

Craig Jessup slipped into the courtroom just before the afternoon session was about to begin.

'Have a minute?' he asked Dana.

'Sure,' she said. 'What's up?'

'Does the name Tom Kirby ring any bells with you?'

Inexplicably, Dana felt the hair rise at the back of her neck and her heart begin to race. 'Why do you ask?' she said, somehow knowing, with a sinking heart, that she knew the answer before she heard it.

'According to the information I was able to get, he's a tabloid journalist who spent several months up here, covering the case,' Jessup told her. 'Also according to my information, he wrote the article in *Probe*. I'm still working on his source.'

Dana sank slowly back into her chair. 'Thank you,' she said tonelessly. 'Never mind the source. You can go on to other things now.'

'Are you okay?' he asked, concerned because her face had gone pale.

She squared her shoulders and tossed her head. 'Sure,' she said automatically. 'I'm fine.'

Fortunately, she had little time to think about what Jessup's news meant before court resumed and Damon Feary came to the witness stand.

The unofficial leader of the support group was a gangly redhead with a pockmarked complexion. He walked down the center aisle with huge loping steps, wearing cowboy boots with metal tips, smiling and grasping hands with the half dozen or so group members who were in attendance for the day's session.

'Mr. Feary, what is your occupation?' Dana began.

'I'm a carpenter,' he replied. 'But I do a little counseling on the side.'

'What kind of counseling, exactly?'

'In simple terms, I help people figure out how to deal with grief.'

'Would you say that kind of help requires a pretty good understanding of human nature?'

'I guess so.'

'Mr. Feary, are you acquainted with the defendant?'

'I am,' Feary replied.

'In what capacity?'

'He's a member of a support group I belong to.'

'Will you describe for the jury what kind of support group that is?'

'We're just a bunch of folks who get together every week or so to work through the grieving process that comes with the death of a child, and we try to help others work through it, too.'

'When did Corey Latham join your group?'

'It was sometime at the end of last November, I believe. He was a referral from Tom Sheridan over at the Puget Sound Methodist Church.'

'And what did you understand to be the circumstances of Corey's joining the group?'

'His wife had an abortion while he was out to sea, and he was trying to come to terms with the loss of his baby.'

'Ballpark figure – how many meetings would you say Corey attended?'

'I've been told that he was there just about every time the group met, from the first day he joined until the day he got arrested. Firsthand, I know he was there at least a couple dozen times between November and early February.'

'Were you able to detect any changes in his attitude or his behavior over the course of those meetings?'

'Absolutely,' Feary asserted. 'He learned that it was okay to be angry. So many people think they have to bottle it up, you know, and not let it show. But you can't deal with grief if you're swallowing the anger all the time. You have to get it out in the air.'

'Corey was having a hard time with that, with knowing what to do with his anger?'

'Yes.'

'Was that unusual?'

'Oh no,' Feary said. 'All of us had been there, walking around in his pain. That's the benefit of a group like ours. We speak from experience. We can all tell you how much it helps someone like Corey to know he's not alone, that he has someone to lean on, someone to draw strength from.'

'Why is that, do you think?'

He sighed. 'Because there is no greater grief one can know than the loss of a child.'

'So you would say his anger was normal?'

'Of course. Anger is a very normal part of the process.'

'And how did Corey respond to your group?'

'Slowly, at first, even though we were meeting three and four times a week.'

'Why so often?'

'Because that's what we generally do when a new person comes in, all raw and not knowing what to do with his anguish.

413

At first, Corey was withdrawn, which is typical. He sat by himself, listened a lot, said little, and didn't interact very much.'

'How long did that last?'

'I think it was during the fifth meeting that he stopped shrinking when members of the group came up to hug him. At the sixth meeting, he let himself cry for the first time. By the time we got to the seventh meeting, he was able to start letting it all out. After that, he began to heal.'

'You're very precise,' Dana observed.

'I take notes,' he told her. 'It helps.'

'And how long would you say the healing took?'

'Well, healing is an ongoing process,' Feary said. 'Sometimes, it can take years, sometimes it's never fully accomplished. But Corey was working on it, that much was clear.'

'You said before that he learned it was okay to be angry. Was there any point where you felt he was able to let go of his anger?'

'I don't know that anyone ever really lets go of anger the way I think you mean. Mostly, it gets redirected down more constructive avenues.'

'What do you mean?' Dana asked.

'Anger can be useful in effecting change,' Feary explained. 'Most of the great advances in history were made by people who were distressed by circumstances that surrounded them. People who were angry about conditions in their homeland founded this country. If we're disgusted enough with the behavior of our politicians, we remove them from office. If we don't like a law, we lobby to change it.'

Dana didn't particularly care for where she sensed he was heading. He seemed to be getting on a soapbox, and she had no intention of joining him. 'But we're not talking about global change here,' she said smoothly. 'We're talking about one man's struggle with grief. At what point would you say that Corey Latham had reconciled to the loss of his unborn baby?'

'By the middle of December, I would say, was when he seemed to be back in control of his emotions,' Feary said agreeably. 'He had indicated to us by then that he had forgiven his wife,

414

which is always an important step. He was participating in meetings with an outward focus rather than inward, extending compassion to others. He seemed much more relaxed, much more open, and ready to move on with his life.'

'Thank you,' Dana said with a nod and a smile, and took her seat.

'Where are you from, Mr. Feary?' Brian asked pleasantly.

'I live in Woodinville,' the witness replied.

'No, I mean where were you raised?'

'Oh, sorry. I was born in Oklahoma.'

'Went to school there and everything, did you?'

'Yes.'

'Anywhere near Tulsa?'

'Not far.'

'Were you there when that abortion clinic was vandalized, and all their equipment destroyed? I think it was in 1985?'

'I was still there in 1985, but I don't recall that particular incident.'

'And where did you go from there?'

'I went to Colorado.'

'And that was when?'

'Sometime in 1986, I believe.'

'Anywhere near Denver?'

'Yes.'

'And were you still there when two doctors from a clinic in Denver were shot? I believe it was in 1989?'

'As a matter of fact, I was,' Feary said easily. 'I heard about it on the news. They never caught the shooter. But back then, as I recall, there were things like that happening all over the country. I think a lot of people were very disturbed about how things were going.'

'Where did you go from Denver?'

'To Oregon.'

'And when was that?'

'As I'm sure you already know, it was in 1990.'

'Yes, you're right,' Brian conceded. 'I did know. And when did you move up to Washington?'

'About five years ago.'

'And that's when you started your little support group?'

'Well, not exactly,' Feary clarified. 'The group just seemed to come together about four years ago. I didn't start it.'

'You said you did grief counseling for these people, did you not?'

'Yes.'

'Do you have any accredited training as a counselor?'

'No. Just personal experience.'

'This group you counsel is for people who've lost a child, is that what you said?'

'Yes.'

'Then if you're counseling them from experience, I assume that means that you're also grieving the loss of a child?'

'Yes,' Feary said.

'Under what circumstances did you lose your child, sir?'

'My first wife had an abortion.'

'When was that?'

'About six years ago.'

'Where?'

'At a clinic in Portland.'

'I see,' Brian said deliberately. 'All right, let's go back over some of your previous testimony. You've told us that the defendant redirected his anger. Can you tell us where?'

'I'm sorry?' the witness said.

'You said that no one lets go of anger, it just gets redirected. I assume you were speaking from personal experience, as well as observation. So, I'm asking you, as an experienced observer, where do you think Corey Latham redirected his anger?'

'I wouldn't necessarily know that,' Feary replied.

'Why not?'

Feary arched an eyebrow. 'Well, to be accurate, I never asked, and he never told.'

'Well, if you didn't ask, and the defendant didn't tell, and you don't know, doesn't that mean he could very well have redirected his anger toward Hill House?'

Feary paused for what might have been a second too long.

'Anything's possible,' he said finally. 'But that doesn't make it probable.'

At that, Corey glanced up at the witness with a puzzled frown.

'But you can't rule out, absolutely, that the defendant might have turned the full force of his anger away from his wife by finding another target at which he could aim it, can you?' Brian persisted.

'Well no, not absolutely,' the witness allowed. 'After all, you can never be absolutely sure about anyone but yourself.'

'What's he doing?' Joan Wills murmured.

'I think he's equivocating,' Dana told her, feeling an unpleasant sensation along her spine.

'Does your support group advocate violence, sir?' the prosecutor inquired.

'Our support group?' Feary declared, looking out at the members among the spectators with a warm smile. 'Hardly. These people know all about suffering. They have no interest in causing anguish for others.'

'What about you?'

'Me?' Feary asked.

'Yes, sir, do you advocate the use of violence to promote your beliefs?'

The smile turned cynical. 'Are you asking me if I'm a terrorist, Mr. Ayres?'

'Are you?' Brian countered.

An expression that Dana had never seen before crept into Corey's glance as he waited for the witness to respond.

Feary leaned back in his chair and crossed one knee over the other. 'Let me assure you that my work with the support group is about forgiveness, not violence,' he said. 'These people have nothing to do with terrorism.'

'Then what about your work outside the group?'

'What about it?' Feary replied. 'I'm a carpenter.'

'That's how you earn your living,' Brian responded. 'I'm referring to your extracurricular activities.'

'Other than the group, I don't know that I have any.'

'Really?'

417

Feary sighed. 'Look, I'm not sure where you're trying to go with this, but let me help you. I build things, I repair things, and in my spare time, I try to help people.'

'Yes, of course,' Brian responded. 'Where is your first wife now, sir?'

The man shrugged. 'Last I heard, she was in Virginia.'

'And the clinic where she had her abortion, where is that?'

'It was in Portland.'

'Was?'

'Last I heard, it wasn't there anymore.'

'Can you tell us what happened to it?'

'I heard someone set fire to it, burned it right down to the ground.'

'I see,' the prosecutor said thoughtfully. 'When was that?'

'I don't know,' Feary said. 'Maybe five or six years ago.'

'I see,' Brian remarked. 'Which would have been not too long after your former wife had her abortion there, is that correct?'

The witness shrugged. 'I guess so. I never thought about it.'

Damon Feary now had Corey Latham's full attention. The defendant's eyes were narrowed and he was leaning forward in his chair, intent upon the witness. It was the most interest Dana had seen him display since Elise had taken the stand.

'Well, I've been thinking about it, Mr. Feary,' Brian declared. 'So tell us, as the guru of your support group, do you think it's possible that the vandalism in Tulsa, or the shootings in Denver, or that fire in Portland, might have been a redirection of someone's anger?'

'Objection,' Dana interrupted. 'Your Honor, it's patently clear that all the prosecutor is trying to do here is sling mud against the wall, in hopes that some of it will stick.'

'Don't I have the right to inquire into this witness's veracity?' Brian argued.

'Approach,' Bendali said, turning aside his microphone as the attorneys came to the bench.

'I was willing to give him some leeway,' Dana said. 'But first he tries to suggest that Mr. Feary is a terrorist. Then he goes

418

on to suggest that he recruits other terrorists. And while it makes for fascinating listening, it is without any foundation or relevance.'

'Mr. Ayres?' Bendali inquired.

'I'm just trying to determine how competent the witness is to assess the defendant's anger.'

'No, Your Honor,' Dana argued. 'What he's trying to do is put in the minds of the jurors the idea that Mr. Feary is a terrorist who may well have gotten away with vandalizing a clinic in Tulsa, shooting at doctors in Denver, and burning down a clinic in Portland. Without offering a shred of evidence to confirm any of it. He then wants the jury to jump to the inescapable conclusion that, because my client happens to be acquainted with Mr. Feary, ergo, he must be a terrorist, too.'

'Do you have any evidence to present to the jury on this matter, Mr. Ayres?' the judge inquired.

'No, Your Honor,' Brian conceded.

'Then I'm inclined to agree with defense counsel.'

'In that case, I withdraw the question,' Brian said.

Bendali repositioned his microphone as the attorneys returned to their seats. 'The witness is instructed not to answer the last question,' he declared. 'And the jury is instructed to disregard it.'

Brian regarded the witness. 'You've made a lot of statements here today about how the defendant "seemed to be this," and "indicated that,"' he said. 'But the truth is, you really can't say, with any assurance at all, that the defendant did not plant a bomb in the basement of Hill House, and blow the place to smithereens, can you?'

'No,' Damon Feary admitted, 'I can't.'

'That's all I have.'

'Absolutes and assurances aside,' Dana asked her witness on redirect, 'as a person who's been involved in grief counseling for the past five years, would you say that Corey Latham fits the profile of a terrorist, of someone who would deliberately turn his anger on innocent people?'

At that, Feary almost chuckled. 'Not from where I sit,' he

said, not sharing the joke. 'In fact, I can't say as I know anyone who fits it less.'

'Was it a mistake to put Feary on the stand?' Joan asked, as court adjourned for the day, and they were being escorted back to Smith Tower.

Dana shrugged. 'We needed him.'

'He was certainly singing a much more positive song both times we interviewed him,' Joan reflected. 'I wonder what happened on the way to the courtroom.'

'I don't know,' Dana said. 'But there was something about him when he got on the stand that I couldn't quite put my finger on.'

'Good heavens, you don't suppose he really did have something to do with those clinics and those doctors, do you?' Joan asked.

'Who knows?' Dana said with a shrug. 'But if Brian had any hard evidence, he wouldn't have hesitated to nail Feary with it. How could he resist trying to tie Corey to an antiabortion terrorist?'

The Magnolia house was still dark and silent when Dana unlocked the door. No Molly came tumbling down the stairs, no music floated from the stereo, no tantalizing smells emanated from the kitchen. And there was still no word from Sam.

It was then, walking through the empty rooms, that Dana realized just how much she had always taken him for granted, assumed his forgiveness and his forbearance. Raised in her father's image, she had always believed that she ran the show, made things happen, moved the earth. When all the time, it was really Sam.

She had never before let herself admit how dependent she had become on him. Only now, when it was too late, when she had done the unforgivable, and was face-to-face with the consequences, was she willing to acknowledge the truth.

It would be easy to blame Judith for what had happened, but Dana knew it wasn't her fault. Judith may have betrayed a confidence, but Dana had betrayed her husband. She had lived with that guilt for almost five years. Now Sam would live with the reality for the rest of his life.

How had she gotten to this point? It was simple, really. She had tried to have it all, and because of that, she had lost it all. The real question was, now what? But Dana knew she couldn't face the answer to that question tonight. Not when tomorrow was the most important day of the Hill House trial, and she needed all her wits about her to get through it. Nor could she face going into the kitchen to fix herself something to eat. She dragged herself upstairs and went to bed.

25

'**A** re you ready?' Dana asked.

Seated beside her in a freshly pressed uniform, Corey nodded. 'Yes, ma'am,' he replied.

Dana smiled to herself. He must be nervous, she thought. He hadn't called her that in months. She stood up and smoothed the skirt of her jade green suit.

'At this time, the defense calls Corey Dean Latham,' she said in a clear voice.

The defendant rose, stepped out from behind the table that had shielded him for so many weeks, and made his way deliberately to the witness stand.

From the first row of spectator seats, Barbara Latham watched her son, so bright, so confident, so proud. It reminded her of the first time Corey had ridden his two-wheeler without help, the ceremony when he made Eagle Scout, the evening that he got up on a stage and became Hamlet, the day he graduated from Annapolis. The milestones of a mother's life, she thought.

Evelyn Biggs had been in court every single day of the trial. Now she squeezed Barbara's hand, and gave her a reassuring smile. Tom Sheridan was there, too, sharing the first row with Barbara and Evelyn, intending to lend whatever support he could to them all.

Across the aisle, the Hill House section was packed with survivors who had waited nine months to hear from the man accused of bombing their clinic and murdering their friends and loved ones.

Frances Stocker had been studying Corey Latham since the beginning of the trial. She wanted more than anything for the police to have gotten it right. She wanted him to be guilty. She wanted his conviction to erase the image of Grace Pauley from her nightmares. But as the days and weeks went by, the psychologist was finding it harder and harder to believe that the young man who now sat in the witness box was capable of such evil. She hoped his testimony would tell her he was.

Ruth Zelkin had never seen the defendant. She had spent her days in court listening to other people talk about him. Now she moved as far forward in her seat as she could, not to miss a word he said.

Joseph Heradia had made a point of being here today. He no longer knew whether Corey Latham was guilty or not, and he was anxious to hear what the young man had to say for himself.

Betsy Toth Umanski sat in her wheelchair. She, too, was waiting to hear from the man that the police were certain had denied her the ability to bear children.

Marilyn Korba was seated in the first row. Painful though she knew it would be to actually hear the voice of her husband's killer, she had been unable to stay away.

Joe Romanadis would not have missed this day for anything. He was confident he would know whether this man had murdered his wife and his unborn triplets just by looking in his eyes and listening to his voice.

In the third row, Helen Gamble and Raymond Kiley sat together, holding hands. They hoped Corey Latham was guilty and would be convicted so they could at least have some closure, if not peace. But neither one of them was very sure anymore.

'Do you swear or affirm to tell the truth, the whole truth, and nothing but the truth?' Abraham Bendali asked.

'I swear,' Corey said firmly. 'So help me God.'

'State your name.'

'Corey Dean Latham, lieutenant, j.g., United States Navy.'

'Be seated.'

'All right, Corey,' Dana began, 'you've been sitting in this courtroom throughout this trial. You've listened to all the testimony that's been presented. What do you think?'

'All those people killed, all those others hurt,' he said. 'I think it was a terrible thing that happened.'

'And how do you feel about the state's efforts to prove that you were responsible for all those deaths and injuries?'

'Sick and scared,' he replied.

'Why sick?'

'Because I was raised to believe in the sanctity of life, and anyone who knows me knows that.'

'And why scared?'

'Because the jury doesn't know me, and after listening to all that testimony, I couldn't blame them if they wanted me to be guilty.'

'Corey, why don't you tell the jury something about yourself, about how you came to be who you are,' Dana invited.

'Sure,' he said with a boyish smile, and turned to the jury. 'I was born and raised in Cedar Falls, Iowa. If you've never been there, it's an awfully pretty little town, with really nice people. I can't think of a better place to grow up in, but the truth is, not very much ever goes on there. I have two older sisters. They're both married now, with kids. My dad is a professor at the local college, and my mom – she's sitting right over there – is on a leave of absence from her job at a preschool.'

He looked over at Barbara and smiled warmly at her, and Dana was pleased to note that every single juror followed his glance.

'I guess you could say I was a pretty normal kid. To be honest, I think I was too scared of the minister at our church to get involved in anything bad. He has these eyes, you see, that all us kids were positive could look right into you, and I always thought he would know immediately if I did something I wasn't supposed to do, and he'd tell God, and then I'd really be in trouble.'

Several of the jurors smiled at that. Dana almost smiled herself, thinking of her childhood priest.

'Anyway, much as I love Iowa, by the time I got to high school, I was just itching to see what the rest of the world was like,' Corey continued. 'And there were these recruiters who

424

would come to the school and tell us all about the travel benefits associated with military service. You know, join the Navy,
see the world. Now, you folks probably wouldn't understand,
being from here and all, but in Iowa, well, there's not exactly
a lot of ocean nearby. And the idea of sailing around the world
sounded like a great adventure to me. So I decided I wanted to
go to Annapolis, and I managed to get accepted. I have to tell
you, I struggled my first term. Life away from home was a big
change for me. But then I adapted, and six years later, here I
am. I haven't seen much more than a lot of deep water so far,
but I have hopes.' He frowned then, as though remembering.
'Well, I did have, anyway,' he said, 'until all this happened.'

'You're an Eagle Scout, aren't you, Corey?' Dana prompted.

'Yes, I am,' he replied.

'And you were president of your senior class in high school,
is that right?'

'Yes, I was.'

'For several years, you taught Sunday school at your church,
didn't you?'

'Yes, I did.'

'And you were twice named Outstanding Teen of Cedar Falls,
weren't you?'

'Yes, I was.'

'And in your graduating yearbook, what did your classmates
name you?'

He seemed to be embarrassed by the question. 'Well, I'm not
a Catholic, you see, but they said that was just an oversight on
God's part, and they named me "Most Likely to Become Pope."'

'Why do you think they did that?' Dana inquired.

'I think it was probably because they knew how important
my faith is to me.'

'Tell us about that.'

'I'm not sure anyone can really explain his faith,' Corey said.
'It's such a personal thing. But mine is pretty much what gets
me up in the morning and lets me sleep at night. It guides me
every step of the way. I guess you could say it's what gives my
life its meaning. I always try to do as much good as I can, and

425

as little harm. I pray every day, and I depend on God to show me the way.'

'And has He?'

'Well, not meaning to be disrespectful, because most of the time, He's done just fine,' Corey replied. 'But all things considered, right now, I kind of wish I'd stayed in Iowa.'

A ripple of amusement flickered across the courtroom, and Dana smiled to herself. He was pulling them in. They were listening, and in spite of themselves, they were beginning to relate to him.

'Do you think maybe God made a mistake?' she asked him.

'Oh no,' Corey said hastily, as though he were afraid he might have sounded too flippant. 'He doesn't make mistakes. I figure this is a test. God's a great one for testing our faith.'

'Do you think it was a test when your wife had an abortion?'

He sighed deeply, and even from the second row of the jury box, Allison Ackerman could see the pain in his eyes.

'It must have been,' he replied. 'Or why else would it have happened?'

'Were you angry when you found out?'

'Yes,' he said. 'I have a pretty even temper most of the time. I'm usually slow to boil. But looking back, I think I must've been very angry, probably as angry as I've ever been in my life.'

'Did you blame Elise?'

'At first, yes,' he conceded. 'I couldn't help it. She'd killed our baby, a precious new life God had given us to love and nurture. It took me a while to understand.'

'To understand what, Corey?'

'That Elise doesn't perceive life the same way I do. You see, I believe life begins at the moment of conception. But Elise, she thinks life begins at birth.'

'And when you understood?'

'Well then, you see, I couldn't be angry at her anymore. I mean, if she doesn't blame me for my beliefs, how could I justify blaming her for hers? The thing of it is, we probably didn't know each other well enough before we got married.'

426

In the Hill House section, Betsy Toth Umanski began to wonder where the monster was.

'Do you think you and Elise know each other a little better now?' Dana inquired.

'Yes, I think so. At least, we got the abortion situation straightened out.'

'How do you mean?'

'We've decided we aren't going to start a family until Elise is ready.'

'When you got over being angry at Elise, were you angry at the people at Hill House?'

He looked puzzled. 'Why should I be?'

'Because that's where Elise went to have her abortion.'

'Yes, but the people there didn't come to her,' he said. 'She went to them.'

'All right, Corey,' Dana asked then, 'where were you on the night before the bomb went off?'

'I was at home,' he replied. 'I was at home that whole evening. Elise was out with some people from her office. She came home around ten, just like she said. We watched the news, and we went to bed.'

'The prosecution has tried to imply that you may have drugged her cocoa on the way to bed. Is there any truth to that?'

He shook his head in disgust. 'I had no reason to drug my wife's cocoa,' he said.

'Did you tell the police you were home that night?'

'Of course I did. I told them I took the five-twenty ferry to work in the morning, and didn't stay up late during the week. Elise told them, too.'

'What did they say?'

'They said she wasn't a reliable alibi, because she was my wife, and she'd say anything to protect me, whether it was true or not.'

'So the one person who could substantiate your alibi for where you were in the middle of the night was immediately discounted by the police?'

'Yes.'

'All right,' Dana said, 'let's move on now to the "mountain of evidence" that's been presented in this trial. First, the trace materials that were found in your sport utility vehicle and in your garage. Let's start with the fibers. How do you explain the police finding fibers from a duffel bag?'

'I'm in the Navy,' he replied. 'I use duffel bags all the time. They're standard military issue. I would have been surprised if there hadn't been fibers.'

'The police also claim to have found sulfuric acid. How do you explain that?'

'I guess the same way anyone else would. I bought a new battery for my car. I kept the old one in the garage until I had time to take it to the dump. It must have been leaking.'

'Where did you buy this new battery?'

'At Bay Auto Supply in Bremerton. That's where I buy all my auto stuff. It's convenient to the base.'

'All right, what about the fertilizer?'

'Well, you've got me there,' he said. 'I am guilty of buying ten pounds of fertilizer from Swanson's Nursery. The house Elise and I were renting had a lovely little rose garden out front. Only the roses weren't doing so well, and Elise thought maybe some fertilizer would help.'

'What kind of fertilizer did you buy?'

'I don't know, whatever they said would work for roses. But it was all for nothing,' he added with a sigh. 'Elise told me the roses are all dead. The media people trampled them.'

'Now tell us about the aspirin,' Dana prompted.

'Aspirin?' He gave a short, hard laugh. 'If you'd ever served aboard a submarine, Ms. McAuliffe, you'd know that headaches are an occupational hazard. I swallow aspirin by the ton. I keep them in my pockets, in my bathroom, in the kitchen, and yes, even in the garage. I also happen to keep a bottle in the glove compartment of my car. If I'd had any idea that something as ordinary as an aspirin could get me in this much trouble, I'd have learned to live with the headaches.'

'Speaking of your car,' Dana said. 'Is there any chance it

could have been the one seen parked outside Hill House that night?'

'My car was parked outside *my* house that night,' he replied. 'And the key was sitting on the top of my dresser.'

'Do you know Carl Thorson?'

'Sure, he's my next-door neighbor.'

'Did he interrupt a loud argument between you and Elise?'

'Yes, he did,' Corey said, 'and I'm very embarrassed about that. I don't think it's proper to involve neighbors in personal affairs.'

'Were you in Carney Toland's auto parts store on Aurora Avenue, in December of last year, and did you purchase a car battery at that time?'

'No,' Corey replied. 'As I said, I bought my battery in Bremerton.'

'And how do you explain Joshua Clune, who claimed to have seen you at Hill House on the night before the bombing?'

'I can't explain it, except to say that the man made a mistake.'

'A lot has been made of the fact that you are a military man, trained to kill. Why would bombing an abortion clinic be any different than, say, bombing Serbia?'

'I think there's an enormous difference,' he said. 'Because one would be termed a defensive act, while the other would be termed an offensive act. The Navy protects, it doesn't provoke. I'm not a killer, Ms. McAuliffe. I'm a defender. Would I kill to defend my country? Yes, I would, because that's my job. But most military people, at least the ones I know, hope and pray it never comes to that.'

'In that case, I have one last question,' Dana said. 'Did you plant the bomb at Hill House that was responsible for killing one hundred and seventy-six people?'

'No, I did not,' Corey Latham said emphatically. 'As God is my witness, I did not kill those people.'

'He made a hell of a witness,' Mark Hoffman observed during the lunch break.

'Better than I expected,' Brian Ayres conceded grudgingly.

429

'McAuliffe's good.'

Brian nodded. 'She did her job. He was perfectly coached.'

'I was watching the jury,' Mark said. 'He had them practically eating out of his hand. I hate to admit it, but you know, he almost had me convinced there for a bit.'

Brian sighed. 'He told a good tale, and he told it well.'

There was a pause. 'You don't suppose the police screwed up, do you?' Mark wondered idly.

The prosecutor smiled a bit, because a similar thought had crossed his mind. 'Well, if they did,' he said, 'it wouldn't be the first time.'

'So what are you going to do?'

'Proceed as planned,' Brian told him. 'Go after him. See what jiggles loose in his testimony. Guilty or innocent, no one's ever going to be able to come back at me over this.'

'Okay, tell me the truth, how'd I do?' Corey asked his attorneys.

'You did just fine,' Dana assured him.

'You had the jury all the way,' Joan added.

'I'm just glad it's over,' he said.

'Well, don't be too glad too soon,' Dana cautioned. 'Only the easy part is over. The hard part is still to come.'

'Good afternoon, Mr. Latham,' Brian began in his most engaging tone.

'Good afternoon,' Corey replied, sitting ramrod straight in the witness box.

'I have just a few things to go over with you.'

'Sure.'

'You know, I listened to your testimony this morning, very carefully, and you seem to have an answer for everything,' Brian said. 'How is that?'

'Wasn't I supposed to?' Corey replied, looking just a bit startled.

'Well, the thing is, you see, most innocent people can't account for absolutely everything. Because people are only human, and there's always something they have no explanation for. But there wasn't anything you couldn't explain.'

There was no question pending, so Corey blinked but did not respond.

'On the contrary, you were very smooth, and well rehearsed, and you were very convincing. Truth be told, as I sat there, listening, I was even inclined to believe you, myself. But you see, I'm the prosecutor, and I know better. Because I've got all these coincidences I don't know what to do with, and a good prosecutor is always suspicious of coincidences. Oh, one or two maybe can be explained away. But over a dozen?'

'I can't explain that,' Corey said.

'No, I'm sure you can't,' Brian said with a slight smile. 'All right, Mr. Latham, let's see what we've really got here. We've got a witness who reports seeing a sport utility vehicle, consistent with the one you drive, parked in front of Hill House the night before the bombing, right?'

'"Consistent with" doesn't mean it was mine, does it? It just means it was similar to mine.'

'True,' Brian agreed. 'But the witness also identifies a military sticker on the windshield, doesn't he?'

'Yes, but he couldn't say what base the sticker came from.'

'No, he couldn't, but still, you have to admit it's a coincidence that you just happen to drive a vehicle similar to the one that was seen, and it just happens to have a military sticker on it, isn't it?'

'I guess you could look at it that way,' Corey granted with a little frown.

'And there's the fact of your being in the Navy, isn't there? And not just in the Navy, mind you, but a weapons officer with training that assuredly qualifies you to make a bomb. Another coincidence?'

'I think it was established that you don't have to have military training to be competent to make a bomb,' Corey said.

'Point well taken,' Brian allowed. 'But then there's poor Joshua Clune. He testifies that he saw someone deliver packages to the basement of Hill House the night before the bombing, doesn't he?'

'Yes.'

'Further, he says the man he saw wore a windbreaker and a seaman's cap, just like two items of clothing that were retrieved from your home, doesn't he?'

'Yes.'

'And finally, he identifies the man he saw as you, doesn't he?'

'Yes,' Corey said. 'But he was mistaken.'

'Yes, of course, but a coincidence nonetheless, wouldn't you say?'

'I suppose so.'

'Now, add to that an anonymous letter that tells the police there's an officer at Bangor who's very angry over the fact that his wife had an abortion at Hill House while he was out to sea, and what do we have but another coincidence, don't we?'

'Yes.'

'And then there are all those trace materials found in your car and in your garage. True, you justified every single one of them – aspirin, sulfuric acid, fertilizer, and duffel bag fibers – but here we are again, faced with coincidences, aren't we?'

'Yes, but that's exactly what they are.'

'As, I'm sure, is the fact that two people from two different auto parts stores both identified you as having bought a car battery at their shop within a four-day period, right?'

'The second man was mistaken,' Corey said, and although it was cool in the room, Dana noticed little beads of perspiration forming on his brow.

'And your neighbor, Mr. Ram, was he also mistaken when he said he heard your car start up around midnight on the night before the bombing?'

'I think my wife showed in her testimony that he could have been mistaken.'

'Oh yes, which brings us to another coincidence: Your sleeping wife is your only alibi. Do you see what I'm getting at here, Mr. Latham? You had motive, you had means, and your wife notwithstanding, you had opportunity, which no one else under suspicion did. How do you explain that?'

432

'Maybe you didn't have the right people under suspicion,' Corey suggested.

'You might have a point,' Brian said, 'except that an investigation is a process of following leads, of going where the evidence takes you, not the other way around, which isn't always scientific, but usually gets you to the right place.'

'Except this time it didn't.'

'How do you feel about abortion, Mr. Latham?'

'I'm opposed to it.'

'For yourself, or for everybody?'

'For myself, certainly. I cherish life, as God wants us to. But I can't really speak for anybody else.'

'You don't have any burning desire to see *Roe v. Wade* overturned?'

'I'm not very political.'

'But you're pretty religious, aren't you?'

'Yes, I am,' Corey replied.

'You said earlier that you pray every day, and that you depend on God to show you the way, is that correct?'

'Yes, it is.'

'I assume that means you pretty much follow God's way, is that true?'

'I would hope so.'

'Well, let me ask you this, if you were pretty sure that God wanted you to go in one direction, even if you thought maybe you should go in another, would you follow Him?'

'Man may be fallible,' Corey replied with a smile, 'but God isn't.'

'So you would be inclined to go in God's direction?'

'Yes, of course.'

'Every time?'

'Probably.'

'But what would you do if, say, God wanted you to go in a direction that might require you to do something, commit some act that was in conflict with the laws of man?'

'I believe that, by its very nature, an act of God can't be wrong,' Corey told him, without thinking. 'I also believe that man should strive to live harmoniously with God. So if there is truly a conflict, then maybe man's laws should be reexamined.'

A brief murmur fluttered around the courtroom, and several of the jurors looked a bit uncertain.

'Thank you,' Brian said, satisfied. 'That's all I have for this witness.'

'Corey,' Dana asked on redirect, 'the prosecutor just asked you, in essence, if you would be willing to commit an illegal act if you thought it was the will of God. Did you intend to say you would?'

'No,' he replied, startled. 'I thought he was speaking in generalities about my beliefs.'

'Then let me ask you in the specific. Did God direct you to kill all those people at Hill House?'

'No,' he replied. 'Of course not. I would never have done that, and God would never have asked me to.'

'In that case, Your Honor,' the attorney declared with an elaborate shrug, 'the defense rests.'

26

Abraham Bendali rarely discussed a trial outside the courtroom, and even more rarely did he discuss one with his wife.

'I wouldn't want to be on that jury,' he said at the dinner table that night. 'Not for anything.'

'Don't worry, no one would ever let you,' Nina Bendali reminded him with a chuckle. 'You know too much.'

'Judges are supposed to safeguard the presumption of innocence,' he told her. 'But so many of us just pay lip service to that. We're supposed to be impartial. Well, at least we're supposed to maintain the illusion of impartiality. But most of the time, we know exactly what's what.'

'Of course you do.'

'Well, not this time. This time I'm as confounded as everyone else. And it's giving me a headache.'

'I'll make you some chamomile tea,' Nina offered.

'I'm tired,' he told her. 'I'm so tired.'

'I know,' she said. 'That's why this is going to be your last trial.'

He looked at her in surprise. 'How did you know that?'

'What?' she replied. 'Did you think I could be married to you for forty-three years and not know everything there was to know about you?'

'Everything?' he questioned, knowing such a notion should dismay him, yet feeling oddly comforted.

'Everything,' she declared, looking him directly in the eye.

Dana and Joan worked late into the night on closing arguments, ordering dinner in, bouncing ideas off each other, polishing, perfecting. Although both attorneys knew that the jurors probably didn't need any further persuasion, the final word was considered almost as important as the whole rest of the trial.

It was past ten when Dana finally dragged herself home to Magnolia. The crowd of media people had dwindled to almost manageable proportions, and were now more interested in her take on the trial than in the state of her personal life.

She gave a polite 'No comment,' and closed the front door firmly on the cries of protest. In the dark, the red light on the answering machine blinked.

Finally, there was a message from Sam. It was brief, giving her his new address and a telephone number, and asking about Molly. But Dana couldn't believe how good it felt just to hear his voice again. Without thinking of the time, she reached for the receiver and dialed.

'Hi,' she said when he answered.

'Hi,' he replied.

'How are you?'

'I'm doing okay,' he said. 'How about you?'

She opened her mouth to tell him about the trial, to tell him how Corey's testimony had gone. 'I miss you,' she said instead. 'I miss you so much I don't know what to do.'

She heard him sigh at the other end. 'I miss you, too,' he said, and there was no mistaking the pain in his voice, even over a telephone line. 'How's Molly?'

'She's fine,' Dana told him. 'She's still with my folks. I thought it would be best to leave her there for a while. My fifteen minutes of fame appear to be over, but just in case, there's no reason to expose her to any of it.'

'I think that was wise,' he said. 'Would it be all right if I went out to see her?'

'Of course it would,' she told him. 'She's been asking for you.'

'I'll go tomorrow then,' he said. 'If it's clear, maybe we'll go up to Hurricane Ridge.'

Dana caught her breath. Hiking in the Olympic Mountains was something the three of them had always loved to do.

'Sam,' she said tentatively, 'could we talk?'

436

'Yes, we'll have to talk,' he said. 'But not yet.'

'Okay,' Dana said, her heart soaring, although his words were hardly committal. 'I won't push. When . . . whenever you're ready will be just fine.'

27

Standing before the jury in his best charcoal gray suit and crisp white shirt, Brian Ayres looked every inch the confident, dedicated public servant that he was.

Like a seasoned actor, he had rehearsed his closing argument in front of the bathroom mirror for over a week, until he had memorized every word, refined every nuance, practiced every change of tone. Now all he had to do was interpret the script for the jury exactly as he had performed it for his reflection.

'Ladies and gentlemen, this has been a very difficult trial for me, as I'm sure it's been for all of you,' he began in a somber tone. 'I didn't lose a loved one in the bombing of Hill House, but it isn't hard, looking over at that special section of spectators who have courageously insisted on coming to court each day, to imagine how horrific it would have been.'

It was ten o'clock on Wednesday morning, and for the next six and a half hours, interrupted only by the customary breaks, he went back over the evidence, piece by piece, showing how neatly it all fit around the person of Corey Latham.

He dragged out some of the slides used by the medical examiner, just as a reminder, although the jury needed no reminding. Dr. Pruitt's testimony was still as vivid in their minds as it had been on the day it was first presented.

He brought into court the ingredients of the bomb, as had been determined by the FBI, set them up on a table in front of the jury, ordered the windows opened, and then donned a mask and two layers of surgical gloves. As he began to grind aspirin tablets into fine powder, he spoke about the death of Corey Latham's unborn baby.

'Abortion is a very personal issue,' he said. 'When two people come up against it, without the proper foundation having been laid for their relationship, the results can be explosive. But make no mistake about it, this trial isn't about abortion. And it doesn't matter which side of the issue you're on. This trial is about the cold-blooded murder of one hundred and seventy-six people, sixty of them innocent babies, and there can be no justification for that.'

As he mixed the powdered aspirin with the methyl alcohol, he spoke about Milton Auerbach's sighting of the SUV.

'The man reported what he saw,' he said. 'He didn't make it up. He had no reason to lie. Without knowing whether it meant anything or not, he simply told a policeman that he had seen a dark-colored sport utility vehicle, with a military sticker on the windshield, parked in front of Hill House on the night before the bombing.'

As he drained the sulfuric acid from a car battery into a glass beaker, he brought up the anonymous letter.

'Someone who, for whatever reason, didn't want to be identified, knew something that he or she thought the police should know. If you had lost a loved one in that horrible tragedy, would you have wanted the police to discount the information just because they couldn't authenticate the source? No. You would have wanted them to do their job, which was to follow up on everything that might have been connected to the Hill House bombing.'

As he combined the acetylsalicylic acid crystals with the sulfuric acid, warmed them in cooking oil, and carefully added the sodium nitrate, he spoke about Joshua Clune.

'That young man saw *something* on the night of the bombing. He almost certainly saw the man who planted the bomb. He identified a windbreaker and a seaman's cap, owned by the defendant, as being consistent with what he saw the delivery man, as he called him, wearing. He says he saw the defendant. Now, whether you accept his testimony or not, he gave it, under oath, and to the best of his ability.'

As he dumped the aspirin mixture into a bowl of crushed ice, and waited for the bright yellow crystals to form, Brian detailed the trace materials found in the defendant's possession.

'How many coincidences must we have before they stop being coincidental?' he asked.

As he pulverized the yellow crystals into powder, he talked about redirected anger and frustration.

'How do we get rid of real anger? We vent it, that's how. But the defendant couldn't take it out on his wife, because he loved her. So he looked around for something that would serve as a surrogate target, and give him that needed sensation of triumphing over his humiliation. Because that's what Corey Latham's anger was all about, humiliation. His wife had taken something away from him, without his permission, and he was powerless to do anything about it. She had destroyed his seed, without a second thought, and he was furious. Carl Thorson told you how furious he was. So furious that he couldn't simply forgive his wife and forget it ever happened, as he would like you to believe. No, he had to do something with that anger. And we know what he did with it. He redirected it at Hill House.'

And finally, as he mixed the powder with the proper measures of wax and Vaseline, he turned to religion.

'You heard the defendant, ladies and gentlemen. He said it himself. In a conflict between God's will and man's law, God wins. He as good as told you, not just that he did it, but why he did it. Who knows what he thought, in his anger and frustration? Who knows what twisted logic his mind must have followed to convince himself that God wanted him to destroy Hill House, and that he'd get away with it? We may never know. But what we do know, what all those grieving people over there in the spectator section know far too well, is the result.'

He picked up the plastique he had created, and held it out to the jury. 'Make no mistake about it, ladies and gentlemen, Corey Latham did it,' he said slowly, deliberately. 'And this is what he did it with. Make him pay for it. Find him guilty as charged.'

The jurors stared in fascination at the yellowish blob. The Hill House survivors wept softly. Brian Ayres took his seat. Dana McAuliffe sighed. Court was adjourned for the day.

*   *   *

Abraham Bendali cleared his throat. It was Thursday, and it was November. The skies were heavy with rain, and the trial of Corey Latham was drawing to an end.

'Ms. McAuliffe, are you prepared to begin your closing argument at this time?'

'Yes, Your Honor,' Dana replied.

'You may proceed.'

'Thank you, Your Honor.' Dana rose, buttoning the jacket of her burgundy suit as she walked slowly toward the jury.

'It occurred to me during the prosecutor's argument yesterday what he and I are really doing here,' she began, looking each juror right in the eye. 'We're spinning.'

She noted confusion in several of the jurors' expressions.

'That's right, we're spin doctors,' she told them. 'We've taken identical pieces of information, and we've twisted them and turned them, and painted them, and dressed them up until we think we've got them supporting our particular position. Now you may ask, how is that possible? How can the identical information be interpreted in two such totally opposite ways? And of course our answer would be: because there are always two sides to a story. And just like politicians who want your vote, we try to put the most convincing slant we can on our side of the story. Because, in a way, we're asking for your vote.'

Understanding replaced confusion and Dana even caught a slight nod from John Quinn.

'Do we have two sides to this story?' she asked. 'You bet we do, and they're about as opposite as they can be. Yesterday, the prosecutor told you the state's side. Today, I'd like to speak for Corey Latham. And don't worry, I'm not going to divert your attention from the facts by standing up here and making a bomb while I talk. On the contrary, I want your total concentration to be on what I'm saying. Because it's the cold, hard facts that should decide this case – not some sleight of hand.'

The jurors, with perhaps a modicum of relief, seemed to relax in their seats.

'The prosecutor has suggested that the police followed the evidence where it led them. But I suspect it was just the opposite.

After all, there they were, Seattle's finest, working for a solid month on the biggest case in the city's history, with nothing to show for it. The truth is, ladies and gentlemen, sad and frustrating though it may be, not every crime has a resolution. Sometimes, there's just not enough evidence to make an arrest or to get a conviction. But they couldn't let that happen here. No, this crime was different, and the public and political pressure on the police to solve it was enormous. Then one day, from out of the blue, an anonymous letter conveniently arrives. And from that moment on, this case had nothing to do with following the evidence, and everything to do with finding the Navy officer the letter referred to, and selecting the evidence that would best fit around him.'

With a twinge of regret, Brian noted that the jury seemed just as caught up in his opponent's presentation as they had been in his. Karleen McKay's eyes were fairly popping.

'Did they have a perfectly good candidate already at hand in Jack Pauley?' Dana asked. 'Of course they did, but somehow he just seems to have slipped through the cracks of a shoddy investigation. And he's just the one we happened to find out about. There could be others. But no, the police zeroed in on Corey Latham, decided they could make him into a viable suspect, and stopped looking.'

Here, Dana paused deliberately, and Allison Ackerman smiled to herself, thinking that the defense attorney's sense of timing was sheer perfection.

'Now, on the surface, finding those trace materials, reputedly from the bomb, in Corey's car and in his garage might seem significant,' she acknowledged, 'except that, when you look a little deeper, you find a reasonable and corroborative explanation for every single one of them. What I find significant here are the ingredients they *didn't* find. No traces of methyl, no wax, no Vaseline. Are they trying to suggest that Corey was sloppy, or that he was very selective in how he cleaned up after himself?'

She shook her head. In the jury box, Stuart Dunn frowned. 'The prosecutor refers to all these coincidences as reasons to convict, when in reality, coincidences are all they are,' she continued. 'Cliché or not, Corey just happened to be in the wrong place at the wrong time. And when there's an avalanche coming down on top of you, there's not a whole lot you can do to get out of the way.'

Dana paced up and down a few steps and then stopped.

'And look what they did to Joshua Clune,' she declared. 'They grabbed him off the street, locked him up in a cell, and scared him half to death. I wouldn't be surprised if they threatened to throw away the key if he didn't do what they wanted him to do. So Joshua, who couldn't identify my client from either the newspaper or the television just six weeks after the crime, eight months later positively picks him out as the person he saw bring the bomb to Hill House.'

She nodded thoughtfully, and noted Rose Gregory nodding as well.

'Now, did Elise Latham have an abortion?' Dana continued. 'Yes, she did. No one contests that. Was Corey angry about it? Yes, he was, and understandably so. Because she didn't just kill his baby, she tried to deceive him about it. When he found out, he got angry, very angry, justifiably angry. But by everyone's account, he went to counseling, he forgave his wife, and he came to terms with his grief. And the prosecution offered absolutely no evidence to the contrary. Not a single witness suggested that he was still dealing with anger in January, much less by February. And speaking of Elise, she was sleeping right beside Corey on the night the bomb was planted. She told you herself that she was a light sleeper, and that she would have awakened if he'd gotten out of bed. And what did the police do? They ignored her, because to accept her word would have destroyed their flimsy case, and they couldn't allow that to happen. In desperation, the prosecutor even tried to suggest, without a shred of evidence to back it up, that Corey had somehow managed to drug her cocoa. But the plain fact is, she didn't wake up, because Corey never *got* up. It's just that simple.'

For a moment, Dana seemed to debate with herself over something and then come to a decision.

443

'I could keep on going,' she suggested, 'and detail all the flaws in the state's case. But this trial has already lasted long enough. It's time for you to do your job. And as you go into the jury room to debate the fate of Corey Latham, I ask you to remember that the prosecution was unable to produce a single piece of reliable evidence that ties my client to this crime. Not one. Everything they gave you was coincidental, speculative, or just plain fabricated. And you can't simply say it doesn't matter because you think he did it, or you want him to have done it, or if the police say he did it, then he must have done it. It has to be "I have listened carefully to all the evidence presented, and I have determined, past any reasonable doubt, that he is guilty." If you cannot do that, then Corey Latham is not guilty.'

She stopped for a moment then, and looked at each juror in turn.

'The bombing of Hill House was a terrible crime,' she told them. 'A great many people died for no rational reason, and the anguish we all feel about that is as valid now as it was the day it happened. But you must find a way to set aside that anguish, to shut out public opinion, and to avoid outside pressure. Most of all, you must resist the urge to convict Corey Latham out of hand, simply because you believe *someone* should pay for what happened, because that would be just as terrible a crime.'

At this point, Dana seemed to square her shoulders for what was to come next.

'I have to say a word now about the messenger,' she said with quiet dignity. 'We usually say, if you don't like the message, don't shoot the messenger. But in this case, given all the recent publicity which I'm sure you could not have avoided seeing and hearing about, I would ask you not to discount the message because of what you may think about the messenger. Whatever I may have done in my personal life has no bearing on the matter before you. In the final analysis, trials aren't about judging the attorneys, they're about judging defendants.'

She sighed.

444

'I've come to know Corey pretty well since this all began, and to know him is to understand that he could never have committed this crime. Not just because it goes against everything he believes in, but because it goes against everything he is. Now I realize that you don't know him as I do. Rather, you know what the witnesses told you about him, you know what the attorneys told you about him, you even know what Corey's told you about himself. But you don't really know him. So you must judge him based solely on the information you've been given, and on your instincts. I've sat here watching you for the past six weeks, probably just as closely as you've been watching us. And you know what I think? I think Corey can trust your instincts. I think he can trust them with his life.'

Thoroughly drained, Dana sank into her chair because this was what it had always been about – pushing everything else in her life aside to pull out the best that was within her in defense of her client. It was what she had always been about. She wondered why it felt so hollow.

28

Allison Ackerman arranged for a neighbor to take care of her animals. Then she packed her suitcase, as she had been instructed, although she had no idea how many days she would be away. Since it was the first time she had actually served on a jury, she had no idea about a lot of things. For example, how disturbing it was to have an actual person's life in her hands.

Her mystery novels usually ended with the apprehension of the guilty party. They rarely got to trial. They never dealt with the issues or the emotions of jurors. And neither had she. She wished now that she could make some kind of an excuse, or get sick perhaps, or just plain quit. But of course she couldn't. She was stuck in this mess for the duration, whatever that meant, and she would have to make the best of it.

Stuart Dunn could barely contain his excitement as he packed his bag. This was the American justice system in action, and he was a part of it. What a tale he would have to tell his students.

His wife brought him fresh underwear. 'How many days are you packing for?' she asked.

'I haven't a clue,' he replied happily. 'But I can fit enough for three days in here, so I guess that's as good a place to start as any.'

She shook her head and smiled. 'You're just like one of the kids,' she told him.

The history teacher shrugged. 'I guess some people would consider this a burden,' he said. 'I consider it a privilege.'

Rose Gregory's granddaughter packed the suitcase for her grandmother, while Rose sat on the edge of the bed and directed.

'No dear, not that dress, it'll get too wrinkled. Not that one, either,' she said, wrinkling her nose. 'It isn't flattering.'

'And just who are you trying to impress?' her granddaughter asked with a mock frown.

'Well, there's a nice gentleman named Ralph, who's a barber,' Rose replied with a little giggle. 'And I've noticed he has an eye for the ladies.'

'Oh now, you stop,' her granddaughter chided. 'This isn't any church supper you're going to, you know.'

Rose sighed. 'I certainly do know that,' she said. 'And I don't mind telling you, it's been keeping me up nights.'

'I'm not surprised,' her granddaughter said.

'I know it's my civic duty to serve on this jury, and I'll see it through. But between you and me, I'd really rather be someplace else.'

Karleen McKay's idea of packing for the weekend did not include spending the better part of it in a courthouse jury room. It had more to do with sun and sea. Nevertheless, she dutifully ironed a selection of blouses, and matched them up with skirts and sweaters, and then added a slinky negligee, just to satisfy her own sense of humor.

She had no idea how the rest of the jurors felt about this trial, but she was tired of it all. There had been too many witnesses, saying too many things, for the defendant, against the defendant, and now it was all a muddle in her mind. It wasn't that she didn't take jury duty seriously. She knew how important it was to put away the bad guys and exonerate the good guys. It was just that she didn't want to be the one to make the decision.

John Quinn's wife was nervous as her husband packed his battered suitcase. Although there had been no further harassment after the grisly photograph incident, she didn't like the idea of him being gone from home overnight.

'I can talk to you every day on the telephone,' he assured her. 'If anything's wrong, you can tell me, and I'll report it. You and the kids will be fine.' As if to underscore his words, the family dog bounded into the bedroom and began to wag his tail. 'See,' Quinn said, 'you have Mutt to protect you.'

'Do you really think serving on this jury is going to help your business?' his wife asked.

'It can't hurt,' he told her with a shrug, 'unless we come out with the wrong verdict.'

'What's the wrong verdict?' she asked.

Quinn shrugged. 'I guess we won't know that until we come out with it.'

It took the judge most of Friday morning to charge the jury, explaining to them what they could and could not consider, and what they could and could not do, and how they had to do it. As soon as he finished, court was adjourned. The four alternates were excused but asked to stand by. Robert Niera then led the group of twelve into the jury room, where the smell of fresh coffee wafted from a large percolator, and two big platters of sandwiches sat on the table, along with twelve pads and twelve pens. The luggage they had brought with them had already been tagged and removed to the nearby hotel where they would stay as many nights as necessary.

Robert made sure the door leading into the corridor was properly secured and then turned to leave. 'I'll be locking this door behind me,' he said, referring to the courtroom entry. 'If you need anything, just press the button here on the wall.'

With that, he was gone, and the jurors heard the sound of a dead bolt sliding into place.

'I hope none of us is claustrophobic,' David Reminger, the computer programmer, worried. 'It could get pretty tight in here.'

'At least we won't go hungry,' Allison observed.

'It's a good thing we all sort of like each other,' Ralph Bergquist, the barber, said tentatively.

Eliot Wickstine grinned. 'So far, anyway,' the pilot said.

'I guess the first thing we should do is pick a foreperson, shouldn't we?' Elizabeth Kwan, the technical writer, reasoned.

'Why don't we all sit down,' Aaron Sapp, the community college professor, suggested.

Glad to have a starting point, they pulled their chairs up around the table.

'How do we pick a foreperson?' Kitty Dodson, the cosmetician, asked.

'We elect one,' Stuart Dunn told her. He glanced around the table. 'Any nominations?'

'I nominate you,' Karleen McKay said.

'Why me?' Stuart asked.

'Because you're levelheaded,' Karleen told him, 'and because you already know how to work with kids.'

'I agree,' Allison said.

'Then let's make it unanimous,' Ralph declared. There was no dissent, and the barber promptly vacated his seat. 'The foreman gets to sit at the head of the table,' he said, and exchanged places with the history teacher.

'What do we do now?' Kitty asked.

'Have a sandwich?' Eliot offered, helping himself to a ham and cheese on rye.

'Maybe we should take a preliminary vote,' Stuart suggested. 'Sort of get a feel for where we stand.'

Kitty looked at the pad and pen in front of her. 'Should we write it or just say it?' she asked.

'Write it, I think,' Stuart said.

'What do we write?' Elizabeth wondered. 'Guilty or not guilty?'

Stuart nodded. 'I'm pretty sure that's how it's done.'

There was a general murmur of assent, and each of them proceeded to write something down, and then tear the page off the pad, fold it in half, and pass it down the line. Eleven pairs of eyes fastened on the foreman as he read each vote.

'We have seven votes for guilty,' Stuart summarized, 'four votes for not guilty, and one vote for undecided.'

'Undecided?' Eliot Wickstine complained. 'Who said undecided?'

'I did,' Allison replied mildly.

'That wasn't an option.'

'Maybe not, but it's how I voted.'

'Now what do we do?' David Reminger asked.

'I guess we talk,' Stuart told him.

'Where do we start?'

'I have an idea,' Eliot said. 'Why don't each of us – if we want to, that is – just say how we feel, and why.'

Stuart looked around the table. 'Any objections?' he asked. There was no response. 'Okay, Eliot, you want to begin?'

'Sure,' the pilot said. 'He's guilty. I think the prosecution proved its case.'

'Beyond reasonable doubt?' Aaron Sapp asked.

'Beyond any of my doubts,' Eliot replied. 'He had the motive, his wife's abortion. He had the means, he knew how to make a bomb. And I figure he found the opportunity, even if his wife *was* a light sleeper. I think they even showed he was one of those religious nuts who thought he was answering the call of God.'

'I voted guilty, too,' Karleen said. 'I think the prosecutor pretty much did his job. Some of the testimony may have been a little flaky, but most of it was solid. And I think he did it.'

'So do I,' Ralph Bergquist declared, 'for the same reason as Karleen just said. I think he had some good answers when he got on the stand, but it didn't change my mind. Certainly not after listening to the medical examiner's testimony.'

'I voted guilty,' Elizabeth Kwan said. 'I have questions about some of the testimony we heard, and about what his real motivation was, but on whole, I think he probably did it.'

'I voted not guilty,' Kitty Dodson said. 'I listened very hard to what the defendant said, and I believed him. I believed what he said about the aspirin and the battery acid, and stuff. I thought about all the products I use in my work. I know some of them must be deadly, and I'm sure there are traces of them all around my apartment and in my car, and I don't even realize it. So what he said made sense to me.'

'I voted not guilty as well,' Rose Gregory said. 'I liked the defendant, and I didn't like the police detective. I think he coerced the testimony from that poor homeless man, and that makes me wonder what else he did that was wrong.'

'I voted guilty,' John Quinn said. 'When I added it all up, there were just too many things that pointed at the defendant, circumstantial or not. And I think he could've drugged his wife's cocoa.'

'We're not allowed to consider that,' Stuart reminded him.

'Why not?' John asked.

'Because the prosecutor can't make a statement that he has no evidence to back up.'

'Well maybe not,' John grumbled. 'But I heard it anyway.'

'I liked the prosecutor,' David Reminger said. 'But I didn't like the way he tried to slip that in. I didn't think that was fair. I could tell the judge didn't like it, either. And I had questions about some of the other evidence he presented, too. Like the anonymous letter just showing up like that. It seemed awfully convenient to me, and no one could explain where it came from. So I voted not guilty.'

'I also voted not guilty,' Aaron said. 'It's not that I don't think he did it. To be honest, I actually think he did do it. But I'm not sure the state proved its case beyond a reasonable doubt.'

'Well, I voted guilty,' Bill Jorgenson, the Boeing worker, said. 'I thought that defense attorney was a little too slick, like she wanted us to think she had all the answers. Whatever the prosecution witnesses had to say, she always had a comeback ready to trip them up, make them seem stupid or dishonest. When the prosecutor finally had the chance to lay out all the evidence at the end, I realized just how overwhelming it was.'

'And I voted guilty,' Stuart said. 'I think the defense attorney did a good job trying to refute the evidence, but there was just too much of it. Too many coincidences, as the prosecutor said. I listened very closely when the defendant was testifying. I don't know, it's just a feeling I have, but a lot of what he said sounded a little too rehearsed to me.'

Eleven pairs of eyes turned to Allison.

'I think he may be guilty,' she said. 'Or maybe it's just that I want him to be guilty, because it was a monstrous crime, and

I feel that somebody ought to be held responsible for it. But I can't vote to convict unless I'm certain he's guilty. And I'm not yet. The medical examiner's testimony was powerful, yes, but he couldn't implicate the defendant in any of those deaths. The bomb expert's testimony was also effective, but he couldn't connect the defendant to that bomb. I believe the eyewitness saw something, but it's not clear to me what he saw. And as for all the trace evidence, I thought the defendant had reasonable answers for a lot of it. On the other hand, I feel as some of you do – how many coincidences do you pile up before it isn't coincidence anymore?'

29

Friday became Saturday, and still there was no word from the jury. Dana split her time between Magnolia and the jail, her cell phone always on, and never out of reach.

'The waiting is always the hardest part,' she told her client. 'After you've done all you can do, and it's out of your hands.'

'What does it mean,' he asked, 'that they're taking so long?'

'It means they aren't unanimous yet,' she replied.

'Is that good or bad?'

'Well, there's an old maxim that says the longer the jury is out, the better it is for the defendant. But all things considered, I wouldn't put too much faith in that.'

'You mean, I'm guilty until proven innocent?'

Dana shrugged. 'Given the circumstances, probably something like that.' She could have said that she was growing more cautiously optimistic as each hour went by, but something stopped her. She told herself it was because she didn't want to get his hopes up, but she knew it was more that she was afraid to get her own hopes up. She had likely lost her career, her best friend, and her husband because of this case. She couldn't stand the thought of losing the case as well.

'But what if they can't get to unanimous?'

'Then we have a hung jury,' she said. 'And we start all over.'

Corey shuddered. 'You mean, go through another whole trial?' he said.

'If that's what the state decides, and I'm fairly certain it would.'

'I don't think I want that,' he told her. 'I think I want a verdict right here – whatever it is. It's the not knowing that's driving me crazy.'

'Well then, let's hope that we get one, and that it's the right one,' she said, as much to bolster herself as to bolster him.

The jury was still at it. They had debated for six hours on Friday and ten hours on Saturday, and they were beginning their fourth hour around the table on Sunday.

'It feels so strange, not going to church,' Rose observed.

'I know what you mean,' Ralph said. 'But I'm sure God will forgive us.'

'Well, where are we with this thing?' Karleen asked, thinking that it wasn't church she was missing, it was the income she was losing.

'We're at nine for guilty, two for not guilty, and one still undecided,' Stuart replied as he finished tallying the vote they had just taken.

'That's the same as it was last night,' Eliot said with some exasperation. 'At this rate, we'll be here till Christmas. Has it occurred to anyone but me that the day after tomorrow is already Election Day?'

'Well, what are we supposed to do about it?' Elizabeth asked.

'I think we have to talk some more,' Stuart replied with a sigh. He looked at Kitty, and Rose, and Allison. 'Those of us who believe he's guilty have been pretty much doing all the talking. Maybe we should hear from those of you who don't. Maybe you can tell us what's hanging you up.'

'I'm not hung up, young man,' Rose said archly. 'I just think Mr. Latham is too fine a person to have done such a terrible thing.'

'And I still have too many doubts,' Kitty added.

'I had doubts, too,' Aaron said. 'But after we looked again at all the evidence, I realized it couldn't add up any other way.'

'I'm sorry,' Allison said. 'I don't know what to say except that I'm just not sure in my own mind yet.'

'It's funny,' Karleen said. 'Of everybody here, I was certain you'd be the first to find him guilty. I guess I don't understand why you won't.'

'It's not that there isn't a lot of evidence,' Allison tried to

454

explain. 'And it's not that I think the defendant isn't guilty. I still suspect he probably is. But I keep doing what the defense attorney asked us to do. I keep stepping into Corey Latham's shoes, and asking myself if I'd want to be convicted of this crime based solely on what was presented by the state. So far, my answer is no, I would not.'

Karleen shrugged. 'I forgot all about that.'

'So did I,' Elizabeth agreed.

'Well, I expect most of us did,' Rose said.

Aaron Sapp looked at Allison. 'You're a mystery writer, aren't you?' he inquired.

'Yes, I am.'

'Do you generally have all the loose ends tied up at the end of your books?'

'I try. I prefer not to cheat my readers.'

'Well, may I make a suggestion?'

'Of course,' Allison agreed, 'anything.'

'Why don't you pretend that this is one of your stories. Play it out for us the way you would if you were writing it.'

'You really want me to do that?' she asked.

'It can't hurt,' Aaron said, 'and it might help to see where you're coming from. It might help Kitty and Rose, too.'

'Anything to get this over with,' Eliot said.

Brian Ayres knew he didn't have to be in his office on a Sunday afternoon, that there was a telephone at home, and that nothing would happen before he could return to the courthouse. But he sat at his desk anyway, alternately moving papers around and staring at the wall.

'You did everything you could do,' Mark Hoffman told him.

And Brian knew that he had. But he also knew he had been counting on a quick verdict, and it hadn't come.

'Do you think you did the best with what you had?' the King County prosecutor asked.

'Yes,' he replied.

'Then that's all you have to worry about.'

It was heartening to know that his job wasn't going to be

on the line, whichever way the verdict went. But it didn't stop the nagging feeling that, despite the polls, despite all the rhetoric, despite the climate of the community, he had somehow misjudged the most important case of his career.

The jury notified Robert Niera that they had reached a verdict at ten o'clock Sunday evening. Contacted at his Kirkland home, Abraham Bendali instructed his bailiff to send the jury back to the hotel for the night, and to inform everyone that court would convene at ten o'clock Monday morning.

Seattle was braced for the verdict. A formidable police presence greeted Dana on her way into the courthouse. Decked out in full body protection, and armed with tear gas, pepper spray, and rubber-pellet-firing weapons, they lined the streets – an estimated one for every two demonstrators. The chief of police had issued direct orders that gave his personnel the go-ahead to use whatever force was deemed necessary to maintain order.

Local networks covering the crowds had moved their camera crews to the safety of windows and rooftops. Inside the building, the ninth floor was chaos, with reporters and their cameras jamming the corridor, knocking into one another, almost blocking the entrance to Abraham Bendali's courtroom. In New York, Peter Jennings, Dan Rather, and Tom Brokaw were all standing by.

Robert Niera knocked lightly on his judge's door.

'Come in, Robert, come in,' Bendali invited.

'We're ready, Your Honor,' the bailiff said. 'Whenever you are.'

'Everyone present and accounted for?'

'Yes, sir.'

The judge heaved his massive frame out of his chair. 'Well then, let's not keep them waiting any longer.'

'No, sir,' Robert said with a grin, because he knew it was one of Bendali's favorite pleasures to keep attorneys waiting.

Five minutes later, court was called to order. The gallery was packed. The Hill House section overflowed. The space that had been provided for forty reporters was crammed with close to sixty. More than a dozen of Corey's supporters were in attendance, including his father, who had flown in on Saturday. Zach Miller had gotten permission to attend. Elise Latham had taken time off from work. There was standing room only.

'Mr. Foreman, do I understand that the jury has reached a verdict in this matter?' the judge inquired.

'Yes, Your Honor,' Stuart Dunn replied, rising.

At a nod from Bendali, Robert walked over to the jury box, secured the multipaged jury form, and passed the document up to the bench.

Neither the judge's expression nor demeanor changed as he read through the pages. After a moment, he returned the document to Robert, who then handed it back to Stuart.

'The foreman may read the verdict,' Bendali instructed.

At the prosecution table, Brian Ayres sat almost at attention. At the defense table, Dana grasped her client's hand as they rose and found it icy.

'On the first count of the indictment, the death of Susan Marie Abbott,' Stuart read, 'we the jury find the defendant, Corey Dean Latham – not guilty.'

There were verdicts on one hundred and seventy-five other deaths and numerous lesser charges to be read, but it didn't matter. The first one told the tale. The courtroom exploded.

Joan Wills grinned like a Cheshire cat.

Dana allowed herself a little smile and one small pump of her right arm, and wondered, fleetingly, why, when she had just won the biggest case of her career, she wasn't more elated.

Corey Latham, after almost eight months of uncertainty, sat down in his chair, drained of all emotion, his head in his hands, tears falling unheeded onto the table in front of him.

Brian sank slowly back in his chair, wondering why he wasn't more surprised.

Mark Hoffman shook his head in disbelief.

Among those in the Hill House section, Marilyn Korba gasped, Frances Stocker shrugged, Joseph Heradia nodded,

Betsy Toth Umanski sighed, and Joe Romanadis groaned.

'How could they have done that?' Ruth Zelkin demanded.

'What happened?' Helen Gamble asked.

'It's over,' Raymond Kiley told her, shaking his head in disgust. 'Let's go home.'

Corey's family and friends rejoiced, while other spectators alternately cheered and jeered. Reporters dashed out, tripping over one another in their haste. And Abraham Bendali, his face a perfect mask of impartiality, watched it all.

It was well into the afternoon before the formalities and the paperwork were done, and Corey was truly a free man, but he didn't mind. What were a couple more hours, when he knew he would sleep beside his wife tonight?

After a quick courtroom embrace, duly noted by the cameras, Elise made her apologies. 'I have a project at work that absolutely has to be finished today, but I'll see you at home,' she murmured to her husband, and escaped.

If Dean and Barbara Latham thought that odd, they didn't mention it. At three o'clock, they took their son out to a late lunch, insisting that Dana and Joan accompany them. It was a joyful occasion, filled with the kind of food Corey hadn't seen since his arrest, a lot of laughter, and champagne. Despite uncontrollable bouts of grinning, Corey couldn't stop eating, while Dean and Barbara were so ecstatic they could barely get a bite past their lips.

'We owe you everything,' Dean said to Dana and Joan, but mostly to Dana. 'In spite of the bumps and the detours, you stayed on course and never wavered, and you gave us back our son. We can't ever express our gratitude.'

Reaction to the verdict came swiftly.

In the privacy of his office, Roger Roark tore up his final check to the law firm of Cotter Boland and Grace.

The governor of Washington expressed disappointment that there would be no closure for the families and friends of the victims, or for the people of Seattle who had lost their clinic.

The mayor of Seattle urged the public to stay calm.

The chief of police made it clear that he saw no purpose in reopening the investigation. 'However, the file will remain active,' he said. 'Should any new information come our way, we will certainly look into it.'

Coming up on an election that was too close to call, the Democratic presidential candidate also publicly expressed concern over the lack of closure for the victims of Hill House. A spokesperson for the Republican candidate suggested that the absence of a conviction signaled a clear shift in the country's attitude about abortion. Privately, both candidates were furious.

Across the country, religious leaders on both sides of the issue counseled restraint.

In Port Townsend, Jefferson Reid leaned back in his chair, brought his feet in their heavy brown boots down on top of a stack of files on his desk, and grinned.

Craig and Louise Jessup took Al Roberts and his wife out to dinner.

When he heard about the verdict, Detective Dale Tinker went out and got drunk.

'I thought you were going to be on that jury forever,' Allison Ackerman's daughter declared. 'What do you think? A book about the experience?'

'No,' Allison told her firmly. 'I have no intention of ever talking – or writing – about anything that went on there.'

'Are you at least satisfied with the verdict?'

Like mother, like daughter, Allison thought. The young woman had a knack of always digging the tip of the knife right into the softest part of the meat.

'Yes,' she replied. 'And no.'

'Well, after all was said and done, did the trial turn out to be everything you'd hoped for?' Stuart Dunn's wife asked.

The jury foreman considered for a moment. 'I think my students are going to learn a lot from what I have to tell them,' he said, finally.

'I must admit, I never really thought you'd find him innocent.'

'We didn't,' Stuart told her. 'We simply found the state not to have proved its case beyond a reasonable doubt.'

'Is there a difference?'

At that, Stuart sighed. 'There's supposed to be,' he said.

'Our prayers have been answered,' Jonathan Heal told his flock during the Prayer Hour. 'Young Corey Latham is free, and a mighty blow has been struck against the forces of evil that would have condemned him for an act of deliverance. To those of you who helped support his cause, be proud tonight, very proud.'

Rose Gregory shook her head, and snapped off the television. 'The man's a fool,' she told her granddaughter crossly. 'I don't know why I ever admired him.'

'Well?' Larry King asked his two special guests for the evening.

'As you can imagine, Larry, I held my breath all morning until I heard the good news,' Prudence Chaffey of AIM exclaimed, 'and I'm positively elated. The jury sent a very clear message. This is a day of true vindication for the rights of the preborn. Now all we have to do is carry the message through tomorrow's election.'

'We have yet another horrible miscarriage of justice, on a growing list of such occurrences,' Priscilla Wales of FOCUS retorted. 'This acquittal declares open season on women's clinics for every lunatic in the country. Nothing good is going to come of it. I hope people will remember that when they go to the polls.'

'I've heard a lot of talk since the verdict came in,' King said, 'about jury nullification, and bad police work, and shaky evidence. But do either of you ladies entertain the possibility that Corey Latham might in fact be innocent?'

Both women seemed surprised by the question.

Prudence shrugged. 'What difference does it make?' she declared.

'Who cares?' Priscilla echoed.

460

30

When Dana and Joan returned to Smith Tower, they found a magnum of champagne cooling on Angeline Wilder's desk.

'It's for you, of course,' the receptionist cooed. 'You're the talk of the office, you know. The phones have been ringing off the hook with new clients. Mr. Grace wants you for two meetings on Thursday. And I've already taken calls for interviews from *Dateline, 60 Minutes,* and the *Today* show. Between you and me, low-profile be damned. Everyone around here is just tickled pink.'

Well, maybe not everyone, Dana thought to herself. 'Stash the bubbly in Mr. Cotter's refrigerator,' she instructed Angeline as she made her way down the hall. 'Ms. Wills and I have already had our celebration.'

'And I don't really care that much for champagne, anyway,' Joan confided.

'Close the door, will you,' Dana said when they reached her office.

It was an unusual request, and the associate was instantly alert. 'What's up?' she asked.

Dana sat down at her desk, and removed a sealed packet and a letter from a locked drawer. 'I wanted you to be the first to know this,' she said. 'I'm resigning from the firm, effective immediately.'

Joan's jaw dropped. It was the last thing she had expected. 'Resigning?' she sputtered. 'Why?'

'The reasons aren't important. I've just decided that it's time for a change,' Dana replied. 'And it seems appropriate to leave on a high note.'

'But didn't you hear Angeline? All those new clients, they're calling because of you, because of what you did. You're top of the heap now.'

Dana smiled. 'And if I'm not here, it's only logical they'll come to you. After all, I didn't represent Corey Latham all by myself.'

'What are you going to do?' the associate asked. 'You're not giving up the law, are you? Are you going to go out on your own? If you did, you know, you could probably take most of those new clients with you.'

'I haven't decided yet. I'm tired. I may just take a break for a while. Get some things sorted out.'

'This place won't be the same without you,' Joan said, and truly meant it.

'I think you know you're on a fast track to make partner here,' Dana said. 'Who knows, maybe even faster once I'm gone. And I wish you well, if that's what you want.'

Joan grinned. 'Oh yes, I want it,' she said, 'and I figure being on the winning end of the Latham case ought to seal the deal.'

Or scotch it, Dana thought. 'Whatever,' she said, 'I'm going to give you something,' and passed the sealed packet across the desk.

'What is it?'

'Let's say it's an insurance policy, if you ever need it. Hopefully, you never will. But hang on to it anyway. Put it away somewhere, and keep it safe, just in case.'

'How will I know if I need it?'

'You'll know,' Dana assured her. 'You'll know.'

She picked up the letter. Paul Cotter's name was written on the front of the envelope. 'Now I have the pleasure of delivering this.' She stood up, and put out her hand. 'Good luck,' she said.

It was six-thirty when Corey Latham came through the door of his West Dravus rental with a large bouquet of roses in hand, expecting to find Elise. But the house was empty. He supposed she must still be working on the project she had mentioned that morning, but he had thought she would be home by now. It

462

was almost eight months since he had made love to her, a lot of lost time to make up for. And not a night had gone by that he hadn't thought about it.

He put the roses down on the kitchen counter and took the few belongings he had been allowed to have in jail into the bedroom. It was pristine, no clothes hung over the back of the chair, the shoes were gone from the floor, and the bed was freshly made. Elise was an indifferent housekeeper, but she had obviously made an extra effort to clean up for his homecoming. He took his personal items into the bathroom and noticed the sink counter was no longer cluttered with her assorted creams and lotions and makeup. She had even put her toothbrush away.

Corey smiled and opened the medicine cabinet to stash his shaving stuff. The cabinet was empty. The smile slowly became a frown. He looked under the sink, but found only a few household cleaning items and some extra toilet paper. With a strange sensation starting in the pit of his stomach, he went back into the bedroom and opened the closet. His off-duty clothes and his uniforms, all clean and pressed, hung on the bar by themselves. There were no dresses or blouses or business suits keeping them company. Frantically, he pulled open the dresser drawer where she kept her underwear, and then the drawers where she kept her shirts and sweaters. They were empty. All trace of Elise was gone.

He walked slowly into the living room, wondering what was going on. The logical answer, of course, was that she was staying with someone in her family, not to be alone. But he didn't understand why she wouldn't have mentioned it, or why she would have had to take her entire wardrobe with her. He was still trying to figure it out when Elise burst through the front door.

'I'm sorry,' she said breathlessly. 'I thought you'd still be with your folks, and I would get here before you did. I really wanted to be here, but we got stuck in traffic.'

'We?' he asked.

'Oh, a friend drove me over,' she replied carelessly.

'Where's all your stuff?'

'Well, I want to talk to you about that,' she said.

'Are you staying with your parents?'

'God no,' she replied with a short laugh. 'My mother as good as disowned me months ago.'

He looked at her in confusion. 'Then what's going on?'

'Well, you see, I'm staying with a friend now,' she told him, 'an old friend.'

'You mean, you were, while I was gone,' he said.

'No, I mean, I *am*,' she corrected him. 'Look, the last eight months have been pure hell for me. I've been analyzed, and scrutinized, and brutalized. I never told you any of it, since you had your own problems, but it was awful, and it never stopped. And what I need right now is to be away from here for a while.'

'But you're coming back soon,' he said.

'No, not for a while, I don't think.'

'What are you talking about?' he asked. 'We're married. You're my wife. We belong together. We can move someplace else if that's what you want. But I've been dreaming of this moment the whole time I was in that awful place. The moment when I could hold you again, and kiss you, and tell you how much I love you.'

He got up off the bed, and tried to take her in his arms, but she slipped away from him.

'Please don't,' she said. 'I'm just very confused right now. I need time to think things through, work things out.'

'Can't we work things out together?' he wanted to know. 'Isn't that what married people do?'

'Please,' she said, 'don't make this any harder for me than it already is. I need to go. I just came to tell you that I'll be in touch.'

'Wait a minute,' he cried. 'Which friend? What's her name? What's her number? How can I reach you?'

'I'll call you,' she said. 'I promise.'

Before Corey could comprehend what was happening, she was gone. Dazed, he stumbled after her, yanking open the front door in time to see her climb into a shiny black BMW and drive away.

He stared in the direction of the car long after it turned the corner and disappeared. What had happened, he wondered, dazed, his head throbbing. What had it all been for? He couldn't think straight. All he ever wanted was to serve his country and live happily with his wife. He had survived months of hell, and headaches, and nightmares, and gastroenteritis worse than anything he had experienced on the *Jackson,* clinging to that dream, and now here he was, with his career probably in ruins, and Elise gone. He didn't understand. What had it all been for?

'So tell me, was it the right verdict?' Nina Bendali asked.

'Legally, it's always the right verdict, you know that,' her husband told her.

She gave him a nudge. 'Yes, I know that,' she said. 'But that's not what I'm asking you. And I'm not asking you to breach any legal ethics, either. I'm simply asking if you think justice was served.'

Abraham Bendali shrugged because he was unbearably tired and ready to put the trial behind him. 'Who knows?' he replied.

The doorbell in Magnolia rang at seven-fifteen. Thinking it was one of the more brazen reporters who were still laying claim to her lawn, Dana peered through a side window. Judith Purcell stood on the front porch. It was a long moment before Dana could bring herself to open the door.

'Oh good, you *are* here,' Judith said breathlessly. 'I was beginning to think you weren't.'

'I haven't been answering the door,' Dana told her, nodding in the direction of the newshounds for explanation.

'I just heard about the verdict,' Judith explained. 'I took a chance you'd be home.'

'Did you?' Dana murmured.

Judith looked dreadful. She wore no makeup and there were heavy dark circles under her eyes, her hair was all stringy, she had probably lost ten pounds, and she looked as though she hadn't changed her clothes in days. With a deep sigh, Dana stood aside and let her in.

'Congratulations,' the friend from childhood said. 'You pulled it off. I have to tell you, I didn't really think you would.'

'Thank you.'

'Well, I mean, I knew you *could*, but considering all the public pressure there was to convict, I didn't think the jury would have the gumption to acquit.'

'It was a strong jury,' Dana said.

Judith looked around, noticing the emptiness. 'It sure is quiet around here,' she observed. 'Where's Sam? Where's Molly?'

'Molly's in Port Townsend, visiting with my folks for a while.'

'Good idea,' Judith said with a nod. 'And Sam?'

Dana squared her shoulders. 'Sam's gone,' she said.

'Gone where?'

'Gone wherever husbands go when they discover they've been deceived, I guess. He's left me.'

'Left you?' Judith gasped, her hand flying to her mouth as if to keep her words in, and she looked as if she might actually faint. 'Oh my God, you never told him?'

Dana shrugged. 'I meant to,' she said. 'And then, as time went by, I guess it was just easier not to.'

'I never dreamt – I wouldn't have – I didn't realize . . . I am so sorry.'

'Well, that's the way things go, sometimes.'

'But it's all my fault,' Judith cried, tears filling her eyes and beginning to stream down her cheeks. 'It's all my fault.'

'Is it?' Dana asked without expression.

'I'm the one who told,' Judith sobbed. 'I didn't mean to. I thought he cared about me. I thought I could trust him.'

'Why would it even have come up?' Dana wondered wearily. 'Why would my personal life have become food for conversation in the first place?'

'It was all a mistake,' Judith whimpered. 'I'd just come from the bank. They were going to foreclose on my house. Tom told me I could make a lot of money if I had a story to tell, and pay off all my debts. He was sure I knew some juicy tidbits about you.'

'So you did.'

'But I told him no, I wouldn't do anything like that. I didn't

466

care how desperate I was. But then he gave me wine to drink, and I was so upset I guess I drank too much of it. And it just slipped out. I didn't think anything of it. I thought he was a handyman, and that I mattered to him. I didn't know he was a reporter.'

'You know you could have come to me if you were in trouble.'

Judith shook her head. 'I've always come to you, and you've always bailed me out,' she said. 'But even you couldn't have helped me this time. Aside from the mortgage, I was more than fifty thousand dollars in debt. You weren't in any position to get me out of that kind of trouble.'

Dana opened her mouth to tell her about the gallery in Pioneer Square, and closed it again. What would be the point, she reasoned. What was done was done. 'I see,' she murmured.

'Oh God, I can't believe how stupid I was,' Judith said. 'I thought he loved me. I was actually planning a future around him. I wouldn't blame you if you never wanted to see me again. And if I've cost you your marriage, I don't know how I'm going to live with myself.'

Dana wanted to hang on to her anger, because it was easier to blame Judith than to blame herself. But even as she tried, she felt it slipping away.

'If it's cost me my marriage, it's *my* fault, not yours,' she said heavily. 'Go home, take a hot bath, eat something fattening, and go to bed. I forgive you.'

Joshua and Big Dug sat in their favorite bar, nursing a beer, and watching the reaction to the verdict on television. Sporadic street fights had broken out, there were a few spontaneous demonstrations, and a little vandalism had taken place during the afternoon and on into the evening, someone having thought it appropriate to smear graffiti across the entire north face of the courthouse. But nothing happened that the police weren't able to handle quickly and efficiently.

'What does it mean?' Joshua asked.

'I guess it means, in the eyes of the law, he didn't do it,' Big Dug told him.

'But I saw him,' Joshua said.

'No, you just think you saw him,' Big Dug corrected him.

Joshua frowned. 'Is everyone mad at me because he's not in jail anymore?'

'Who's mad at you? No one's mad at you,' Big Dug told him. 'The reason he's not in jail has nothing to do with you. He's not in jail because the people who decide these things decided that he didn't bomb Hill House.'

'And it's not my fault?'

'No, it's not your fault.'

Joshua digested this information for a moment. 'But if the delivery man didn't set fire to Hill House,' he said finally, 'who did?'

The call Dana had been hoping for came at eight-thirty.

'I just wanted to say congratulations,' Sam said. 'I know how much winning this case meant to you.'

'To tell you the truth,' Dana replied, 'it didn't turn out to mean as much as I thought it would.'

'Well, I guess now it's on to the next big one. After this, there'll be no stopping you.'

'I quit Cotter Boland today,' she said.

There was a sudden silence at the other end of the line. 'Why did you do that?' he asked slowly.

'For a lot of reasons,' she told him. 'Not the least of which is that I think I need to reevaluate my priorities.'

'But I don't understand,' he said. 'You got Latham off. You won the biggest case in Seattle history. You could write your own ticket at the place now.'

'You may be right,' she concurred. 'On the other hand, maybe getting to that point didn't turn out to be all it was cracked up to be.'

'What are you going to do? Join another firm or hang out your own shingle?'

'Right now, I'm going to go out to Port Townsend for a while and be with Molly,' she said. 'Who knows, maybe I'll even stay out there, and go to work with my father. We always talked about doing that. Reid & Reid, we were going to be. Well, I think Reid & McAuliffe sounds pretty good, too.'

'It would be a very different kind of life,' Sam observed, and she knew what he meant: less demanding, less dramatic, less star-studded.

'That's true,' she allowed. 'But maybe I don't really need some of the things I always thought I did. I'd like to think that I'm not totally intractable, that I can change.'

'I would, too,' he murmured.

'Anyway, it occurred to me that there's no point in your keeping another place now,' Dana went on. 'You could come back and stay here. It's your home, and it's where Molly should be able to come when she wants to be with you. And I won't be around.'

'Sure, I can do that,' he said tentatively. 'But I'd like to think I can come out to Port Townsend, too, sometime.'

'Of course you can,' she said quickly. 'Anytime at all. I didn't mean to imply you wouldn't be welcome there. I just meant . . .'

'It won't be for a while though, you understand,' he cautioned her. 'Maybe a long while.'

'I understand,' she said. 'I didn't mean to rush you. Whatever you want. There's plenty of time.'

They were silent for a moment then.

'So you really quit Cotter Boland, did you?' he said, and there was a mixture of wonder and delight in his voice.

'I really did.'

'I never would've thought it.'

She smiled into the telephone. 'I love you, Sam,' she said softly. 'I know I haven't shown it like I should have, and I know I did an awful thing that you have every right not to forgive me for, but I do love you. The irony is, I'm only now beginning to realize how much. Now, when it might be too late.'

There was a pause then, and Dana heard a deep sigh before she heard his words.

'I know,' he whispered. 'I know.'

*　*　*

It was nine o'clock when, uninvited, Corey made his way through a persistent rain to Damon Feary's home in Woodinville.

'Hey kid, you're looking great, all things considered,' Feary said, breaking into a big grin when he answered the knock at the door. 'I heard about the verdict. You beat the rap. That's good.'

'Yeah, no thanks to you,' Corey said. 'You almost did me in on the witness stand.'

Feary gave a careless chuckle. 'You mean about the terrorist stuff? Well, I had no choice, now did I? I had to answer their damn questions. But no harm, no foul, as they say.' He still stood in the doorway. 'Listen, I hate to disappoint you, when you've come all this way, but there's no meeting tonight.'

'I know,' Corey said. 'It's you I came to see.'

'Oh?' Feary responded. 'Well, I'd like to oblige, but this isn't a real good time.'

Looking past him, Corey could see that the inside of the little log house was filled with packing boxes. 'Going somewhere?'

'As a matter of fact, yes,' Feary acknowledged. 'The wife and I decided it was time to move on.'

'You mean, your work here is done, and it's time to find another city with another clinic . . . and another patsy?'

Feary shrugged. 'I guess you could say that.'

Without warning, a right arm swung around with mighty force, the fist catching the carpenter full in the jaw, smashing it, and sending him sprawling.

'You son of a bitch, you set me up,' Corey cried.

Feary lay on the rough wood floor, bleeding from his nose to his mouth. 'We had to steer the cops to someone,' he slurred through the pain, 'so there'd be a trial.'

Corey stared down at him. 'All those months I rotted in jail, I thought I'd screwed up. I was sick with the guilt. But I didn't screw up, did I? It was *you*. Right from the start. You rigged that timer. I set it for two o'clock in the morning, so that no one would get hurt. I made that very clear. No one was supposed to get hurt!'

'Grow up, kid,' the carpenter retorted, spitting out a dislodged tooth. 'You jumped at the chance to play in the big leagues.' Grasping the edge of the door, he slowly pulled himself to his feet. 'What did you think this was all about? Something nice and antiseptic like Portland? We found out just how much good *that* did – a couple of paragraphs in the local paper. Sorry, but this time, we were after everyone's attention. And to get it, we needed a body count.'

Then calmly, but firmly, he shut the door in Corey Latham's face.